ABUSE OF PROCESS

By the same author

The Right to Silence

ABUSE OF PROCESS

Rankin Davis

Hodder & Stoughton

Copyright © 1996 by Keith W. Rankin and Anthony J. Davis

First published in Great Britain in 1996 by Hodder and Stoughton
A division of Hodder Headline PLC

The right of Keith W. Rankin and Anthony J. Davis to be
identified as the Authors of the Work has been asserted by them
in accordance with the Copyright, Designs and Patents Act 1988.

10 9 8 7 6 5 4 3 2 1

British Library Cataloguing in Publication Data

Rankin, Keith
    Abuse of process
    1. English fiction – 20th century
    I. Title II. Davis, Anthony
    823.9'14 [F]

ISBN 0 340 65785 5

Typeset by Palimpsest Book Production Limited,
Polmont, Stirlingshire
Printed and bound in Great Britain by
Mackays of Chatham PLC, Chatham, Kent

Hodder and Stoughton
A division of Hodder Headline PLC
338 Euston Road
London NW1 3BH

To the barristers of England and Wales; the truth is out there, find it if you dare.

But *for* Sarah and Julie, my 'wives'.

ACKNOWLEDGEMENTS

It is impossible to write a novel thick enough to act as a wind break and twisting enough to cause rollercoaster nausea without the vital help and support of so many colleagues and friends. In research, Toby Hedworth QC (a deserved promotion) and Roger Cooper, junior barrister (but your time will come) were invaluable in sharing their experience of the prosecution of a notoriously complicated trial and gave me a home in 'Holmes'.

'Spymaster' boggled the imagination in their help with the amazing array of surveillance equipment available and allowed me to be 007 for an all too brief period. Kate Lyall Grant and all the support team at Hodder for their patience and continued belief that there is more to a barrister than a wig and a huge brief fee (most certainly the latter) and to Sara Peacock, though now many miles away, still close enough to make a difference. To Phil Pride for my face and Michael Mallett for my name.

To Sarah, Julie, Hollie, Tom, Rebecca, Hannah and Barney for keeping the author smiling when the characters were as awkward as a Judge with a raging hangover.

Jane Gregory and Lisanne Radice for unmissable lunches and advice.

And to Rankin Davis, the man who never was, but might be.

Warmest thanks.

R.D. County Durham. 1996.

Curse not the King, no not in thy thought;
for a bird of the air shall carry the voice, and that
which hath wings shall tell the matter.

Ecclesiastes 10:20

PROLOGUE

Jonathan Berkeley stood in the neon glow of Piccadilly Circus, coat collar pulled high around his neck. It was 10.15 p.m., there was an icy breeze and the theatre crowds were beginning to swell the already busy streets surrounding London's most famous little lovelord. The dubious smells from a nearby greasy burger bar assaulted his nostrils and affronted his own expensive tastes. He made a final perambulation of the historic terminus and rested in a shop doorway at the corner of Regent Street. Taylor was late. The envelope felt damp in the warmth of Berkeley's pocket, folded tightly as if he wanted it to disappear altogether.

Shortly afterwards, a ragged youth with Mohican hair and a rusting shopping trolley pushed his way through a group of Japanese tourists laden with London memorabilia to Berkeley's left. The youth slumped in the doorway and retrieved a can of lighter fuel from a filthy plastic bag. Berkeley watched in abject fascination as he inhaled. The strobe show of camera flashes from the excited Japs spasmodically lit the pathetic still-life portrait. In a moment of perverse jealousy, Berkeley wished they could swap lives. The youth stared vacantly in his direction, a spider's-web tattoo etched across his weathered young face.

'You always did have an eye for the unfortunates,' a familiar voice whispered into Berkeley's ear, making him start. 'Looking at him reminds me of where I could have been – before you, of course. Go on, throw 'im a tenner – you can afford it. Maybe you can make friends.' The voice belonged to a striking young man with black hair gelled back from a bronzed, sculptured face. He wore a tailored blue cashmere overcoat with a velvet collar against a pristine white shirt and distinctive Hermès tie.

'Bastard,' spat Berkeley.

'Oh that's nice, Jonathan. Had a hard day? Not made enough

1

money, is that it? Or is it just that your bed's too cold these days?'

'Take the cheque and go, you worthless piece of shit,' Berkeley hissed, holding out the crumpled cream envelope from his pocket. The well-dressed young man smiled arrogantly, took the envelope and carefully began straightening out the creases.

'Shame you have to be so bitter about things, Jonathan. Sometimes, you know, I think we could still make a go of it, sort of for old times' sake.' He reached up to Berkeley's face and stroked his cheek. Berkeley pulled away sharply, his eyes ablaze with anger.

'I'll see you dead, Taylor!'

'Somehow I don't think so,' the young man sniggered, while producing a lizard-skin wallet from his jacket. Returning Berkeley's stare he pushed the envelope into the zipped compartment and took out a crisp twenty-pound note. 'Same time next week; make sure you're here or the video plays.'

'There *is* no more: the Boatman account is dry.'

'Shame. Best put your greedy little brain into top gear then, hadn't you? My partner and I have our own expenses to meet. I'm sure your friends will help you out.'

'They still don't know.'

'Not my problem.' The young man turned to walk away, but then took a step towards the spaced-out mess still slumped in the corner. He let the twenty-pound note drift down beside the punk. 'Don't thank me, thank him,' Taylor said, laughing and patting Berkeley's arm. The Mohican inspected the money through marble-glass eyes and looked at Berkeley as if he were the second coming.

'You see, Jonathan, charity. Don't you just love it!'

CHAPTER ONE

The telephone's insistent ring cut through Jack Forth's recurrent nightmare. He was drowning. Lungs strained against his injured ribcage, arms reaching out on a vague but vital quest that they would never complete. The brass bell continued to hammer through his unconsciousness. Jack sluiced back his black curls, which were wringing with dreamscape sweat and, groaning slightly, plucked the Bakelite mouthpiece from its cradle.

'Jack, it's Tom Leath.'

He groaned again. Leath was his boss at the agency. Jack had booked the day off to watch Hollie, his eight-year-old daughter, in the school swimming gala.

'Not today, Tom, I've got commitments. Hollie will never forgive you if I'm dragged away again.' Nor me, he thought, conscious that he had missed her recent birthday party on account of his unhappy vocation.

'You know I wouldn't call unless it was vital. Hobbs has gone AWOL again.'

'If he's gone on a bender I'm not going to take a hangover for it.' Hobbs was one of the best courtroom sketch artists in the business – he could make a defendant look guilty or innocent, depending on how he viewed the case – but more often than not these days he preferred the pub to the canvas. The agency had become increasingly reliant upon Jack's talents.

'You know who's up today, Jack.' Of course he did; the entire country did.

'I turned you down on that one last week. I still don't want to touch it.'

Leath was insistent. 'Look, Jack, it's only the magistrates' court. There won't be any evidence given; it's just the committal hearing to Crown Court. Come on, it's, what, half an hour at worst, and

3

the pay is good. I've got three nationals who want it. All I want is your drawing of "King Arthur".'

Though the heavy, goose-feather duvet was drawn snugly around his body, Jack shuddered at the mention of the defendant's pet press name. But Leath had been good to him. When Jack had returned haunted and exhausted from sketching the horrors of the Gulf conflict, Tom had offered the disillusioned war artist an opportunity to forget the evil of the Bazra Road: but it was simply another kind of evil he was asked to record. Hour upon hour sitting gazing into faces of murderers trying to show what was clicking in their minds was like trying to scream without being able to open your mouth.

'If you swear that I won't be asked to cover the trial . . .'

'Jack, I know how you feel about this one, everybody with a daughter feels the same. Come on, you'll still be able to see Hollie. Look on it as your contribution to keeping that scum off the streets.'

'He hasn't been convicted yet,' Jack muttered into the mouth-piece.

'Question of time. The prosecution are confident. Christ, even the defence have given up the ghost: they've briefed Sedgewick,' Tom offered.

Jack had seen the Old Bailey hack in action in several wine bars. Brilliant with a bottle and a genius with a glass, Jeffrey Sedgewick QC was as charming as he was incoherent come a courtroom appearance.

As Jack's reluctance faltered, Leath seized his opportunity. 'It's listed at the magistrates' for ten. I'll expect the sketch by lunchtime. Give Hollie a kiss from me. Gotta go now,' he rattled quickly before the line went dead.

Jack Forth reluctantly pushed back the quilt, then stretched away his inertia. He padded through the glass-walled studio that abutted his bedroom. Negotiating a path through the easels of half-finished work, paints, charcoals and pieces of wire-mesh sculpture, he made it to the bathroom. Sunlight pushed into the room through the frosted glass above the freestanding Edwardian bath and lent the pine-clad walls a warm honey glow. Jack looked at his reflection in the mirror of the bathroom cabinet above the toilet. He looked tired. Knowing, green-grey eyes returned his steady gaze; he had seen too much to appear innocent even to his naked self.

4

He fingered the stubble on his chin and toyed with the idea of a shave before coffee. As usual, the coffee won: tempting him in the background was the gentle hissing of the best Christmas present he'd ever thought of buying himself. As a compromise, he splashed cold water over his face and through his hair. He reached for the towel and buried his head in it. His face reappeared in the mirror. He looked his thirty-five years. Sun-etched wrinkles had brought him up to date with his body clock; it was only Hollie that kept him feeling young. Little Hollie. He smiled at the thought of her small, serious face and her constant concern about his wellbeing.

'You look thin, Daddy: too many late nights, too many girl-friends.'

'You know you're the only one for me, Hollie.' And it was the truth. Since the death of her mother, when Hollie was fifteen months old, there hadn't been, couldn't be, anyone else. Jack pushed away the memory of the accident: it still wasn't time, he still couldn't deal with it.

The aroma of Colombian ground beans drifted in, saving him again. He followed the scent to the kitchen and pulled a mug from the rack above the island. His computerised Coffee Buddy bubbled softly in the corner, offering black gold and telling him it was 7.30 a.m. As he removed the stainless-steel beaker from the hotplate, the chirpy American voice cut in. 'Gooood mornin', Jack Forth,' it yammered. He'd paid an extravagant £130 to a gadgets mag for the privilege of being greeted this way every morning, but he loved it. He poured and took his first sip in preparation for the second, which was always the best, he thought, when taste buds have taken the initial bitter assault and could then settle to seek out the finer nuances of the flavour. He replaced the beaker on the machine. 'Have a nice day, Jack Forth.' He doubted it.

Jack moved to the multi-gym in the spare room, where he donned shorts and a singlet for his morning workout. God, he hated exercise, but it helped him to focus on the day ahead. He began with some loosening exercises, then, supine on the rubber matting, crossed his ankles and began fifty sit-ups. Through the constant seesaw of motion, he reviewed his task. He had ample time to make his way to the magistrates' court. The lawyers would waltz through the formalities while he gazed upon the face of 'King Arthur'.

'Fifteen, sixteen,' he counted, breathing twinned with his rocking. The nation would follow this one through to the end. The defendant was the most reviled killer since the Yorkshire Ripper – and reviled with good reason.

'Twenty-six, twenty-seven.' For five long years, until the defendant's arrest, the parents of any young girl who was more than ten minutes late home would feel the drying of their mouths and the grip of fear that their daughter had been selected.

'Thirty-three, thirty-four.' Seven had been taken and seven had later been found mutilated, their eyeballs forced from their sockets. The first body had been discovered floating in a culvert near Dosmary Pool on Dartmoor. The press soon had the angle it needed when it happened upon the legend that the stale old fell pool had been the home of Excalibur, King Arthur's sword.

The first body, that of a teenage runaway girl, set a precedent for the vicious reign of sexual deviancy that followed. Each of the other victims had been a girl of similar age, abducted sometimes only yards away from her home, then dumped in a different watery location around Devon and Cornwall. All had been sexually assaulted before their breath was snatched from seared lungs by the cold waters. 'King Arthur' was their sovereign and they were his 'Ladies of the Lakes'. Jack felt his own breath become laboured by exertion and the unimaginable horror the victims must have experienced at King Arthur's hands.

'Forty-four, forty-five.' Rivulets of sweat ran from his armpits down to the cutaway material of the sports singlet while his heart cruised into overdrive.

'Forty-nine, fifty.' Jack slumped back and fought to control his lightly ragged breathing. He stretched out to his full five feet eleven inches. Six feet dead had been his intended height: Jack had even taken to hanging by his arms from a push-up bar with weights around his ankles until his father had told him that tall people could be very small people too.

He moved to the bench and began to press weights until his shoulders cramped with pain. Replacing the barbell in its slot, Jack lay back once again and thought about the girls' murders. Twelve months before, Trevor Speakman, the alleged killer, had been found asleep in a layby at the wheel of his heavy goods vehicle. In the lorry's trailer a heavily drugged girl had been discovered by the police. As Tom Leath had said, it was only a matter of time before Speakman was convicted. But there was something about the killings that troubled Jack. It wasn't only the fact that the girls, like his wife, had suffered a watery death: it was something else – the wisp of a memory that skirted his conscious mind like a wraith. He shook his head with the effort of impotent retrieval; it was useless.

Sighing heavily, he made his way to the shower. Soon he would see the face of the beast.

As Trevor Speakman slopped out his remand cell, a breakfast meeting at his solicitors' offices was in progress. In typical pinstripe style, the conference room was full of senior partners witnessing another kind of cleaning-up exercise. They all studied a bundle of identical documents. The tall, dark-eyed man in the centre of the table continued to stare at the Piet Mondrian paintings that he so adored on the wall opposite. No one spoke during the pause. He cleared his throat as though instinctively aware that it was to him the others would look for guidance.

'In short, therefore, we have a situation, gentlemen.' He paused again, distractedly, but precisely realigning the coffee cup to his satisfaction. 'When we pulled out of criminal casework a year ago the Speakman file was overlooked: he was not transferred to another firm of solicitors in line with our other clients at that time and essentially we still represent him. The matter was brought to my attention by a call from the Attorney General's office only a matter of days ago. It seems that the prosecution are somewhat anxious, naturally enough, to make progress, the committal proceedings being set for today. They were concerned that they had not heard from us with prospective guilty pleas. Needless to say, I became very concerned myself, considering the disastrous affair which led to the disbanding of the criminal department in the first place.

'I did not, however, reveal my astonishment to the Attorney General, in the knowledge that some time in the not-too-distant future I shall be leaving you all for different office . . .' He looked at the smiling faces surrounding him, then reciprocated their shared and privileged secret with a barely disguised, self-satisfied curl of his own pencil-thin lips. He went on, 'I did not want the honour about to be bestowed upon our firm to be sullied by another enquiry. While it is therefore regrettable that the Speakman case has not received the attention it should have done, it is nevertheless unlikely that a great deal could have been achieved in any event, given the overwhelming nature of the evidence against him. So, gentlemen, in consultation with the management committee, and of course with your approval today, I have assigned a solicitor to go through the motions in Speakman's defence and I hope in due course the entire matter will be forgotten alongside that monster when he is convicted. The alternative course would be to acknowledge our oversight and risk the stench that would follow, for he would surely complain once a new set of solicitors see that so little has been done.'

'Can we sack anyone for the mistake in creating this compromising position?' A hunting call was made.

'It appears that we have already done so, although I have little recollection of the individual personally. A chap called David Taylor. He was an articled clerk at the time. He was present at the original interviews; went off to work in the City some time ago.'

'Shame.'

'Yes, it is, rather, but the reality now is that this matter must be concluded quickly with the minimum of fuss. I intend to travel to the magistrates' this morning with the only person left in the firm who has any experience in this field. Given the history of things, you may agree it is an admirable choice should things backfire at all.'

The tube journey passed with typical claustrophobic anonymity. The continual heave and press of bodies avoiding human contact at all costs depressed Jack intensely. All eyes were downcast, either gazing at the floor or scouring the pages of compact newspapers for escape from a mundane existence. Jack had his sketchpad and pastels secured in the battered brown briefcase that lay across his lap. He was already regretting his decision to take this commission. He felt his fingers drumming on the surface of the case, each finger in perfect syncopation with its twin on the opposite hand. He hadn't felt this nervous since his last few days in 'The Mother of all Wars'. He forced himself to breathe deeply: this wasn't a combat zone, it was a courtroom.

The approach to the magistrates' court was teeming with reporters and cameramen. Jack hoped he had missed the obligatory pursuit of the prison van when, lenses held high above heads, the paparazzi loped alongside, flashguns exploding in a furious effort to catch the killer's profile. He pushed his way through the crowds, past the ugly Victorian splendour of the court's frontage, along the relative quiet of the car-encrusted side street, to the rear entrance.

Jack wasn't alone in his abhorrence of the crowd's crush. Twenty yards ahead, unusually for this area, a chauffeur-driven Daimler was parked adjacent to the kerb. As Jack approached, a tall, athletic woman, dressed in demure black, emerged from the limousine. Ash-blonde hair pulled back carefully into a chignon accentuated the sombreness of her outfit. She clutched a large black Gladstone bag and looked angry. She seemed to hesitate for a moment, then leaned down below the roof line to bring herself level with the car's interior. As he approached, Jack could see that there was a man inside, though the driver and the window posts prevented a full-face encounter, but he could hear the woman's voice. Jack was right: she was angry.

Her accent was hewn from the suburbs of Sydney with the edges softened by English familiarity. Jack was approaching them fast, but his suede desert boots gave no advance warning of his arrival. He kept walking, dipping down as he did so, his artist's curiosity urging him to catch a better glimpse of the car's passenger; but the interior seemed unnecessarily dark. He was five yards away when he heard a deep, cultured voice:

'Just look after King Arthur, Miss Stern.'

Jack Forth stopped dead in the street. He could not move, and he didn't know why. As he stood frozen to the spot, the car drove past him and away; the woman whisked up the steps and he still could not move.

What the hell's going on? What's wrong with me?

As Jack felt the inexplicable terror begin to dissolve, he wondered if he was having a flashback. Or was it the cocktail of injections they'd given him before the Gulf? Whatever it was, it pinned him to the ground motionless. He tried to get a grip of himself. He was here in a peaceful side street on his way to work. He thought for several seconds in an effort to isolate the moment when his body had rigidified, but the moment had gone. Inexplicably he was wrenched from his reverie by the voice of his Coffee Buddy:

'You're cracking up, Jacky-boy: the shrink warned you it would come.'

Shaking his head, he made his way into the building where 'The Crown v. Speakman' would take its first tentative steps towards the defendant's imprisonment for life.

The double-height Victorian corridors were packed. An air of apprehension seeped through the familiar dense blue smoke from a hundred cigarettes. Jack sidestepped the outstretched legs of arrogant teenagers sprawled along the old oak benches, and eventually came to court number seven. Signs had been hung around the exterior doors to the public gallery entrance, indicating that it was full, but still the crowd questioned the uniformed police officers posted to protect it. Jack worked his way a little further down the corridor to the press entrance and flashed his pass. Once he was inside, it was only a matter of moments before the bench was assembled and Jack caught his first glimpse of the country's most hated man.

'Are you Trevor Speakman?' the black-robed clerk of the court asked the miserable figure in the dock. He was flanked by two stern-faced prison officers, the harsh lighting reflected from the bright steel of the securing handcuffs that joined the three together. Jack studied the face of the defendant.

Speakman looked like a bodybuilder who had put away the weights and piled on the pounds. His face was wide and flat, with oval startled eyes that failed to comprehend the proceedings.

'Are you Trevor Speakman?' The clerk's irritated voice rose a decibel.

'Yes, I am.' The defendant's voice was faltering and unsure. A scream of 'bastard' erupted from the public gallery. The lone voice was joined by others, all screaming their hatred of the murderer.

'Silence,' commanded the elderly usher, his half-hearted command drowning in the loud vocal display of animal loathing. The chief magistrate took up the quest for order:

'I shall have the public gallery cleared if there are any further interruptions. Be quiet or you will be in contempt of this court.' The noise subsided to a steady hum, then down to expectant silence. Jack studied Speakman while all this was happening. The man's terrified eyes were glazed over like a newborn babe's. The two prison officers continued to stare straight ahead impassively.

'Now,' the clerk resumed, 'I shall put the charges to you. Who represents the defendant?'

'I do,' a woman's voice replied. It was recently familiar. Jack swivelled away from his view of Speakman to the row of lawyers. She still looks angry, he thought. A strong, rather than beautiful, face stared back at the court clerk.

'Leone Stern, Teal, Windle and Crichton.'

Jack was surprised that she had introduced herself: normally these facts were known well in advance of the hearing. The clerk went on to read the seven charges of murder and one of abduction. To each and every one, his voice barely a whisper, Speakman pleaded 'Not guilty'. Jack began to make a preliminary sketch of the courtroom layout and the personnel it held. The three magistrates he drew in outline, the lawyers for the Crown Prosecution Service the same, the public gallery a hostile silhouette. Then he fixed upon the face of the beast.

That was why he was here: to draw the face of the killer of the girls. It was never easy. A courtroom sketch artist was meant to capture more than a likeness. It was his job to catch the mood of the court and the soul of the accused. There were any number of pictures available to the press to show the public what Speakman looked like, but Jack was there to show what he was *really* like. Speakman refused to look bored or angry, petulant or proud: he merely appeared afraid and confused. Try as he might, Jack could not get the picture right: it wasn't what the papers wanted.

Suddenly, he was vaguely aware that the proceedings were winding down. Leone Stern agreed that the case could be committed to the Crown Court for trial without delay. She went further, insisting on expediency. Jack saw the unhappiness in her face, her chin thrust firmly forward.

'I make no application for bail on behalf of the defendant.'

In the moments that Jack had listened to the last legal formalities he had continued to doodle in an attempt to draw the murderer. He looked down at his latest rendition. His head began to carousel when he saw what he had drawn. On top of the shoulders of Trevor Speakman he had grafted the features of a much younger, more familiar man. Taking out his green pencil he drew in the eyes, sat back and stared into the unmistakable features of the face that greeted him in the mirror every morning.

CHAPTER TWO

Leone couldn't bear to look behind her as Speakman was led away down the cold, grey, stone steps to the holding cells below the main court, the public gallery following every movement of the pitiful convoy with fresh abuse.

She shuffled her notes back into the black bag at her feet and in doing so knocked over one of Richard Dexter's aluminium crutches propped up against the lawyers' bench. A loud clatter reverberated around the emptying courtroom as she looked up apologetically to the senior Crown Prosecutor.

Richard Dexter was probably the best technical lawyer the Crown employed. Strongly principled and with a reputation for being unswervingly fair, he had never contemplated a career in defence work, although many firms had tried to lure him away. He had suffered from polio as a small child and, although the infantile paralysis could have left him bitter, there was no person more positive and determined. It was little surprise to Leone that the committal to Crown Court was being handled by him.

'Talk about sweeping a man off his feet,' he whispered to Leone as she scrambled around retrieving the crutch.

'Sorry, Richard,' she replied smiling up at him. 'Guess it's not my day: I've had better, I can tell you.'

'Want to talk? Someone from your place has got to sooner or later.'

'Yeah, I know. I've just seen the correspondence file. What the hell has been going on?'

'Hey, I'm only the other side! How should I know? Suits me fine if Speakman doesn't want to give you instructions. Makes our case easier. But I'm bound to say we did think it a little peculiar, this close to the trial, that nothing seems to be happening at your end. Now, if you were to tell me that it's going to be a guilty plea at the end of the day then terrific – it saves the families an ordeal

– but otherwise you're playing a very dangerous game: this case is what you could call *water*-tight.'

Dexter didn't expect Leone to respond to the tasteless pun: he was serious. Hauling his bulky frame onto the crutches, he nodded to the doorway at the side of the court. Leone winced a little as she saw the strain manifest in glistening sweat across his brow, but she knew better than to offer any assistance. He clattered through the lawyers' row, colleagues parting the way like interrupted filmgoers at a 3D festival.

Leone had been away from the criminal courts for twelve months but none of the faces had changed. For the most part, the assembly of sad-looking solicitors had been here when she had left, doing the same cases with the same clients all playing legal-aid lottery; there were few winners.

Nodding her acknowledgements along the line, she emerged into the corridor that led to the solicitors' room, towards which Dexter was heading, wasted legs trailing behind. Leone followed him into the room and closed the door. He reclined against a table covered with back copies of the *Law Society Gazette* and piles of user-friendly leaflets for criminals. He pulled out a crisp white cotton handkerchief and began assiduously working it between the collar of his shirt and his thick neck.

'So, you decided to come back.'

'Kind of; I didn't get much of a choice.'

'I won't even ask what that's supposed to mean; just glad to know that someone with a bit of sense has got on board at last. But remember, Leone, this one is a no-favour case; orders from so way up that you'd need oxygen and a Sherpa for your handbag.' He gestured to the sky with his finger.

'Spare me the hype, Richard. What's the party line?'

'Seriously, Leone, Speakman's had it. Everything is so well recorded and above board that there's no possibility of an appeal. This is a genuine state trial whether we like it or not!'

'Stupid me: there was I just beginning to think all those ghouls had turned up to watch the road traffic court. Give me a break.'

'Look, this investigation has spanned five years – the Assistant Chief Constable has just about devoted his career to catching this bastard – and they won't be palmed off with anything less than a full confession or conviction before the court. If you're thinking of any deals, you'd better think again. Seven counts of murder and one abduction: that's all we'll take, Leone.'

'My instructions are "not guilty" to anything. What more can I say?'

'Level with us. Listen, I understand that Speakman will want to keep his privileges while on remand but it's putting off the inevitable; all these tactical pleas won't get you any credit.'

Leone was well aware that defendants who had been remanded in custody pending trial were treated differently from convicted prisoners because of the age-old maxim, 'innocent until proven guilty', but that wasn't the case here. Speakman had been unable to alibi himself for any of the abductions, and could hardly deny the strength of the evidence against him, but according to the file he was so blocked on methadone that he couldn't give rational instructions.

'Have you briefed for the trial?' she asked.

'Roger Fry QC leading, Jeremy Kelly as junior, and a noting junior.'

'Some line-up.'

'What about you?'

'Don't ask.'

'I'll find out sooner or later, Leone.'

'Well, when you do, tell me because the way things are at our place I'll be the last to know.'

'You're playing games again, Leone. I've had frequent conferences with the barristers and they tell me that Sedgewick has got his hands on it: if that's true, then God help Speakman. Do you realise that there's something like seven hundred thousand statements logged onto the HOLMES computer as unused material? Somehow I don't think you'll be able to get through that lot in a hurry, but of course you're welcome to try. On the other hand, you could help us both out by making admissions about some of the evidence.'

'Such as?'

'Well, it seems pretty clear to me that you won't be able to challenge any of the evidence on Speakman's employment history for starters. It's a fact that he worked for Bigg Truck Haulage as a driver.'

'So what?'

'So we can prove categorically that his work schedule places him close by each one of the abduction points.'

'How?'

'As a long-distance lorry driver he had to have diesel. His company issued him with an account card. You know the sort of thing: it acts like a credit card, only the bill goes to the company. All he does is sign the receipts. We can trace his movements on the days in question by a combination of witness statements and these till receipts, which are all timed and dated. So there isn't much point in denying that he was near the scene. We've even got an analysis of the tachograph inside the cab of his lorry to back those facts up.'

'But that's all circumstantial: as I understand it there's no eye-witness account, or anyone who saw him dispose of the bodies.'

'True. But he was found with a young girl drugged in his trailer; he still lives in Exeter at a point central to the places the bodies were discovered. It all fits, and he doesn't have a word to say in his interviews with the police. In my book that adds up to sure-fire guilt. Now, do you want to talk about those admissions?' Dexter finished forcefully.

'I can't really say anything until I've had a chance for a proper conference with Speakman. I wouldn't like to step on counsel's toes by admitting things which they may wish to con-test.'

'What about the parents of these girls, Leone? We all want to be able to tell them that it's over, that they can eventually put their daughters to rest and get on with the rest of their lives.'

'That's below the belt, Richard, and you know it.'

'Maybe, but this case has got everyone wound up and, judging by today's performance, it doesn't look like *you're* going to be making things any easier.'

'I don't think you understand me. I won't be putting pressure on Speakman to change his pleas; you should know I don't work like that. If he says he's not guilty then it's a trial no matter what. But I've only just got on board; it may change.'

'So be it, Leone. I expect I'll be hearing from you in due course. The pre-trial review's set for the first of October. Have your list of witnesses ready before then and put on us notice of any applications you may wish to make.'

Leone held Dexter's gaze with a growing unease; there was a lot he wasn't telling her and a lot she had to learn. She headed out of the room and walked along the main corridor towards the front doors of the court building, where she knew the press would be waiting for her.

CHAPTER THREE

L eone had expected trouble, but not this. The hostility of the waiting crowd mirrored the hatred of a united nation. Though she had arrived by the back entrance, her instructions from above were to give a press conference after the day's business was done. This could only be held at the front of the magistrates' court. Leone walked into the belly of the beast.

A throbbing phalanx of reporters pushed forward to take what they could. Each hard, eager face searched for an exclusive angle.

'Miss Stern, will the case be contested at the Crown Court?'

'Is King Arthur going to plead?'

The crush of disorderly journalists, all of them thrusting forward tape recorders and microphones, began to push her out of stride. Leone stopped dead and glared at the encroaching throng.

'If you stand back I will read a prepared statement.' Her voice was far from inviting.

The milling reporters withdrew slightly as she straightened her back and removed the one-page document from her Gladstone bag. Flashguns popped, TV video cameras whirred, as she took a calming gulp of air and began.

'Trevor Speakman has answered the charges truthfully. He unequivocally denies the allegations against him. While no application was made for bail, this should not be taken as acceptance of the charges. He remains in custody for his own safety because of the hostility of the public . . .' Leone read the script flatly before the reporters became bored with the usual statement of innocence made by the guilty. The inquisition resumed, one voice joining another. One stood out above the rest.

'Miss Stern, a drugged girl was found in the back of Speakman's cab: how does that square with his innocence?' It was a good question, and one she had asked herself repeatedly in the hours since this case had been passed her way.

'All these matters are *sub judice*. When the jury are empanelled *they* will decide the case, not the press.'

The shouting began again.

In the press box, Jack Forth viewed his work unhappily. This wasn't what Tom Leath wanted. Everyone knew what Speakman looked like, everyone knew what he was, but not Jack. This picture before him came from somewhere within his psyche riding on the back of a grating, uncomfortable, but as yet elusive awareness. Something tugged at him: an undertow of uneasiness indicated something was wrong. Why had he drawn his own face?

When news of the first abduction and murder had sown the seeds of parental terror five years before, he had felt a prod of distant familiarity. When the peculiar method of binding the girls' bodies was muttered by a journalist, he felt the sleepy awakening of recognition. When the same insider described how the girls' eyeballs had been forced out of their sockets, it felt as if the back of his head had knowledge it refused to share with the front. The proliferation of the watery deaths hadn't surprised him.

Jack pushed the inadequate sketch into his briefcase. The truth was there somewhere. He didn't know why he knew that, but he did. One thing was for sure: the agency couldn't possibly use his drawing. He snapped the case shut in the hope that out of sight meant out of mind.

The court continued with other, less controversial, business. Another drink-driver was being hauled up to answer for his inadequacies. The defendant looked uncomfortable in what was probably a borrowed, tight-fitting suit. It was time to go.

Jack had plenty of time before he retrieved his daughter from his parents. His work had designated him a weekend father. Hollie understood, but didn't accept that it would always be that way.

Pushing through the double, frosted-glass, swing doors, he tightened his grip on the case and walked slowly en route to the front door. The court foyer was ringed with self-pitying defendants, pregnant girlfriends and shell-suited children with filthy mouths. Why did criminals believe their prodigious breeding rate was a mitigating rather than an aggravating feature? Jack believed children were a joy, not an excuse.

Court staff, security men and nosy lawyers, mixed with criminals; they all peered out through the large windows. Jack sidled up to Nick

Rice, the weasel-faced guru of the gutter press, who was standing in a prime spot.

'What's going on, Nicky?' Jack asked.

'It's Speakman's solicitor. She's having a rough time of it,' he sniggered.

'I'm surprised you're not out there with the pack. What's up?' Jack had always disliked Rice. He stank of hypocrisy, rubbishing other people's lives on scandal-strewn pages where his own would not be out of place.

'Nope, I'm afraid you might say I've been appointed head of the deferred gratification committee.'

'Come again?'

'Queen Guinevere!' he said, gesturing over his shoulder to a bench behind them twenty yards away.

'You mean Speakman's married?' exclaimed Jack.

'Used to be, five years ago; divorced before the first murder. We got to her ages ago; left the *Sun* on the starting blocks. Fifty grand and she's singing the sweetest fucking tunes since Elvis Presley. I mean the whole lot. You know the shit: "How I was gagged every night but didn't think to tell the police".'

'What the hell is she doing here?'

'Getting some shots of her to run after he's convicted.'

Jack looked over to the bench where an ordinary-looking woman dressed in what were quite obviously newly bought clothes perched nervously on the edge. Jack shook his head in disgust. He didn't know who to blame most: the wretched woman for taking the money or the press for offering it. The whole thing was like a circus, from the big-top courtroom action to the tacky little sideshows like the one he was witnessing.

Just then the slanging match between Leone Stern and the media notched up a decibel. He watched as she snapped her bag shut and began to wade into the hostile public gallery, which had moved in behind the press corps. Almost without thinking, Jack set off into the mêlée.

The dark-blue backs of several police officers greeted his descent to the steps. Outside, the crowd surged forward to swallow Speakman's solicitor into its midst. Jack could see that the officers were striving ineffectually against them. As Leone Stern pushed through the encroaching, booing mob, the sleeping policemen pulled back to enjoy some lawyer abuse.

Everyone knew Speakman was guilty. They wanted to show it and live it. Didn't they understand? The solicitor was just doing her job, not fighting a crusade. Jack shoved his body between the hateful face of an outraged pensioner who was muttering 'bitch', and a screaming skinhead who punched the air. He could see the solicitor being manhandled on her way to a taxi. Jack was surprised that the costly Daimler he had seen earlier had not re-emerged to whisk her away.

The swell of the crowd forced him towards the heaving shoulders of the Australian solicitor. He watched in horrified fascination as a bald, blazer-wearing, middle-management executive hawked up a gob of phlegm and propelled it accurately to Leone Stern's right cheekbone. It caused the surging group to pause, momentarily, before the success of the defilement, and the police officers' reluctance to act, propelled the anger to meltdown point.

This wasn't right. Jack pushed through the ranks of foul-mouthed skinheads, punks, mothers with children, all united in their common hatred of King Arthur. He could feel the heat of the taxi's exhaust against his leg as he wedged himself a gap, and Leone Stern a way out. Her coiled hair had been freed by the hostile actions of the crowd, grabbing and pulling. Jack gripped her left arm, thrust open the door of the black cab and began to bundle Leone inside. As her long, black-stockinged leg slid across the seat, she turned momentarily to look upon the face of her saviour. Jack looked back. Though her mouth was downcast and stern, he could see the panicked gratitude in her eyes.

'Thanks,' she mouthed through the noise as he began to push the door shut.

Though her hair was tousled, the tendrils framed a beautifully contoured face. She pulled her hand up to her left ear: her earring was gone and she looked back briefly to the pavement for its whereabouts. Jack watched but could feel the punches to his back: the coliseum populous hungry for blood. He quickly snapped the door shut to a gratifying look from the cabbie, a loud diesel rev later she was gone.

He scanned the floor. Directly above the gutter, a pearl earring sat inoffensively on the pavement. The police officers were watching the fleeing taxi with amused pleasure. While their vapid features were fixed on Leone's departure, Jack swooped down to retrieve the fallen earring.

She was Speakman's lawyer – perhaps she could tell Jack why he felt so disquieted by the case. Something was very wrong with all this. Her unhappiness outside the court supported that precognition; her forced abruptness in the court had cemented his view; but why did he feel so apprehensive?

A couple of hours later, he was still tussling with the concept while walking down the street to his parents' Hertfordshire home. The house occupied a large corner site of the twisting 1920s cul-de-sac in a small village just in danger of being swallowed by St Albans. It had been his parents' one desire after his father's years of military service to retire here and, as he approached the house, Jack realised that the older he got the more he understood why. The air carried the smells of the country. Fresh and light; not a trace of fumes anywhere. He walked through the gates still thinking about Leone Stern, and made his way in through the front door.

Hollie's voice gently interrupted his autopilot journey.

'Daddy!' she said with a big grin. 'I thought you'd forgotten.' Her long, autumn-brown hair slipped from a lemon ribbon as she dashed across the polished ash floor of his parents' large country kitchen. His father, or the Colonel as he was known in the village, nodded his head in his customary shy, agreeable manner. His mother moved away from the range and kissed him lightly on the cheek while Hollie hung from his arm in delight.

'How's my girl then?'

'Which one?' Hollie offered, as she took her grandmother's hand.

'Both,' he added, and smiled at Hollie's acceptance that there was more than one important woman in every man's life.

'I've got my swimming things, Daddy.'

Then, with a slick change of demeanour that would have put an Olympic athlete to shame in the concentration stakes, she was solemnly saying goodbye to her grandparents as if she were about to swim for the gold. Jack and his parents smiled at each other in memory of Fiona.

'Absolutely nothing like her mother, is she?' The Colonel winked as Jack was unceremoniously dragged out of the door by one very determined eight-year-old.

During the leaf-clouded walk to the school baths, Jack marvelled at the enthusiasm of his daughter's stride.

23

'You're getting tall, too tall for me to keep up with.'

'I'm only growing up. Remember what a pain that was?' she said, eyes straight ahead, focused and bright with energy.

Of course he did; the years sat uneasily in his mind. He recalled the moment when he thought he had truly grown up. It was the point at which his dad had stopped being a hero and had become a man. After twenty-three years, the Army decided that Colonel Forth's services were no longer needed: 'surplus to requirements', as stark as that. It always seemed to work that way: once you were good at your job, then it was time to be replaced.

They ate up the ten-minute walk, fuelled by Hollie's excitement.

'Come on, Dad, you're lagging behind. I've got two races to swim.'

They reached the swimming pool entrance and waited in the queue behind a photo-fit family complete with identical twins and crying infant. Jack looked around the 1960s under-designed concrete foyer and sniffed the dubious qualities of chlorine; it took him back. Everything seemed to take him back – so far but not far enough. Why wouldn't his mind let him return?

Inside the public gallery of the pool, Jack wrinkled his nose at the antiseptic smell. Several sets of enthusiastically biased parents half smiled at his entrance. They were the PTA, the FBI and R&B of the school, and recognised a flake when they saw one. He sat alone and apart.

He thought again for a moment about Leone Stern but didn't really register why. More and more, his concentration was deepening with the echoing qualities of the silent pool water. Fifteen minutes passed before he noticed Hollie emerging from the changing rooms to join her friends at the poolside. He stood to wave, placing his hand on the seat in front, but it slipped off and he nearly lost his balance. His palms were sweaty; he hadn't realised. One or two people around half nodded in their concern for him but would never have dreamed of making further contact. Hollie didn't see him among the crowd and sat excitedly talking with the other little women, oblivious of the growing dryness that was developing in Jack's throat.

He slumped to the seat, his knees loose and weak. It was always the water. He looked down at Hollie wishing her to catch his eye.

A potted version of her beautiful mother. The images came quickly: too fast to rationalise, too blurred to focus, and too painful to really want to remember.

The gala continued to unfold before him. The screech of feedback over the PA stabbed his brain as they announced Hollie's race. Thin, broad-shouldered girls, hair consumed by rubber caps, made their parent-ignoring way to the seats behind their launch pads. With towels around excited frames, they readjusted froglike goggles and moved forward for the off. Hollie was swimming in lane seven. Her eyes scanned the audience in a final sweep for his familiar face. She looked so tiny, so vulnerable; he was suddenly overwhelmed by an urge to cry out to her but couldn't, and he didn't know why. Jack knew this was an eliminator for the county trial. Of all the sports for Hollie to have developed an interest in, it had to be this. He'd said nothing to Hollie about her mother's death. Years ago when she had asked in earnest, Jack had told her Fiora had gone to sleep in the water and since then it was as if Hollie had to be near the water too. He sort of understood and his own phobia was never mentioned. But Hollie loved the water.

The sweat-suited starter called the girls to order. Disrobing, Hollie appeared grimly determined in her quest. She didn't look like a little girl any more: she was a mirror image of her dead mother. Steady eyes gazed down the pool ahead. The set of her shuddering shoulders told Jack how ready she was for this, and he knew it was for him. Hollie prepared to dive flat to the whistle. Arms held out, she readied herself for the first push.

Suddenly a false starter to Hollie's left could no longer hold to the waving pistol and in she went. The others followed, the movement captured in their peripheral vision.

Hollie got the dive wrong. Jack could see that she had attempted to pull back once the girl's false start had been ratified. Instead of spreading on the top of the water she went deep, too deep. The other contestants pulled themselves back over the lip of the pool, all except Hollie. Jack shouted to the starter as he vaulted across the barrier and slipped on the wet tiles surrounding the pool.

'She's down there, can't you see?' he cried.

Pulling himself up, he moved towards the water, pursing his hands together in anticipation of a dive, flexing his legs to push, then froze: not even the momentum would carry him to the edge.

He could see how still her body was; it was no more than a stain on the bottom of the pool. He was shouting, shouting as a number of the other girls screamed in panic. A young teacher came from nowhere and dived headlong into the blue depths. A second later two attendants followed him and the panic began to spread and sizzle among the spectators. Jack could feel the rush of sickness and helplessness run through the gathering crowd. Suddenly the surface smashed open, the young teacher gasping for air, his face red with fear. He was shouting but Jack could barely make out the words through his own confusion. 'She's trapped in the air vent . . . scissors . . . her hair . . .'

Within moments of each other, the attendants broke the surface, gulping fresh air, then resubmerged. The crowd at the poolside parted to let someone through. Hollie had been under for over a minute. Jack screamed into the face of the teacher, 'Get her up, get her up.'

'She's got a wound to the side of her head; we have to cut her hair to free her . . .' He was still gasping air into his lungs as he spoke. The crowd opened up again, allowing the first-aid kit to be passed forward, and a pair of bandage cutters was handed down. The young man disappeared beneath the water and Jack held his breath. Seconds later large clumps of Hollie's hair began floating to the surface. Children were screaming as parents clutched onto them. Jack was cursing and praying. Well over two minutes had elapsed: if Hollie was unconscious, her lungs would have filled with water by now. 'Come on, come on,' he shouted at the pool.

Hollie broke the water first, spilling onto the floor like a wet fish. Jack reached forward for his daughter and placed her flat on the floor to begin resuscitation, but the teacher pushed him aside, not wanting to risk a second failure to act. Jack fell down on his backside as the competent educator breathed new life into his daughter. Her chest began to push as she turned sideways and vomited onto the tiled flooring.

Jack had almost lost her again.

CHAPTER FOUR

R ichard Dexter's nose twitched rapidly, sniffing the air with short intakes as if trying to minimise the amount of pipe smoke his lungs would have to endure. Two days after Speakman's committal proceedings the prosecution were moving the case forward. It was always the same when he came to this place. He was sitting in an uncomfortable plastic chair, which had lost one of its rubber feet, and he had to use his crutches to stop the seesaw motion. To his left were three young boffins, notebooks in hand and pencils at the ready: obviously students, but they hadn't been introduced to him. Opposite him, puffing slowly on a huge barrel-shaped ebony pipe, sat Dr Ian Coombs, Home Office pathologist, Bachelor of Science, Chartered Biologist, Fellow of the Institute of Biology, and unquestionably the country's leading expert in DNA analysis. Coombs was a big man with a purple face achieved by years of claret abuse. He had a shock of white hair in the style of a monk, and friendly brown eyes.

They were entrenched in a conference room at the Home Office Forensic Science Laboratory in Northditch. Unlike most other government departments the occupants of Northditch lab never complained about the distinctly tatty surroundings provided for their comforts; they were more interested in acquiring the latest scientific equipment. Dexter was waiting for the final forensic reports from Coombs, hoping that he would find evidence to nail Speakman unequivocally to the cross. The preparation of the forensic evidence had been unusually difficult because Speakman had only been caught as a result of the drugged girl found in the back of his trailer. To tie him forensically to seven murders over a five-year period with only the original autopsy files to go on was going to be almost impossible.

Coombs looked up from the papers he had been reading and

noted Dexter's discomfort through the brown smoke that lingered between them.

'Sorry, Dexter: forgot you were there for a moment. I trust you won't mind if my pupils sit in on this one,' he said loftily while striking the wooden pipe twice with the palm of his shovel-like hand. The smouldering embers flashed out and fell into a glass ashtray on the table.

'That's all right, Doctor, what's the verdict?' replied Dexter nodding at the large bundle of documents.

'Not good, at least not good from your point of view.'

'Why?'

'We've encountered a number of problems, especially with the first victim.'

'Give me the lowdown. I've got to tidy this lot up fast: the barristers are screaming for your reports.'

'OK, but I don't think you're going to like it.' He manoeuvred his large frame out of the chair and looked over to his students. 'You may wish to note the evidence-gathering techniques here, gentlemen.'

Three pencils moved swiftly across notepads in perfect unison like a formation dance team.

'The first victim's body was discovered lying face down in a culvert some two feet square. The culvert itself was designed to take the overflow down the hillside from Dosmary Pool on Dartmoor. The bottom was rough and stony and the water is very free-flowing at this point. The victim was found with her head pushed deeply into this culvert and her hands were tied by means of diver's twine in front of her. As with all the other victims, the whole body was immersed. By way of general background, the post mortem revealed few external symptoms of drowning but there was certainly white foam around the nostrils and mouth. As you are probably aware, drowning results from a combination of the effects of water on the blood and air prevented from entering the air passages and lungs by water.'

'How can one be sure that death did in fact occur by drowning, Dr Coombs?' asked one of the students.

'Well what can be stated with certainty is that, although the severity of post-mortem signs of anoxia will depend on how much the victim struggled while in the water, if *no* signs of anoxia are present then the cause of death was not drowning. In the present case the victim was probably unconscious when placed in the water because there is little evidence of debris such as water weeds or stones from the bottom in her hand, which was clenched as a result of a cadaveric spasm. There were, however, five strands of human hair found wrapped around the fingernails of her left hand. Autopsy revealed the lungs to be pale and distended; the trachea and bronchi also contained foam. There is of course muddy water lodged in the cerebral cavity given that this victim like all the others had her eyes removed from their sockets. If she hadn't drowned she would inevitably have bled to death.' Coombs reached onto the table and extracted a black and white photograph which he handed to the students, who peered at the mutilated body dispassionately. Coombs looked pleased with their detached scientific appraisal. He went on.

'As you can see from the photographs, the body carries evidence of a significant number of injuries. In view of the fact that changes in the blood occur when the body is submerged in water, we cannot say with any great confidence whether the injuries were sustained before or after death, but for what it's worth I suspect that most of them were inflicted before. There is clear evidence that the girl had been sexually active and the reports identified four different samples of semen from her body.'

'That stands to reason,' Dexter interjected, his voice disappointed.

'Why?' enquired Coombs.

'She was a prostitute, abducted from central London.'

'Although my experience of such individuals is limited, I consider it a little odd that she would have acquired the semen voluntarily. Is it not the case that prostitutes are notorious for insisting on sheath protection given the inherent risks of contracting the AIDS virus?' Coombs said.

'I suppose that must be right, but surely you can't be suggesting that she was murdered by four different people!' Dexter exclaimed.

'I'm not suggesting anything, Mr Dexter, merely pointing out that four separate and distinct semen samples were recovered from her body. You have to remember: we are scientists here, not police officers, lawyers or indeed clairvoyants,' Coombs shot back, mainly for the benefit of the student audience, who smirked adoringly at their guru.

'All right, point taken, Doctor, but it could be the case that she was in the habit of soliciting for unprotected intercourse. It's a common enough activity among those prostitutes who are desperate for the money. Perhaps she was a drug abuser.'

'I'm afraid not, Mr Dexter.'

'How do you know?'

'Because it is routine procedure in drowning cases to carry out tests simply to ascertain whether there could have been any extraneous factors which contributed to the death.'

'Like alcohol or drugs, Doctor?' a student half asked, half surmised.

'Precisely, but also disease or illness.'

'What about this case?' Dexter pushed, a note of annoyance creeping into his voice.

'No evidence whatsoever of any long-term narcotic abuse, but we did discover something which certainly links all seven victims.'

'Go on.'

'In each case there was carried out what is known as specific-gravity testing of the blood found in the heart. Principally this was done to ascertain whether the drowning occurred in fresh or salt water.

'The results showed evidence of a rare phenobarbitone derivative, which is a powerful depressant especially when taken intravenously. The doses were so powerful that just a small amount would be enough to knock the victim out almost instantaneously.'

'So you're saying that each victim at the point of abduction was injected with the same drug as was found in the one girl who survived in the back of Speakman's trailer.'

'It's a strong scientific probability.'

'Oh, that's beautiful. How rare is the drug?' Dexter seized on the point.

'I should say exceptionally rare. It is more frequently used in the United States but nevertheless it is still prescribed in Britain.'

'I wonder where he got it from?' Dexter mused. It was certainly something he would have to take up with the officer in charge of the case for further enquiries. If they could pinpoint a prescription issued to Speakman by his own doctor or perhaps identify an unsolved burglary of a chemist in an area he had visited, then surely that would be the final nail in his coffin.

'I'm afraid that's about the high point of your case, though, Mr Dexter.' Coombs interrupted his temporary euphoria.

'What about the intimate samples we sent to you for analysis?'

'Ah yes, I subjected the sample of Mr Speakman's hair to some STR profiling to determine whether or not there was any cellular connection with samples taken from the first victim. As you know, there wasn't anything at all useful in the other cases.'

'Is that a form of DNA profiling, Doctor?' posed one of the students.

'Yes: the remarkable factor about this type of analysis is that, because DNA is a material found in cells throughout our bodies, it remains the same irrespective of the source.'

'So if we can recover DNA from, say, a person's blood, will it be the same as that found in other body tissue?'

'Exactly the same. It also applies to body fluids such as semen and saliva and other things like bone marrow. Mr Dexter here forwarded us samples of Speakman's hair taken with his consent and asked us if we could compare it with the five strands of hair found in the victim's clenched fist.'

'And?' Dexter prodded impatiently.

'And they don't match.'

'Shit!' said Dexter uncharacteristically. The collected academics looked appropriately offended at his bad language. He blushed slightly and quickly went on – but soon wished he hadn't. 'Is it possible that there may have been a mistake?'

The high priest of biotechnology turned sharply on him. 'Mr Dexter, DNA carries genetic information which is unique to each one of us except in the case of identical twins. STR profiling is a process dependent upon DNA amplification, enabling us to isolate single loci and, thereafter, short tandem repeat structures. It has taken over ten years to perfect at a cost of many millions of pounds. I can assure you that in my humble experience neither I nor my staff are in the habit of careless use of the samples or the very expensive equipment we have striven so hard to acquire. In short, there is no mistake, no cock-up and more importantly no evidence whatsoever of DNA to link your suspect with that body, or any of the others for that matter.' The doctor's face had coloured significantly during this outburst. Dexter held up his spare hand in surrender.

'Sorry, Doctor, just checking.'

'Check all you like, young man, but it will do no good: there is no link and that's final. I've already noted all of this in my report, which I trust you will disclose to the defence in due course.'

'It'll probably end up as unused material, Doctor Coombs; after all it doesn't establish one way or another that Speakman was at the scene, does it?'

'I'm a scientist, Mr Dexter. It doesn't matter to me, but I would have thought that from a moral point of view the defence might find it useful because it shows that it is definitely not Speakman's hair that was found in the girl's hand.'

'Looking at it from the prosecution's perspective, that hair could have come from anyone. You said yourself that the culvert where the body was found was fast-flowing. There's nothing to stop bits of hair drifting past and becoming entangled with the body.'

'That's one explanation, Mr Dexter,' said Coombs acidly, glaring at the lawyer. His contempt unmasked, he reached for his pipe and began reloading.

CHAPTER FIVE

The children's ward of the hospital was silent apart from the tread of the night nurse's crêpe shoes as they squeaked against tired linoleum flooring. Jack held his daughter's hand. Hollie had drifted off into tranquillised sleep. Her last muttered words, before she lapsed into her eight-year-old dream world, were:

'I would have won, Dad, I would.'

Jack watched as the REMs began to flutter across the fine lids of her eyes.

'I'm sorry, sweetheart.'

He felt a hitch in his throat as he remembered his inability to act. What kind of a father was he? His own parents had left an hour before, smiling too much at their granddaughter, attempting to make light of a near-disastrous occurrence. They were careful not to ask him too much about the accident.

Jack shook his head in misery at his failure to save her. At least Hollie wasn't expected to suffer any long-term effects. The doctors said she wouldn't remember a thing but had to be kept in for observation. Jack hoped so but feared to imagine what went on behind those delicate eyes. The brain scan had failed to show any abnormal waves or patterns. Her reactions had been thoroughly tested.

She's fine, he told himself, fine.

The ward was half empty, or should that have been half full? Were you an optimist or a pessimist where beds in a children's ward were concerned? Jack liked the idea of its emptiness. It seemed that there were fewer sick children that way. Everybody was being so kind, so understanding. The nurses made Hollie relax immediately; he wished they could do the same for him. Even the agency had been understanding about the sketch of King Arthur, under the circumstances.

It began to occur to him that, despite everything that had happened, and the trauma of the last twenty-four hours, out of sight didn't mean out of mind after all. He was drawn to his briefcase, still locked at his side; he hadn't been home since the accident. Jack withdrew the sketch and held it across his knees. The agency had asked for a drawing of Speakman and in response he had drawn a portrait of himself. He knew what Speakman looked like; what was the problem?

He crossed his legs and tutted at his inability to draw a simple face. It hadn't always been that way. When he was a child, Jack could take one look at a building, a face, a street scene, no matter how complex, and faithfully reproduce the original on paper. He could take one glance at a landscape and then capture every object in it with accuracy. They called it 'eidetic' memory – each picture a photograph of the chosen scene. Jack had achieved childhood notoriety when appearing on a nationwide TV programme that studied people with gifts. They called his a phenomenon; but it felt nothing like a phenomenon to him, who had always had it.

That was all before the Cyprus trip. The trip may even have caused it, no one was sure. There were so many blanks to fill in his life.

Hollie shifted around in the crisp linen sheets and pushed against the safety frame at the side of the bed. When she had seen the juvenile restraint, intended to stop her falling out of bed, she had pulled an insulted face. She didn't have to say, 'I'm not a kid'; her expression got the message across to the smiling ward sister.

He looked down more closely at the drawing. The silhouetted public gallery seemed so empty and he felt a goading compulsion to fill it with colour. It was an urge he hadn't felt in years, the sort of feeling he used to have when he was a child, just the pure drive to empty everything out onto the paper from his mind's picture.

He focused his memory of the courtroom and tried to recreate his feelings. What was it about this Speakman case that snagged at him? Suddenly he decided to try again. There was a simple trestle table in the middle of the corridor. Checking Hollie was still, he moved to one of the children's chairs and squatted down gently into its tight bucket seat. There were stray soft toys straggling along the table's top.

'Round-up time,' Jack whispered as he cleared space to work. He laid a virgin piece of paper on the table and weighted down the two vertical sides with one-pound coins. Next he removed the pastel pencils from the teak and brass box and laid them in a perfect regimental line. He could see the courtroom clearly. He could feel the hostility it contained, but he couldn't draw a line.

The light wasn't right, that was it. But that was every bad or lazy artist's excuse not to work, as well he knew; the light was fine, it was he himself who wasn't. Things looked different from this height. Adults didn't sit in children's seats or dream their dreams. Kids weren't just small grown-ups: they were people with a different perspective and a different approach. That was what he needed.

He looked around to test his theory. The walls were crammed with simply drawn pictures. They had used pen and ink, paint and wax. Wax! Why not?

Jack reached for his own pencils, then stopped. They weren't the sort he wanted – it had to be done in wax. He searched the toy locker for his working tools. Eventually they offered up half a dozen chewed and stubby crayons of varying colours. They felt like an old memory in his hand. The tacky texture of their surfaces rolled around between his fingers. He was ready.

He began by sketching out the courtroom plan with a fine-nibbed ink pen. He placed the prosecution and the position of the Australian solicitor, Leone Stern; he captured her face at the end of the row where she had perched so unhappily. He drew in the magistrates' bench and the dock. He added the public gallery; the layout was complete. He put the busy and bored court staff in next: the clerk of the court, stenographer and prison officers.

He reached for the wax crayons and began to fill the picture with bursts of colour. He was forced to combine his own pencils as second after second the paper began to fill with colour at a furious pace. A woman in a bright green coat sat next to a bald man in a navy-blue blazer. A reporter with a red tie and a redder nose slumped over his notebook. A woman with beautiful azure eyes. He was working in a whirlwind of memory retrieval.

The fine detail he was working into the picture was lost on him; the trance was deepening. He could see and draw the anguish on a bereaved parent's face, the fury on the lips of another, the colour of their hatred. Jack had no idea of the time – he was trapped in a fugue he had not experienced for years. He didn't know whether he was hating it or enjoying it; he was just doing it.

He saved the face of the killer until last. The rest of the players were all there: the gallery was full, everybody had a face, everybody had a place on his canvas except the defendant. There was still just a torso. Jack's crayon lay like a wet fish in his hand; he couldn't do it. He had come so far and then failed. Even the desire to draw his own face had disappeared as if his previous drawing had led him to this point. But strangely, he could see Speakman's face in his mind's eye. It was clear to him.

He threw down the red crayon; it scuttled across the tabletop and plopped down to the floor. He picked up the sketch and stared at it for what seemed like an age, then his eye picked him out. He was sitting in the back row of the public gallery. The body wore a finely cut serge pinstripe suit but the face was that of Trevor Speakman. Jack felt the bilious warning of vomit. Unconsciously, he had removed Speakman from the dock and placed him on the shoulders of an innocent bystander. He could ask himself only one question: where was the face of the man in the blue serge pinstripe suit?

CHAPTER SIX

L eone kept her head firmly down as she rode the wooden escalator at Holborn Underground. She reached the top and had to sidestep a tramp asleep on the cold tiled floor close by. His face was covered by a four-day-old copy of the *Daily Telegraph*. She caught a glimpse of her own face staring out from the front page, broad forehead clenched in a spasm of fear as the mob pressed themselves past the slack wedge of policemen.

Leone had spent the last few nights reliving the scenes outside court: the thunderous abuse, the weight of the crowd, the overfamiliarity of the press – 'This way Leone, love. Come on, girl, gi's a shot.' Cold, frozen memories chilled her as she emerged into daylight.

The sudden anonymity of London's rush-hour mania freed her from the memory as she meandered along High Holborn with the Tuesday-morning army of office drones. Eight hundred yards later she rounded a corner and walked through the passageway past the Inns of Court School of Law. The September wind bit against her pale green gabardine overcoat and whipped around her cheeks as she turned left towards the offices of Teal, Windle and Crichton. The building stood at the eastern corner of Gray's Inn Square like a proud, stony-faced general.

She walked through the ancient archway and briskly past the gaggle of chauffeurs waiting to take their pampered employers to power-breakfasting clubs. She looked at the expensive motor cars parked all over the square, testimony that the recession had no effects here. Her entire salary wouldn't cover a parking permit for this place. Eventually, she made her way up the steps worn down by generations of eager lawyers. The firm was one of the finest, but not the oldest, in the city, built on a reputation of straight talking and fast dealing. It had risen unremarkably through the seventies, practising a mixture of specialities from white-collar crime to society divorce, but it was the cash-rich 1980s that had catapulted the firm into the super league. Commercial property leasing and corporate finance had become the firm's major income earner. Forty-three equity partners shared a purse of millions as a result.

Leone knew that she would never be offered a partnership. For a kick-off she hadn't graduated from Oxford and at full-time she was a woman. Not that TWC could ever be seriously accused of prejudice. In fact, there were two female partners who both worked as consultants in the Hong Kong office, as far away as possible from the London headquarters. But even they were rowing blues from Balliol. When it came down to it, Leone didn't much care for the prospect anyway. She'd been ambitious once, but not any longer. As far as she could see, getting to the top involved too much 'yes, sir' and not enough 'but what about this . . . sir?' None of her contemporaries at the firm would ever dream of questioning the partners' approach to case management, but she did.

Her heels clicked over the green Italian marble in the reception area as she nodded good morning to the security staff milling around the reception desk.

'Miss Stern,' the dark-haired young woman sitting behind the desk called out.

'Yes?'

'Message for you from upstairs.'

The girl had deep red lipstick framing the most perfectly matched white teeth as she smiled at Leone.

'Saw you on television the other night: it must have been terrible. I just couldn't believe the way those people were behaving, spitting at you and everything. Anybody would think you were on trial instead of that monster.'

'He's innocent until proven guilty, Mandy,' Leone replied, halfheartedly.

'I know, but what he's done . . .'

'Allegedly,' Leone corrected more firmly.

'What do you think, Miss Stern?'

'I'm not paid to think, Mandy; you know that. Now, the message?'

'Oh, yes,' Mandy replied huffily. 'There's a partners' management committee meeting at nine and you're invited.'

'Thank *you*, Mandy,' Leone said sarcastically and checked her Swatch: it was 8.58. She scowled and headed for the lift.

Five storeys later she was gliding along the partners' silent corridor: softly lit, large, gilt-framed portraits adorned salmon-pink, regency-striped wallpaper. A pale green carpet over Burmese teak stretched out in front of her. The corridor led to a beautifully crafted double doorway of deep mahogany topped with a carved pediment, the wood and brass so highly polished it looked almost impenetrable.

Leone sat at the right-hand side of the door on a long leather Chesterfield and waited for the secretary to call her in. No one was ever late for meetings at Teal, Windle and Crichton: no one except Leone, that was.

Within a few moments a blonde, busy woman was escorting her across the threshold. Three men sat at the end of a long conference table. All three stood as Leone made her way down the room.

'Miss Stern, good morning.' A grey-haired man with bulbous nostrils and broken veins around his cheeks offered a big fleshy hand to Leone. Frederick Foster was sixty-two and enjoying every minute of it. He spent three days a week on his farm in Norfolk and drank real ale as if it was coming into fashion. He carried the look of someone who knew he had presence, despite his vertically challenged status.

'Fred, how are you?' Leone returned, shaking his hand and smiling towards the other two men.

'You know Daniel, of course.' Leone did.

'Nice to see you again.'

Dan Morgan smiled broadly at Leone. He looked closer to thirty than the forty-five he was: a real climber and the hottest drafter of commercial writs in London. What was he doing here?

She turned to the third man, whom she knew only too well: Ronnie Pearsal. Ronnie and Leone went back a long way. They nodded without a word. Fred Foster opened the batting.

'I'll come straight to the point, Leone. There's been some criticism of your handling of the Speakman case. Now, before you start blowing up, we all appreciate that you'd only had the case four days, but we did warn you that this was as big as they come. It's not as if the proceedings themselves are difficult: it's just that you knew you'd have to deal with the press and handle the lynch mob. We thought you could deal with all that; we thought you were ready. This is a show trial, Leone. Why didn't you read the rest of the statement to the press? Didn't you think that was important?'

'Of course it was. I just couldn't stand there any more and take that crap.'

'But you won't get another opportunity to ask for witnesses to come forward.'

'It doesn't matter. Speakman is as good as convicted already. You weren't there, any of you!' She wanted to raise the temperature. 'You should have heard those people; they want him dead. Try finding a jury who would dare acquit him. Talk about maximum prejudice: even our receptionist thinks he did it. Be realistic, Fred.'

'Irrespective of that, Leone,' Dan Morgan chipped in, 'it's our firm which is representing him and while that remains the situation you have to remember we're all on show.'

'Look, either you want me to run this case or you don't. This sort of interference doesn't motivate me, gentlemen. First of all I pick up the files and find that nothing has been done on the case. I spent last night looking through Speakman's medical records. Were you aware that the man is barely able to give lucid instructions? He suffers from blackouts occasionally. But hold on, he didn't tell his employers about it for fear of losing his licence and so he can't alibi himself for any of the abductions. Worse still, since being remanded he's taken to smack in a big way: the prison hospital's dosing him up to the eyes with methadone to keep him stable, but God knows what else he's getting his hands on inside. The guy's an addict. Then I'm told that the brief was delivered to a has-been silk. This is eight weeks from trial and you're now telling me to look for potential defence witnesses. This is a poisoned chalice and you know it.'

'Well, if you're not up to it we can always give it to someone else: it's just that this is one way of proving that you've got over the Bradley mess.'

'Oh, that's brilliant, Ronnie. I wondered how long it would take for you to drag that up.'

'Well, have you?' Pearsal pushed.

Leone looked at the faces opposite her. Not a day had passed in the last twelve months when Ian Bradley's lost eyes hadn't burned into her mind: a young man who entrusted his future to Leone Stern and who ultimately took his own life in a juvenile remand centre while awaiting trial for a crime he surely hadn't committed. The family had blamed Leone, although the inquest later upheld a verdict of suicide while the balance of his mind was disturbed. A

40

formal investigation by the Law Society followed complaints by the parents that Leone hadn't dealt with the case expeditiously. Ronnie Pearsal had been on the case with her but he was made a partner before the fan was switched on and managed to avoid any suggestion that he was in any way to blame. Leone knew differently.

The inquiry eventually cleared her and the firm, but there was no doubt that she had been scarred. The criminal department had been disbanded after the débâcle. She hadn't wanted to see another criminal case anyway, so for a year Leone worked in the family law department. The order had come from the top: 'Do the Speakman case or leave the firm.' If only she could.

'Of course I'm over it,' she replied, but knew that they didn't think so.

'Good. I'm sure we're all delighted to hear it. How are you proposing to progress?' Fred Foster enquired while glaring at the crassness of his younger partner, Pearsal; these things should always be done subtly.

Leone recovered quickly.

'I'm preparing instructions for junior counsel, now that the committal documents have eventually arrived. Then I'll arrange a full conference with both barristers and Speakman.'

'Who are you going to brief?'

'I thought about Toby Sloane: he's quick and keen enough to do the legwork that Sedgewick doesn't. I still can't believe that we sent him the papers in the first place!'

'Leone! Sedgewick is a good man, maybe a little eccentric, but he's still got what it takes. Look at the way he defended the Gordon case. He got the result.'

'Fred, time flies. That was over three years ago. Things have changed. Everyone knows he drinks too much. This case involves papers which have to be transported by articulated lorry. There's over a million computer pages alone. You seem to forget Speakman's instructions are "not guilty". Whatever state he's in, it doesn't matter: we're going to have to put the Crown to proof. Now, if he feels for one moment that the job isn't being done properly we'll have another Bradley on our hands, only this time it won't just be me in the firing line because this time everything I do is well recorded. I'm amazed he hasn't complained already.' She turned sharply to Pearsal, who remained impassive.

'Clients' instructions have been known to change. I'm sure

41

Sedgewick will bring some clear reasoning to the case. A plea of insanity might be satisfactory. You will instruct a psychiatrist?'

'It goes without saying.'

'What about Chris Bayfield for junior? I've heard that he's very good and he's worked alongside Sedgewick before.'

'He's as bad as Sedgewick, if that's what you mean,' Leone blurted. 'This case needs someone who's computer literate. We may even have to ask for a link-up to the HOLMES database on the police computer. Bayfield wouldn't have a clue. Why are you being so insistent that Speakman be represented by Sedgewick and Bayfield?'

'I've already mentioned the case to Bayfield at the Club; he seemed very interested,' Dan Morgan said. 'Do you have a problem with that?'

Leone knew all too well how the network of men in positions like those of Bayfield and Morgan operated, and she realised now why Morgan was at the meeting in the first place: jobs for the boys. She said that *she* didn't have a problem: but she had made plans to make sure that if Speakman wanted a trial he was going to have at least one barrister on board who would give him a voice. Shortly afterwards, she left the meeting determined to do just that.

CHAPTER SEVEN

Jack had slept fitfully. When he did sleep, several clashing images demanded his brain's attention. Hollie: her hair swimming, with dead-fish eyes, mouthing through the chlorinated water, 'Why didn't you save me, Daddy?' A man in a black overcoat: twisted and crushed, body streaming blood into the same pool, shaking his head disappointedly, whispering, 'He didn't save me either, Hollie.' Then behind him, just beyond his vision, Fiona, her voice hard beyond recognition: 'He's used to letting people die, it's his way.'

The harsh apparitions forced him awake, sweating and exhausted, until he submerged once more into the dream. Eventually, at 4 a.m., he had slumped through to the kitchen for a large whisky and temporary sanctuary. It was at that time he decided he had to speak to Helena Dwyer. She more than anyone might be able to give some calm meaning to his dreams and all that had happened over the last few days. Helena had helped him in the past. Her professional demeanour and soothing ways had been a balm over the last few years. But he had never needed her insight more than he needed it now.

His usual exercise routine abandoned through fatigue, he had showered quickly, not wishing the caress of the warm water to relax him into a waking dream. Jack had telephoned the hospital at 8 a.m. and spoken to his daughter briefly. Kids were amazingly resilient. Her voice had been bright and full of questions. But in his mind's ear he kept hearing her question from the dream, 'Why didn't you save me, Daddy?'

He still didn't know the answer to that: the meeting with Helena Dwyer, his psychotherapist, would have to provide the answer, whatever it took.

Jack watched from the back of the lecture theatre as Dr Helena

43

Dwyer shuffled the notes in her hands. He knew she would not refer to them during the lecture. They provided a necessary prop to underline a point or underscore a proposition. The auditorium was dark save for a single spotlight that illuminated the lectern where she awaited absolute silence.

The audience, clinical psychology students in the main, waited in ghoulish anticipation. Helena had a reputation for bringing human drama to the complicated enigma of the human mind. Her speciality, trauma-induced amnesia, often revealed a darkness brighter than the light. The surface babble and shuffling of notebooks subsided to a hum, then stopped as she gazed patiently into the darkness.

'The study today is a male subject: we shall call him Turner after the artist famous for his impressionistic seascapes. As we know, Turner was partially blind; this explains his unusual visions of the subject matter. Our study is also blind, blind in parts of his memory; that is effectively what amnesia represents. Through sustained therapy his impairment is capable of repair, but only when his subconscious is ready to allow the transfer of information.

'The subject is thirty-five years of age, in prime physical condition, with an intelligence quotient well above the average. His childhood development provides us with an excellent base core for comparative evalution. It was discovered when the subject was an infant that he possessed an eidetic memory: that is one which provides vivid mental images resulting in the ability to gaze upon a complicated scene, then reproduce it later with near-perfect detail. It is a trait sometimes found in autistic children, the so-called "idiot savant", but unusually Turner did not exhibit the more unfortunate idiosyncrasies or symptomatology of that group.'

Aware that the students were already gripped by the factual history of her patient, Helena continued.

'His talent was recognised and the young Turner was granted a place at a school dedicated to gifted children. All was well for some years; there was little indication that any problems existed. The psychological profiles show a well-balanced if serious boy.

'However, we know that, during a visit to his family in the summer of 1974, a trauma intervened. Turner's father, a career soldier, was stationed abroad when the island of Cyprus was invaded. Something happened: to this day we don't know what. As a result his eidetic gift was displaced. He believes it to be lost entirely; I believe it to be merely misplaced by his brain.

There was a sight or experience so overwhelming that, in order to protect itself, the brain blanked its memory. That memory still remains somewhere, waiting for the right trigger to release it.

'In teenage years, Turner became prone to nightmares and enuresis. He became morose, antisocial and increasingly phobic to water. This was long before he became a patient of mine, but so deep-rooted is the trauma block that his phobia remains twenty years later. In the meantime he was prescribed strong tranquillisers and given counselling. He was unresponsive to both.

'A distinctive change of direction came in his artwork, where his subjects were no longer architecture or complicated landscapes, but portraits of human misery. Turner showed great willpower in attempting to rebuild what was left of his adolescence. He graduated from art college and married in his early twenties.'

A hand reached up from the darkness. Helena knew to whom it would belong.

'Yes, Mister Compton.' A northerner with a chip on both shoulders, he possessed a keen mind but little patience.

'The trauma event was over twenty years ago; that's hardly news.'

'Perhaps not, but in order to understand a subject we must know the origin of his character. Besides, that is not the end of the intervention of tragedy in his life.'

The young man returned to his notes.

Helena continued. 'Having made the best of his life, the trauma still buried deep, he found happiness with his partner and they had a child after trying for some years. The tranquillity did not last. A tragic accident, resulting in the death of his wife, occurred only months after the birth. Again, his mind blanked out the episode, though there were several eyewitness accounts, exonerating him from all blame. His water phobia returned with savage ferocity but he now had a baby girl to raise on his own. His parental duties forced the issue away but did not resolve it. After some time, however, his guilt over his wife's death did resurface. Turner accepted a three-year commission in the army as a war artist. This in turn took him to a place with scant water: Saudi Arabia and the Gulf War.'

Helena paused and looked up into the blackness of the lecture room.

'Please note how Turner distanced himself from that which he

45

loved, his daughter, and that which he feared, the water, as if he felt himself cursed by circumstance and did not wish those around him to be tainted by his world. The carnage of the war is well recorded in every medium, but never more accurately than Turner's haunting canvasses of the event. There is a unique sadness and anger at the pointless loss of human life on each side.'

A voice interrupted: Compton again. 'Doctor?' Helena nodded her encouragement. 'Are there any signs of Turner suffering "Gulf War Syndrome"?'

Helena firmed her chin before replying. 'For his sake I sincerely hope not, but evidence suggests that GWS has a medical origin, due to the various vaccines injected into the troops' bodies. What concerns me most is if his Gulf War experiences have further set back the process of healing his other devastating experiences.'

Helena didn't want to be sidetracked from the main thrust of her observations. She continued. 'He came close to suicide on occasions and was intent upon self-destruction. That was when he was referred to me. We have worked together for several years attempting to isolate each trauma. As yet, he is unable to remember either incident.'

Helena was reaching the end of the lecture, when it would be thrown open to questions.

'The memory has skins, like an onion. It is possible to peel them back, layer by layer, until the bare core of the trauma lies naked before us. But in that method lies madness. The revelation, if premature, might be more than the subject's brain can accommodate. He has to be ready to remember. There must be a blinding spark, something more important to the subject than his own fear of what he will discover, before he can free himself. Turner has chosen to forget: I believe we must reverse that situation.'

Helena listened as the students took down these words verbatim; they would appear scholarly and mature on an examination paper. They didn't know that 'Turner', or Jack Forth as she knew him, was sitting at the back after begging an emergency appointment. He had sounded distressed. Perhaps the time was approaching when she could peel back the layers of his mind and discover the torments of his life. Several hands pushed through the air, grasping for further information. In one hour she might know more herself.

CHAPTER EIGHT

Helena's office was a place of calm. There were no buzzing telephones to interrupt the patient's concentration at a vital moment; the walls were plain and covered in muted fabric. When Jack had first come to this place, years before, he had expected the inevitable leather couch, swinging pocket-watch and mind drivel of a thousand bad films: instead there were two deep comfortable armchairs that threatened to engulf a body, mineral water and a quietly intelligent woman who spoke warm words but never pushed into a place where she was not invited. Helena sat opposite him, legs outstretched, slim fingers as still and serene as the rest of her body. She had a patient smile on her finely lined face. He looked away to the walls, but their familiarity failed to grant him any inspiration.

'You're not trying, Jack.'

Jack swivelled his gaze back to Helena Dwyer. The olive-skinned psychiatrist seemed sombre but her professional excitement could not be disguised.

'I know you've come to talk, but I've only heard my own voice so far,' she blurted after a long silence.

It was six days after the swimming baths incident and Jack was far from fine. He couldn't sleep, he felt as though he was trying to scream without using his voice. Helena's office, or therapy suite as she preferred it to be known, offered him little comfort, but desperation had driven him here.

'Hollie was down there. I could see her, but I couldn't move. I wanted to, I really did, but I was nailed to the floor.'

Helena nodded her encouragement for him to continue.

'I knew that every moment I lost was another moment closer to her death, but it took someone else to hack it.' His heavily set shoulders lurched forward and he grabbed the sides of his head in both hands.

47

'You know why, Jack, don't you?'

He returned her stare, knowing what was coming next. Why the fear? Isn't this what he had come to face?

'You've been coming to see me for years, but you have never been right back to the time of your wife's death, not properly.'

'You mean hypnotherapy?'

'Your only way forward is to go back,' she said solemnly.

Jack knew she was right. He had to find out what held him in this state.

'All right. What happens if you can't put me under? If I'm fighting against this memory as hard as you think, won't I fight you?'

Helena considered.

'It's possible, but you have been having the dreams again, haven't you, Jack? You've been back there already; this is a short step from there.'

'So what happens? Do you produce a pocket watch and tell me I'm a chicken, or something?'

Helena smiled appreciatively as she went about closing the wood-slatted blinds. She looked over her shoulder at Jack sitting nervously in the padded chair.

'You joke because you are afraid. I don't blame you. It was a terrible time, it's left deep wounds; we have to heal them.'

Helena was right again: he was afraid to face the past, but terrified about the future if he didn't.

'I just want you to relax, think warm thoughts. Uncross your arms and feet, then take a deep breath, allowing the muscles in your neck and shoulders to relax as you breathe. See your mind as a blank canvas, so white it dazzles you. But you are an artist, and to you a blank canvas needs to be filled. Your mind draws a picture of a face, a woman's face, Fiona's face. She looks happy, her eyes are alive with joy. Smile back at her, Jack, show her how happy she makes you.'

Helena stared at his face. His eyes were firmly shut, but at the corners of his mouth the beginnings of a smile began to form.

'That's it, Jack, look: she's laughing.'

Jack began to smile more broadly.

'Think of Fiona and listen to the sound of my voice counting down.'

He was gone, travelling deep into his mind.

'Fiona is still your wife, and will always be Hollie's mother. The fact that she is no longer here doesn't change that.' Helena reinforced the hypnotic trance to fix time and space in his mind; the more real his image of Fiona the better.

'How did you meet?'

How did they meet? Suddenly the years peeled away.

A picture spun into his mind: a young woman in a flowing black coat stood at the door of his art-school flat. As the young Jack Forth rubbed the sleep from his eyes, they cleared to allow him a better view of the fresh-faced girl. Eyes the colour of almond butter gazed over impossibly long lashes. An amused smile skimmed across a full-lipped mouth. She waited patiently for him to come to his senses.

'I read your advert on the bulletin board. Is the room still available?'

His flatmate had dropped out two weeks before leaving Jack with a burgeoning overdraft and twice as much rent to pay.

'Yes, it's still free but I hadn't expected a—'

'Woman?' she interrupted, raising finely sculptured eyebrows in mild irritation.

'The place isn't too clean. I mean, washing up isn't a priority.'

'Good,' she said firmly. 'Then we'll get along fine. Can I see the flat or would you prefer me to stand on the doorstep while you describe it?'

She had moved in and never moved out. They married two years later.

He reran the happy partnership through the VCR of his brain: a home, a daughter, a future, then the accident. They had been in Rhodes for a perfect week, with one week left to enjoy. Hollie was sleeping well and Fiona had never looked more beautiful. She still carried a delightful childbearing roll around her midriff and Jack loved to nuzzle that soft flesh.

He had wanted to see the island. As their villa was up in the mountains he hired a car with a baby seat in the back for touring. Fiona had packed a picnic and Hollie dozed peacefully as the journey began. The day had been perfect – too perfect: something had to spoil it. As the quick dusk gave way to Aegean darkness he noticed the brakes' sponginess. As the drive progressed he was pumping the pedal more frequently.

'I'm worried about the car. I don't think it's safe.'

'Come on, Jack, it's getting late. Hollie needs a feed. We aren't that far from the villa.'

They were passing the harbour wall when the thin dog ran out into the road. Jack stamped the brake pedal, but the car didn't slow down. He swung the wheel away from the sprinting mongrel; the little Fiat pushed through the harbour chain-link fence, plunging fifty feet into the depths of the clear water. The car floundered in the sucking grip of the harbour, then began to sink. Fiona turned and reached towards her tiny daughter, panic in her eyes. The car rocked to the side and settled on the ocean bed. Jack struggled to click off his tangled, webbed seatbelt. Once the car was full of water they would be able to swim out. Until then the force of the watery crush would prevent them from opening the door. He reached for his wife's hand and squeezed it.

She was attempting to loosen her own seatbelt: there was no blind panic to her actions, as if she had already come to the same conclusion.

Hollie was screaming water into her lungs. Fiona's long auburn hair swam around her shoulders as she pointed to Hollie and Jack and then to the surface. She wanted him to get Hollie out first, then come back for her. Jack forced open the car door and, reaching back for his infant daughter, he loosened the baby restraint and pulled her over the seat. As he did so, Fiona took the girl and breathed her own last breath into Hollie's mouth. Jack kicked up to the surface, where waiting hands in the circling boats above took his charge. He gulped in a vast lungful of air then kicked back down. It was the seatbelt, the fucking seatbelt. He dived down three times until, lungs screaming, he returned to the surface. He had nothing to cut the thick strap with. Fiona was pronounced dead thirty minutes later.

Helena watched as tears began to course down Jack's cheeks. He was gulping in more air and clawing at his throat, his hands searching for his own windpipe to throttle the life out of himself. Jesus, this was dangerous.

'Jack, you must come back to us.'

His hands continued their search and this time fixed on his throat. His face began to turn bright red: if she didn't act quickly he would soon turn blue, but it was too dangerous to snap him awake – she had to find something to bring him back.

'Jack, the baby's crying, Hollie's crying, she needs you. She's on the surface waiting for you to take her home.'

His hands seemed to hesitate, then dropped away. Colour returned to his cheeks as he gasped for more air.

'Hollie's safe, Jack. You've spoken to her at the hospital. She wants to see you soon. Come back now and see her. It won't take long.' Jack nodded solemnly. 'But you must come back to me first: if you don't they won't let you see her.' A frown shot across his face. 'You know how they are, silly rules.'

'I know,' he muttered.

'You see a dazzling white canvas.' Helena realised how panicked her voice sounded; she forced herself to remain calm. 'You want to draw a picture on it. You draw yourself in my office, comfortable, relaxed, happy, but you will remember everything that you have just seen and accept that you were not to blame. Now when I clap my hands you will open your eyes.'

Helena brought her hands together sharply. His eyes opened instantaneously, focused for a moment, then filled with tears.

'It wasn't your fault, Jack.'

Helena's voice brought him back from the past.

'The point is you saved your daughter and yourself. Your wife loved the two of you more than life itself. You have to respect that, and learn to respect yourself again. You have to go back in the water. The water is a symbol: it is life. You have been avoiding the living because of your guilt about the dead. Participate again: act, don't just react.'

Jack now knew her words were true. Since the accident he had gone through the motions without any real emotion. As he sat sweating and shaking in the chair, Helena touched his hand, her face flushed with the adrenalin of success.

'You've had a breakthrough today. But we have to go back further.'

Jack narrowed his eyes. 'There is no more.'

'Oh, there is and you know it, but not today. You must be exhausted. Listen, Jack, and listen carefully: there is something you have buried even deeper. The breakdown you experienced as a child was caused by something you saw, did or had done to you. Like a dentist, we can get to the root this way and extract the rotten tooth.'

Jack rose, reached forward and kissed Helena gently on the cheek.

'I know. It's just that I'm afraid of what I'll find, but I'm sure it has something to do with this.'

He reached inside his jacket pocket and produced the wax crayon drawing created in the feverish hours at Hollie's bedside. He laid it flat on the desk top.

'Have you been following the Speakman case?' he asked as she opened the blinds. Light poured into the room.

'You mean King Arthur?'

'If he is King Arthur. Everyone seems so sure, but I'm not.'

'Why?'

'I don't know. Call it gut feeling, intuition or whatever, but I was hoping you could shed some light on it.'

'What about memory?' she said slowly.

'I was afraid you'd ask that,' he replied and she ignored him as she scanned the drawing.

'You have so much detail in the drawing but not the facial features of the main subject. It's astonishing. This represents almost a total return to your pre-trauma abilities. Look at that, you've even drawn the clock in at ten minutes past eleven; look at the second hand! This is a scene lodged in your mind right down to a fragment of a second. Extraordinary: a "living photograph in your mind".'

'Thanks for the compliments, but it doesn't help me.'

'It does.'

'How?'

'I assume your instructions were to draw the face of the killer.'

'Yes, why?'

'Such a didactic instruction must have prevented you from drawing Speakman in the dock because of something you know, something buried in your mind.'

'I don't know anything.'

'You might not think so, but it's there, Jack: it's the only explanation.'

'What if you're wrong?'

'What if I'm right?'

Jack reached into the pocket of his leather jacket and touched the contour of Leone Stern's earring. There was only one way to find out. It was time to enter the combat zone.

CHAPTER NINE

The following day, at half-past nine, Richard Dexter was perched uncomfortably in the back of a black cab heading towards Inner Temple and the chambers of Roger Fry QC. The recent cold snap had given way to the promise of an Indian summer. Early-morning sunshine cut through the listless dusty air and swirled gracefully inside the cab. The chain-smoking driver weaved a perilous route through London's side streets, periodically leaning out to remonstrate with equally reckless despatch riders.

Dexter was thankful that at least he didn't have to endure a pointless conversation and switched his mind to the conference ahead.

This was to be the last in preparation for the first appearance of Speakman at the Crown Court, when the prosecution team would at last be given some indication of how the defence case was to be run. He reflected on his conversation with Leone Stern at the magistrates' court a week ago and cursed silently that he had failed to extract any information from her other than that Speakman was unable to accept his undoubted guilt.

They passed the griffin statue at Temple Bar marking the ancient boundaries between the cities of London and Westminster. A security guard at Middle Temple gate waved them through without hesitation, catching a glimpse of Dexter in the back. Seconds later they were pulling up outside Fountain Place, tucked away in the central courtyard.

He was in the middle of a venerable group of buildings which spread from Fleet Street on the northern boundary to the natural delineator of the Thames Embankment on the south. The 'Temple' was founded on this land in the fourteenth century, taking its name from the ancient order of Knights Templar, the original owners. Since then, it has been the exclusive province of the Inns of Court where barristers cluster themselves in establishment chambers.

He struggled out of the car, tipping the cabbie precisely ten per cent, and was met immediately by the noting barrister on the case. When it came to trial it was her job to make detailed notes of the evidence for leading and junior counsel to analyse at the end of each day. Dexter had been highly impressed with her perseverance so far and had no doubts that with a few more years under her belt she would become a fine prosecutor. For the past eight months she had sifted through the case notes under the supervision of her pupil master and consequently had an encyclopaedic knowledge of the depositions.

She was dressed in the traditional uniform for female barristers: high-necked, white cotton blouse under a tunic-like black suit with a mandarin collar. Her black hair had an auburn tint and was scraped back in a dramatic coiffure, exposing a square-shaped forehead from which a long, straight nose protruded. Although severe-looking, she had a quiet, confident manner coupled with a minimum of bodily movement, giving her the aura of someone who was in complete control: a rare quality for one so young.

The pair moved to the thickly painted black door of number twelve Fountain Place, the girl carrying Dexter's briefcase. She pushed open the door and waited while he moved past her into the hallway. To the left, the clerk's room was noisily careering its way through the last-minute business encountered before the courts sat at 10.30 a.m. Dexter heard Tusker, the chief clerk, berating an unfortunate solicitor on the telephone who, it appeared, had neglected to engage the services of a barrister for a case starting at 11 a.m. He nodded briskly to Dexter before placing the solicitor on hold with a perfunctory 'I'll see what I can do'. He walked the few yards towards them with his palm outstretched. Dexter slipped his arm out of the right crutch and they shook hands warmly. Tusker shook hands with everyone warmly so long as they were giving *his* barristers business. The accepted pleasantries over, Dexter was led down the now familiar corridor to a large conference room on the ground floor of the building. It had been specifically set aside for the Speakman case.

The room was typical of a set of successful chambers: large oil paintings donated over the years by members adorned two walls; the rest of the space was crammed with leather-bound volumes of case reports dating back centuries. In contrast to the ancient opulence, a decrepit coffee percolator squatted bubbling in the far corner; next to that sat the man whose narrow shoulders carried the responsibility of ensuring that Speakman was convicted.

The top half of Roger Fry's head peered over a copy of *The Times*, his half-moon, gold-rimmed spectacles teetering delicately on the tip of a finely chipped nose. Flashing eyes swivelled to Dexter, then to the other occupants of the room in the manner of a kestrel on the lookout for prey. It was a trait he was renowned for, constantly moving as if no part of his body were fixed. When excited he would gesticulate, twist, turn, point, but always remain like a still-life portrait when called upon to listen.

In one swift motion he folded the newspaper and rose from the brown leather armchair. He possessed a deep throaty voice, each syllable clipped into position with a definitive rasp. It was the sort of voice that made people listen or squirm. Only the faintest trace of his Cornish roots remained; instinctively lilting but perfectly controlled.

'Mr Dexter, how pleasant. I think that's everyone now. Come, do sit down.' He waved his arm in the direction of a seat next to Jeremy Kelly, the junior, at a large round walnut table by the window.

'Good morning, Mr Fry. I hope I'm not late,' replied Dexter, shuffling to the seat. 'I thought it was ten a.m. we had arranged.'

'True, true, but we were all anxious to hear news of the committal proceedings and Doctor Coombs' report. Forgive me if I sound impatient.' A smile broke the barrister's face and his nose twitched rapidly for a moment before serenity was restored.

Dexter sat with the usual difficulty and accepted a black coffee from the girl he'd met at the door. Reaching into his briefcase he retrieved his notes of the committal proceedings. All in the room listened intently as he recounted the conversation with Leone Stern.

'Well, that forces our hand, doesn't it, Roger?' said Kelly.

'Mmm, I believe you're right,' replied the Cornish silk.

'What do you mean?' enquired Dexter.

'Given that the defence will not, or cannot, make any admissions with regard to the evidence, it's up to us to make the case out in its entirety,' said Fry. 'We are essentially relying on similar-fact evidence, which means we will be asking the jury to look at the circumstances of the last abduction where the girl survived and then conclude that Speakman is guilty of the seven murder counts because of the striking similarity in the methods used.'

'I don't see any legal problems in that?' Dexter pushed.

'I beg to differ. Firstly, the defence could make an application to sever the indictments, which, if it's successful, would mean that Speakman is entitled to have each count tried separately.'

'In other words, we wouldn't be able to present any evidence to the jury of the other cases because he has to be tried on the facts of each one individually.'

'Precisely, giving him a much better opportunity of getting off. The evidence on each murder is purely circumstantial. We need to have all matters tried together.'

'What's the second point?'

'If the trial judge, for some bizarre reason, allows separate trials, I believe there's a prospect that the defence will say it will be impossible to find any jury who could not have been prejudiced by all the publicity surrounding the case. It's a classic trial-by-media situation.'

'Do you have any inkling as to what the trial judge's attitude will be to all of this?'

'Justice Singleton is well aware of the situation, I can assure you. I bumped into him only the other evening at the Inn. We had a frank exchange of views and you might say we are *simpatico*,' Fry said solemnly, looking only at Dexter; the other two already knew how things were played at this level.

Dexter looked around, secretly cursing their privilege but not envying it. He understood only too well what this implied familiarity with the trial judge's feelings was meant to convey to him: the public wanted someone to hate and they were going to get their man at whatever cost. Judge Singleton was the presiding judge for the South-West circuit. He had assumed responsibility for the trial and obviously wasn't intending to stand in Fry's way. Dexter braced himself as he saw Roger Fry reaching for the Northditch laboratory report.

'Now then, what has the good doctor managed to unearth? I wonder.'

'I think you'll find some parts of it disturbing,' replied Dexter.

Dexter chewed his lip for five minutes while the contents of the report were digested by the barristers. Roger Fry remained impassive as he read the conclusion, then gently tossed the papers onto the table.

'It means very little to us: we can serve the factual analysis of the post mortems on the defence but not any of his forensic findings about the hair sample and the DNA cross-matching. If they want to go searching then let them get their own expert. Put the conclusions in unused material on the HOLMES database: they'll never come across it.'

'The doctor isn't going to be very happy: he realises that his findings could be important to Speakman's defence, at least in relation to the first victim,' Dexter objected.

'So what? They probably won't require Coombs to give evidence. If they only see the first part of his report there's nothing controversial in it: all it's saying is that, from a forensic point of view, there's nothing to link Speakman specifically to the bodies. We omit to mention the hair sample. It doesn't assist us, and there's nothing in our job description that says we should build his case for him. So we bury the conclusion. What the hell? It's only one scientist's opinion. They're ten a penny these days.'

'Except it's not an opinion, it's a finding of fact: Speakman doesn't match the hair sample. I'm beginning to think if they find this on top of the other stuff that's already in the unused files—'

'Have you forgotten, Dexter, what it is that we are supposed to be focusing on here?' Fry said sharply.

'Well of course not, but—'

'No buts; a but is something a goat does, not something we use to start questioning our judgement at this stage. We three are firmly committed, Mr Dexter, to achieving no less than full public satisfaction. We will not deviate from the fundamental obligation to the families of these girls: they know we have the right man, *we* know we've got the right man, so all we have to do now is to make sure the right man is put behind bars and then forget about it until the next one comes around. Now I was obviously under the misapprehension a moment or so ago that you had developed some sort of motivational problem. If that is the case then I'm sure—'

It was Dexter's turn to interrupt: he knew how Leone Stern must have felt when he'd delivered a similar, though less elegant, rebuff to her at the magistrates' court. 'You don't have to go on, Mr Fry.

I'm just anxious that there should be nothing lurking around that could prove a frustration.'

'I'm very glad to hear it, because I'm relying on you to make certain that the defence don't find anything that may assist to that end.'

'What do you mean?' Dexter asked uneasily. He heard the others in the room shifting in their chairs.

'I anticipate that the defence will wish to link up to HOLMES. They can only do that at Scotland Yard, and obviously we will be required to oversee the search of the unused material. The officer seconded to prevent them from straying into the entire intelligence network is Inspector Barnes. I am reliably informed that she is an excellent officer who can be relied on to toe the party line, so to speak. You will liaise with her: I'm sure that, between the two of you, you'll find some way of ensuring that it isn't made easy.'

'Hold on a moment, you're asking me to bury this material outside of the Speakman files—'

'Not bury, Mr Dexter, merely temporarily inter, then miraculously resurrect once the search is over. They'll soon get bored.'

'But that's—'

'Your duty, Mr Dexter, your duty,' Fry said solemnly.

'An abuse of process, I was about to say,' replied Dexter, holding his stare. 'An abuse of process.'

'Call it what you like and then tell the mothers of these girls what it was that let Speakman off: a few technicalities might cover it. Yes, that's what you could say. "Dreadfully sorry, Mrs Bridges, I'm afraid your daughter's murderer walked because the Crown experienced a few technicalities." That's what it amounts to, isn't it?'

Dexter's jaw tightened and for the first time in his entire career he wondered how deep you had to sink before there was no chance of coming back to the surface.

CHAPTER TEN

'Where had you hidden the camcorder, Jonathan?' The man's voice was steady, though his dark eyes sparked with barely controlled rage as they bore into Berkeley's face.

'On a shelf inside the drinks cabinet,' he whispered.

The other nodded once. 'There will be time for punishment later.'

Berkeley swallowed hard but did not dare to voice any complaint at the pronouncement.

'In the meantime we must consider the problems this causes.' He smiled bleakly at the terrified financier. 'Now, although you may well have viewed this sequence for your own pleasure on many occasions, I have not yet had that opportunity, so put it up on the computer screen.'

'But—'

'Now.' As always, his voice was terrifyingly calm and undeniable.

Berkeley shuffled across the corner office on the top floor of Teal, Windle and Crichton. His trembling fingers tapped in the Internet code now indelibly scorched into his own memory base. Within seconds the familiar tinny-sounding electrobeat was echoing around the room. It heralded the arrival of the two-minute pay-to-view compuvid. Slowly, the pixels began to crystallise into focus and Berkeley vacated the chair, allowing his inquisitor the dubious privilege. After fifteen seconds he'd seen enough.

'How long has it been running?'

'I don't know: ever since Taylor left me, I guess.'

A look of superior distaste crept over the face opposite him.

'You're sure that none of the faces has been descrambled?'

'Two million pounds' worth of sure.'

'At least that's something, but where did the money come from to pay Taylor?'

'Where do you think?'

'Not the Boatman account?'

'It was the only way. I did it for all of us.'

'How touching, but if your loyalty is to be believed shouldn't this information have been shared with me a little earlier?'

'I'm sorry, but what else could I have done?'

An icy stare told Berkeley the answer to that one.

'How did you get the money without my signature?'

'Forged.'

'How did you pay Taylor?'

'At first in cash, but when the Boatman account ran out I started to give him some personal cheques. Now, though, there's no more left. It won't be long before they discover discrepancies in my clients' accounts at work.'

'Your naïveté is as ever quite breathtaking. Blackmailers do not have a code of honour. There is no such word as "enough" in their vocabulary. Whilst you still have a stick of furniture or a five-pound note in your wallet it is never enough.' He measured Berkeley with a steady gaze. The banker dropped his own to his hands, which twisted wetly together.

'I'm sorry, I thought I was doing the best thing: I thought I could handle it.'

'Will you stop saying that. It doesn't mean anything to me. You should have got rid of that scumbag rentboy when he discovered Boatman. That was the deal, wasn't it? But now you're telling me that you didn't get rid of him, that you put him in a job in the City because you couldn't stand to live without him. You've lied to me because of him; years of friendship gone. Me, I'm the one who made things happen for you. I made you, and this is the way you repay me.'

'I truly am sorry, believe me.'

'Being hypothetical, Berkeley, I'd say that it really doesn't matter any more. As far as I'm concerned you would be better off finishing it yourself: you have no idea of the ramifications of this.'

'You have to help me,' Berkeley pleaded. He rose from the chair and stood in front of the desk. 'I'm not going to prison,' he shouted, slamming his palm into the desk.

The tall man glided up from his seat with the grace of a shark and in one brutal, savage motion brought the polished steel blade of the letter opener crashing down through the web between Berkeley's thumb and forefinger, pinning him momentarily to the wood. He stared into Berkeley's speechless face.

'If I say you will go to prison, then to prison you will go.' He twisted the blade through ninety degrees, and clamped a hand over Berkeley's mouth before the scream could erupt. 'If I tell you to fuck your mother, then you will carry out that act.' He stared into Berkeley's tear-filled eyes. 'Do we understand each other, Jonathan?'

Berkeley nodded dumbly, the pain coursing up his arm like a snakebite.

'You have jeopardised more than you can ever understand. When I remove my hand you will not scream or whimper; if you do then the pain will return.'

Berkeley shuddered as the blade pulled through his flesh and gasped as the silver point was withdrawn; the blood flowed.

'Mop that mess up, then leave. There is nothing for you now. There never will be anything for you again. Do you understand?'

'Please!'

'It's too late, for you at least.'

'Oh God.'

'You have lived without honour; redeem yourself.'

He moved towards the door of the office suite. 'Isn't there anything . . . ?'

'Samurai Bashedo states, "He who has lived badly must die well".'

'I'm not a fucking samurai,' Berkeley shouted as he wrapped his hand in a handkerchief.

He was looked up and down with disdain as the door was opened for him.

'That, my dear Jonathan, is sadly obvious.'

As he passed through the portal, Berkeley turned to stare into his oldest friend's eyes: they sparkled with power and sly amusement.

'I'm sorry. Just give me one more chance.'

The other reached down to his injured hand and squeezed it tightly. The pain was terrible, but Berkeley did not dare to cry out.

'There are worse things than death,' he whispered, and in that moment Berkeley knew it was the irrefutable truth. The other watched the figure of the financier reel away to the lifts and the brief time that was his future.

Four floors down in the same building, Leone was pleased with her morning's work. Earlier, she had spoken on the telephone to the chief clerk to the chambers of Chris Bayfield, the barrister who had been promised the Speakman brief. She had just completed a scam. Late the previous afternoon she had spoken to the junior clerk at the same set of chambers. Posing as a solicitor from another firm, she engaged the services of Mr Bayfield to advise in conference a most important chemical company on a delicate contractual dispute. Mr Bayfield had been delighted to be able to assist. Leone knew that there could be no comeback on her from Danny Morgan if Bayfield wasn't available for the Speakman trial. All he was interested in was money, and all she needed was a fighter.

'Ah, Miss Stern. Nice to know you're back in circulation,' the clerk said.

'Yeah, thanks, Colin. It's been a long time since I've needed a criminal barrister.'

'I heard you were on the Speakman case.'

'Believe you me, I didn't ask for it.'

'Sedgewick's leading, isn't he?'

'Yes, so I gather,' she said, leaving the clerk in no doubt that *she* hadn't made that decision.

'Who were you thinking about for junior? I heard from Mr Bayfield that he was being talked about at your place.'

'Yes, I think he's worked with Sedgewick. What's his availability like?'

'Hold on a sec, let's have a look on the computer.'

Leone held her breath, hoping that the junior clerk had taken down the bogus dates properly. The clerk was soon back on, grumbling, 'The Speakman trial is set for when?'

'The second of November, but there's a pre-trial review on the first of October. We'll need him for that, and a conference with Speakman later this week,' Leone replied.

'I'm afraid Mr Bayfield has commitments already, Miss Stern. He's involved in a civil case of some significance. He's doing a lot more commercial work these days. This one is a huge chemical dispute; very high-profile.'

'That's too bad,' she said, a bit too glibly, and hurriedly went on. She would have given anything to be present when Bayfield eventually found out that his lucrative civil brief had vanished after turning down the slightly less well-paid Speakman case. Toby Sloane was available. She booked a conference and arranged to have the brief delivered later by messenger.

No sooner had she replaced the receiver than the telephone's light flashed. The receptionist informed her that a man calling himself Jack Forth was in the foyer hoping to return something she had lost. Jack Forth, who was he? And what had she lost? She told the receptionist that she would be right down, and quickly left her office.

The lift doors opened smoothly and a man stood inside, his right hand thrust inside his black overcoat, which hung loosely over his shoulders like a cape. He nodded with a thin, sickly smile. Leone hardly acknowledged him, only checking him over once to glimpse the security pass stuck to the lapel of his coat. No one else interrupted the lift's descent and shortly afterwards they were spilling into the reception area, the man brushing past Leone in his hurry to exit the building.

Jack was inspecting the impressive original oils lining the walls of the ground floor when he saw them emerge. As he walked to greet Leone halfway, the man in the overcoat sidestepped him neatly, his head down, apparently deep in thought.

Jack held out his hand as Leone approached. She took it, and he was surprised at the strength of her grip.

'Mr Forth, now I know. Outside the magistrates' court: you helped, didn't you?'

'That's right. I couldn't be sure whether you'd remember.' He looked into her sea-green eyes. She looked a little harassed but still formidable.

'I didn't get a chance to thank you. It was all rather strained.'

'That's OK. I didn't come for any awards, Miss Stern: I came to return this to you.' He held out his hand to reveal Leone's missing earring.

'Oh, that's ever so kind of you. It's just a cheap one, but so nice of you to take the trouble,' she said, smiling and touching her delicate ear lobe as if realising for the first time she was missing her jewellery. 'What were you doing at the court, Mr Forth?' she asked, suddenly but politely.

'Working,' he answered. 'I'm a sketch artist. I was there because I was meant to be drawing your client.'

'I see, and did you get what you wanted, Mr Forth?' The question was posed with a distinct change in attitude. He guessed from her performance outside the court the other day that she didn't care for the press, however remote the connection.

'Not quite.' He was about to explain to her that he hated the job as well, and was reaching for his briefcase to pull out the Speakman courtroom sketch when something stopped him: a flashing image sprinted across his mind. Then, before he had time to assimilate the feeling, the most piercing screech split the air. Jack instinctively looked to Leone, only to see her staring over his shoulder towards the front door as a scream from the receptionist rose above the sudden commotion.

'Oh, my God,' Leone shouted. As Jack looked through the open doorway he could see the jackknifed container of an articulated lorry spewing across Gray's Inn Road. The scene drifted past at what seemed like a third of the speed of real time as the lorry headed inexorably towards the figure walking slowly across the road. They could only wait helplessly for the moment of impact; the deathly dull thud and breaking glass were enough to sicken even the most hardened of individuals.

He exited by the main door. The crowd was too numbed by the horror of the scene to react; Jack wasn't. He heard the rumble of the engine and could see two twisted legs protruding from underneath a huge tractored wheel; they were twitching. Jack used the driver's step to climb into the cab. The driver was bleeding from a head wound. He reached for the keys and turned the motor off.

'He jumped in front of me,' the driver muttered.

'I know, you'll be OK,' he soothed, jumping back down. Voices were raised in collective trauma as he pushed past the shocked gathering to the injured man. He had seen death before but still took a moment to steady himself before inspecting the body beneath the wheel. The man's stomach was crushed flat. All that it had contained now lay outside, spread in a visceral smear on the crimson tarmac. Jack bent down, swallowing the unbidden bile from his own stomach. The man's face was parchment white, bloodless, but he was breathing shallowly.

His continued twitching told Jack that he was still alive, but only just.

Strangely there was no injury to the victim's face and Jack recognised him as the man who had emerged from the lift with Leone Stern. Jack squatted next to him, using his own jacket to prop up his lolling head. As he did so the eyes flicked open and fixed momentarily on his own.

'Will somebody please call a fucking ambulance?' Jack shouted, though he knew a hearse was the only proper form of transport. He swallowed hard again – the stench from the man's spilled body was overpowering – and forced himself to return the desperate gaze.

'You'll be OK, really, just hang on.'

The man began to spasm and tremble; his chest convulsed, then a torrent of thick blood spewed from his mouth and over Jack's hands and arms. He was trying to speak. Jack could see his lips were moving, mouthing a word of two syllables. His eyes were beginning to glaze over like a dying junkie's. Jack put his ear closer: whatever he had to say was important: it could be the last words to his wife and family and, despite his own horror at the gross scene, they needed to be heard. The blood in the man's mouth was making it difficult to hear, so Jack placed his left ear directly over the dying man's mouth. He could hear two words, could just make them out: the man repeated them three times in a mantra.

'Boat Man,' he whispered, 'Boat Man, Boat Man,' before exhaling deeply and finally and forever.

CHAPTER ELEVEN

J ack had slept more fitfully than usual. Every time he had dozed off the image of the hideously mangled man had returned to burn itself across his dreams, the only difference being that this time he carried the contents of his stomach cavity in a holdall in front of him and kept walking up to Jack inviting him to have a 'peep' inside. Jack had woken, startled at the tricks the human mind played and sweating profusely with the terminal horror of the scene. He had given up on sleep at around 5 a.m. He attempted to understand what the dream might mean, how his unconscious had wrestled with the actuality and returned with the strange nightmare. But he was beaten back by the effort. Jack watched the grim dawn break and bring with it more rain. Eventually he climbed exhausted from his bed, donned a worn towelling bathrobe and moved into the hallway.

The banner headline of the morning newspaper attracted Jack's eye immediately.

FRAUD SQUAD PROBE AFTER BANKER'S DEATH

He reached down to where the paper lay on the doormat and took it with him to the kitchen table. As Coffee Buddy bubbled his morning brew he spread the paper before him at the solid-oak breakfast table and smoothing the wrinkles flat he read the article.

A merchant banker killed when he was hit by a lorry in London this week may have been at the centre of a major fraud scandal, it emerged last night.

The Serious Fraud Office is refusing to confirm or deny that 45-year-old Jonathan Berkeley had left a legacy of deceit at one of the City's oldest firms. A spokesman would say only that Mr Berkeley's dealings were 'under investigation'.

The incident happened at the upper section of Gray's Inn Road . . .

Reading between the lines, Jack could see that the journalist had omitted to refer to the death as an accident.

. . . The news of the SFO's investigations has set the City buzzing with rumour and speculation about Mr Berkeley's dealings.
The driver of the articulated lorry has been interviewed about the death, but no formal charges have been made. . .

The accompanying picture showed a very different Berkeley from the one who died before Jack's eyes: a young man in Oxford graduation gown, his entire future before him. Jack had witnessed the end of that. Now the police wanted a statement from him about the death. He had half an hour before the chief inspector arrived to chronicle the last few minutes of Berkeley's life.

Jack mentally cancelled breakfast. The recurring vision of the mangled man had driven away his appetite.

He showered lazily, rubbing apple soap over his tired body. He was reaching for the bath towel when the doorbell rang.

'We're a little early, Mr Forth.' A warrant card identified the speaker as Chief Inspector Latham from the Serious Fraud Office. He introduced his sergeant, a tall, ginger-bearded man, with a nod. 'We can wait outside while you get dressed.' Jack regarded their less than fashionable double breasted catalogue suits and then realised he was wrapped in an inadequate towel. He knotted the top corners around his waist, then smiled sheepishly.

'No, no, come in, please. I'll just get dressed.'

He stood back to allow them through the doorway, then left for the bedroom. Inside the sparse lounge the policemen looked for a comfortable seat in vain. Stark Bauhaus chairs abutted the shrieking white wall with geometric precision.

'Nice place,' the gruff-voiced sergeant was saying as Jack reappeared at the door dressed in denim shirt and chinos.

Jack observed their discomfort, opened the door to the kitchen and gestured to the table. The two policemen moved through the doorway and took more traditional seats.

The chief inspector looked down at the newspaper on the table, still open on the Berkeley article.

'An important man.'

'A dead man,' the sergeant added with a smirk.

'They seem to indicate it was suicide,' Jack said, nodding towards the article.

'And you, Mr Forth, do you think it was suicide?'

Jack shrugged. 'All I know is that he seemed upset about something. He stormed out of the solicitors' office.'

The chief inspector looked puzzled. 'So far as our information goes he went straight from Gabrielle's restaurant to his death. I'm sure we've got a statement to that effect: what office?'

It was Jack's turn to look puzzled. 'Speak to his solicitors; they are—'

'Jessop and Jessop, I believe,' the chief inspector interrupted

'Jessop, Jessop and Jessop.' The smug sergeant repeated the firm's name correctly for him.

'Yes,' Latham went on, his irritation evident, 'we *have* spoken to them. They contacted us last night. A senior partner called to offer his assistance, said that he hadn't seen Berkeley in weeks, but that a verdict of suicide would kill any life insurance money. He wanted to know if Berkeley had said anything before he died – any last words.' The inspector peered at Jack, forcing his eyebrows together in a frown of intimidating intensity. 'Well?'

Jack shook his head. 'No, that doesn't make any sense. Maybe it wasn't his solicitors, but he definitely came out of the offices of Teal, Windle and Crichton.'

'I assure you, Mr Forth, we do not have any statements to support that scenario. A reliable witness has come forward to say he was dining with Mr Berkeley directly prior to the incident.'

'But—'

'Look, Mr Forth, we will take the details and no doubt check it out, but please let's get on. Now, did he say anything?'

'No, he was just fighting for breath.' Jack's mind was fighting for reason. If no one had come forward from TWC it made sense that the so-called reliable witness was anything but. If that was the case, why had the solicitors' firm for which Leone Stern worked lied about Berkeley's presence at its offices? The security tag and appointment register would show that Berkeley had been there and whom he had seen.

'Are you positive, Mr Forth? Several witnesses believe he whispered something to you.'

'If he did, I didn't hear it.'

Jack realised the tone of his voice was too defensive. These two would recognise the timbre of a lie at a hundred yards.

'You will be asked to give evidence at the inquest, under oath, and you know what that means.'

Jack knew only too well: an indictment for perjury if the truth emerged, but how could it? Berkeley was dead, and Jack alone had heard his dying declaration for all it was worth and it had to be worth something to somebody.

'Look, he was delirious, he muttered something – it could have been anything – like "Boatman". It didn't make any sense to me.'

'Are you sure?'

'Yes. I'm telling you what I heard; it was a very shocking situation.' Jack moved to the kitchen door. 'If you have any further questions I'll be delighted to answer them, but not today.'

The faces of the policemen were expressionless as they walked past him. It obviously wasn't what they had been expecting but short of a reliable spirit medium they had no way of fine-tuning.

Jack also knew that someone at Teal, Windle and Crichton was lying, but why? He hadn't been alone when Berkeley had sped through the foyer clutching his hand: Leone Stern had been there too.

Was she aware that her employers were denying Berkeley's visit? If she was, was she involved with the cover-up?

'You need some therapy, love,' the driver was saying.

'No, just a reduction in the fare. You clearly tried to rip me off,' Leone replied confidently. 'Now, what will it be? Are you opting for the report to the licensing authority or are you going to knock, let's say, thirty per cent off the meter reading? You know as well as I do you took an unnecessarily long way around.'

'How come you know so much? You an inspector for *Which?* magazine then?'

'Time's running out: here's my stop.' She ignored the side-track.

'All right, all right, call it a straight twenty, then.'

'No, let's call it a realistic fifteen, shall we?'

As Leone's minicab pulled up outside the huge, blue, iron gates of the prison, she handed three five-pound notes to the cowboy driver and didn't consider telling him the truth: that she'd spent countless hours rehearsing the *London A to Z* with her ex-boyfriend when they'd first arrived from Australia, so he could pass the 'Knowledge'. He didn't make it, but *she* would have.

The reddish-brown, Victorian brick frontage bore the scars of shrapnel bites from the bombings during the war. It looked every bit the sort of place whose goings-on you didn't really want to know. From its vantage point on top of the Heath, Leone could see clearer skies in the distance, but for the moment the rain was still drizzling across the city. She struggled to avoid the deep puddles that pockmarked the gravel forecourt.

She arrived at the special-visits reception and noticed that Toby Sloane had already signed in; but there was no corresponding entry in the journal for Sedgewick. She was ushered through to the beginning of E-wing, which spread out to the west of the main block. It was one of eight tendrils fanning out in a semicircle, each housing one thousand prisoners. The building operated on a 'Pentonville' single-cell system, but in recent times the single cell had statistically and miraculously multiplied into a double and then triple space for accommodation.

The screech and clang of metal doors closing behind her at the first searchpoint forced a sickly memory of the accident outside her offices. Then that man again. Jack Forth. His quizzical green eyes.

'This way, miss, into the bowl, please.' A voice interrupted her thoughts. Leone was being asked to place all metal objects from her pockets onto the conveyer belt. The door opened and a prison officer stepped forward. He searched her bags. Inside, he found nothing but the bulky pages of committal documents in 'The Crown v. Speakman'. In a maximum-security environment every visitor was a potential threat to the order of things. Once satisfied that nothing she carried was a danger, he flicked a switch. The impact-resistant glass partition slid silently aside to allow her access.

Leone had been on prison visits before, but this was different. Normally she would have been surrounded by hard-faced women and cadaverous old men, each of them waiting to see a husband, boyfriend or son. This was maximum security; few got in and no one from the inside got out.

While other remand centres stank of sweat, feet and faeces, Bansworth prison smelled like a large, unfriendly dental surgery. Leone followed the arrows to the next holding area and turned a corner to see Toby Sloane gazing out of the heavily fortified window to a sparse patch of grass outside. He nodded towards the scrubland blanched dry by the long summer and now surrounded by the wooden skeletons of the rhododendron bushes which marked the perimeter of the exercise yard.

'Not much to keep your dreams alive.'

'Not Kew Gardens, that's for sure.' She held out her hand. 'Nice to see you again, Toby.'

'Likewise, although I don't quite know whether to thank you or curse you for this one,' he replied, taking her hand. He had a thin face with energetic eyes. A couple of strands of hair lay foppishly across his forehead and he had a peculiar little half-crescent scar right in the middle of his chin and a slim nose that supported round, gold-rimmed spectacles. She'd always liked Toby. He was quite attractive in that academic, sensitive sort of way: the type who, given long enough, would go to the trouble of cooking an interesting meal and who would impress your mother. But, then again, she wasn't that interested in food and she didn't have a mother to take him home to.

'I thought you might say something like that. Have you had a chance for a first readthrough?'

'Only just. I've spent the last three days doing nothing but and that was only skimming. Why was the brief so late?'

'Don't ask me. I was given it at the last minute. I reckon there's been a huge cock-up at our place and they can't turn their back on him now: the Law Society would come down heavy if they knew the case hadn't been prepared properly. They're expecting that he'll turn in a guilty plea before trial but the instructions are firm: it's "not guilty" all the way.'

'What's he like? Have you met him yet?'

'Only for a short time at the magistrates'. He's totally out of his head. This place has the worst drugs problem in the country.'

'Hey, this just gets better and better.'

'Believe it.'

'Where's Mr Sedgewick, by the way?' Leone asked, her lips pursed sardonically.

'He left a message for me in chambers: something's come up.'

Probably last night's Scotch, she thought but didn't say so. 'He'll be along when he can.'

Leone understood that Sloane had to be loyal to his leading barrister, but wondered how far that loyalty would extend. She knew that Toby would have preferred a different QC. Sedgewick represented just about everything that he hated about the Establishment. The fact that they belonged to very different sets of chambers was testimony to that. Most of the people who had a place in Sedgewick's set were virtually guaranteed advancement to the High Court so long as they kept their noses clean, unlike Sedgewick himself. In Toby's cooperative set you were more likely to find yourself labelled a radical on account of the large amount of anti-government work that was handled. Toby had carved a very decent criminal practice out of an incurable suspicion of the prosecuting authorities.

Heavy footsteps at the other side of the grey door ahead of them signalled that the next area had been cleared for their passage.

Sloane shot the cuffs on his plain white shirt and straightened his yellow paisley tie. He had a shy smile that contrasted sharply with his gaunt face.

'Let's see what Speakman has to say.' He reached down for the heavy aviator's bag, favoured by many barristers, and began to stroll to the next security point.

'Don't you mean King Arthur?' Leone asked testingly.

'If that's what the jury want to call him at the end of the trial then that's fine with me. Until then he's Trevor Speakman.'

It was what Leone had wanted to hear.

The next security search was identical to the first, with Leone becoming impatient, although Sloane appeared inured by many trips down these depressing corridors of retribution. As the door slid back she could see that Speakman was already slumped inside a conference room. He had his back to the wall furthest from the door; a table would separate them.

'Security policy,' Sloane explained. 'We have to be closest to the alarm button in case a situation develops.'

A waiting prison officer nodded a scant good morning as he inserted a plastic security card into a thin slot. It reminded Leone of a key card to a modern hotel room but here the guests could not check out when they had tired of the trip. She heard the triple lock click out in sequence as the door moved a little way away from its jamb.

Speakman's eyes never wavered from the tabletop. He rose from his seat, eyes still fixed on the grey surface. The months on remand had taken their toll. He looked beaten, robbed of hope. The prison-issue remand 'browns' were not designed for comfort or elegance: they were part of the dehumanising process.

Toby took a seat. 'Please sit down, Mr Speakman. My name is Sloane; I am the junior barrister in the case. Mr Sedgewick, your QC, will be along soon.' Leone doubted it. 'You remember Miss Stern?'

Speakman nodded dumbly.

'We met at the magistrates' court, didn't we, Trevor?'

At the use of his Christian name their client looked up for the first time. He had deteriorated further during the last couple of weeks. His face had a drained, yellow pallor and his eyes swirled in bewilderment: heavy lids and red pools.

'What's happening to me?'

Sloane removed a legal notebook from the aviator bag. 'We're here to establish the terms of your defence.'

'Why am I here?' he slurred.

Leone saw the same look of underlying incomprehension that Ian Bradley had exhibited at their last conference, just before he took his own life.

'Mr Speakman, you are here because the prosecution believe you have taken the lives of seven young girls.' Sloane's voice was professionally passionless as he spoke. 'They also believe they can prove those allegations. I will be frank: the evidence against you is very strong.'

'I'm not pleading guilty,' Speakman said bleakly.

'No one's suggesting that you should.'

Not until Sedgewick arrives, Leone thought.

'But if we are to approach the prosecution evidence properly we have to acknowledge the strength of it. I'm not in the business of forcing innocent men to plead guilty. That decision is the jury's, not mine.'

Speakman appeared to accept the sincerity of the young advocate's words, though how much he understood was anyone's guess.

'The case begins when you were found with Joanna Cheem in

the back of your trailer in Exeter outside your home. Have you any idea how she came to be there?'

Speakman's eyes had reverted to a dull glaze; he could only shake his head and shrug. If that was his best answer then the case would be over before it began.

'As you know, that was the starting point of the police investigation,' Sloane continued. 'They cross-matched the abduction with the other missing girls by analysing the similar evidence. They then compared the dates and times of their disappearances and inspected your employer's work records. According to till receipts and a few witness sightings of a lorry similar to yours, you were in the right areas at the right time.'

'It's such a long time ago. How can I remember where I was?'

'Do you deny being in the areas at the time? You see, there are accurately recorded, computerised, credit-card receipts from the company diesel account. They support the despatcher's evidence. They have your signature on them.' Sloane produced a sample voucher and pushed it across the table. 'Is that your signature?'

Speakman looked down momentarily before nodding his acceptance.

'I have checked that sample against the rest of the receipts; they all appear to match.'

'So?' Speakman asked.

'So,' his barrister continued, 'it seems pretty clear that they can put you within a short journey of the abduction spots and the scenes of the murders.'

Leone joined the conversation. The old-time advocates would not have welcomed a female solicitor's input; the new-age versions accepted that this was a team effort.

'Can you remember anything that might give you an alibi? A special anniversary or birthday? An event where people would have seen you? The more public the better.'

'I've tried, Miss Stern, I really have. Since the accident my memory isn't so good as it was.'

Leone knew he was referring to the North Sea disaster, which she'd read about on the file. In 1985 six men had been killed by a faulty decompression chamber, but Speakman's body strength had saved him. He had recovered quickly from the physical effects, but suffering the bends for five days had short-circuited parts of his brain.

'I was never the same since the accident.'

'About the diving,' Sloane pushed. 'When Miss Cheem was discovered in the trailer her hands were tied by a piece of plastic diving rope. It was identical to the ones used on the other victims' bodies and it was tied in a knot commonly used by divers and fishermen. The prosecution intend to point to your diving expertise as another indicator of your guilt, Mr Speakman.'

'I didn't do it,' Speakman said through clenched teeth. 'No one believes me, but I didn't. I know it looks bad. I've been banged up for twenty-three hours every day with nothing else to think about. Christ, I know it looks terrible. You do believe me, don't you?' he said, turning pathetic, pleading eyes to the woman solicitor. Her refusal to give him false hope caused a nervous smile to cross his fleshy lips.

'I might as well plead guilty: you think I killed them. Every villain in this place believes it too. Do you know what "the Rule" is?'

Of course she did: Rule 43. It segregated from the rest of the pack the at-risk prisoners – rapists, paedophiles, informants, child murderers, all thrown together: the lowest rung on the prison ladder.

'I've been on the Rule since I arrived. I didn't ask to be but they insisted. Said I was a target for any lifer who wanted to make a name for himself. You should hear them talk; they're sick people and I'm getting that way. Look at my arm.' He peeled back his shirtsleeve to reveal scabby veins.

'I don't think we should continue with this conference without Mr Sedgewick's presence,' the barrister interrupted, realising he wouldn't get anything useful out of Speakman while he was reduced to this state. 'We'll come back another day. Please help us to help you. Dredge down into your memory for faces and places. The smallest detail may be important: jog your recollection. We have to have something to work with.'

Leone turned to indicate to the guard that the interview was over. Sloane repacked his bag. Speakman had returned his attention to the tabletop.

'Do you have children, Miss Stern?' She shook her head. He wasn't interested enough to look up. 'I used to – two wonderful girls. I wouldn't hurt them or anyone else for that matter.'

The door to the room was closed behind Toby and Leone.

'What do you think?' she asked as they moved to the holding area.

'I think that Mr Sedgewick has been delayed.'

'No, about the case.'

'It's overwhelming. The prosecution evidence is strong enough without Speakman's help. If we put him in the witness box he'll be slaughtered in cross-examination. He has no alibi witnesses and no idea where he was at the relevant times.'

They were passing through the last set of security gates.

'Then we need an angle,' Leone suggested.

'No, missy,' he said, imitating a John Wayne drawl, 'we need a miracle.'

Leone appreciated the dark, accurate humour. They needed a miracle: that was how the newspapers described the continued existence of Joanna Cheem, the girl in Speakman's trailer: 'a miraculous escape'. But it wasn't chance that had taken the police to Trevor Speakman: it was a tip-off, an anonymous tip-off. Why no name? Something was worrying Leone about the whole set-up because that was how it felt: set up.

CHAPTER TWELVE

Back at her cherrywood, leather-topped desk later the same day, Leone swept aside the second delivery of post and logged on to her computer. She accessed the messages column entered by the firm's receptionists. There were the expected complaints from family-law clients all demanding an update on divorce settlements or wishing to arrange extended contact with their estranged children. She flashed these across to another solicitor; if she was dealing with Speakman then the others could cope with some 'social work'.

One message stood separate and apart from the rest. It was timed 11.25 a.m. and it was from Jack Forth. Jack Forth: that man again. The last time she had seen him he was cradling the dying Jonathan Berkeley in his arms. She tried to abandon the image but it stubbornly refused to budge. What could he want that was so urgent? Whatever it was it would have to wait: there were several tasks outlined by Toby Sloane that required attention – like, yesterday. Richard Dexter had telephoned eight times enquiring whether she was ready to do business on the admissions. He'd also faxed the consent form in order that the defence could view all the material that had been collected throughout the investigation but the prosecution weren't intending to use. She shifted the details to the Speakman files and made a note to check the date with Toby. She knew that he always insisted on a full search of documents to find inconsistencies with which to muddy the waters. They were to liaise with an Inspector Barnes at the Commissioner's Office.

She set about the various calls that her rigorous work timetable demanded and was lost for the rest of the afternoon. At 5.30, Leone's personal internal intercom buzzed her attention. It was Mandy, the receptionist.

'It's Mr Forth again. He called this morning. I left the message for you. He's quite insistent.'

'OK, put him on.' Leone sighed with mild irritation, although simultaneously recalling his handsome features and lost-boy eyes. There was something strange yet reassuring about him. He'd acted without hesitation at the accident scene just as he'd helped her at the court that day. But it was something more than that: when she'd talked to him briefly an expression in his eyes told her he'd seen things he wouldn't wish upon others.

After a few seconds she heard his voice. 'Ah, Miss Stern,' he opened nervously, 'I'm sorry for interrupting you but something strange has occurred. I think you may be able to help. It won't take much of your time, I promise.'

'I know, Mr Forth, but I can spare you five. What is it that's so urgent?'

'I was hoping you could tell me why your firm should lie about something.'

'What?' she exclaimed. This man did have the habit of surprising her.

'It's about Jonathan Berkeley.'

'The man who was killed in the street? What about him?'

'It could mean a lot of trouble for your firm: you and I saw him leave.'

'And?'

'After he died, the police arrived. You had obviously left the scene but I gave them my name and address. I got a visit. The Serious Fraud Office came to see me this morning: they told me the dead man, Berkeley, had not been into your offices. We both know that's a lie and now the papers reckon the Fraud Squad are trying to put a nail in his coffin. You don't think that's interesting?'

'I think that it's none of my business and I can't work out why you should think it's any of yours.' As soon as she said the words she knew she hadn't meant it. She had definitely seen Berkeley: for God's sake, she had stood in the lift with him!

'Are you sure, Miss Stern?' Jack's voice gently probed, breaking the brief and embarrassed silence.

'I get it, this is your pick-up routine, isn't it?' she joked unconvincingly. 'Of course, I can't be sure I saw him: I'm a lawyer,' she said, uncomfortably aware that her secretary had just entered the room. 'Now, I've got work to do. Why don't you go and paint or whatever it is that you do?'

'Well, you know what? That's a disappointing answer, Miss Stern. I can see I've wasted your time.'

It must have been the sense of finality in his voice that made her hang on rather than hang up. She cupped a hand around the mouthpiece so that she could keep her words from the secretary's ears and whispered, 'Just a minute. Look, I get the feeling I might regret this but I didn't mean to sound so cool. It's just that I'm extremely busy, you know how it is.'

'Yeah, I know.'

'What if I say I might be able to verify that Berkeley was the man I saw in the lift?'

'If you promise not to interpret my answer as another attempted pick-up line . . .'

'Promise.'

'Well, believe it or not, I want you to see my etchings.'

CHAPTER THIRTEEN

J ack squeezed his way past a lively group of young guns dressed head to toe in city chic. The bar Leone had chosen for their rendezvous was around the corner from her offices and wall-to-wall pinstripe was the dress code. He edged towards the imposing Victorian counter feeling slightly conspicuous in black jeans, turtleneck and a long black overcoat. The place was packed with teatime revellers hungrily slurping real ale before wending their way home to commuter land. He took in an admiring glance from a pretty but bored-looking redhead isolated from her group. They were obviously celebrating a rare day on the markets, drinking pink champagne and tequila slammers at the bar. Waiting patiently behind them and glancing at the redhead, Jack smiled shyly, which did the trick as she nudged her boisterous boyfriend in the ribs and a gap in the throng appeared for his benefit. He ordered a bottle of Australian Chardonnay with two glasses and turned away, searching the background for Leone Stern.

Ten minutes later, perched uncomfortably on a high but low-backed bar stool between the dartboard and the video jukebox, he was pouring himself another glass when he saw her enter the bar. She breezed in with her hair loose. It curled around her face and danced on her shoulders. As she stopped to talk to someone he looked at her profile, more delicate than he could remember. She was dressed in a navy two-piece with short jacket and long, tight skirt. Suddenly he began to wonder what he was doing here in the middle of a load of suits about to accuse one of their own of some sort of conspiracy. And for what? Why didn't he just walk away? 'Go on, walk outa here, Jacky Boy. It's someone else's problem,' crooned the voice of Coffee Buddy deep inside his head. But somehow, before he could make the decision, she had spotted him, waving her arm and gesturing towards a space at the rear of the pub. Gratefully slipping off his pedestal, Jack made his way round to her. They settled at a new resting place around an old cooper's barrel.

'Good choice,' she said, nodding towards the bottle of honey-coloured Hunter Valley wine.

'I thought I'd make you feel at home,' he replied, pouring her a glass.

'It's me who should be getting the drinks. I feel guilty about the way I spoke to you on the telephone.' Her blue-green eyes narrowed to pinpoints as she took a deep draught with some satisfaction.

'It doesn't matter: you're here, that's good enough,' said Jack. 'Sounds like you had a tough day.'

'Are there any other kind? That place drives me up the wall.'

'You surprise me. I thought all lawyers loved their work.'

'You're kidding. If you're a senior partner sharing the purse then it might be tolerable, but the rest of us are just cleaning up the scraps. Anyway, you didn't come here looking for another mouthful of abuse. Tell me exactly what the police said to you about Berkeley.'

Jack recounted the visit from the police officers while she listened intently, never interrupting, simply staring into his eyes making him feel like he was talking to a human tape recorder. Lawyers – they were enough to make anyone uncomfortable. When he had finished she turned away without a word and reached into her handbag retrieving, to his surprise, a packet of cigarillos. Carefully peeling back the Cellophane wrapping she slid one of the little brown shoots out of its sheath and gripped it between her teeth. A small grin appeared as she registered his quizzical expression.

'What's the matter?' she asked mockingly. 'You never seen a woman smoke a cigarillo before?'

'Now you come to mention it, I don't think I have. Maybe in a circus.' He flashed a smile.

'Do you mind?'

'Not in the slightest. I guess it creates a good image for a high-flying brief.'

'Nothing to do with image. I only smoke when I'm nervous: tried cigarettes, pipe, cigars, even pot. I think it's something to do with reading about Churchill when I was a kid. Besides, I'm trying to give up. Watch.' She reached inside her handbag and fished out a brass Zippo lighter. She flicked open the top and struck the flint. 'See, no petrol.' She smiled, then proceeded to take a deep, imaginary draw on the full-bodied cigarillo. Jack looked suitably bewildered.

'Something I said made you nervous?' Jack ventured hesitatingly.

'You said that the police told you someone from Jessops already telephoned them to say that the Berkeley estate was concerned about a finding of suicide.'

'That's right.'

'They do a lot of things at Jessops but probate certainly isn't one of them.'

'Then who rang the police?'

'One step at a time. I'm a lawyer, remember; I like things slow. Are you sure they were police officers?'

'Course I'm sure.'

'How? Did you check their warrant cards?'

Jack straightened up and stared at her.

'OK, so I'm not sure. Remember, I'm *not* a lawyer. But they certainly acted like police officers. I mean, why would anyone go to those lengths to find out whether Berkeley had said anything before he died? They had to be police officers; come off it.'

'You could have been followed or traced through a detective agency. That quite often happens after a road traffic accident. Could be insurance investigators: the insurance companies need all the information they can get, especially witnesses, if it looks like they may have to pay out a substantial sum,' Leone persisted, but she knew it was only a half-hearted attempt to ignore the obvious. Someone at TWC was lying and that made her very nervous indeed. She took another long draw on the unlit cigarillo.

'All right, but why the charade? It would have been a lot easier just to say they were from the insurance company, wouldn't it?'

'Granted,' Leone replied grudgingly: he was right and she knew it.

'OK. Next step, counsellor. Surely it wouldn't be difficult to establish that Berkeley was at your offices. But hey, I'm only the amateur sleuth to a pro like you.'

'Don't count your chickens,' Leone cautioned.

'What do you mean?'

'After you called yesterday I made enquiries: something odd is going on.'

'Are you going to level with me?' said Jack.

'Mr Forth, we're not just talking about your fantasies as a private eye, we're talking about my career. You've got no idea what this firm is like,' she said, sounding a little too superior.

'Tell me about it.'

'I can't.'

'Why not?'

'I'm breaching my contract already, talking to you about internal affairs. If they discover this, I'm out.'

'Look, don't worry, I just want to find out what's going on: I certainly won't be telling your employers. I don't want to cause any trouble for you. But I saw that man come out of your building: others must have too.'

Leone jolted back a little. There it was again, that odd feeling: it seemed to happen when he looked at her. It was like a compulsion, strong and powerful. She knew she should walk away from all this, but she couldn't.

'Wrong!' she asserted confidently.

'What do you mean, "wrong"? There's the receptionist: she must have seen him.'

'Think! When I came out of the lift she wasn't at her desk. She came out of the little girls' room just to see a man crossing the road; she didn't know he'd come from our offices. I asked her specifically whether she could remember signing him in but she was on a call at the time, so the security guard would have completed the formalities and handed over the security tag worn by all visitors.'

'So the guard will remember: it's not as if it's weeks ago. It was only last Tuesday.'

'The guard's gone.'

'How do you mean, "gone"?'

'Exactly that, gone: kaput, disappeared, whichever way you want to put it; he's not around any more.'

'Explain.'

'Speculation at the office seems to be he got the push.'

'Convenient?'

'Maybe; maybe not.'

'Come on.'

'Don't worry about it. Apparently, he failed to mention his criminal record; that's an instantly dismissable offence as far as

TWC are concerned. So maybe there was a reasonable explanation.'
Leone looked over her shoulder at the sudden upsurge of noise from
the group of young stockbrokers: one of them had collapsed during
a beer boat-race and was spread-eagled on the floor.

'It's stretching it to believe this is all coincidence,' Jack said,
topping up their glasses.

'If you think that's bad, wait till you hear about the visitors'
book.'

'Don't: destroyed in a freak fire?'

'Just as suspect. Some water was spilled over the page relating
to that day; the handwriting's illegible.'

'Stunningly convenient, Leone,' he said, raising his eyebrows.
He realised that he had subliminally slipped into using her Christian
name, but she didn't seem to mind.

'I asked our receptionist, and she told me she had found a vase
of flowers strewn over the reception desk. She assumed someone
knocked it over, accidentally.'

Jack gave her a look of incredulity. 'Yes, someone knocked it
over all right. It leaves one interesting point.'

'What?'

'You and me.'

'Come again?'

'That only leaves you and me who saw Berkeley leave your
offices.'

'And whoever it was he was there to meet.'

'Exactly. On the assumption that whoever it was isn't going to
make a song and dance about it I'd say we were on our own.'

'Correction, you're on your own: I can't afford to get involved.'

'But you are involved, aren't you?'

'Only in so far as I can say that I saw a man who may have
resembled the deceased. I could be wrong. Besides, I learned a
long time ago that just about everything happens for a reason.
I don't really want to know what he was doing in our offices.
I've got enough problems of my own,' she said unconvincingly.
If TWC were involved in Berkeley's dealings then there would be
some very unhappy clients. A lot of commercial banking business
would go elsewhere for legal advice.

'I see, toeing the party line. I guess I'll just have to go to the
police and give them your name, then. You'll be able to verify
everything I've said.'

'Look, if you go to the police with this information, what are they going to do about it? Do you honestly believe that they'll come rushing over to TWC and start interviewing the entire staff? Why? To discover that there is no record of Berkeley being there in the first place? He could have entered the building by mistake for all we know.'

'Leone! This guy was up to his neck in something that stinks. The bogus witness and telephone call to the police are sure to be followed up. There's a conflict between what I've said to them and the information they received by phone. Discrepancies don't go away, not when the Serious Fraud Squad is involved.'

'Have you thought about this? TWC do a lot of City business: it may well be that the police have already had a satisfactory explanation for Berkeley's visit. Some things are best left unsaid and undisturbed.' It came out wrong, every syllable, and she knew it.

He fixed his eyes on her once more: it was as if he had the ability to control the temperature between them.

'So that's the real reason you don't get involved, is it? Make sure that your firm doesn't get caught in any shady business. What a club! Funny, I never had you down as bent!' he fired as if he knew it would burn her up. She fell into it.

'How dare you! It's clear that your understanding of the legal world is limited, Mr Forth. Things don't work that way for me. Let's get this straight. I don't mind the club – I might even be forced to admit on occasion that I think the club works well – but the club doesn't own me, get it?'

'From where I'm sitting you look worried that you may lose your membership,' he said.

'Why are you so interested, anyway?'

'Not interested, just involved, in case you'd forgotten. I like mysteries, got a lot of friends in the press.'

'Then you're no better than—'

'What? Give me a break here.'

The voices rose again behind them, preventing further sparring, like the bell at a boxing match. Suddenly it dawned upon her why she felt so strange here, locked in a confused little tryst with this man. That's what she saw in those green eyes that so fascinated her: lost boy, lost girl. Sometimes they had to find one another

'Don't say anything else to them, will you? Not till I've made some more enquiries,' Leone pleaded.

'Why are you so worried: you've got nothing to hide, or have you?'

'It's a long story.'

'I've got the time.' He held her gaze.

It was a strange interlude. She'd met him only a couple of times and yet there was that feeling again, almost forcing her to justify herself. Something told her that he was going to be around for a while and somehow she knew there was no choice. She had to level with him.

'I've had to work very hard to get this far.'

'I don't doubt it.'

'But I wouldn't have got anywhere if it hadn't been for this firm. I owe everything to the chance TWC gave me.' She peeled another cigarello from the box.

'Come off it, you're a big girl, Leone. If—'

'Listen, my family got into a real mess way back and if it hadn't been for the job here I just don't know what would have happened . . .' She trailed off in hesitation and drew on the unlit cigarillo.

'What sort of mess?'

'My father, he became very sick, depressed, as a result of money pressures on his business. And he, er . . .'

'Look, don't tell me if it's hard for you. I didn't mean to upset you. It's none of my business.'

'No, it's just that it's very difficult to tell anyone when I know the reaction I'll get.'

'Try me.'

'My father was a very successful man. His construction company built most of Sydney's downtown commercial centre and we were privileged. I was his only daughter: private education, rich friends, great lifestyle and bright future. Then a lot of people let him down. Suddenly, I remember a change at home. I stopped visiting at weekends. There was a lot of pressure on Dad. The press were on his back seeking to persuade the public that he was involved in corruption with the city council for building contracts. I was in my final year at uni when things went mad. Dad's bankers started calling in loans. Other creditors lost confidence and he was in way too deep.'

'What happened?' asked Jack. 'How did he take it?'

'Huh! You really don't know, do you?' Leone smiled ruefully. 'I guess people do forget. But I never can.'

'I'm not following.'

'He woke up one morning to find that the bank were calling for a suspension of his company's shares on the market. He got dressed, drove down to the city, stopped off at a gun store and walked into the main offices of the bank at eleven-twenty-two a.m. At eleven-fifty-two eighteen people were dead. He killed himself at twelve noon. I changed my name by deed poll.'

'I'm sorry, Leone.'

She stared into her wineglass before taking another slug. 'Some inheritance, isn't it? He knew what he was doing – he just didn't have the guts to take the consequences. Mother never recovered. After the news broke she was devastated. Deep shock set in. Cut off from her so-called friends on the social circuit with no money and the press hounding her, she lost it: admitted to a sanitarium in Adelaide. She didn't even recognise me. So there was no point in trying to get a job in Australia with that family background. I stayed in New Zealand until the heat went down, changed my name to Stern after my grandfather and made a last visit to her. When I was sorting through her things after the funeral I came across a letter from an English solicitor, who said that he had always respected my father and if there was anything he could do to assist she only had to ask. She couldn't, but I did. So seven years on I can look people in the face without fear of them prejudging me because of my father's crimes.' A harsh conflict between pride and shame flickered in her eyes.

'Who else knows about this?' Jack asked, gently touching her hand clasped knuckle-white around the stem of her glass.

'Only a few close friends: I live a very private existence. So, any hint of disloyalty and I'm pulling the noose around my neck: there's no way I could work again. That's the only reason I'm telling you now.' She pulled her hand away. 'But when it comes down to it I'm getting sick of the pantomime so if you want to go ahead and tell the scandal sheets you can earn yourself some easy money. "The long-lost killer fraudster's daughter": good headline?'

'Easy. I won't be saying anything, trust me.'

'There's no such thing.'

'You've got to some time.'

'Not true, Jack. You see, nothing about human nature surprises me. Can you imagine that? I don't think so.'

'You'd be surprised at what doesn't surprise me,' he winked, forcing a smile to cross her face briefly. 'It's your round.'

Leone stubbed out the untouched cigarillo and made for the bar, shaking her head. Why had she told him that? At the same time she still felt a kilo lighter in her mind. She didn't know why she trusted this man. When she returned he had spread two pictures out on the barrel top.

'My etchings,' he said flatly; his mood seemed to have changed – colder and remote.

Leone looked at the first, and saw a portrait of herself alongside the other players at Speakman's committal sketched in minute detail. She did a double-take when she noticed Jack's face grafted onto the body of the man in the dock.

'Spooky stuff,' she said after he pointed out Speakman's face at the back of the public gallery.

'You're telling me,' said Jack, shaking his head.

'But what's all this got to do with you? Why have you put yourself there?' she said, relaxing a little in his company. It felt familiar.

He raised his eyes, catching her smile. 'As I said, I have no idea. I was hoping you could help me. It's like I know this man is not a killer.'

'You haven't seen the evidence against him,' she replied. 'It'll take more than a picture to convince a jury.'

'Take a look at this.' He peeled out the second drawing from underneath the first.

Leone turned her head sharply away. 'That's sick.'

'No, that's reality: bites, doesn't it?'

Gingerly she brought her eyes down upon the canvas: before her was a perfect graphic scene of Berkeley's body, dark red blood seeping in a purply black shadow around his fallen frame. She looked away once more, scrambling around in her bag for the cigarillos.

'You don't see it, do you?'

'I've seen enough. Is this the way you impress girls?'

'Have another look.'

She turned once more to the picture as he slowly moved his right index finger across the background of greying buildings to the one office block that stood out more intensely than the others. She immediately recognised it as the one she entered every day. TWC. He tapped his nail three times at a large window she knew to be the side-entrance staircase, fourth floor. As clear as daylight stood the figure of Trevor Speakman dressed in a blue serge pinstripe suit.

David Taylor tied a Windsor knot in his Hermès silk tie. The light blue reflected the colour of his own sharp, avaricious eyes and contrasted neatly with a dark bespoke blazer. He grinned at himself in the mirror. The phone call arranging the meeting had saved him the trouble of fixing the appointment himself.

The death of his ex-lover, if one could refer to the insignificant merchant banker in that way, had caused him real upset. How on earth could he live his chosen lifestyle without regular 'donations'? Now a new but not unknown donor had come forward. Taylor and his partner had planned to invite him into their intrigue shortly but now he had saved them the trouble.

A car horn sounded outside his mews apartment. Looking through the sweeping bay window and down to the leafy street below, Taylor could see the black cab double-parked awaiting his attendance in the muted darkness. He keyed in the code on the alarm pad, patted his jacket in the search for his wallet then, satisfied that it was there and would be fuller by the end of the evening, stepped from his rooms and into the corridor.

He whistled patiently as he watched the lift ascend from the underground car park without pausing. The numbers flashed by quickly, then, with a cheerful ping, its doors slid apart and he stepped in. In it a man stood with his back to the new entrant.

Takes all sorts, Taylor thought as he turned and pressed the brass button to the ground floor, mildly puzzled that anyone would want to ride up and then down. But then he heard a rustle of movement before a sharp pain to his lower back propelled him around. The man had turned to him.

'You!'

The solicitor smiled. 'Thought I'd bring the meeting forward a little.'

Taylor felt his vision begin to double, then triple as his knees began to buckle under his weight. The solicitor pushed him gently to one side, pressed the cancel button on the lift's command panel, then depressed the button that would speed them to the subterranean car park.

'David, we really need to talk. It's been such a long time, so much catching up to do.'

Taylor could hear, he could feel. He thought he had known fear before and now knew that he had been wrong.

CHAPTER FOURTEEN

The continuous flow of fuggy prison air drifted languidly through various air vents and into Trevor Speakman's nostrils. His bulky frame was squeezed uncomfortably into the lower white metal bunk. This was the third cell he'd seen since the arrest. Above him a new cellmate muttered in his sleep about the lovely boys, so young, so perfect. Speakman winced. Every inmate he'd met was some kind of filthy sexual deviant. He read the newspapers – he knew what scum these kiddy-fuckers were. He rubbed his clenched fists into wretched eyes, and his mouth formed a sickly smile at the irony of it all; that was what they all thought of him. Stripped down to his vest and boxer shorts, Speakman could see the expanding roll about his gut pushing against the accepting cotton.

He was hurting for a fix, but what he had to do to get it turned his stomach. How low could he eventually be driven? The days didn't pass quite so slowly when he tripped. It was easier to get smashed than to think about what it all meant. He had long since given up trying to protest in this place. Besides, it was probably safer in here. He only got the odd kicking from the screws these days and on the wing he was a celebrity. Some celebrity – selling his mouth for a wrap of smack.

Speakman had never been a soft target: he'd had his share of brawling in the oil-supported ale houses of Aberdeen; never turned away from a fight. This was different. The lisping innuendo of sexual favours worked its way into every conversation: he'd never had to face opponents like these before. Besides, he didn't think he had any fight left in him.

At least the Rule wing meant only two to a cell: plain walls, no window, two chairs, no comfort, two beds, no sleep. A single bulb was screwed into the ceiling, a girdle of steel wire around its pearly glow. The prison was a net and all the inmates a floundering, cold-blooded catch. He shouldn't be in here: not with them; not at all. That's what they all said in here. Every one of them had been set up, or tricked, or misunderstood: they all maintained their innocence, but he really *was* innocent. No one would believe him.

The solicitor had tried to be kind but she wouldn't lie to him when he asked her what she thought. He liked that about her: she was straight, blunt, truthful. The barrister was a cold one: not aggressive, mind you, just clinical. Sloane reminded him of a dentist called McCay on an off-shore oil rig. He had tutted at the state of Speakman's teeth and then extracted three of them without explanation or apology; it just had to be done.

He would see them all soon: all the lawyers, the press, the angry public. His first appearance in the Crown Court was only hours away, though the time would draw itself out slowly. He wondered if you ever got used to that, the speed of real hard time. Then he pushed the thought away. He still had hope. Trevor Speakman felt his huge shoulders begin to shake, then heave. He began to weep as he recognised hope for the slippery impostor it was.

It had been three days of panic getting all the papers together for the plea and directions hearing. Leone had to prepare witness lists, alibi notices, defence exhibit bundles and everything else Toby had demanded. She had seen Jack again the previous night, before she left for Exeter. All those strange feelings she had just kept on coming. He had told her about his little girl and the accident but said nothing about his wife. Leone stupidly hadn't asked. Was he divorced or separated? Worse still, married and lying to her? She shook his face out of her head as she headed up the ramp towards the stainless-steel and glass revolving doorway. She saw Sedgewick at the entrance, shaking a tatty umbrella. He joined her at the lift.

Two distinctive but different smells drifted into Leone's nostrils as she was elevated to the fourth floor of the newly con-structed court complex. The semicircular glass lift was one of three that adorned the outside front face of the building like huge transparent arteries. First, the overpowering aroma of the freshly laid blue- and grey-flecked carpet predominated through the building; second, she detected the more subtle but malt-fuelled breath of Sedgewick. He leaned against the chrome rail beside her, avoiding contact with the other occupants. Nobody talked.

The lift emptied its cargo of criminals eager to avoid their fate on the third floor where the majority of courtrooms were situated, enabling Leone to move subtly away from Sedgewick. When they stopped, he gestured for her to precede him as they emerged into the corridor leading to the barristers' robing room and solicitors' common room.

'Just give me ten minutes, please, Miss Stern, while I robe up and locate our learned junior,' Sedgewick said, his sobriety-challenged voice sounding like car tyres crunching over wet gravel.

'I have a couple of calls to make anyway. I'll meet with you back here before we go down to see Mr Speakman.' Leone could see the watery hue glazing over his eyes: sickly yellow with tiny, burst, blood-red veins where there should have been white. As an articled clerk many years before, she had been told by her principal always to be polite to barristers irrespective of their appearance, but that wasn't appropriate today. His distressed black and greys hadn't been cleaned probably since the day the wool was sheared off the back of the sheep. As he walked unsteadily before her she noticed the worn heels on his scuffed Oxford brogues with a loose hem trailing raggedly behind. He didn't deserve respect or politeness. The thought that the only reason he was here was because of his friendship with the partners at her firm only made matters worse.

They reached the door to the robing room first and he trundled in, slinging his floppy briefcase to the floor beside a row of lockers. The robing room was traditionally a place where solicitors were frowned upon; a place where the bar could close the door and indulge in secret discussions. Called 'counsel to counsel', it meant whatever was said would go no further. Privately held views on cases were exchanged here before the combatants entered the real arena.

Pupils, juniors and silks were busy adorning the accoutrements that separate the professional advocate from other lawyers. Starched white, bat-wing collars and legal bands replaced soft collar and tie. Horsehair wigs covered bald patches and flowing black gowns were swathed around the men and women who shoulder the responsibility of administering legal-aid justice.

Roger Fry QC adjusted his silk waistcoat in a full-length

chevalier mirror. Beside him, and already robed, were his junior and noting junior, looking as fresh and as hungry as two unblooded prize fighters. The atmosphere was heavy with anticipation. Till now, all the prosecution could do was prepare their own case, attempting to anticipate what line of defence would emerge from the Speakman camp. Today was different: they would know.

Toby Sloane was waiting patiently at a small table beside the large window looking through a case report. Roger Fry looked over to him and nodded, his eyes steady and cool. Toby returned his greeting and noticed Sedgewick alongside the prosecuting silk, fiddling unsuccessfully with his collar stud. Toby reluctantly headed over to where his learned leader stood.

'Ah, there you are, Sloane. Give me a hand, will you?' Sedgewick asked. 'I don't seem to have the delicate touch these days.'

'Certainly,' replied Toby, who effortlessly slipped the small brass stud into the corresponding hole at the back of Sedgewick's collar.

'I trust you will be handling Mr Speakman with great care, Sedgewick, old boy,' interjected Roger Fry, smiling beside them.

'Ah, Fry, how are you?'

'Can't complain. Of course, I'll be much more comfortable when we've got this little mess sorted out. I was so glad to hear that you had got the brief on this one. In fact, I said to my junior only the other day that a man with your experience is bound to give proper advice. He's as guilty as sin, is he not?'

Toby waited nervously for Sedgewick's response.

'I don't think you'll have to worry too much about a long contest, if there's to be a contest at all. An appalling catalogue of crime, what! I was hoping we could put our heads together and look carefully at what you can really prove against him. I have an idea that if you give me something to lever him with, say a diminished-responsibility plea, then we can tidy this up and let the doctors work out where it is that he went wrong. What do you say?'

Toby cursed silently: Sedgewick obviously hadn't read the psychiatric report Leone had commissioned but, at his request, had not yet disclosed to the Crown. Fry shook his head.

'I'm afraid not this time, Jeffrey.'

'Oh. You surprise me.'

'Yes, it rather surprised me that the senior Crown Prosecutor and the Director of Public Prosecutions are taking such a robust view, but it seems to have got everyone a bit hot under the collar: so you see, my hands are rather tied. No deals, Jeffrey.'

'I see. Mind you, I can't blame them,' Sedgewick replied, pulling from his waistcoat pocket a packet of indigestion tablets. 'If you can't get a conviction for murder here I don't know where you can. Sloane tells me the evidence is entirely circumstantial, but my reading of it is that there can be no other reasonable explanation, circumstantial or not: he did it!'

Toby coughed a little too deliberately as the Crown's team smiled at Sedgewick. Here he was with the leading barrister for the defence virtually giving up the fight before it had begun. He knew all too well that Sedgewick didn't want to swear in a jury on this case: all he wanted was to persuade Speakman to throw in the towel and go guilty, then he would walk away with a hefty brief fee for very little effort. Toby began to wonder whether Sedgewick had looked at the papers at all. He realised that, with Speakman being unable to give clear instructions and Sedgewick pressuring for a guilty plea, he was going to have to cover his own back.

'We're about to go down to see him now,' Toby stated, trying to ignore what had just been said, but the damage had been done: it was clear to all that if Sedgewick couldn't persuade Speakman to change his plea then the trial would be a charade. They moved off into the corridor and found Leone talking to Richard Dexter outside the lift. The little gathering subconsciously split into two teams, each waiting for its own lift. The defence team were quiet. Fry, on the other hand, was telling the tale of the last murder he'd done in the old Exeter Assizes in 1962 when the black cap was still in operation. He often referred to them as the good old days. Just as the lift doors opened it hit Leone that she had been born that year: when they were still hanging people like Trevor Speakman.

Once inside the lift, Toby pressed the button for the basement where the holding cells were situated and, looking at Leone, raised his eyebrows in an exaggerated movement. She gave a questioning frown and then realised he was indicating towards Sedgewick.

They eventually made it to the thickly painted red door marked CELLS. They were admitted by a surly prison warder who was munching on a forlorn ham sandwich with one hand and opening and closing the heavy metal doors with the other. Eventually they were shown into holding cell number three and there opposite them sat the most hated man in Britain. Speakman looked up as they entered, his eyes bleary red – not unlike Sedgewick's but obviously not caused by the same brand of depressants. There would only be five minutes or so for brief introductions and Sedgewick's 'overview' of the case before it was called on upstairs.

'Hello, Trevor. Mr Sloane you know,' said Leone as brightly as she could. 'I'd like to introduce you to Mr Sedgewick QC: he will be conducting the case on your behalf. We will have to arrange a fuller conference in due course, but for the moment I'm sure he will be able to put your mind at rest that everything possible is being done to assist you.'

Speakman didn't say a word as the lawyers took seats surrounding him. Sedgewick leaned back into the hard wooden chair and regarded him with the look of a teacher to an unruly pupil.

'Good morning, Mr Speakman. How is life on remand? I trust they're keeping you on the Rule.'

'Yeah, but it doesn't make much difference: still a load of nutcases everywhere I turn. You have to get me out of there, Mr Sedgewick. I know it looks bad but I didn't do nothing.' Speakman's words slurred into one another.

'Ah, well, that's not what the Crown are saying. I believe they've got as good a case as I've seen in thirty years as a barrister: it's uphill all the way, I'm afraid. But when I come to see you we'll have a much longer chat about things. In the meantime you may want to focus on your options.' Speakman's head dropped once more to re-examine the concrete floor. 'You do understand what it is that I'm saying to you? I know it will be hard for you to come to terms with.'

'With what?' Speakman erupted, jumping off his chair. 'What is this? You sound like you're fucking one of them.' He had a demented look about him, pulling at his greasy hair and pacing to the back of the cell angrily.

'Calm down, Trevor,' Leone said. 'Mr Sedgewick was only saying that you have—'

'Calm down! Is that all you can say? I know what he's like,' Speakman shouted, pointing at Sedgewick. 'I've heard all about him inside. "No chance," they say, "he'll make you try and plead guilty." Well, that's no good to me, Miss Stern. I'm not guilty, do you hear me, not guilty?' He moved to the corner of the cell and began slamming the wall with his fist. Leone pressed the alarm button near the door and the sound of heavy boots could be heard pelting along the corridor.

Sedgewick looked visibly shaken by the outburst: obviously it hadn't occurred to him that his reputation had reached the ears of prison inmates along with all the other people who'd received second-rate advice from his whisky-sodden brain. He turned to Toby, who sat unmoved by the pantomime. 'The man is clearly insane,' Sedgewick blustered.

The door was flung open and two warders burst through, grabbing Speakman roughly by the arms: he began to let out a slow gurgling whine like a battered cur as he was dragged forcibly out of the cell.

'Not according to Malcolm Hurst he's not,' Toby Sloane said as they walked along the same route back to the lift.

'What's that, Sloane?' Sedgewick asked, looking quizzically at his junior.

'Malcolm Hurst, the clinical psychiatrist.'

'Yes, yes, I know who he is, but what did you say about him?'

'I said that he doesn't think Speakman is insane; far from it, in fact.'

'What are you talking about, man?'

'You haven't seen the report I sent you, then?'

'I never received a report.'

'You should have done: I had one sent around by messenger last week to your chambers.'

'Ah . . . erm . . . I, er, haven't been to chambers for a little while: been off circuit in a long fraud.'

'Oh, I see,' lied Toby: he knew perfectly well Sedgewick had been around because he'd seen him in the Frog and Firkin. But Sedgewick had been so pissed he couldn't remember.

'Well, what does it say, man?'

'In short, it says that there is nothing whatsoever in Speakman's background or make-up which suggests that he could be capable of these crimes: the only rogue factor is that he suffers from blackouts as a result of a diving accident when he worked on the rigs. Notwithstanding that, Hurst firmly believes that his psychological profile tends to point to an ordinary heterosexual male who may be suffering some mild anxiety syndrome as a result of marital breakdown and general depression. He's developed a drugs problem, which has complicated the diagnosis somewhat, but certainly no delusional paranoia or organic psychotic tendencies. In short, the signature of the crime doesn't match him.'

'He's clearly got it wrong then, hasn't he? It's obvious the man is suffering from some great inner turmoil which manifests itself in severe bouts of anger. You said it yourself: he has probably blanked out and doesn't know what he's done when he wakes up next to a corpse. We've just witnessed it, for God's sake!'

'Well, that wasn't quite my reaction, but don't you think that it seems rather odd? Here we are preparing for one of the biggest cases likely to be seen for some time and we have a defendant who doesn't seem on the face of it to have the right sort of mentality for murder, irrespective of this drug problem. These girls were severely mutilated, Sedgewick, and that's a lot different from banging your hand against a brick wall: some would say that that is the sort of reaction one might expect from an innocent man drugged up to the eyes and falsely accused. But what would *you* say? You're in charge.' Both Toby and Leone looked for a response as they walked onto the third floor and headed for court number six.

'He's probably buried it so deep that he can even fool the trick cyclists,' Sedgewick said rather unconvincingly.

'Really,' replied Sloane as he opened the door to the court for Leone: she shot him a 'thank God you're here' look and they all took their places in the well of the court.

Shortly afterwards, the clerk to the court walked down the steps from the entrance to the judge's chambers and whispered that Mr Justice Singleton wanted to see counsel in his room before the case was called on. The rest of the court watched as five wigs disappeared in single file through the door. They emerged into a corridor with several sets of electronically controlled doors and trooped along to the very end. Toby could see the judge's book-lined room through the door. The clerk rapped on the name plate.

'Gentlemen, come in, sit down, please,' snapped Mr Justice Singleton. He was balanced precariously with his back to the delegation on a small stepladder too fragile-looking for his large frame. The scarlet red robes with ermine collar and cuffs, banded together with a black sash, hung around him like a Bedouin tent.

He eventually retrieved a green leather-bound volume from the top shelf. As he descended he indicated for them to remove their wigs: his own full-bottomed grey mane was hanging on a faceless dummy on the edge of the desk. He sat and flicked through the pages of the tome, looking up only once to smile at the noting junior for the Crown and apologise for omitting to refer to her as a lady upon entering – 'political correctness being what it is these days,' he added dryly. She blushed and the waiting went on for several minutes. Toby looked around at the huge ancient portraits hanging rather incongruously in the newly constructed room. Having little interest in marriage, Singleton was the last in a long line of judges and the portraits displayed were unmistakably those of his ancestors, all carrying the family's distinctive flaming red hair and broad rugged features.

Eventually he looked up from his book.

'Mr Sedgewick, Mr Fry.'

'My Lord,' they replied in harmony.

'I have grave reservations about this case being contested in the full public glare. I was told by the Lord Chief to anticipate a great deal of publicity. No surprises there, gentlemen. When it comes on for trial, there are to be television cameras from New York to Moscow outside the court building every day, reviewing the evidence, reviewing the performance of the lawyers and quite probably reviewing my own performance as well. I do not, I repeat, do *not*, want some sort of gruesome media circus dictating the conduct of this case. If you must have a trial, Sedgewick, for what it's worth, please ensure that you do as little as possible to sensationalise the evidence. We do not want this to be remembered as a showcase for how things should not be done in this country's criminal justice system.'

'Yes, my Lord.'

'Good. Now then, are we ready to proceed with plea and directions today?'

'It may be, your Lordship, that in due course I will have some news which will find favour with the court. Mr Speakman is considering his position and I think I can safely predict that the television cameras will be despatched fairly rapidly,' Sedgewick said grandly.

'Very sensible, Sedgewick. There's only one verdict the country wants to hear in this case. Will your client enter his pleas today?'

'Well, not quite, my Lord. You see, it is rather delicate getting him to see reason.'

Lying bastard, thought Toby.

'Quite, quite. That's unfortunate. You will just have to try your best. I'm sure with the very able assistance of Mr Sloane you will eventually be able to make him see sense and have this resolved as quickly as possible. Think of the families.'

'There's just the small matter of applications for severance of the indictments, my Lord,' Toby intervened quietly yet firmly. The Crown barristers all looked over at him and he felt the warm rush of pressure creeping into his veins. He had to at least get it on record early. He wasn't playing Sedgewick's game. He wasn't playing anyone's game.

'The what?' Justice Singleton enquired sharply.

'I, or should I say we, are instructed at this stage to apply to your Lordship for separate trials on each of the counts.'

'But I thought Sedgewick said this is likely to go off as a guilty plea. What on earth is the point of such an application?' Singleton said, irritation ripe in his voice.

Sedgewick looked stunned and fumbled around in his pocket for another indigestion tablet. 'Ah, yes . . . em . . . er . . . Of course, your Lordship, Speakman does have moments of rare clarity and his solicitor is anxious to avoid any suggestion that we did not try, how shall I put it, every avenue,' he stumbled.

'Humph . . .' the judge growled. 'Well, you can tell Miss Stern that however many applications she is instructed to make will make very little difference to her client's position: this is a well-precedented position in the law and unless there are any ground-breaking and unique arguments to put before me all these murders will be tried together by the same jury – do you hear me?'

'Yes, my Lord,' Sedgewick replied obsequiously.

Roger Fry sat back with a smirk and a 'told you so' wink to his juniors.

'Mr Sloane, do *you* hear me?'

'Loud and clear, my Lord,' Toby said.

CHAPTER FIFTEEN

Leone woke with a start, reaching out from under the duvet to thrash the radio alarm. She hadn't arrived back from Exeter until midnight. It had seemed a good idea to set it for 4 a.m. then, but now she wasn't so sure. She showered and dressed quickly nonetheless, going over the events of yesterday in her mind. Speakman's trial had been set for 2 November. That left four weeks to prepare a defence that at the moment didn't exist.

Toby had arranged with her to view the unused files starting on Wednesday at Scotland Yard. He had seemed very edgy after the hearing, saying only that he was concentrating on the circumstances of the first murder and would catch up with her when Sedgewick wasn't around. And then there was Jack. She still wasn't sure if he was some kind of psycho himself, but the more they had talked the more she had become intrigued. Why was he so concerned about Speakman? Why had they become embroiled in this ludicrous charade over Berkeley?

She only just avoided a serious collision with the milk boy as she stepped outside her front door at 5.30 a.m. The lad was more shocked than she when they stumbled ungracefully on the old lichen-covered step of her mews home. As he couldn't see her smiles of apology the startled youth hurriedly made an exit down the cobbles and Leone followed him, still smiling but wondering where the next laugh was coming from. Instinctively, she realised that her long-planned-for, quietly relaxed future was becoming more complex and infuriatingly out of reach by the day. But equally that same instinct told her she must go on.

The air was clear, crisply chilled and still cooling, aided by the persistent October wind. She felt the simultaneous heat and biting cold around her mouth as she breathed through the scarf. Ten minutes later she had walked along an almost deserted King's Road and was boarding the tube heading into the city. She was determined to find an answer to at least one of the questions responsible for complicating her existence. Who had Jonathan Berkeley arranged to see at TWC?

The carriage was virtually empty and smelled of disinfectant. The rubber flooring still glistened from the morning swill. She fell back into a semiconscious state as the train headed deep underground. As it waited briefly at Bank station she registered the annoyingly monotone voice of the platform tannoy: 'Mind the gap, mind the gap,' it announced repeatedly, triggering another image of Jack. He'd told her about the missing parts of his life: about Fiona, about Hollie and about the first time he'd laid eyes on Speakman. Why was he so disturbed by the case? Why couldn't he bring himself to draw Speakman in the dock? Why had he drawn Speakman in the picture of Berkeley's death? Where was the face of the man in the blue serge suit? Surely it didn't mean anything. It was the mind playing tricks. She was a lawyer and more comfortable with facts and logic, not vague feelings. But, then again, what if Jack was right? His crazy pictures, crazy and vivid – no, more than vivid; more real than real. And something else. What was it? They had to mean something, didn't they? When she had challenged him about the serge-suited figure in his sketches he refused to accept that there could be any number of suits like that one.

'Look,' he'd said, his eyes holding hers in a grip of honest intensity, 'I need answers, perhaps more than you do. I'll know when the right one comes along; believe me, this is reality, Leone, it's not a game. I know it sounds mixed up and may come to nothing, but it's happening to you and me. No matter what your brain tells you, it's what your instinct forces upon you that counts.' His eyes pleaded for a response, while he tapped his temple, slightly embarrassed at the outburst, but desperate to make her understand.

'I guess so,' she replied reluctantly. He waited for her to go on. 'I think I follow you,' she said, but didn't.

And then he told her. 'I *knew* when I painted this figure,' he said, pointing to the blue suit on the canvas. 'It's in the colours, the same combination of colours – exactly the same as the first picture. I didn't even have to think – it's just there. I don't know what it means, but it's there for a reason, believe me, please.' And in those few moments she knew she did.

*　　　*　　　*

Gray's Inn Square was deserted save for three or four students gathered in a huddle outside the library. Mock exams, she guessed. Christ, she was never that keen. As she walked past they smiled a collective grin. It was as if she was an endorsement of their future. Long hours, dedication, industry and, yes, we too can be like you. Leone returned their smiles and thought, If only they knew.

It was no easy matter persuading the night security guard to allow her access to the building at this hour, especially since she had forgotten her identity badge, but eventually he succumbed to her begging and she was safely installed behind the terminal at her work station by 6.15 a.m.

Where to start? One of the sacrosanct rules of TWC was that, although the entire firm used the same network of computers served by a mainframe, invasion of other solicitors' files was strictly forbidden.

Events last year had been testimony to exactly how forbidden 'strictly forbidden' was in the TWC rule book.

A friend of hers in the commercial leasing department had been dating a man who happened to be a divorce client instructing Leone at the time. It turned out to be a stormy relationship and things got out of hand when the client complained that his date seemed to know a great deal more about him than he would have liked. Leone confronted her friend, who owned up and begged Leone not to inform the partners. Leone kept her confidence on condition that the file snooping would stop. Sometime later the couple fell out in a drunken tiff, and the client was told by his lover that Leone's personal case notes were pessimistic about his chances of success. The client complained the next day to the senior partners. Five minutes later one unhappy-looking friend was clearing the contents of her desk into cardboard boxes.

Leone waited for the dying whispers of guilt to pass, then allowed her mind to take over: as Jack said, there was no way of ignoring some things. Internal inhibitions and ethical barriers eradicated, she plunged straight into the entire client list of TWC. She had only two hours before the automatic billing system clicked into operation: every minute of lawyers' time between 8 a.m. and 6 p.m. was automatically clocked according to which reference was typed by the operator. The system then instantaneously allocated the time spent to the correct client, thereby never wasting a second of potential profit. As this would be classified as overtime, and charged at a higher rate, Leone was obliged to clock on manually. She entered the reference for Speakman's file then immediately pulled down the main client list over the top. Now she could flick quickly between screens and no one would discover that she wasn't working on legitimate business.

A large menu appeared on the screen dividing clients alphabetically into categories of work. She hadn't navigated these waters before and doing it without a map, like a techno-pirate, turned her heartbeat up. She tried the criminal file first on the basis that Berkeley was clearly in serious trouble, having his life mauled over by the Serious Fraud Office before his body was cold. Active cases were listed in the usual manner. She pressed the page-down button and skipped through the As, rapidly getting to the section containing surnames beginning with B. The list contained seventeen entries. No sign of Berkeley anywhere.

She paused and sat back in her chair: this could take her hours, scrolling through the whole list of departments in the firm. There had to be a shortcut. Then suddenly it occurred to her: the day Berkeley died he was already in the lift when she joined on the sixth floor. It was a ten-storey building and, excluding the possibility of a conference with the janitor on the rooftop, that left four floors. She mentally walked through the building trying to remember which floor housed which departments.

On the seventh floor the Admiralty lawyers shared with entertainments; the eighth was solely the domain of tax experts. European bilingual solicitors and personal-injury section occupied the ninth and the top spot belonged to commercial litigation and corporate finance.

Which way? She hesitated: top down or bottom up? She chose the latter and at 7.55 a.m. she was cursing. She figured that, as Jack had told her Berkeley had uttered the word 'Boatman' to him, it might have something to do with shipping. The Admiralty section, as the name implied, dealt with all manner of commercial shipping disputes and tended to classify files according to the vessel's name. It had taken Leone over an hour to establish that there were no ships which even sounded like *HMS Berkeley* or *Boatman*. This was demoralising as it caused her to reflect for the first time upon the magnitude of her task. After all, Berkeley could have been visiting in his capacity as part-owner of a ship, a Lloyds name seeking information, or a board member of an export agency – literally anything: he was a general financier, after all. Eventually she decided to push on with the same tactic notwithstanding her waning enthusiasm.

She exploded the files marked ENT and the screen burst into life, spilling its eerie green data. The firm, as everyone knew, had established a large following among media celebrities, but Leone hadn't quite realised just how many famous rock stars, actors, actresses and TV pundits were reliant on TWC for legal advice. She checked the whole list more out of fascination than expectation of finding Berkeley's name hidden inside the web. She had wasted two hours and still nothing.

The office was beginning to fill up and she didn't want anyone to stumble across her enquiries. She logged off and wandered down to the solicitors' lounge to grab a coffee. When she returned, the Speakman files seemed to glare at her from their undisciplined heap in the corner. She began ploughing through notes of additional evidence which had arrived from the Crown Prosecution Service offices. Yet more diesel receipts from various filling stations used by Speakman in his travels around the country. It appeared that the net was closing around them. If they didn't come up with something more concrete than the psychiatric report then she was afraid that Sedgewick would cause problems. Although he was a drunk, in situations like this everyone was sure to cover their backs. In Sedgewick's case that could involve his writing a formal opinion to the Legal Aid Board stating that he had offered advice and it was futile to fight the case. This would probably mean that the board would question the future financing of the case. All she could do was to wait – wait and hope.

Toby had requested that she begin the laborious task of going through the transcripts of the tape-recorded interviews with Speakman after his arrest. In all, there were twenty-two hours of questions and answers, spread over three days, dealing with all seven murders. Although Speakman had maintained his denials throughout, and despite the fact that he had the benefit of legal advice, Toby still wanted her to check the transcripts against the actual tape in case there were any important but convenient omissions.

She leafed through the preliminary pages to the first interview bundle and began to feel tired. What's the point in all this, Toby? She could feel her eyelids getting heavier. Locating her Walkman and inserting the cassette, she pushed back into the recliner and started the tape. Her eyes closed as the interviewing officer introduced those present in the room and cautioned Speakman . . .

Twenty minutes later she was losing interest in the monotonous delivery of the officer.

'Where were you on the night of the seventeenth of April 1994?'

'I don't know.'

'Where were you on the eighteenth of April 1994?'

'I can't remember.'

'I'll tell you where you were, you scumbag. Abducting little girls, that's where, Speakman. Now, where were you on the twenty-third of November 1993?'

Suddenly Leone snapped open her eyes and switched the tape off. There was something niggling at her. She rewound the tape. Somewhere near the beginning, she was sure of it. She started it again. Yes, there, just after the caution.

'Do you understand why you have been arrested?' the officer asked.

'Well, yes, I suppose so, but I can't really help you. I have been advised by Mr—'

'I've explained the procedure to Mr Speakman,' a voice interrupted quickly, too quickly. It was vaguely familiar and she reran the segment several times, but the voice was too far from the microphone to have real definition. She checked on the transcripts for all the interviews looking for a name behind the voice of Speakman's legal representative. It could only be one of a handful of people who worked at TWC in the old criminal department.

Thirty minutes later she was heading down to the typing pool and still confused. She had decided to hunt down her former criminal secretary, Debbi Ludlum, to get some answers.

She entered the secretarial department and fought her way through the forest of pot plants surrounding Debbi's desk. There she found her hunched over a word processor.

'Debbi, you're sure to know the answer to this one,' Leone said breezily.

'Probably,' replied the secretary in a world-weary Liverpudlian accent. She had a spongy pliable face and blonde hair cut in a sixties pageboy style. She was almost like an institution to the younger women. In her mid-forties, she carried that unassailable sort of confidence that comes with experience but not necessarily deep understanding. She had been with the firm since its inception and what she didn't know wasn't worth knowing, a fact she never let solicitors forget.

'I've just been going through the Trevor Speakman file and your reference appears on the correspondence.'

'I remember doing some work right at the beginning but that was before the criminal department was disbanded. I've been in commercial litigation for over twelve months.'

'Who's been doing the secretarial work on it then, if it's not your reference?'

'I've no idea, but I can ask around; it could be that nobody's bothered to change the reference on the computer. Which solicitor had the case before you?'

'I'm not sure. The correspondence is signed Teal Windle Crichton with an indecipherable scribble.'

'Nothing unusual there: but you must know who had the case before you did. Didn't they tell you?'

'No, I was brought in at the last minute. Basically, he's been overlooked. How did we get this case in the first place?'

'Through his employers.'

'Why?'

Debbi adopted the manner of a smug matron. 'It was all laid down in a long memo. The drivers at Bigg Truck have some sort of loyal insurance policy through the company. It covers them for their legal costs if prosecuted for offences committed at work: you know, careless driving, speeding, that sort of thing. But don't ask me, I'm only one of the typists.'

'Fighting a murder case is only slightly different, wouldn't you say?' Leone enquired. 'Who told you to create the file?'

'Er, I can't rightly remember just now but it's bound to be on that memo.' The typist's voice pitched a little higher and her aura of confidence faltered for a moment.

'Would you mind showing me where?' Leone demanded, aware that her own temperature was beginning to rise.

A painfully slow search by Debbi revealed nothing: no memo dealing with the funding of the case in sight. It was the last thing Leone needed. She knew of no insurance policy that offered free legal advice in a murder case. Slowly, her stomach began to tingle.

It looked like the partners of TWC would have to fund the entire costs of the case.

Fresh questions sprang into her mind. Something was brewing at the bottom of her stomach and she could already taste its bitterness. It wasn't long before logic began to impose its authority. There was something seriously irregular about this – but, more importantly, she was in the hot seat.

'Miss Stern, you'd better take a look at this.' Debbi's earthy northern tones drifted into Leone's ear.

'What?'

'I still can't find the memo but here's a file note from David Taylor; it's the same guy. He was the solicitor dealing with it.'

'No, that can't be right. I'm sure he was an articled clerk in another department. He never handled any criminal work: I would have remembered.'

'I'll check it out, but you know I think you're right. I seem to recall that he left us just before Speakman was arrested. He went to work in the City at some American stockbroking outfit. I went to his leaving do.'

'All right, Debbi, but what does the note say?' Leone asked impatiently: the tingling was getting worse.

'Oh yeah, it says that all the original documentation – custody record and charge sheets – from the police station following Speakman's arrest should be on file.'

'Well that should tell us a bit more. But why would David Taylor's name be on that note? He couldn't have been at the police station.'

'Well according to this, you should know, Miss Stern.'

'What are you talking about?'

'He's cited your name at the bottom of the note as his supervising solicitor; you must have authorised him to do the interviews at the police station.'

'That's bullshit. Give me a look.' Leone grabbed the piece of paper. She hadn't been near the Speakman case before, let alone given any supervision to an articled clerk called David Taylor. What the hell was happening? Her mind raced on.

'Have you seen this before, Debbi?'

'No,' replied the secretary quietly.

Leone had to see that file: any material over twelve months old would be stored in the file archives, but she should be able to find them on microfiche. Every page contained in the file would have been photographed before transfer to the archives. She was shaking as she strode down the office to the library.

Her heavy tread caused a few heads to turn in the book-lined silence as she clattered across the wooden floor, plugged in the microfiche viewer and selected the correct index. Within seconds she had scanned onto a scrappy sheet of TWC paper headed TELE-CON. She read:

West Street Police Station. 21 April 1995: 2.45 a.m.

Client: Trevor Speakman

Arrived at police station following telephone conversation with custody sergeant. Client arrested apparently on serious charges: certainly abduction and probably murder. Advised client of rights. Custody authorised pending further enquiries. Telephoned Miss Stern at home to confirm I would re-attend when client is re-interviewed tomorrow at 10.00 a.m.

David Taylor (Articled Clerk).

Her heart kicked in an extra thump. She tried desperately to remember. At the time of Speakman's arrest the Bradley mess had surfaced and she was under extreme pressure. What if Taylor *had* spoken to her? But no, she was certain he hadn't. Think, Leone, think. She plunged both hands into her thick hair, pushing her fingers into her sore temples and circling them in opposite directions. Her chair screeched along the polished floor attracting disapproving glances. As she stood there motionless, the message began pounding in her chest: set-up! But why?

She quickly retreated without any apologies and made her way along to the lift, her head whirling in panic. There was one waiting; she pressed LG. A couple of minutes later she was bristling past the archives clerk who was reading a *Superman* comic at his desk. The basement was a huge area which housed all files for up to six years after they were deemed dead. Although it had been ages since she'd been down here, as an articled clerk herself, Leone threw the young man a look that told him she didn't need any assistance. She made for the criminal section. The entire room was covered in steel shelving from floor to ceiling, packed with papers. At one end was a secure vault where various deeds and ultra-sensitive material were stored for safekeeping or, in most cases, safe burial. Access to that part was restricted to partner level.

Although she was shaking inside she calmly located the old criminal files; there weren't many left. In theory, there shouldn't have been any since the firm had stopped doing criminal work, but they still took on the odd drug possession charge against their celebrity clients. Speakman's stood out, being fatter than the rest. She took it to a small reading table against the painted brick wall and searched frantically for that scrappy sheet of paper. She couldn't find it. What she did find was the custody record confirming that David Taylor had attended Speakman. Her frustration erupted.

As she slammed the file shut a creeping sense of inevitability swept over her. David Taylor. Then suddenly another thought occurred to her: his personnel records must show when he left; and if he did leave before Speakman's arrest, who the hell had visited the defendant and advised him through the interview? It was only then she realised that, if she was right, there was a very good chance that whoever was using Taylor's identity could be watching her. But why?

She hurried over to the archive clerk's desk and grabbed his telephone quickly.

'Here, what's going on?' he said, aggrieved at the intrusion.

'I'm ringing Mr Pearsal,' she replied simply, returning his indignant stare. Ronnie Pearsal, despite their differences, was the only partner she could trust with this, and even then it was a risk: what if all the partners were aware of what was going on? She dialled his mobile number and noticed a tremor in her fingers as they clasped the handset.

'Hi, Ronnie, it's Leone Stern.'

'What's the problem?'

'Sorry to disturb you but something very odd is going on.'

'So what's new,' he replied distractedly. 'Look, I'm on the fifteenth fairway, a sand wedge from the green and two down: can't someone else help?'

'I didn't know who else to turn to.'

'Go on then, make it quick.'

'Can you remember an articled clerk called Taylor who worked

here, about twelve, maybe eighteen, months ago? David Taylor?'
she prompted cautiously.

'Vaguely. What about him?'

'I've found some paperwork on the Speakman file indicating
he worked on it.'

'So?'

'So he couldn't have; he'd already left the firm by then.
Somebody has been masquerading as Taylor.'

'Impossible; there must be some mistake.'

''Fraid not.'

'Does it matter?'

'I was hoping you could tell me that.'

'Can't help on that one. Maybe you should just check first on
the personnel records. I can't remember how the oversight of
Speakman's case came about in the first place. All that happened
was a memo from the senior partners saying we were representing
his interests and that was that. Then I saw you after the committal
hearing. Say, is this going to cause some problems, Leone?'

'I'll let you know,' she said and was glad the line wasn't
good.

'What's that you say?'

'Nothing. Do you know where this guy Taylor did work when
he was here?'

'I think he was assigned to the Bigg Truck account.'

'Speakman's employers,' she whispered to herself. Then she
asked, 'Why did he leave?'

'I don't think he was regarded as the right sort, if my recollection
serves me properly. I think he got his articles here by the back door:
son of one of the partners' friends or something like that.'

'Who was his principal solicitor?'

'No idea; you'll have to check his records.'

'They're in the vault: I need authorisation.'

'Tell the clerk you have mine then . . . Oh, good shot,
Charles . . . Sorry, Leone, best I can do. Let me know how
you get on. Bye . . .'

The line went dead and she replaced the telephone gently,
looking at the vacant-faced clerk, who stirred into action in
the manner of one who likes to hear a grovel. He even stood
his ground for a couple of moments before Leone invited him
to check for himself with Mr Pearsal.

'If you try now you may just catch him teeing off at the sixteenth.'

A minute later, the vault was being opened with elaborately slow movements and a false reverence. Leone crossed the threshold into the cabinet-lined room.

The personnel files were marked in the right-hand corner. She quickly located the correct drawer and began sifting through the suspension files. A small gasp escaped her as she passed the space the Taylor file ought to have occupied. She searched either side but it wasn't there. She slammed the door, the metallic clatter echoing throughout the basement followed by a disapproving and slightly superior grunt from the far corner.

What the hell was going on? She slumped with her back against the cabinet and let out a deep sigh. As she lowered her gaze from the ceiling she inhaled slowly, then something caught her eye on the cabinets opposite. There on the drawer right across from her in bold black lettering was a recently familiar word: Boatman.

CHAPTER SIXTEEN

Leone nursed a pounding headache all afternoon. She rescheduled her appointments and sought the solitude of a conference room on the fourth floor of TWC. Moments earlier she had tried tracing the Boatman file on the computer, but it had recently been deleted, just as the archive files had been emptied in a hurry. The only thing she discovered was that Boatman was a limited company. A single letter-headed page bearing the logo of a pair of crossed oars embossed with shiny gold lettering had been trapped in the back of the filing cabinet. It bore a registered office address in the City but when Leone called the number she was told it had been disconnected. There were some scribbled figures across the page, which seemed to be a calculation relating to Deutschmarks. It was dated March 1990. None of it made any sense to her. One thing was certain, however: Jonathan Berkeley's visit to TWC had been no mirage. What should she do now? What would they do now? After all, she was the lawyer. Jack would have every right to say they should go to the Fraud Squad with the information. She had to find out more before she spoke to anyone.

She decided to use the stairs and leave early. She walked along the corridor, out onto the landing, and stood for a moment in the spot where Jack had pictured Trevor Speakman. She looked out onto the road below and saw the long white gouge marks in the tarmac made by the lorry that had killed Jonathan Berkeley. She thought about David Taylor and his missing personnel records. Where was it all going?

Hailing a black cab at the corner of Gray's Inn Road and Cheapside, she set off for Companies House, where all information on limited companies is held. The cold evening air was beginning to settle over London as the taxi made an uneventful journey through the permanent rush-hour traffic. She wedged herself into the seat and pulled her Katherine Hamnet polar jacket tighter around her body. She had no idea what was going on or whether this had anything to do with Speakman, but one thing was clear: she was stuck. It was drawing her in.

As she passed along the glowing Embankment she looked over at Tower Bridge; it triggered a memory of her father. At least something in his own streetwise, boorish philosophy had been right. They had been standing on the terrace outside the concrete umbrellas of Sydney Opera House looking up at the great suspension bridge. It was the last time she'd seen him alive and had no idea of the chaos his empire was in. She remembered telling him that she wanted to travel to England after university. He pointed up to the bridge and told her that London wasn't like Sydney. He said the first thing she should do was to take a look at Tower Bridge and watch the people walking over it. 'Every second there's a mug passes over that bridge. They walk straight, they keep dry but they still get covered in leeches. Don't you be one of them, girl: keep wet, get slippery, act like an eel and move like a shark, because as sure as damn it they'll suck you dry.'

The only thing about that, Daddy, she reflected, is that you weren't even brave enough to hear people call you one, were you? But thanks for the advice, anyhow. Mug, bastard, same difference to me, she thought.

An acidic burn gripped her stomach as she turned everything over. The fact that she had been brought onto the Speakman case so late, Berkeley's death, the stroke she'd pulled to get Sloane on the case, the mystery of David Taylor, Jack Forth's weird paintings, Boatman Limited . . . The list was growing, becoming ever more real. She laid her head back, closed her eyes and felt the leeches clamp.

Jack winced at the sudden rush of light as he reached inside the refrigerator for the bottle of Highland spring water. Too many nights in the deserts of Kuwait, too cautious for sleep, had awakened in him an ability to judge the time in even the blackest of skyscapes. He knew it was 4 a.m. when all the good people of the world were dreaming dreams. But not Jack's dreams. He walked to the window smoothing the cool surface of the blue bottle over his brow. The pains in his skull were becoming intense now – clean and sharp like a polished scalpel, probing more accurately than before. He wedged open the wooden slatted blind and looked out to the dreary

120

street below. Deep silence lay heavily over the rooftops, broken only by the distant blues of a lonely tomcat.

He watched in blind concentration, trying to visualise the wind. All he could see was Speakman rotting away, paralysed and impotent. He knew that the real beast was out there – still free, planning, pacing, plotting and controlling. He couldn't see him yet but he could feel him. The bottle's lip leaked a drip of liquid. Water, it was always the water. He slugged a mouthful from the bottle, then splashed some more on his face vigorously.

He had to sleep. He tried to think about Hollie, and visualise her petite oval face. He tried to hear her voice soothing his pain away. He thought about the scrapbook they were making, full of the postcard paintings that they had garnered from the finest galleries in the world. Underneath, in her careful handwriting, Hollie had delivered her personal critique of history's most celebrated artists. He longed for her naïveté.

He flopped backwards onto his bed. He didn't want to be alone any more. He watched the dancing patterns of the curtains and could see the face of a girl. It was always the same girl – dark-eyed and screaming – but no sound, only his own shallow breathing increasing in rhythm as she writhed. Then she was gone. He reached for something in his mind – anything to replace that. The pain went on, bringing with it the voices. He heard a different language – the words tumbling over one another in a riot of sound. It pierced his brain. Then the silence. Blue skies and calm green sea rushed past, each frame almost imperceptibly different. The big picture never changed. He could see his own small feet pounding the goat's track that snaked away forever into the distance. His destination was always out of reach. The damp sheet around his shoulders focused him. He had sweated another hour of the night away. It was futile to try to sleep.

Jack rose and plodded through to the studio, where he switched on the television for company or distraction; it didn't matter. Old B-movies and primetime-reject shows crammed the airwaves. He settled into a chair and surfed the remote control mindlessly until he came across a documentary programme featuring a group of men struggling to erect a tent in torrential rain. All the men wore stiff little Romany moustaches, giving the whole scene a strangely comic feel. But these were real men, not clowns; they were acrobats in a circus from Eastern Europe. The programme showed animals being herded into cages as the storm intensified.

As Jack gazed at the screen his own memory monitor ground into gear and he drifted once more to a stone-built harbour on a bright sunny day. Small, whitewashed cottages surrounded the inlet with deep purple and pink flowers clutching the stucco sides and reaching to the eaves. Children were playing, singing, chasing gulls away from the brightly coloured fishing boats until a whole flock of them circled and hovered above him. There was a boy at the end of a long jetty. He was sitting on an upturned fish crate with his hands cupping his chin watching an old man with dark, olive-coloured skin and dreamy black eyes. He was mending a net, periodically snapping bits of twine and working it into the holes, tying intricate knots while the boy looked on. No words passed between them. Just the boy watching the old man and Jack watching them both.

It felt as if the scene had lain in his psyche for years and it was only the whip-weary roar of a tamed lion in the circus parade that brought him out of his trance. The pain eased slightly, then suddenly snapped completely away like a wily old pike at the end of a taut nylon line. He half fell out of his chair while scrambling around on the reading table for a pencil and pad. Then he began to draw, the dark scaly lead skating across the paper faster than he could think. He sketched a rope threading through a loop, then another; he drew in an arrow pointing downward. Then as quickly as he had drawn it he ripped it from the pad and sped through to the kitchen, frantically searching through the junk drawer. Seconds later he found a length of string. And then, as if he'd sailed the seven seas seven times over, his hands went about tying the most elaborate of maritime knots. When he had finished he stared at his handiwork. Where it had come from in his past he had no idea, but the deep familiarity was too strong to ignore. He had to see Leone.

Leone took another slurp of coffee and wrapped the towel around her head, still wet from the tepid shower. It had been a fitful night's sleep, her mind heavy with confusion and no one to share the burden with. She had returned from Companies House with a complete history of Boatman Limited and had spent until the early hours attempting to make sense of the paper. She walked over to the pile of documents glaring at her in front of the living-flame gas fire and crouched down beside them.

The gentle purring of her mobile made her get up again. She could hear it somewhere beneath the pile of paper. It was Jack Forth.

'Hi, Leone, I knew you'd be up.'

'Just going through some stuff.' She had decided not to tell him anything about Boatman until she was sure. At the moment, however, she was still stuck in pitch-black ignorance.

'I'm sorry, I was just wondering if you fancy breakfast. Isn't that what lawyers do, working breakfasts?'

'Two decaffs and a slice of crispbread. I've already had the first, I'm drinking the second and I'm looking at the crumbs of the third. You've got to get up earlier to be in my club, Jack,' she said, using a transatlantic drawl.

'Maybe you should meet my Coffee Buddy: you'd get along just fine,' he replied.

'What?'

'Never mind. Look, I've got to go in to collect Hollie from the hospital around lunchtime. Why don't we hitch up?'

'Ah, yeah, that would be . . .' She hesitated. Christ, she thought, she really was heading for the deep end. Coffee machine, kid: it'll be the mother next. Everything seemed to be happening so quickly. Or was it just that she had shunned so many over the years? What was it about this man? 'I'll see what I can do. I'm still up to my eyes.' She compromised between her head and heart.

'OK, I understand, but if you change your mind I'll be at St Luke's about twelve-thirty.'

She put the telephone down and turned back to the papers smiling to herself. She'd just realised that it wasn't the gas fire that was warming her up.

The first file was full of Boatman Limited registration documents. Jonathan Berkeley was one of the directors, and there was another name she didn't recognise. The shares were split equally between Berkeley and the other man. TWC were the solicitors and company secretary. It had been formed in the late seventies as a general investment company. More questions. Her brain was beginning to reel again.

As usual, the figures made little sense to her but she knew enough about company accounts to understand that on the face of it Boatman Limited was a very successful concern. According to the balance sheet, at the end of the previous year it had nearly four million pounds in cash reserves but had made no investments since 1991. It immediately occurred to her that, as Berkeley had been involved with it, likely as not the money was dirty. It was beginning to look like a classic little insider-dealing scam. Furthermore, it was looking increasingly likely that the police didn't have the remotest idea that it existed. Above all, it struck her that, as whoever was in on this at TWC was prepared to mislead the police, they certainly wouldn't be pleased to discover she knew about it. Drawbridge up, Leone, she said to herself.

She dressed quickly, collected the papers and walked out of her apartment just after 7 a.m. She reached the foyer still fiddling with the pieces in her head like an unruly and unsolvable Rubik's cube. It was another wet morning and she stopped momentarily at the front external door to adjust the hood on her coat. She didn't really take any notice of the postman as he bustled past her, collar up and cap pulled down against the weather. He grunted something and waved a registered letter in the air. But Leone had soon rounded the corner and was out of sight.

The postman crept up the single flight of stairs to the woman's apartment. Gaining entry was as simple as he had envisaged. The thin pick slid silently into the Chubb lock, its greased surface moving smoothly over the internal mechanism. There was a satisfying click of the tumblers and he was inside. He removed his rubber overshoes on the rush matting and quickly pulled a small leather pouch from the postbag.

Five and a half minutes later the postman snapped off his surgical gloves and activated the transmitters on all three bugs. The first was a CSS, UHF-powered telephone socket: this replaced the old one identically and would monitor all calls. The second was a standard, working, 13-amp twin plug adaptor, which would monitor conversation in the lounge. The third was a standard bug hidden in the photograph frame beside Leone's bed. He recognised the man in the picture and smiled with the knowledge that *he* would have appreciated the lengths to which one had to go for success.

They all had a range of 700 metres. That allowed him to designate a pick-up point for the tapes well out of sight of her home. It was all so simple, yet oh so necessary. Delighted with his handiwork, he exited the apartment whistling a cheerful Mersey Beat song. Inside his head, the lyric ran in tandem to the tune.

'Listen. Do you want to know a secret? Do you promise not to tell?'

CHAPTER SEVENTEEN

L eone kept a low profile during the morning, trying to let her
discoveries about Boatman distil in her mind. She spoke
to no one – apart from Debbi to ask her to divert her
calls – and worked steadily through the remaining interviews
with Speakman. She considered calling Ronnie Pearsal about
Taylor's missing employment records but quickly abandoned
the idea. He had confirmed her suspicions anyway. Although
nothing had gone terribly wrong at the police station, it still
bothered her. Taylor definitely hadn't worked in the criminal
department and he definitely hadn't telephoned her on the night
of Speakman's arrest. Ronnie had said Taylor worked on the Bigg
Truck account, Speakman's employers. It could be that Taylor had
been sent there as an emergency measure when the employers
found out that Speakman had been arrested. But no, that couldn't
be right: she was sure that Taylor had left the firm before the date
of Speakman's arrest. The whole situation was bouncing around
in her mind again.

Anyway, who removed the damned personnel file? Who emptied
the Boatman file? Were the two connected in any way? And, above
all else, if she was right about Taylor's date of departure who
the hell was masquerading as Speakman's solicitor at the police
station?

She delayed the urge to rush out and find Taylor herself: that
would have to wait a little while. For the moment she had to read
through the prosecution summary of evidence before the following
day's meeting with Toby at Scotland Yard.

The summary was more thorough than anything she had seen
before. At the time of each of the girls' disappearances a huge
number of potential witnesses had been contacted and interviewed,
but as the manhunt had stretched from months to years the volume
of material had ballooned to gigantic proportions. It wasn't until

Speakman became the number-one suspect that the police were able to search through the entire case files to find anything relevant to link him.

The main difficulty was that after such a delay none of the witnesses could reliably identify Speakman as being close to the abduction sites. It was because of this fact that the police had concentrated on his work routes at least to put him in the general vicinity. Leone was still only up to the evidence in connection with victim number three, a teenage girl from the town of Windermere in the Lake District who had been abducted on a warm summer's night in August 1993.

The area had been bursting with tourists at that time of year, families enjoying the vast open countryside that surrounds the largest of the lakes. The victim was a local girl who was well known and liked in the town. During the long summer nights her parents would allow her to walk down to the lakeside promenade to play with her friends, happy in the knowledge that she was a sensible girl who always came home when instructed. But not this night. Leone traced through the statements, which recorded the last hours she was seen alive. A neighbour had seen her with friends heading towards the amusement acrade by the marina, but had not taken much notice of a man lingering around the slot machines who seemed to be staring at the children. Other witnesses had taken only a subliminal note of the same man with descriptions ranging from scruffy and dishevelled to well-groomed and touristy. After all, there was no reason to be diverted from their own business: it was just another ordinary summer's evening.

A couple of minutes before nine o'clock a man from the travelling fair on the green at the side of the lake recalled the teenager asking to change a twenty-pound note at the cash kiosk and returning to the side of a tall man whom he had presumed to be her father. They were alone. At the same time the real parents were becoming a little anxious and sent her older brother out to search the area around her home. They searched in vain. Although the fairground was only half a mile from her front door the girl had already disappeareed into the night.

Leone remembered the emotional plea made on national television the following day by the girl's distraught parents and the overwhelming but ultimately useless response from members of the public anxious to lend their support. The girl's broken body was found three weeks later in the River Tale, Devon, over three hundred miles away. A group of young boys out shooting with air rifles had spotted the body floating down the river close to the edge and had managed to drag it to the side. The original pathologist's report stated that the body had been quite well preserved and all the indications were that she had died by asphyxia due to drowning. The report concluded that she had probably been alive when dumped into the water but most likely unconscious, owing to the fact that her eyes had been removed from their sockets.

As with the first two murders a number of statements followed dealing with the initial findings of the investigation by the local police force. The temperature of the River Tale had been taken at the time of discovery and had proved to be different from the body temperature. This indicated that the body had probably been further upstream for some time before it had been discovered. Police had spoken to the technical staff of the water company responsible for the upkeep of the waterways in Devon and were able to conclude that the body had been dumped higher up the river or in the River Clyst, a tributary of the Tale. The smaller river proved to be several degrees centigrade cooler, coming as it did from higher ground on the Black Down hills. On its route downstream the body would have encountered many obstacles, which could have captured it for considerable periods of time. It was only the recent rain that had probably forced the body loose and caused it to float downstream. There were many injuries recorded but it was clear that she had been viciously sexually assaulted. The conclusion was eventually reached that the body had been dumped in the river at a point close to the junction of the A38 and the M5 motorway. When police began collating Speakman's journeys they discovered that he would often use that route on his way home to Exter, and, furthermore, his work schedule had shown that he was in the Lancaster area of the north-west at the time of the abduction: easily within striking distance of the Lake District. The owner of a transport café just off that particular junction had come forward after the arrest and made a statement to the effect that Speakman was a regular visitor.

Leone looked up from the papers with growing despair. Speakman couldn't deny any of the facts being put forward in support of the case against him, but they really were only circumstantial. Not for the first time since this mess began she recalled the old wives' saying that there is no smoke without fire, but they still had a strong psychiatrist's report saying he didn't fit the profile. But, then again, maybe the report was way off the mark. Speakman wasn't able, or wasn't willing, to help himself: the last hospital report concluded that he had tested positive for amphetamines, LSD and heroin, all illegally obtained inside. The report probably wouldn't stand up in court against the real background of Speakman's increasing dependency. She glanced at the clock on her computer: it was time to find David Taylor. But first she had to see Jack Forth.

The taxi ride to the hospital took only ten minutes. She had decided upon a gentle introduction to the most important thing in Jack's life: Hollie. She found herself practising as the vehicle stopped. Her palms were getting sweaty as she approached the front entrance. She asked the way to the children's ward and was directed by a surly youth in a brown jacket. He pointed out the blue signs and turned his back without a word. She made for the eastern wing. By the time she had reached the third long corridor she had chickened out of lunch. this was a bad idea.

She could see inside most of the wards as she passed by. Old people, bandaged people, sick people. Shot people. She stood still for an instant as her memory raced back to the television news the day it happened. Blood everywhere, women screaming, stretchered victims in white sheets, doctors in shock and her own father's smiling face at the end of a list of the dead. Every TV station in the world had carried that bulletin. Her pain was soul deep. What was it you used to say, Dad? she thought bitterly. 'Don't admit, think twice before you commit, and never ever quit.' Well you sure made it easy for me to forget that crap, didn't you, Daddy?

When she got there, the children's ward was bustling with overworked, eternally cheerful nurses and painfully sick kids. Leone walked along the corridor searching the beds for Jack. He was nowhere to be seen but someone else caught her attention. A young girl was straddled across a bed improvising a glove puppet show. The tiny hairless boy with pale translucent skin who was her audience managed a toothless grin as the little cloth doctor and nurse danced around on the girl's hands. Leone recognised the same focused intensity around the girl's eyes but her smile was easier than her father's.

'It comes from her mother's side.'

Leone swivelled round quickly to see that Jack had joined her, watching with obvious pride as his daughter continued her improvised show.

'How is she?'

'Wicked, as they say in the third form: her hair has yet to grow back and she won't forget the accident in a hurry, but otherwise she's ready to come home. Are you OK? You look pale yourself.'

'Yeah, I'm fine. What about you?' Leone retorted quickly.

'I'm OK, I guess.' His eyes shot away, defensive and distant.

'We have to talk,' she said. 'This whole thing's getting weird. I've just come to say I can't make lunch.'

'That's too bad. I have to take Hollie back to her grandmother's anyway. It would be a rush. What about dinner tonight?'

'All right. I may know a little bit more by then anyway. Give me a call when you're back and we'll arrange something then.' She made as if to go.

'Would you like to meet her?' He stared straight at her: a challenge. She knew it wasn't something he was used to asking and her face flushed slightly at the implications of this invitation into his private life. Meeting the kid shouldn't be a problem but the space between her and Jack was heavy with future promise. She realised that to him it must seem strange, her being at the hospital like this, watching his child from a distance. But she just felt she had to see him, be near him.

'Think twice before you commit, Leone,' her dad's voice warned. *Get out of my head, you bastard.* 'No . . . I mean yes . . . but not now.'

'She'll wonder who you are.'

'Yes, who are you?' A shrill and squeaky Punch and Judy voice broke the moment.

They turned around together to see Hollie peeping at them between the two puppets from the door to the ward. Jack's face cracked into a smile while Leone grinned nervously like a teenager on a first date.

'Hollie, this is Leone, she's a friend of mine.'

'Hi, Hollie, great show,' said Leone.

'Leone – that's a funny name,' mused the girl.

'Don't be rude, Hollie. Leone is from Australia.'

'Wow! Do you eat kangaroos?'

'Only on Tuesdays.'

Hollie eyed her suspiciously.

'Have you got a boomerang?'

'Sorry, left it at home today.' Leone winked and Hollie's brow wrinkled in defeat. 'How's your head?'

'Oh, it's fine; Daddy's taking me home today. Are you coming as well?'

'Now that's enough, Hollie. I don't think Leone came here to answer your questions all day. Come on, let's get you packed up and get out of this one-hospital town. Say goodbye to Leone.'

'Bye, Leone, nice to meet you.'

'Nice to meet you as well. When you get better I'll maybe show you how to fly a boomerang.'

'Really? That would be great.'

'Sure, why not, but you'd better get going now.'

'Yeah, come on; let's go and see if we can spring you,' smiled Jack, taking his daughter's hand. 'I'll call about sixish; good luck this afternoon.'

They turned and headed back towards the sister's duty office.

'She's lovely, Jack,' she whispered.

Leone crossed the city on her way to Threadneedle Street. Debbi had eventually remembered the name of the stockbrokers Taylor had gone to work for and it wasn't long before she reached number 56, the home of Michigan Mutual Bank. All she could do was hope that he still worked there.

As it turned out she couldn't miss the huge glass skyscraper that housed a number of foreign banks and stockbroking outfits. The plush lobby area carried a large brass nameplate declaring MMB trading headquarters to be on the twenty-first floor. A turbo-charged elevator left her stomach at ground-floor level and she emerged into the reception area feeling less than comfortable but determined to confront Taylor. She marched over to the receptionist.

'Good afternoon, may I help you?'

'I certainly hope so,' Leone replied. 'I'm looking for someone who works here. His name is David Taylor. I believe that he's in the Eurobond department.'

'David Taylor, er . . .' she hesitated uncomfortably. 'I'm afraid he's no longer employed here, or at least I don't think he is, Miss . . .'

'Stern, Leone Stern.'

'Miss Stern,' she smiled like an automaton, 'may I enquire of anyone else in the same department?'

'Nobody else can assist me with this: it's a personal matter. What do you mean you're not sure if he's employed here?'

'Look, let me get someone who may be able to help you.' The girl attacked the switchboard, whispered something into the mouthpiece and indicated to a nearby sofa. Leone was puzzled but figured she would go with the flow. Two minutes into a lifeless back-copy of *Bankers Monthly* she heard footsteps behind her.

'Miss Stern.'

'Yes.' Leone turned to see a heavily pregnant young woman with flaming red hair and full red lips standing over her.

'You're looking for David Taylor?'

'That's correct, Mrs . . .'

'Miss, actually, although I understand the mistake. Shirley Hutchinson,' the woman explained, holding out her hand. Leone guessed she was in her mid-twenties.

'David Taylor was my fiancé,' she said, sitting down carefully next to Leone. Her accent was carved from the East End.

'Oh, I see. Then you may be able to help me. I'm a solicitor from Teal, Windle and Crichton: perhaps you know David used to work there some time ago.'

'Yeah, he told me; what do you want him for?' the woman asked cautiously.

'Do you know where he is today? I need to speak with him urgently.'

'So do I, Miss Stern,' she replied, patting her bulge gently.

'I don't understand.'

'He disappeared four weeks ago.'

'He walked out on you!'

'I guess you could call it that; more like ran away.'

'What do you mean?'

'He got into a lot of trouble trading Eurobonds on his own account with the firm's money. He was gambling the markets big time; I mean millions. They were going to find out and I guess he just couldn't face up to the pressure, so he just upped and left.'

'He didn't tell you?'

'Nah; not his style. You obviously don't know him too well.'

'Evidently, but he seems to be making a habit of it.'

'Come again?'

'It doesn't matter,' Leone went on. 'Listen, do you have any idea at all where he could have gone?'

'Not a clue. I tried tracing everyone who knew him but it was useless; he was a compulsive liar, the sort of person who didn't have a past. Best lead I had was an old girlfriend who was helping him with cash when he knew he was going to be discovered here.'

'What happened to her?'

'It was when he first came here: he said he was living with her, told me he left her to make a new life with me. I even tried a private detective to trace her to see if he'd gone back, because he always said she had a lot of money and that's what he liked most of all: money.'

'And?'

'The only thing I had was her name: J. Berkeley. I saw it on the cheques he used to get from her but that wasn't enough to go on . . . Miss Stern, are you all right?'

Leone was suspended somewhere in an empty hinterland of confusion but had the look of someone who's just begun to get the hang of the map.

CHAPTER EIGHTEEN

Jack rattled along on the train returning to central London after making sure Hollie was settled back at her grandparents'. The rhythm of the carriage and the stolen hours of the previous night began to take their toll. It was ten past five. The garish red and blue stripy seats of the tacky plastic interior around him were empty. As the train drew to a halt in the last station before Euston he could see grey-faced workers crushed against the glass of a train heading out of the city. He felt himself gently drifting with the motion. Outside, the chocolate-orange glow of sodium lighting prepared the metropolis for another night. He allowed his shoulders to relax and succumbed to the weight of eyelids pulling him closer to oblivion. A deep sleep consumed him.

Now he was free of the turbulence he found in daily reality, peaceful yet dark. Then suddenly he was undulating over light patches, riding a strange rollercoaster. It wasn't long before he registered the distant chanting – a familiar religious mantra from within, somewhere inside him. There were the answers he sought. Then he glided like a free bird over the landscape, being drawn inevitably towards the chant. He could see himself huddled below a leafless winter sycamore. There was a summer sun shining bright and strong. He was a little boy again, this time cowering on top of a barren brown hill, yet the landscape was lush and green. The darkness lifted and he entered, his childhood eyes gazing at the whitewashed chapel below. He could see the mourners, old women with dense black veils crying over an empty coffin, and in the distance the noise of gunfire.

He woke with a throbbing head and was glad to leave the train. He quickly found a telephone and rang Leone. Her Sydney tones soothed his ears as he listened to her recorded message. He was just leaving his own when a breathless version of the real thing jumped down the line.

'Jack, hi, it's Leone. Christ, you just don't know what we're getting into here; this is dynamite.'

'Slow down, will you?'

'Jack, this is really something. I just hope it doesn't blow up in our faces.'

'It's definitely ours now, is it?' he asked, gently reminding her of her initial reluctance to take him seriously.

'OK, OK, I've just got in and I'd apologise if we had the time. Just meet me at the Via Venetia on Claremont Street in Chelsea. I'll be there at eight.'

Later that same afternoon, his hair still greasy from the postman's cap necessary to the disguise, he listened with mounting apprehension to the contents of the call between Stern and her friend 'Jack'. He had retrieved the tape from the drop without difficulty. She sounded genuinely frightened by what she had learned. He needed to share that knowledge. Knowledge was indeed power, but force was as yet too abrupt a card to play. He would observe: see them, but they would not see him.

He knew of the restaurant Leone had mentioned and accordingly was aware that he would be unable to watch them from inside its intimate geography. Very well. He pondered what equipment would best suit his purposes and decided on the Lynx-10 Second Generation Plus Intensifier. It operated in very low light and, with the aid of an inbuilt laser, in total darkness. It also accepted a 35mm camera lens. Say 'cheese', Jack and Leone. Smile for King Arthur.

A long, golden ciabatta bread sat between them on the small window ledge at the rear of the busy little restaurant. To the side of the bread, a roasted garlic bulb emanated its pungent breath-threatening odour. They both eyed it nervously, awaiting the waiter's departure as he poured from a bottle of Lazio Chardonnay. Jack looked over to Leone, the tension between them more than mere discovery: it was the first time he had seen her dressed as a woman rather than a lawyer. The formal chignon had been released into free-fall sun-hugged curls that softened and framed her face. Starched black and white traded places with yellow and blue. The former, a delicate silk evening shirt, the latter a battered, war-weary, revealing pair of 501's. With a '*buon appetito*' and a swivel of his tiny Latin waist, the waiter moved away.

'So what's going on?' Jack pleaded.

'Someone is being very naughty at TWC.'

'Who?'

'I don't know yet but when you hear what they've been up to I think you'll agree that they don't want to be found easily.'

'What do you mean?'

'I figured out Boatman. Boatman was, or should I say still is, a limited company which was used as a front to purchase shares on the German stock market with inside information.'

'Hold on a second. I don't want to spoil your fun, but where did you get all this information?'

'I stole it!'

'You did what?'

'Well, more borrowed really.'

'So you can break rules!'

'Look, Jack, what I've got here is so incriminating it really doesn't matter what it is or where it came from. Just bear with me, OK?'

'I bet you're the first lawyer ever to say that,' he joked.

'Smart ass. Be quiet and listen.' She waited for a moment for her victory to sink in. Not so much in control now are you, Jack Forth? she thought. 'Boatman made a lot of money around the time that the Berlin Wall came down.'

'How?'

'The shares it invested in were almost exclusively in one company called Eurofreight. It controlled the major contracts for commercial goods traffic to Eastern Europe. The routes had never been important before, but then the Wall was about to come down. Those contracts for haulage were going to be very special. Boatman took its holding to just under five per cent, the legal maximum, one month before rumours began to circulate that Sir Colin Bigg decides he wants to buy the thing.'

'He's the guy who owns Bigg Truck Haulage, isn't he? Yeah, I know his face.'

'Which also happens to be TWC's most lucrative account.'

Jack let out a soft, low whistle. 'So someone is really inside.'

Leone went on. 'The share value of the target company, Eurofreight, went through the roof when Bigg Truck's bid was

confirmed. Boatman ended up with a great wedge of cash and a
lot of very valuable Bigg Truck stock in exchange for its holding,
which was vital in the takeover battle.'

'Let me guess: Berkeley is in there.'

'He was an equal shareholder with someone else, I reckon
someone using a false identity at TWC.'

'Do we go to the Fraud Squad with this?'

'You need to know the rest.' She had to level with him. 'Because
TWC was company secretary, all documentation lay dormant in the
archives at our offices for years: it wasn't even listed as a client.
No one, as far as I'm aware, knows about it, not even the police.
It was just lying there: Berkeley's, and whoever else's, nice little
pension fund. Then about twelve months ago, just before Speakman
was arrested, a young barrow-boy type called David Taylor was
working for TWC. He stumbled across the Boatman scam and this
was the result.' She reached into her handbag and pulled out
a floppy disk. 'Taylor took all the paperwork and blackmailed
Berkeley with exposure.'

'Brave lad.'

'Maybe, but I'm assured no worse a scumbag could you hope
to meet,' she said in deference to his unborn child.

'What's on the disk?'

'It's all Taylor's figures and workings in relation to Boatman.
He had Berkeley stitched up but he didn't know the identity of
his partner at TWC.'

'Is this what you sto— I mean, borrowed? Where did you get
it?'

'Hold on, will you? So it turns out that Taylor got sacked from
TWC. Surprise, surprise, but then he lands a job in the City trading
bonds for a bank called Michigan Mutual.'

'You think Berkeley had something to do with him getting
that.'

'What do you think?' She went on quickly, telling him about her
visit to MMB's offices and her meeting with Shirley Hutchinson.
'So I asked the compliance officer at MMB a few questions.' She
blushed, remembering the outrageous flirting. Her embarrassment
must have shown.

'The which officer?' Jack asked.

'It's the person who deals with irregular activities by employees:
they're a bit like gamekeepers of the City institutions. You see, the

girlfriend had already told me that Taylor was in big trouble at work. He'd gambled a lot of his firm's money away on his own account. Since Nick Leeson brought down Barings the City's been paranoid about rogue traders. Anyway, they were onto him, but the officer tells me that Taylor kept covering his losses with vast sums from a private source. He had a boxload of floppies downloaded from Taylor's PC. I saw one of them had Boatman labelled on it and I, well, sort of picked it up.'

'You mean you stole it, Leone?' Jack seemed highly amused that she wasn't prepared to admit to theft.

'Whatever. It shows that Taylor got about four million pounds' worth of blackmail money.'

'So now do we go to the police?' asked Jack, spreading his arms and narrowly missing the wine bottle.

'We can't: Berkeley's dead and Taylor's disappeared.'

'What?'

'Vanished, and as far as TWC is concerned, it was like he wasn't employed there at all. His personnel records have gone and I don't know what to do next. Jack, I'm scared. Something even stranger turned up yesterday, something to do with the Speakman case.' She had to trust him now – there was no one else.

'Go on.' He filled her glass.

'It doesn't make any sense but David Taylor started at MMB three weeks before Trevor Speakman was arrested, so he wasn't physically working for TWC any more. You with me?'

'Yeah, but so what?'

'Someone assuming his identity attended the police station when Speakman was interviewed.'

'That's odd.'

'There goes your gift of understatement,' she mocked, but he could see that she was worried sick. 'What's going on, Jack?'

'Your guess is better than mine, but at least you know someone else has an interest in the Speakman case.'

'But not why.'

'Not yet,' he corrected, trying to instil some confidence. 'Now, you can start looking at a different angle in his defence.'

Jack was still thinking about Boatman. Wherever there was money, real money, and serious reputations to protect, then danger was never far behind. They sat in silence.

David Taylor was the key to this. Leone had described him

as a Cockney barrow boy. If so, what was he doing at TWC, an establishment firm who were used to employing top-class graduates? It didn't make sense. How did he get the job there?

'Did Taylor's girlfriend tell you anything about him?'

'Enough. How much do we need to know? He was a blackmailer. He bled Berkeley dry and he's disappeared with the money.'

'I thought blackmailers never quit.'

'They do when the money runs out.'

'There's something not right about this. With that much money at stake I would have thought Berkeley, or whoever else is involved, would have been able to either buy a get-out-of-jail-free card or just take the scumbag out altogether. But I can't accept he would just keep on paying. It has to be something more than Boatman: surely it would make more sense.'

Leone stared out of the window thinking about Jack's comment for a short while, idly playing with her wineglass. Suddenly she made some connections from the thousands of pieces tumbling around in her head.

'Got it!' she exploded. 'It could be a sex thing.'

'Why?'

'Taylor told his girlfriend that he used to live with a girl. She assumed he was telling the truth and even sent a private investigator to trace her, but we know the person he was in fact referring to was Jonathan Berkeley. That's why he couldn't be found; they were looking for a woman not a man.'

'I still don't get it.'

'Look, Taylor was described to me as a person without a past.'

'Meaning he just didn't talk about it too often. I suspect many blackmailers do the same.'

'Exactly. So what if the past he was trying to conceal involved Berkeley? What if they did live together?'

'It's no big thing.'

'Right, but there must be other secrets Taylor learned through Berkeley. So much so that Berkeley would do anything to keep him quiet, pay anything. Look at the evidence, Jack! First of all Taylor gets a job in a very prestigious firm of solicitors more used to recruiting from Oxbridge than the East End. Some graduates with excellent qualifications have been known to want to work for free just to get a start with TWC. Berkeley has connections there.

Makes sense, doesn't it, that when Taylor subsequently stumbles across the Boatman scam, Berkeley's partner at TWC wants rid of him? So he's sacked and left for Berkeley to deal with. Berkeley can't just get rid of him: he's still sharing the bed. He's given a job in the City, he keeps quiet for a while, and in the meantime meets Shirley Hutchinson.'

'I thought we were working on the basis that this guy is gay.'

'He's young: a mover, remember. His only love is for money. If he was prepared to blackmail Berkeley we can safely say that loyalty doesn't come very high on his priority list. In about three months' time there's going to be three-dimensional evidence that he swings both ways.' She raised her eyebrows, referring to the girl's pregnancy.

'Yeah, I see the point.'

'Taylor then gets greedy and more intimate with the girl. Berkeley is shoved out. Taylor starts gambling on the stock markets, gets out of his depth, and Berkeley refuses to cover his losses. They split and the blackmail begins again while Taylor's living with Hutchinson.'

'But no one's gonna pay four million quid for the privilege of not coming out of the closet.'

'Depends how dark the closet is,' she countered.

'It does make more sense, I know, but we're still no closer to finding out what the hell Taylor had over Berkeley that would cost four million. What about the girl? Do you think she knows more than she's prepared to tell you?'

'Nah. She's as mad as hell about him disappearing, leaving her to clean up his mess. I reckon Taylor is a genuine snake. He wouldn't tell her anything because, as you said, what he's got has to be something very, very important.'

'Leone, you'd better tread carefully because, if you're right, it looks to me like whoever was in the frame with Berkeley has got his teeth into Speakman as well.'

Jack gazed out of the window, his mind trying to work out the unworkable. He didn't take any notice of the one car in the street with its engine ticking over and its driver staring right at him.

CHAPTER NINETEEN

Richard Dexter meandered his way to the fifth floor of Scotland Yard at 9.10 a.m. He passed through a door marked CENTRAL COMMUNICATIONS COMPLEX TO25 and moved down the corridor, bypassing other doorways leading off to Central Traffic Control, the Message Switch Office and the Central Casualty Bureau. At the end, two more nondescript teak doors stood side by side. The one on the left housed the Special Operations Room. He pressed the intercom for access to the Information Room on the right. Nearly two hundred police officers and civilian workers staffed the unit, which was by far the largest within the Central Communications Complex. The door was answered by a young WPC who directed him to the 'Wendy House', as it was unofficially known. This office, occupied by a chief inspector twenty-four hours a day, controlled the entire complex.

Dexter hobbled past hundreds of consoles manned by the operators responsible for running the Metropolitan Police Force's communications systems. No one even looked in his direction as they gave rapid instructions into their headset mouthpieces.

Chief Inspector Lee, a large man with a benign expression and square jaw, rose to greet Dexter as he knocked on the glass door and entered the Wendy House. Beside him, a smart-looking woman in traditional white shirt and checked cravat was stooped over some papers.

'Ah, Mr Dexter, good morning.' The CI held out his enormous hand.

'Pleased to meet you, Chief Inspector,' replied Dexter, returning the gesture.

'Likewise. May I introduce Inspector Barnes, who I believe you have already spoken with on the telephone. I'm just filling her in on the final details.'

The woman stepped forward. 'Hello, Mr Dexter, it's nice to put a face to the name at last.' She had short, mousy-coloured hair framing a plain face with no make-up. Dexter had imagined her as taller and more robust. In fact, she was quite petite with pixie-like features and doughy brown eyes magnified under tortoiseshell spectacles.

'I'm sure you'll be sick of the sight of me after a while, Inspector,' Dexter smiled, shaking her hand.

'Not at all. It will be a pleasure to work with you.'

'Inspector Barnes tells me that Miss Stern and Mr Sloane are expected at half past nine,' said CI Lee. 'We've allocated the special ops room for their use subject to any major emergencies arising. How long do you anticipate they'll need?'

'It's hard to tell, but Sloane especially has a reputation for thoroughness.'

'I see. Well, the sooner we get them out of the building the better. The Assistant Commissioner isn't best pleased that they're here at all.'

'No option, I'm afraid,' Dexter sympathised. 'I have hopes that they'll run out of steam before too long, though.'

'Good, well I shall leave you in the capable hands of Inspector Barnes as far as the technical side is concerned. I gather that Roger Fry's leading the case for the Crown. How is the old dog?'

'I think he'll be substantially happier when this search is over.'

'Really? Nothing to worry about, is there? I thought the case against Speakman was nailed on!'

'Yes, it is really, but if the defence look hard enough they might come across some statements which could muddy the waters somewhat.'

'I see,' the CI said solemnly. 'Well, Inspector Barnes is totally at your disposal, Mr Dexter. Her major function is to ensure that the defence don't stray onto PNC2 or any on-line investigations within HOLMES, but we're all on the same side here so feel free to consult with her for any assistance you need. I've chosen the access codes personally and I don't think they'll be broken.'

'Thank you,' said Dexter, looking over at Barnes, who remained impassive. Her smile was still in place but strangely he detected just a hint of resentment in those big brown eyes.

Chief Inspector Lee offered his hand once more and Dexter

followed Barnes out of the room. A message was waiting, saying Sloane and Stern had arrived and were on their way up to the fifth floor. Five minutes later they were all in the corridor outside the Information Room.

'Your console is here, Mr Sloane.' Inspector Barnes pointed the barrister towards a blinking screen inside the Special Operations Room. That was the deal: they would have access to the HOLMES computer database on the police's terms and on their territory. The chosen battleground was a grey box without a window; a strip light's mean glow accentuated dark rings under the policewoman's eyes from too many hours of staring at computer screens.

'Thanks. Can I stick my bag down here?' Sloane had already deposited the weighty holdall in the middle of the room; he strode towards the leather-backed chair that stood before what was to be his work station for the foreseeable future. Leone sat down beside him.

'There's a coffee machine down the hall.' Barnes forced a fixed, public-relations smile across her elflike features. 'If there's anything else . . .'

Toby could sense the career woman's hostility to his presence and the access he had been granted. He nodded his head. 'Thanks, you've been really—'

'Helpful?' Dexter offered.

'Forthright,' Toby concluded.

'Let me just get the set-up right,' he muttered to Dexter as his information-hungry fingers began to flex above the keyboard. 'The judge granted us access to HOLMES.'

'Limited access, yes,' the prosecution replied cagily.

'And whatever I access will be monitored by your operator on another console in another room,' Toby said, turning to Barnes.

'I didn't make the rules, Mr Sloane.'

'I am not complaining yet,' Toby said. Barnes raised an amused eyebrow. 'Who decides what I am allowed to see?'

Inspector Barnes smiled thinly. 'You will be allowed to see everything that is pertinent to the Speakman case and nothing else.'

'And pertinence is a question for . . . ?'

'Me, Mr Sloane,' she said firmly. But Toby persisted.

'And if I disagree?'

'You are entitled to your opinion, as I am to mine; there is no appeal.'

Sloane appreciated her position. The HOLMES system was seen as a living, breathing organism linked to the entire criminal-intelligence network. So far as the police were concerned, they had solved the case of King Arthur over a year ago; all they needed was a jury to agree with their findings. The inspector was watching his reactions carefully. No doubt Special Branch would have supplied a copy of his file that would explain her polite hostility. Any accurate research on his career to date would have detailed his work in immigration appeals, for animal-rights activists and his appearances in the Court of Appeal for convicted women murderers who had done no more than defend themselves against a violent partner. He pushed his round, gold-rimmed glasses further up his slim nose. There was something else about Barnes, something familiar to him, though he couldn't for the moment decide what it was. He shrugged the feeling away.

'If I do need anything, I'll just tap it through on the keyboard; you'll get the message more quickly.'

She moved her hand towards the door handle and spoke over her shoulder. 'I have already, Mr Sloane.' As Barnes and Dexter walked out to return to the Information Room, Leone turned to Toby.

'OK, where do we start?'

'I've been looking at the evidence in relation to the first murder. Colleen Bridges.'

'What about it?'

'Two things worry me. Firstly, she was a known prostitute operating in central London and yet there are no statements dealing with her whereabouts in the days before her body was found.'

'That's not unusual, is it? I mean, it's highly unlikely that any of her punters would come forward to eliminate themselves.'

'Maybe not, but all the same she must have had friends or a pimp or someone who knew her. I'm sure the police would have taken steps to contact those people simply to trace her last movements. If they have, then the findings ought to be in here.' He tapped the console.

'Makes sense. What else is bothering you?' Leone asked, impressed by Toby's reasoning.

'The fact that I can't find any evidence from the employment records that puts Speakman in London around that time.'

'No diesel receipts or delivery forms?'

'Precisely.'

'He could have gone in his own car.'

'It's possible, but did you look through the interviews with Speakman?'

'Yeah.'

'Didn't you notice that he was asked what colour his car was at that time?'

'Vaguely.' She sounded a little defensive.

'It's OK, Leone, you could be forgiven for not latching on to it. The point is, he told them it was a red Vauxhall Cavalier.'

'So.'

'So they must have had a list of vehicles they were interested in. My guess is that it was probably compiled from witness statements taken from people in and around King's Cross Station, which is where Colleen Bridges worked, according to the prosecution summary. I want to see those statements.'

'I should tell you I found something else odd about the Speakman interviews. The custody record indicates that a man called David Taylor acted as his solicitor but the fact is he didn't work for us then.'

'Could it be an administrative glitch?'

'I don't think so, but I can't trace David Taylor to be one hundred per cent. He's been involved in some very serious business,' she said, conscious of the fact that she wasn't telling Toby everything.

'Get an enquiry agent on to it then. I can hold the fort here.'

'OK. You sure you don't need me?'

'I'll be fine. Go on, get to it.'

When Leone had closed the door behind her, the barrister reflected on the mutual antagonism between himself and the police; it had always been so. There was always another agenda. He saw it as his task to detect just what that might be, then use that knowledge to the advantage of his client or the case; the two were not necessarily the same.

Toby had been given his own password for entry to the database and was wryly amused to see what name the inspector had chosen. He typed it in: 'loophole'. Just because they were police officers, it didn't mean they had no sense of humour. The multicoloured screen sprang into activity and invited him to key 'Camelot', the imaginatively chosen operation name for the search for King Arthur. A menu of topics appeared before him. Each dealt with a separate portion of the vast investigation into the identity of the girl's murderer.

HOLMES was a piece of solid, logical computer craft. Since its inception in 1987, the Home Office Large Major Inquiry System had provided forces all over the country with instant access to the tens of thousands of pieces of information collated during any major investigation. Toby looked at the statistics breakdown for the Speakman files, which glared at him ominously. There were 189,677 separate statements, a nominal index of 324,129 names with almost as many addresses, over 500,000 telephone numbers and a full range of specialised information categories and description indexes.

He scanned the list of specialised topics beginning with 'Locations'. This section collated all information about abduction sites and the points at which the girls' bodies were found.

Other topics included 'Transport', which dealt with the sightings of vehicles around the time and place of abduction and abandonment; 'Suspects', as the name implied, was a complete register of sex offenders whose victims were young females; and 'Articles' was the generic description for the rope and other items, such as the injected narcotic, used by the killer to facilitate his crimes.

Overall, there were more than two million separate computer screens of information. Where did one start? Sloane had taxed his brain about this matter for the preceding few days. He had to work on the assumption that Speakman was innocent of these crimes. Whether he shared that view personally was of little consequence to a dedicated barrister. If he accepted that as his starting point, then another person, as yet unknown, had committed the murders. His task was two-fold: to attack the prosecution evidence against his client, and to build a case against the real killer. He was not naïve enough to believe that any researches of his own would lead the police and prosecution to change their minds about the killer's identity, but if he could construct an alternative for the jury, then perhaps Speakman might – just might – get a fair trial. He had four weeks – four weeks to attempt to save Trevor Speakman from a sentence of life imprisonment. He removed his jacket, hung it around the shoulders of the chair, removed the two gold cufflinks from his double cuffs, placed them carefully inside the pocket of his waistcoat and rolled his sleeves up for work. Scrutinising the keyboard, he keyed in his first request.

'I'd love a black coffee, Inspector.'

A moment later a response lit up the screen: 'Access denied.'

'The first of many,' he muttered as he plunged into the immense material at his fingertips.

He stared into the face of his own computer terminal. It had been four weeks to the day since he had extracted the details from Taylor's pitiful and pleading mouth. Victor La Saux. Things were too close to let a second-rate porno merchant get in the way. The picture sat in front of him in technicoloured pixels, plastered over the Internet. page. A slightly different angle from his own recollection, but the same unmistakable bodies. Only the faces were scrambled. A new message every four hours updated subscription count: more and more viewers were hooking into the the two-minute compuvid as word of Electromouth spread among the perverted ones.

In the corner of the screen a personal reminder to him read, '£2 million to play.'

He slammed his fist onto the keyboard. With Leone Stern beginning to create dents in his biorhythms he had to let La Saux into a secret. Nobody had ever broken a secret with him before: they didn't live long enough.

'Access denied.'

Christ, this was becoming irritating. Toby drummed his fingers across the Formica top of the regulation police workstation. Barnes and Dexter were clearly intent upon refusing him sight of the prosecution case map. They would be happy that he was wasting his time trying to find it, but it was the only way ahead. He needed a comprehensive overview of the investigation to help him navigate towards the specific points that interested him. What he was seeking was a master blueprint that would outline key points, both for the prosecution and the defence. The police and the prosecution would be aware of the dangers of refusing to disclose most of the gathered research. What he suspected they had done with this case, because of its notoriety and high public concern, was to hide potential evidence in plain sight under a soaring tower of useless data. In order to do that, they must have been able to identify it, then bury it.

Toby searched his memory for all the Arthurian words and phrases he could remember. The same policeman who had named the operation Camelot might well have been responsible for the code word for the master print of the entire computerised enquiry. He had tried Guinevere, Mordred, Merlin and Morgan le Fay: the computer merely repeated 'not recognised'. He entered the words Gawain, Kay and even Lancelot to no avail. His brain dredged for other references to the Knights of the Round Table and its legends. The Green Knight and Excalibur were no more successful in his own quest. He stopped himself dead: that was the word, 'Quest'. He entered it; again, the computer's hard disk failed to recognise the word as a password.

'Come on, Toby, think.' He was on the right lines, he knew it; it required just a bit more thought. He had to place himself inside the senior police officer's brain. How would he see his task? If King Arthur the killer was unholy, then the officer would see himself as the opposite of that. Who was the holiest, the most pure of the knights? Toby smiled as his memory filled in the gap. Sir Galahad; of course: he was the youngest and the purest; he had been selected for the most important quest in the Arthurian legends; he had been sent to seek the Holy Grail. Wouldn't a policeman with some knowledge of the subject matter see himself in the same light? There was only one way to find out. Holding his breath, the young barrister keyed in the words 'holy grail'. Nothing. He typed, 'holy quest'. Again, the same. Then he entered the words 'Sir Galahad'. The computer screen began to fizz with information and a message appeared.

'Code incomplete.'

He racked his tired brain for some moments. After a minute of deep concentration the knight's full title sprang into his head. He entered 'Sir Galahad the Pure'. The computer screen showed the words 'code complete: access granted'.

He was in at last, but what he would find was another matter.

CHAPTER TWENTY

Eton was an ideal environment for learning the darker needs of others. Victor La Saux had enjoyed his 'carefree' school-days at the ancient seat of learning; many of them had been spent as a provider of recreational drugs, boys and pornography. His best clients were some of the older masters who returned his favours with their own. His school reports spoke of a 'splendid, clear-thinking young man'; anything more derogatory would have brought an embargo against future pleasures.

Though Oxford was an open invitation to the inexplicably popular eighteen-year-old, he had decided to enter the world of commerce. His contacts were as helpful as ever. They needed little reminding of their dangerous liaisons. He had never been a partaker in any of the commercial commodities available; he was a businessman, not a consumer. When working capital was required to expand premises or purchase new stock, La Saux was gratified by the open-palmed help available to the young entrepreneur from his past associates, though he was careful never to kill the tarnished golden goose. He referred to his success as an 'empire of human weakness'. As sexual tastes and deviancies became jaded or more extreme he had reacted quickly to market forces; consequently, his empire grew. At thirty-two, Victor was a wealthy and respected member of the community. His work for charity was held up as a banner of goodness to others less generous, and he intended to get even bigger.

La Saux now had an excellent business opportunity. A friendly Dutch chemist had recently refined the Ecstasy drug to a new specification. The effects lasted longer – and it was cheaper to produce than its predecessors, though this last fact would not be communicated to the consumer. The problem was that the chemist was aware of the potential of his research and wanted a vast retainer to protect the market from a deluge of the drug.

It was simple economics: if the drug, or E+ as he called it, was widely available, it would drive the purchase price down. La Saux was undercapitalised. His compromised sleeping partners did not have the financial wherewithal for this particular venture. He had been about to pass on it when the 'article' had come into his possession. He had been sitting in his Soho office when David Taylor had walked through the door carrying a brown briefcase, wearing a big smile and looking for a partner. Until that moment La Saux hadn't believed in a superior force controlling the universe. Call it God, call it Allah, call it what you want: from then on he saw the light and, what's more, it was shining on him. He watched the home video and cut the deal without hesitation.

Victor utilised his fine business mind and put his quest for venture capital into action. The Internet was a marvellous item of progress. Its speed and relative anonymity created a failsafe haven for blackmailers. Four million pounds netted between himself and Taylor so far, and he hadn't had to break into a sweat. But now, sadly, that foolish man Berkeley was deceased. The money, his money, had disappeared beneath the crunch of the lorry's wheels. Now it was time for victim number two. Proof that he had the article could be seen flicking frame by frame on the Net. He had been patient, waiting for the prey to bite. Today was a good day.

The e-mail message begged him to pull the two-minute piece of Netporn from the Web. Now it was time to reel him in and get ready to do business; at this rate it wouldn't be long before his dreams became reality. It was a pity Taylor seemed to have flipped out of the venture, he thought vacantly, he'd not been around for a while after Berkeley's death. It didn't bother La Saux that he wouldn't be there to share the payout.

A meeting had been arranged. La Saux sat patiently in the Greek coffee bar in Covent Garden. The heavy late-night rain had formed a thin film on the surface of his Burberry raincoat. The warmth of the crowded café caused hazy steam to rise from soggy footwear and sodden jackets. It was 11.05 p.m. The man was late.

By 11.30, his untouched espresso deathly cold, La Saux placed the exact money for the beverage on the aluminium tabletop, pulled his mackintosh belt tight and strolled slowly into the continuing rain. Not a promising start to his relationship with victim number two. His car and driver were parked round the back of the square at the far end of the near-deserted market. Just inside a side street close to the Strand, La Saux pulled up his collar against the wet and felt like a ridiculous Humphrey Bogart in the gesture. He could see the back of the car some fifty yards away and noted the driver's plume of cigar smoke in the reflected light from the pub opposite. La Saux was doubly annoyed. Not only had his meeting been a literal washout, but Jenkins was smoking one of his own Cuban cigars. It would come out of his wages.

Suddenly, he felt a sharp, needled pain to the back of his neck. His knees buckled first. La Saux felt vaguely grateful to the pair of arms that stopped his rapid progress to the wet and grimy floor. They were strong arms but surely their owner could not have been aware that he was guiding Victor in the wrong direction. He was powerless. The car and its smoking driver were receding quickly. He heard a Cockney voice in the distance enquire, 'Is he all right, mate?'

The owner of the guiding arms answered, 'Fine, just too much drink; you know how it is.'

It was a pleasant voice, deep in tone and well educated; a voice one could trust. La Saux, feeling drowsy yet strangely euphoric, attempted to thank the stranger for his kindness but his vocal cords refused to respond to his brain's demands; all he produced was a dull grunt.

The Good Samaritan spoke again. 'Shh, now, just relax. Oh, and, by the way, sorry I'm late.'

The numbed figure of Victor La Saux was dumped inside the rear of a blue Range Rover. His assailant covered the heavily drugged man with a tartan blanket. 'After all,' he whispered, 'it wouldn't help if you died of shock; not yet, anyway.'

It was midnight at Scotland Yard and Inspector Deborah Barnes was exhausted. The long hours watching Sloane's attempts to break the access code had worn her down. Richard Dexter was clearly hiding something. Her experiences told her it was better not to know, but her curiosity had been aroused. She had been briefly tempted to download the files he had directed that she should transfer out of HOLMES and onto PNC2 to keep them from Sloane's eyes. In the end, she had simply followed orders, but it was definitely niggling her.

She had found out years ago just how relentless Sloane was and couldn't help but feel a grudging admiration for the lawyer.

Many would have deserted their task hours before, but Sloane had complete faith in his powers of logical deduction and pursued his task tirelessly. He had correctly deduced the existence of the case blueprint, much to Dexter's surprise. At the moment the files were safe but surely it wouldn't be long before Sloane discovered the black holes. Barnes had warned Chief Inspector Lee of the path that Sloane had chosen, but her vainglorious superior had seen the barrister's pursuit as an intellectual challenge to his choice of code names and love of Malory's *Le Morte Darthur*.

'He'll never work it out, Deborah. Briefs are full of wind and piss; their only original thoughts are about fees.'

Now she was waiting in the Wendy House with the news: he'd got in, transferred a copy of the blueprint into forty different files and had used the colour printer for a hard copy of the information. Her boss would not be a happy man. He would be on his way now from a briefing with the Assistant Commissioner and Dexter.

Barnes had swiftly changed the access code to one she had chosen and one that marked her attitude to the response of Chief Inspector Lee: 'idiot'. It was idiotproof, just as the original one should have been. But it didn't make that much difference now. Sloane was on the inside track.

The door opened abruptly and Lee walked quickly through wearing a dinner jacket and bow tie. She looked at his apparel with understanding.

'Sorry, sir. I didn't realise it was Lodge Night.'

'Not only Lodge Night, but Ladies' Lodge Night. Mrs Lee is not a happy Master's wife.' He was one of many senior policemen on 'the square': it was another of the privileges that Barnes's sex denied her.

'He's cracked it.' Lee gave her one of his slow nodding responses that was meant to convey deep understanding but only served to make him look like a rear-parcel-shelf dog in a Ford Cortina.

Her superior glanced towards the computer terminal on the desk. 'Don't you stand when a senior officer enters the room?'

She climbed slowly to her feet. Too slowly for his liking.

He frowned towards her quickly, then looked away as if suddenly aware how foolish he appeared.

'If you tell me what it is we are hiding then I will be able to perform my job more efficiently, sir.'

'We are not hiding anything, Deborah; if something is discoverable then it is not hidden.' His voice had the quiet menace that had propelled him swiftly to his present rank.

'With respect, sir, I can't function without accurate information.'

'This is a need-to-know situation and at the moment you're not on the list to be educated, Inspector. Is that clear?' he said harshly.

'Now where have I heard that before?' she muttered under her breath.

'What was that?'

'Nothing, sir.'

'What access code have you given the files that are now on PNC2?'

'Idiot, sir.'

'I beg your pardon, Inspector?' he asked angrily.

'The code, sir: I-D-I-O-T.' She spelled it out slowly, beginning to enjoy herself.

'I warned them,' he began, 'told them you'd cause trouble, but no, think of equal opportunities, I'm told: she's been passed over too many times, what harm can she do on HOLMES?' Barnes felt the burn of anger on her cheeks. 'You could have stopped him before he found the right code for the blueprint. Do not insult me by denying it.'

He moved to the console, flicked several buttons on the keyboard and read through the numerous attempts Sloane had made to access the blueprint. 'As I thought. I will enter a report on your behaviour in the morning.'

'But sir . . .'

'No buts, Inspector, this is down to you and I'm going to make sure the ACC knows about it.'

She reached into the top drawer of her desk and removed a document. 'I have my own report, sir. It details the advice I gave before the breach occurred, it goes on to detail the efforts I made to contact you earlier this evening, and repeats my request for new access codes.'

Lee measured her with his gaze, nodded once more and pushed his hands into his dress trouser pockets; she believed that this was to prevent them from encircling her neck.

'Stand-off?' he offered. She nodded, then felt shared ridicule at the situation. 'No reports?'

'All right.'

'All right, what?'

'Sir!'

'That's better. Now I'm going to switch to another code.'

'At least knock out the Arthur references; he's too bright not to follow your thought processes.'

It wasn't meant to come out like that, but it had. CI Lee looked as though he had been kicked in the balls. He turned once more to the keyboard and furiously punched new commands into HOLMES. He stood, looked her up and down with disdain, and left the office without further comment.

Inspector Deborah Barnes let out a long slow breath. She'd been lucky. Not only had he failed to see that her 'report' was an invitation to the Metropolitan Police Charity Ball, but he had also failed to observe that she had keyed in a file copy command on the hard disk. She accessed his recent changes, noted the key commands and looked at the first of them.

'Now then, let's see what we are *not* hiding.'

CHAPTER TWENTY-ONE

'Sorry it's so early, Leone,' Toby said, his eyes still rapt upon the document spread on his desk top. She had been bleary eyed with sleep when the 6 a.m. phone call had plucked her from a dream of Australian sunshine into the grey dawn of London's reality.

'You said it was urgent: here I am. What's it all about?' Knowing the barrister's professionalism, she accepted that, whatever it was, it was important.

'Coffee?'

She had smelled the bitter aroma of freshly ground beans as she walked past the clerk's desk – apart from Sloane the place was deserted. Leone nodded.

'Follow your nose. There are some cups in the bureau in the clerk's room. Too early for the milkman, though.'

'Not too early for you?'

'I have to be back at the Yard by half eight. Inspector Barnes will be expecting me.'

A few minutes later leone returned, steaming mug in hand, grateful that the scorching liquid was unfurring her tongue.

She had enlisted Jack's assistance after leaving Scotland Yard and had spent the previous night roaming around the West End bars trying to pick up the trail of David Taylor. The private detective hired by Shirley Hutchinson had helpfully told her that his investigations all pointed to the fact that Taylor was a frequent visitor to the strip joints and gay bars around Soho.

Three hundred pounds poorer and full of watered-down champagne, they eventually discovered a male prostitute who admitted to knowing Taylor. Although he hadn't seen him for a while he mentioned that Taylor was friendly with someone called Victor La Saux who owned a string of seedy venues in the area. They soon realised it was pointless trying to get an appointment with

157

a man like La Saux; besides, Leone drew the line at entering his live sex show clubs. Still, it had confirmed that they were on the right track. Whatever Taylor had, it was 3 a.m. when Leone had eventually crawled into bed.

Toby was keying something into his laptop as she sat in the chair opposite his desk.

'Have you found anything we can use?' she asked.

'No, what I have is more of a treasure map really.'

Leone was puzzled. He took her silence as an invitation to explain what the map entailed.

'They're worried about some of their information. It's in there somewhere; it has to be. They wouldn't dare destroy it. Even if it takes years, someone with an axe to grind would pop out of the woodwork and blab it to the press. No, I think that what they have done is to move whatever it is somewhere else.'

'Any idea what it could be?'

He shrugged. 'Could be anything: a witness statement, fibre, fingerprint, who knows? The point is that while the blueprint helps me to navigate through HOLMES it doesn't point to where the material is.' He paused for a moment, then leaned towards her, placing the palm of each hand flat against his jutting cheek bones. 'It could take years, Leone.'

She was grimly aware that time was a commodity in short supply.

'What do you suggest?'

'We have to remember that Speakman will spend the rest of his life inside if we don't get this right.'

'Agreed.'

'It's a desperate situation; it calls for—'

'Desperate measures?' It was an argument Leone had grown up with: her father had utilised it regularly in his business dealings with the construction industry of Sydney. If only she had known just how desperate he could get. Toby's eyelids closed once in silent acceptance of her accuracy.

'In my experience that normally involves something illegal,' she ventured.

'Depends what you mean by illegal,' he replied flippantly.

'If you don't know . . .'

'Leone, there's illegal and there's *illegal*.'

She placed her coffee mug down on the crowded desk top: as with every other barrister she had met, a tidy mind did not mean a tidy desk.

'Semantics.'

'Realism, Leone. You can't ignore the fact that every day in some place the police are breaching civil rights, the right to privacy and worse.'

'I don't, but that doesn't mean it's right to repeat that behaviour: it can't justify the committing of a crime,' she said, not pausing to reflect upon her own actions when stealing the disk from MMB. Never admit, Leone.

'What was it Bassanio said in *The Merchant of Venice* when he was pleading for his friend's life?'

She knew, and repeated it from memory: '"Wrest once the law to your authority and to do a great right do a little wrong." Yes, then Portia saved the day with a clever legal argument, didn't she?'

'Lucky. Women lawyers always get a better hearing from a male judge.'

'She was dressed as a man, wasn't she? Anyway' – she dropped her chin down a fraction and held him with a disapproving stare – 'you don't believe that any more than I do.'

'That isn't the point.'

'Then what is?'

'Speakman's innocence.'

'Do you believe he's innocent?'

'That's not the point either.'

'You just said it was.'

He paused for a moment, then smiled broadly at her. 'I'm glad you're not practising at the Bar.'

'So am I,' she replied truthfully.

'At least hear me out so you know what I've got in mind. I wouldn't even suggest this if I didn't think the situation merited it.'

Leone spent the next fifteen minutes listening to the barrister's plan. When he was finished he sat back in his seat and waited for her decision on the matter.

'Can we cut a deal with this for the moment?' she asked.

'That depends on the terms.'

'Fair enough. You remember me telling you about David Taylor? Well I think someone at TWC has more than a professional interest in this case and I'm making my own investigations into that. So you continue with the blueprint for the moment using ethical means and see what that throws up: if that's unsuccessful then we'll talk again.'

'We haven't got long, Leone.'

She knew that all too well.

Victor La Saux awoke from his long sleep. He attempted to pull his hands up to his neck to the sore point where he had been stung, but could not. His hands were bound to the arms of a wooden Carver chair. He blinked away the crusty residue around his sore eyes. His vision stumbled into a soft focus. In front of him, a cracked ochre wall, unadorned by pictures or display, stretched from left to right. He flexed his legs but anticipated that they too would be bound; he was right. He opened his mouth expecting a gag to limit the movement of his lips: his mouth opened wide without restraint. La Saux spat the mixture of bile and saliva onto the floor.

'You will feel a little groggy for a while.'

He attempted to turn his head around to where the voice had come from and felt a sharp needle point insert itself in his neck. He flinched back quickly and sighed with relief when the instrument came out. He felt a trickle of blood from the entry point.

'Forgive me. I should have warned you about that. Luckily for you there is nothing more lethal than a mild painkiller in it at the moment. Funnily enough, if you had turned to the other side, you would have been dead by now.'

He recognised the voice of the stranger from Covent Garden. He attempted to speak, but his throat was dry and cracked.

'Slowly,' the man's voice counselled; 'we have rather a lot to talk about.'

La Saux rolled his tongue around the inside of his mouth, attempting to produce some lubrication for his vocal cords. Eventually there was sufficient moisture to attempt to speak again.

'I need to piss.' His voice sounded dry, husky, as if he had been on a heavy alcoholic bender.

'Go ahead.'

La Saux looked slowly down to his lap to see that a catheter had been inserted into the open eye of his penis. Its tube ran down to a collection bag between his feet. He felt the welcome release of the urine and watched the bag begin to fill.

'That better?'

He nodded his head slowly.

'Only one problem,' the voice behind him warned. 'I'd try and hold it a bit longer next time: when the bag is full it's going straight back in the same way.'

'What do you want?'

'What we all say we want, but don't really: the truth.'

'Ask me and I'll tell you whatever you want.'

'That's precisely the problem: you may tell me what I want to hear but how will I know it's the truth?'

'I'm frightened. If that's what you wanted to achieve then you've won already, believe me: I'm not about to lie.'

There was a moment's silence that seemed to stretch for days.

'Had we met before I might have been able to accept your word, but as it is, us being strangers, I cannot. We have to get to know each other intimately before I can begin to accept what you tell me is the truth.'

'Tell me what this is about and I'll tell you everything I know.' His voice was rising to a pleading whine.

'You will, in time, you will: do not doubt that for a moment. But we are both businessmen. As in any deal or agreement it is necessary to know how determined the other is to achieve true parity and trust. At the moment you are rightly terrified; this shows me your intelligence. You are attempting to rationalise what it is I want; that proves your powers of logic. I, on the other hand, have shown you nothing.'

'I don't want to bargain with you, I want to live.'

'Again you have shown your understanding of the situation and have assessed it accurately. We will get along well.'

La Saux was beginning to swallow hard; his anal sphincter muscle was beginning to pucker.

'I need to shit.'

'Be my guest. Sadly there is no receptacle for the waste. You will have to sit in it. But, then again, as a pornographer you are used to that. It comes down to choice: how badly you wish to defecate compared to you abhorrence of what that will entail.'

La Saux's breath was becoming ragged with fear. 'You are a fucking lunatic,' he screamed. The primal sound echoed around the room.

'Of course, you noticed that I did not gag you? This will have told a man of your intelligence that there is no need; no one can hear you. Desperate, isn't it?'

La Saux felt tears of fear and desperation fall from his eyes; his shoulders shook in tandem with his sobs.

'Ah, you are upset; that at least is a start. You believe I am serious?'

La Saux nodded vigorously, but was careful to avoid the barbs to either side of his neck.

'Good, then there is no need for the little demonstration I had planned, is there?'

Using minimal movement the bound man moved his head in a tiny, silent 'no'.

'But that would be such a waste. I do hate waste, Mr La Saux.'

'Please . . .' he began before his throat began to fill with vomit.

'The collection bag for your urine has a little additive in it: caustic soda. While the pain will be what you consider unbearable you will be wrong: there is worse, believe me. You will know worse until you convince me of the truth.'

La Saux saw the outline of a figure move quickly around to the bag and stamp on it. He wore a black leather mask. The zip to the bondage headwear was open and gaping. Behind it he could just discern a winsome smile. He felt the rush of movement up the tube and then a burning sensation as the adulterated liquid entered his body.

Five minutes later the captor looked sadly at the slumped form of his prisoner in the seat. He wrinkled his nose with distaste at the odour that emanated from it. He removed the bag and replaced it with one containing lye. He left the room of the remote Exmoor cottage and made himself comfortable in an overstuffed armchair. Removing an envelope from his jacket pocket he reread the notification from the Lord Chancellor's department, the realisation of his final ambition: his appointment as one of Her Majesty's Lord Justices.

He would extract the truth from his visitor: isn't that what judges did?

CHAPTER TWENTY-TWO

'It isn't working, Leone,' Toby Sloane said forlornly. It had been three days since their early-morning meeting at the barrister's chambers in the Temple. Now he sat slumped over the self-same desk; it was 7.30 on a cold, crisp autumn night. The sumptuous fan heater, a fixture in many sets of chambers, wheezed out recycled air at foot level.

'I've tried everything I know: it just isn't working. There's a black hole in the blueprint and I just can't get in.'

The barrister looked exhausted. Leone knew that he was logging twenty-hour days on this – so was she – it was the only way forward.

'Every time I think I've turned something up, she,' he said, referring to the inspector, 'denies me access. We need help.'

Leone had reached similar dead ends in her efforts to track down potential alibi witnesses for the trial. She had four enquiry agents following up witnesses who might have information. So far the people who knew Speakman confirmed he was a bit of a loner but never did anything unusual. None of them could alibi him for any of the dates of the murders.

'What kind of help?'

'Family help.'

She raised her eyebrows for him to explain.

'My brother George – well, half-brother, actually – he knows a lot about computers; a lot more than I do.'

Leone was aware how modest the lawyer was being.

'Anyway, I had a chat with him. He thinks he can get beyond the defences and trace the hidden file.'

'How?'

'It's all very technical: I don't pretend to understand it myself, at least not fully, but I'll do my best to explain. You know how computer modems work?' She nodded. 'Well, there's a thing called

163

a baud rate, or reaction rate, on them. He has manufactured a modem with a faster rate than any others available on the market. What he can do is send a request into HOLMES behind one of my requests and use that as a shield. Basically the machine is looking the other way when the question goes through: it thinks there's only one demand, when in fact there are two.'

'Does that fool the defences?'

'He thinks so, but there is a slight complication.'

'What's that?'

'George has to get into Scotland Yard first.'

'Come off it, Toby.'

'Trust me, he can do this.'

'Tell me about him.'

'All right. I said he was my half-brother; that isn't strictly true. My – our – parents adopted him when I was three. They brought him back from some church work in the West Indies. He went to the same grammar school as I, then took a degree in politics at the LSE.'

'Is he a radical?'

'Of sorts, but not a political radical.'

'What other sorts are there?'

'George's sort. He met up with a girl there; she was attempting to promote greater awareness of vivisection techniques in Home Office laboratories. It started then.'

'So he's an animal-rights activist?'

'You could say that.'

'Is he a member of the ALF?' she asked, referring to the Animal Liberation Front.

'He was. Look, it's only right that I tell you the full story. He's been away. He did a year inside for criminal damage to a vivisectionist's lab: rescued some rhesus monkeys as well, not that they mentioned that at the hearing. He was set up with an assault on one of the police officers as well. To cut a long story short, nothing would give him more satisfaction than to get one over on the Met.'

'So,' Leone began, 'you're suggesting that we use the services of a known activist with a criminal record to break into the pride and joy of the police force.'

'That just about sums it up.'

'Not quite: a man on whom Special Branch will undoubtedly

have a file, and who may have been followed on a regular basis, if not his phone tapped: at least one or the other.'

'He's very careful.'

'Not careful enough to avoid being put away for a year.'

Toby flushed. 'He was a lot younger then; it was years ago. Besides, he's not with the ALF any more.'

'What, not militant enough for him? Wasn't economic sabotage sufficient for his purposes?'

'He believes that was a mistake: he doesn't go with the field units any more. He sort of works on the inside now, like a consultant.'

'Inside sounds like where he's heading again. What makes you think he could pull it off?'

Toby looked around the quiet room, and dropped his voice to a whisper. 'He's done it before.'

'With HOLMES?'

'No, but something very similar; something more difficult. Look, I don't want to say any more than that. All I can say is that accessing what he did – and, more importantly, getting away with it – establishes his credentials for the job.'

The heat from the tired fan and the fever of their debate had brought the atmosphere to melting point.

'He's waiting for us, Leone, in a pub around the corner. Meet him. See what you think. If he doesn't impress you then we'll think again.'

Leone was thinking, and thinking fast. If Sloane was this desperate he must sincerely believe that this was the only way to proceed. She wouldn't have gone out of her way to have him briefed in the Speakman case if she didn't trust his judgement; his methods were another matter.

'Do you have the number of the pub?'

He tapped his inside jacket pocket where, she had no doubt, his address book sat.

'Call him. Have him meet us on the Central Line westbound platform at Holborn. Tell him not to approach until we have a space to ourselves. Toby?'

He turned his head slightly to one side, waiting for her to continue.

'Tell him not to fuck up. If I think for one moment that we're being watched or followed then the whole thing's off. Are we clear?'

Sloane grinned broadly.

'Clearer than a judgement from the House of Lords.' She frowned at him. 'Sorry. Yes, completely, crystal, diamond: whatever you want to call it, but clear none the less.'

Gathering up her handbag, she pushed herself to her feet.

'I don't want to hear this; I'll be outside.'

As she turned to go, he spoke. 'Leone?' She froze but remained facing the door. 'What we are doing is right, you know that.'

She walked to the weathered oak door, grasped the tarnished brass knob in her hand and left him to call his brother.

'I hope so,' she muttered, half to herself and half to the dimly lit corridor, 'I really do.'

A light drizzle was falling as they made their way through the silence of Holborn. Unlike other parts of the city, which began to tick only when night fell, it emptied when the day's work was done. Leone had only ever seen snow on childhood Christmas specials on the TV before she'd been forced to move her life to this small island with its odd inhabitants.

They walked in silence. A rickety wooden escalator trundled them down into the bowels of the Underground system. In the distance, Leone could hear 'Cavatina' being plucked mournfully on a cheap guitar, but nobody was really listening. Toby led the way to the westbound Central Line. Along the platform, small groups were gathered. Some wore backpacks; others carried briefcases; others stood alone by choice. She scanned them, trying to pick out Toby's West Indian brother.

'He's not here,' Toby whispered. 'Decided it was safer to meet us on the tube.'

The overhead information screen told them that the next train was due in one minute: it was a long sixty seconds. Leone didn't feel like talking. Toby spent his time looking at the entrance to the platform. The rush of stale air from the tunnel heralded their train's arrival. It stopped with shuddering violence. The graffiti-covered doors slid open reluctantly: they stepped inside and took some seats in the near-deserted front carriage.

'How do you know he'll be on this one?'

'He will, I know George: he gets things right.' It was said with complete confidence.

The train thundered past Tottenham Court Road, Oxford Circus and Bond Street stations; there was still no approach to them. As they headed towards Marble Arch, Leone was becoming impatient.

'What do we do, go around all night until we bump into him?'

Toby sat opposite her, Leone had her back to the driver's cab. She saw him stiffen, then look quickly out of the window. She heard the mumbling of a tube-riding tramp and could smell him before he stumbled into sight. The man was a massive Rastafarian, at least six feet five, with a broad, flat face and a bulk of hair that was almost concealed by a multicoloured woollen hat.

'I'll rest my bones here with the good white folks.' His voice carried the singular menace of the committed Rasta.

Leone looked to Toby: he continued to look out of the grubby window, attempting to ignore a potentially ugly scene. The West Indian collapsed his smelly bulk next to her.

'There are plenty of other seats; try one of them,' Leone said, staring at the side profile of the young barrister.

'But I want to sit witt choo, pretty lady.' He nodded towards Toby, who appeared fascinated by the dark interior of the Tube's tunnels. 'Your man doesn't seem to mind, do you, white boy?' Toby pretended the question had never been asked. 'See, he doesn't mind sharing with one of the brothers, do you?'

Toby's face flashed away from the window and looked the awesome figure up and down with disdain.

'You were the same with my toys.'

Leone stared from Toby to the Rasta with a moment's incomprehension, then smiled at the grinning West Indian. 'Nice to meet you, George.'

'And you, Miss Stern,' he replied in a clipped Home Counties accent.

'Well, you have certainly cleared the carriage,' Toby said, still grinning. Leone spun round; it was deserted.

'Always works. There's nothing like a mean Rasta on a Tube train: gives you all the privacy you could want. If anyone was still here that would be because they wanted to be; it's clear.'

'You're certainly careful.'

'I have to be, Miss Stern, in my line of work.'

'Which is?'

'More than you need to know.' He was polite but resolute.

'Toby has filled me in on your plan. I can't pretend to understand the technical side; I'm more concerned with its chances of success.'

The train was now pulling to a halt at Holland Park Station. Several people entered, dressed for dinner. They took one look at George's swaying figure then moved well away from the smell and the trouble.

'You do stink.'

'It's the dreads; been a while since they saw water.'

Toby nodded, indicating that the way was clear once again.

'Success? Depends on what you mean by that. If we get in, collect the information then get caught, that is not success. If we get in and then get away with it that fulfils my personal definition.' Leone nodded, impressed by his attitude. He continued, 'I believe that with the right planning and the right team it can be done, but we need another body to help.' The train continued to clatter along the hundred-year-old tracks.

'Why?'

'It would take a while to explain and we've talked too long already. Is there anyone you can trust?' He took her hand in his huge paw and turned to stare deeply into her eyes. 'And I mean really trust.'

Leone thought. There was one person: Jack Forth.

'Yes. I mean, I think so.'

'Leone,' George said, using her Christian name for the first time, 'do not think: know!'

'Then yes, I know.'

He relaxed the tight grip he had had on her hand. 'Good. I'm getting off at White City. Stay on until Ealing Broadway then get out of the Tube system, it's dangerous: you meet some desperate characters down here.' He winked at his brother who smiled quickly, then switched to a mean frown.

'Get your hands off her, you filthy pig,' he shouted. The train was grinding to a halt at George's stop.'

'No offence, man,' George whined, his voice returning to a Jamaican drawl. 'Jah strike me down if I cause offence.'

He lurched along the stationary train, then slumped off it and onto the platform. As the train pulled past the confused Rasta, Leone half raised her hand in farewell. She saw George grin momentarily then turn away.

'Amazing man.'

168

'Yes.'

'I trust him.'

'Good.'

Leone left Toby alone to his private thoughts. She had her own: Jack Forth. He was the only one she could trust. Since the discovery of the Boatman account there was nobody in the firm that she dared to trust. What would he say? Where was he now?

CHAPTER TWENTY-THREE

Jack had cleared the spare room of all the clutter of his single life. When Hollie came to stay she preferred the comfort of sharing his bed rather than sleeping in the single he had now moved to the hallway. The studio was too big and light for his needs; he needed a dark space. On the floor he had pieced together a vast blank canvas from several smaller ones; they would be his workplace. It was the dreams that had forced him to this decision. Jack had expected the watery nightmares to disappear, but they had not. The pains had become worse but now small pockets of clarity were beginning to give him a slide show of the past – something infinitely more insidious, dark and wet.

It always began the same way. A brilliant sunshine filled the spaces around him. On glancing down he could see spindly schoolboy legs that smoothed into battered sandals. The air was fresh with the scent of citrus fruits, which told him that this was not England. The countryside was deserted, the sea in the distance; the only noise came from the distant tinkle of a tame goat's bell. He was always in motion during the dreams. At first his pace was a young boy's dawdle through the gorse and there was the undulating movement of the land he walked. Then he could hear the chatter of a busy taverna, but that had to be wrong: it felt miles away from anywhere.

Then suddenly he was sipping a glass of sweet lemonade at a table with a wobbly leg and delighting on rocking the table back and forth to see how far it would tip before his drink slopped over the rim of the scratched glass and down onto the table top. Then an angry drunken voice – a man's voice shouting in broken English. The only word Jack could make out was the word 'leper' over and over again. Then there was the sound of a table being overturned and the patter of swift feet running away.

Then he was back on a mountaintop. The skies were now bleak

and hard as dull iron. Before him was a vast black lake. That was when the pressure on his head began to exert its terrible pain. He was straining to see some movement down at the lakeside but the agony inside his head forced his eyelids closed. He knew something awful was happening down there. He wanted to see it, but at the same time he didn't; or his brain didn't, or something. In his sleep he fought the impulse to close his eyes but they always shut – always. As they did he heard hearty laughter from the lakeshore but there was little humour in it. Despite this, the image of the lake was burned onto his retina: that was what he was going to paint.

Jack believed that if he could faithfully represent what he was dreaming in the light of day, he would free himself from the terrible nightmare; at least, that was the theory.

He hadn't drawn or painted a landscape in years, not since his childhood breakdown. There was something too awesome about all the available space. It was as if he were an artistic agoraphobic. His experience of the Gulf War was limited to the personal suffering of those involved; other war artists could draw the vast emptiness of the massive dunes and miles of flat, unchanging wilderness. Not he.

Jack knew that this would be a long job. He had spoken to Tom Leath earlier, to decline any offer of court work for the near future. His friend and employer was concerned.

'Ever since the Speakman committal you've declined everything I've offered. I wish I hadn't pressured you into it now.'

'You didn't, Tom,' he had replied. 'I would probably have gone along anyway.' That at least was the truth.

Now he had his involvement with Leone: he was sure it was involvement rather than just a common interest in a mystery. He was intrigued by her hard exterior, which contained an inner softness, like a bitter-coated sugar pill.

He thrust his mind away from her and selected the paints he would need. Jack shuddered as he considered the prospect of what he would see when the picture was complete. Helena, his psychiatrist, had told him that his memory was masking a deeper secret than the sequence of his wife's death; now, with the onslaught of the new dreams, he knew that she was right. He squeezed a portion of dun brown paint onto the waiting palette and set about exorcising his remaining demon.

*   *   *

The helicopter flight from Exeter Airport to the rooftop terminal took the customary thirty minutes. As usual, he was the only passenger. That was not surprising: he owned the helicopter. La Saux was holding up rather well, particularly in the circumstances. The saline drip kept his body nourished and his urine flowing. He would return to his 'guest' a little later. For the moment there was other business to attend to. He now knew the Internet code and would shortly withdraw the 'item' from the 'peeping Kens and Dereks' who intruded into its massive catchment. That, sadly, did not end the matter. Victor – they were now on first-name terms – had given up any claim to the money extracted from Berkeley: he had even offered the lion's share of his latest drug deal as well as half of his sordid little sex empire. He was touched by his generosity. But Miss Stern was an added complication. Try as he might, he could not work out how she had connected with the Boatman account; the trouble was that she had.

As his taxi drove into Gray's Inn Square he reflected for a moment on Berkeley's stupidity. Had it not been for him these complications would never have arisen. No matter how prepared, how careful, how methodical he himself was, there was still no accounting for fools. At least he had eliminated the trail: Taylor's body would never be found and La Saux's would shortly be despatched to the same fate. Whatever Leone Stern thought she had discovered, she would never be able to produce any evidence. He strode briskly through the foyer of TWC.

A few moments later the lift deposited him in the interior of his plush, top-floor office. There was no need to inform his secretary, the resourceful Miss Simms, of his arrival: the movement of the lift served to warn her that he was ascending the building. There was always a warm, but not steaming, bone-china cup of Earl Grey waiting at his desk. He had considered asking her how she could manage that feat in the few seconds available before the lift door opened, but believed that everyone was entitled to their secrets.

He would miss this place when he took up his appointment in the High Court of Justice. These jobs didn't just land in one's lap, though; no, not at all. It had taken many years' diligent 'work' to achieve that exhalted position. He was not the first to be granted that status, but he was one of the few solicitors, and certainly the youngest, to have been selected to serve the ends of justice. The

Lord Chancellor had brought in many changes over the years. He was no lover of the Bar or its practitioners and had set about minimising its power within the legal system. Most of them were paper tigers without teeth. Had they managed to band together and form some sort of union then the erosion of their profession would not have been quite so dramatic. Still, that was barristers for you: they were always too busy arguing with each other to argue with anybody else. It had left the way open for people like himself; well, perhaps not quite like himself.

He sipped the soothing drink with pleasure. The small digestive biscuit was always a nice touch; he crumbled it into the bin. Let Miss Simms keep her illusions that she knew him better than anyone at TWC, though he accepted she was probably right. There was little partnership business for him to attend to; all the damages appeared to be operating at full thrust. He would not interfere unless they overstretched themselves or thought themselves indispensable.

Down to the real business.

It took the solicitor scant seconds to withdraw La Saux's compuvid from the Net. He concluded by closing the blackmailer's account with the service.

Leone Stern's activities continued to concern him. An inspection of her work and computer log showed that the diligent solicitor was working flat out on the Speakman case. She was renowned for her work ethic but didn't she have a private life? There was one way to find out. He removed a key, kept on a fob in his waistcoat pocket, and unlocked the bottom drawer of his desk. Within it, a Bang & Olufsen miniature tape recorder sat. The tapes on it were self-loading. He withdrew those it had already passed through its automatic system, then listened, quite bored, to the content of the sounds from inside Leone's home.

She watched little television, listened to too much Mahler and had few visitors. The bugs responded automatically to noise and sparked into life only when someone was present. It didn't take very long at all. He was disappointed. At the very least he had hoped to hear the nocturnal grunting of copulation.

He turned his attention to the telephone tapes; these were much more interesting. There was a burgeoning relationship with a man she called Jack; that must be the man he'd seen her with at the Via Venetia. They were very careful about what was said; perhaps he was married. That might come in useful someday. There was another male caller on the line called Toby. That must be Sloane, the junior counsel in Speakman. While it was not unusual for a solicitor and her barrister to meet to discuss the progress of their case, a 6 a.m. meeting in his chambers was going a bit too far. Perhaps he was her lover? But he doubted it; there was none of the warmth her conversations with Jack contained.

Sloane had sounded worried when he had arranged the meeting, and he was determined to find out why. He would have to speak with Sedgewick, the QC briefed in Speakman's defence. The old soak had been eternally grateful when the all-too-scarce employment came his way. He would ask the silk what progress they were making. Undoubtedly, Sedgewick would claim that they were working miracles with the impossible case. At the very least it would give him an opportunity to enquire about Stern and Sloane.

Satisfied that all was as well as it could be without further effort, he replaced the tapes with a new batch. He was about to push the drawer shut when the recorder bleeped into life. He removed an earpiece and plugged it into the live recording. He heard the ring at the other end of Leone's call sound several times, before a deep, gentle voice answered.

'Jack Forth.'

'It's me, Leone. I need to see you, Jack, soon; it's very important.'

'I've got to see Hollie this afternoon, but I can make it later – tonight?'

'Yes, OK.' She sounded disappointed.

'Look, if it's desperate . . .'

'No, it'll keep till this evening.'

There was a pause before he spoke again. 'Is it about Boat-man stuff?'

The eavesdropper spluttered his tea down the starched white front of his Jerome Street shirt.

'No – but I don't want to talk on the phone.'

'Well, you can tell me all about it tonight.'

She hesitated. 'How's Hollie?'

'That's funny, she was asking me the same question about you at dinner last night; she's dying for you to take her out.'

'Let's take things steady.'

'OK.' It was his turn to sound disappointed. 'Where and what time?'

'Same place, same time?'

'Till then,' Forth concluded.

'Say "Hi" to Hollie from me.'

'I will.'

'Bye then.'

The connection was broken; the eavesdropping solicitor was enraged. He hurled his tea cup and saucer against a cripplingly expensive original painting, where the liquid stained the unprotected canvas and the shattered remains of the china fell to the floor. He sat breathing deeply for some time until his calming exercise was interrupted by the buzzing intercom on his desk. Reaching forward to the speak button he depressed it viciously.

'Yes,' he bellowed.

'Is everything all right, sir?'

He paused and took several more lungfuls of tranquillising air.

'Sir?'

'Yes, Miss Simms, everything is quite all right. There has been a little accident.' But not the last, he thought. 'When I have gone, have the place cleaned up. And Miss Simms . . .'

'Sir?'

'No more of those little biscuits with my tea. I hate those little fucking biscuits.'

The rounded restaurateur at the Via Venetia possessed an excellent memory for faces. He welcomed Leone and Jack with arms stretched wide and ushered them to their table. Leone was edgy, Jack could tell. Her faded jeans and black barathea jacket caused the white silk men's shirt she wore to stand out in the semi-darkness of the restaurant. The Chianti bottles, with their red blebbed candles, cast a pink glow over their faces. They sat at their table towards the back of the tiny establishment.

'Are you OK?' he asked her.

'Yeah, fine.' Definitely edgy.

'You didn't sound it on the phone and you don't seem it now,' he pushed.

Her eyes looked up into his; she smiled. For the first time he noticed the small wrinkles around their orbits. She looked worried.

'Really, I am. How are you?' she managed.

She glanced down to his hands and noticed that there were

flecks of paint around his fingertips. He followed her gaze and shyly attempted to hide his hands under the table, but Leone reached towards him, took them in her own, and placed them flat on the tablecloth.

'Decorating?'

'Something like that.'

'Tell me.'

'Working, on a canvas.'

He picked at the residue of the paint fragments. 'Hollie told me you'd notice.'

'She's a bright girl.'

Though they had not yet ordered, a bottle of the Chardonnay they had shared on their last visit was placed gently on the table. The owner grinned, then bowed slightly before leaving to take the order from another table.

'Looks like we're becoming regulars.'

Leone opened her eyes wide; their extraordinary colour stunned him once more. 'Seems so,' she replied softly.

She reached forward and poured them a glass. Raising hers, Leone opened her mouth, but words seemed to fail her.

'What shall we drink to?' Jack asked. She shrugged. 'Art then,' he suggested as their glasses clinked together.

They each took a long mouthful but never once took their eyes from each other's. She shook her head and broke the moment.

'This isn't why I asked you here.'

He looked away, nervously chewing his bottom lip. 'Why did you?'

'I need your help.'

'Again. You said it wasn't about the Boatman account.'

'Not directly, no, but it involves the Speakman case.'

'Tell me.'

Leone took another large draft from her glass then leaned forward. 'Have you ever heard of the HOLMES computer system?'

The light rain of the previous day had been replaced by the strong winds that scuttled through the Euston streets. They carried with them a deep chill from the north of England. He was grateful for the thick Abercrombie that kept most of the cold out. He had waited patiently outside the Stern woman's flat in a rented car until she emerged, stopped a black cab and proceeded to the restaurant. The traffic was light; he had little difficulty trailing her to the end of the journey. Her escort was waiting chivalrously outside. It must be love.

He noticed a three-storey car park, dark as his own ambition, that skulked adjacent to the restaurant. There were three window-seats inside the warm glow of the eatery and he was delighted that they had been escorted to one of them. He climbed the slippery steps to a deserted vantage point directly opposite their cosy conspiracy.

The matt black image intensifier was slim and portable. With the available light, there was no necessity to use the laser battery. He focused in on Stern and her lover, at least it appeared that way. If they were not lovers, then judging by the proximity of their bodies and the intensity of their conversation, that would soon change. All the better: common sense exited the room when sex pushed open the doors of mortals' perceptions.

He trained the sight on the man. He appeared cloyingly earnest and trustworthy. A handsome face clouded by apparent concern stared unblinkingly into Stern's. But this was much, much more than a mere sex thing, that was all too obvious.

He bided his time. It was something he had always excelled in. During the early years of professional practice, patience, married to a cunning brain, had shepherded him to his present position. On many occasions, this ability had enraged more senior partners in the firm, until, when the moment was right, he struck, always when the opponent's soft belly was exposed and he was hungry. Tonight might be such a night, though instinctively he doubted it. It would be imperfect, too human, not to be aware of all the available facts before embarking on an end game. He whistled tunelessly to the freezing night. They had gone in, they would come out.

'It sounds risky, Leone.'

'I know that. When I think what we are all risking . . .'

They had ordered during her description of all that had occurred. Their food, a joint decision of *Rigatoni Matriciana* steamed away on the plates in front of them, ignored by them both.

'Is everything to your liking, *signorina*?'

They had failed to notice the owner's wife hovering at the table.

Jack smiled as sincerely as he could. What was Leone thinking of? 'If you're caught you'll be struck off. Slinn—'

'Sloane,' she corrected.

'Whatever he's called, will be disbarred. God knows what will happen to his lunatic brother, and as for me I've got Hollie to think of. As if I haven't been a bad enough father to her already; her coming to visit me in prison isn't going to win me any parenting awards.'

Leone couldn't deny the truth of what he spoke. Her voice was husky with disappointment. 'I take it that's a no.'

'I didn't say that. I just want you to be aware of all the risks, and for what? You said yourself the evidence against Speakman is overwhelming.'

Leone's eyes flashed at him. 'I thought I knew you better than that; guess I was wrong. You impressed me as a man who wouldn't just make up his mind without hearing everything first. What if, just what if, he didn't do it? Why are the police making it so difficult for us? Do you care? Because I do, Jack, I really do; it's why I do the job.'

He turned angrily away.

She shook her head sadly. 'Your judgement's slipping, Leone,' she said to herself.

'It's not.' She raised an ironic eyebrow over her wine glass. 'It isn't, Leone, I didn't say no. I'm not saying no.'

'Then what are you saying? Come on, Jack, it's hit-or-sit time.'

'Let me think about it.'

'There isn't time. We don't know what the computer will throw up; it might give us some leads and they could take forever to follow up.'

'What time is it set for?'

'Tomorrow morning.'

'Give me till then?'

She chewed the inside of her lip thoughtfully. Leone understood his predicament, for God's sake: he had a family. Why was she being so unfair? Then it struck her: she wanted to be with him. 'I understand, Jack, I really do. Call me at first light?'

They both knew the evening was at an end. More out of duty than hunger they munched their way miserably through the pasta. Jack refused the offer to share a taxi – he had too much to think about. They said an awkward goodnight outside the restaurant's front door.

179

Jack decided to walk for a while. The wine and the topic of conversation had gone to his head. After ten minutes he flagged down a cab. He was about to give his own address then swiftly changed his mind. Instead, he gave the address of his parents' home. They would all be in bed by now, but he felt the urge to look in on the sleeping form of his daughter and remind himself of what he really stood to lose.

Thirty minutes and thirty pounds later he emerged from the taxi's interior. The wind was whipping up the autumn leaves into whirling spirals. He withdrew the spare key his parents still insisted he carry at all times and let himself quietly into the dark and slumbering house. He wouldn't sleep tonight, he knew it.

At the corner of the street where Jack's parents had lived for many years the man in the hire car noted the house that the man Forth had entered.

'So now I know where you live. Time for bed.'

CHAPTER TWENTY-FOUR

Jack couldn't quell the sense of apprehension he felt as he approached the Docklands warehouse at 7.30 the following morning. As Leone had said, it was hit-or-sit time. The others were already there, hunched over a set of papers and a laptop computer perched on an old milk crate. The hangar was empty save for what looked to be a British Telecom Transit van. Leone looked up as he walked towards them.

'I knew you wouldn't let us down. Thanks, Jack. I really mean that.'

'I hope so, Leone,' Jack said nervously.

'Meet Toby and George Sloane,' Leone said, gesturing to the two brothers. Jack looked a little puzzled, she thought, as he shook hands with the men but seemed to have decided that the less he asked about their lineage the better. George's dreadlock wig had disappeared revealing a short crewcut. He was dressed in blue overalls with the BT logo over the breast pocket. An elaborate workman's belt overflowing with all manner of screwdrivers and electronic gadgetry was slung around his hips. A pair of thick wraparound magnifying glasses hung around his neck and his head. Toby was dressed in a dark blue, chalkstripe, three-piece suit and appeared every bit the legal man with a look of nervous energy.

Leone ushered Jack towards the van and slid the side door open. Inside, a makeshift bench housed two terminals and, opposite that, floor-to-ceiling metal shelving brimmed over with wiring and more tools. Leone picked up a set of overalls and threw them to Jack. 'Here, put these on. You're the driver; you'll need them to get into Scotland Yard.'

'I don't need reminding where we're going, Leone,' Jack said flatly, pulling on the blue boiler suit.

'Yeah, sorry.'

181

'Five minutes, everyone,' George said, calmly joining them, fixing earphones in place.

'For what?' Jack asked.

'Till kick-off. I've set up a jammer on the central switch office at the Yard. It's programmed to start causing problems in the telex machines. They will automatically call BT engineering headquarters. We will intercept that call and promise to despatch a team to clear the lines.'

'Let me guess: that means you and me.'

'Got it in one, Jack. OK, we arrive at the rear entrance and park up in the underground car park. Here's your ID, clip it onto your pocket.'

'What about security? Don't they have officers on the gate?'

'Scotland Yard isn't a police station, Jack, it's just an office block. There's over four thousand people working in the building and half of those are civilians, including the gatemen. They'll have prior notification of our arrival so it shouldn't be a problem. I'll go into the building alone; you stay in the van and look bored. There's a copy of the *Daily Sport*: that should keep you relaxed.'

'Comatosed, I should expect,' Jack replied. 'How long do you expect to be inside?'

'No more than twenty minutes. If I'm right the most logical place for them to have hidden what these guys are after is PNC2.'

'Come again?'

'The Police National Computer, version two. If you're interested in the technical set-up, I need to attach my own modem to the wiring between the special operations computer that Toby's working on and the PNC. After that, it's a simple question of split-nanosecond timing. You'll be able to hear me in the van. Any problems at my end, then you get out of there quickly,' the West Indian concluded.

'How do you get the line in?'

'Secret of the trade, Jack. Look, the less you know the better for you if something goes wrong.'

'Will it?'

'Things do.'

'Terrific.'

'All you have to do is keep people away. It would be a disaster if a real BT engineer turned up.'

Jack looked down at the ignition keys. 'What if they do?'

George slipped off the tiny radio earphones and stared intensely at his new companion. 'We've been through the drill: use your initiative. If that doesn't work then get out of there and forget about me.'

The equipment was a mind-boggling array of precise instrumentation. George had broken into the internal communication in the early hours; it was all set.

'Two minutes to go. Relax, Jack, I've done this kind of gig before.'

'What took you into animal rights?'

'Suffering. No – make that unnecessary suffering. A chimp has to get skin cancer so that some fat old lady can wear some new make-up: that just doesn't work for me.'

'Fine, but why are you doing this?'

'He's my brother; he needs help. What's your explanation?'

Jack could only shrug. That was his problem: apart from a wish to help Leone, he still didn't really know. 'I suppose it's personal.'

'What isn't? One minute. Let's go.'

They all climbed into the van and set off for the Yard. Jack manoeuvred the van along the Embankment and reached the Victoria headquarters of the Metropolitan Police at 8.15. So far, so good: the expected message to BT engineering headquarters was beautifully handled by Leone impersonating an operator. They dropped Toby and Leone in a side street around the corner from the famous revolving sign at the front entrance. And then they waited. Twenty minutes, and Jack would sweep round to the rear entrance.

Inside the information room, Inspector Barnes asked for an update from the HOLMES operator.

'What's our intrepid lawyer been up to this morning?'

The fresh-faced WPC took a sip from a plastic cup of murky coffee, shuddered, then replied, 'Routine stuff for the most part. He's using the blueprint to guide him round all the cars and vans sighted at abduction points.'

'Any matches yet?'

'No. The thing is, he's changed his tack completely.'

Barnes felt uneasy. 'What do you mean?'

Without taking her eyes off the screen, the WPC answered, 'As

I read him, the last two days or so he's been trying to isolate files that were access-denied so he could get them out of the way. I've no idea why.'

Barnes did. 'Is this the first time he's tried routine matching?'

The operator keyed in a number of commands. Inside the displayed box another appeared. 'That's right, ma'am.'

While there were other parts of the HOLMES system to supervise, Barnes decided to stay with this for now. She felt uneasy about something: she'd felt uneasy since her run-in with Lee and what she had learned once he had left her office.

'Pay more than normal attention today.'

'I always pay more than normal attention, Inspector.'

Deborah had annoyed the girl. She hadn't meant to – it was just that she had been uncomfortable since the other night and the knowledge was making her irritable.

'Point taken, Marianne. I just meant be extra careful.'

She moved away from the operator's shoulder and took a seat nearby. Sloane was clever, but was he clever enough?

Toby continued to plough through the routine enquiries he had set in motion. The monitor spewed column after column of car registrations, owners and addresses, all of which had been traced during the five-year span of the Speakman enquiry; he paid them no attention because he knew the information wouldn't be there. Instead, he concentrated on the digital watch on his wrist. When George had handed him the slimline chronometer he had looked at it in disbelief. His experience of this type of wristwatch stemmed from the early seventies when it was considered chic not to be able to tell the time by conventional means.

'It's accurate to a hundred thousandth of a second. It's set to mine exactly. When the moment is right, hit the command. Mine will be linked up to the modem. You can't be a thousandth late, brother, or a dual enquiry will show.'

There were two minutes left before his reactions would be put to the ultimate test.

The security guard didn't even ask for identification as they passed through the gate and parked the van. Jack marvelled at George's nerve, as he watched him from the van, holding the door open for two police officers with pips on their epaulettes.

George looked back with a huge toothy grin and then disappeared through the door.

Five minutes later George was in the Message switch office on the fifth floor. A young woman was busy painting her nails black and took no interest in him as he lifted the access hatch to the wire ducting under the raised flooring to the central communications complex. Scotland Yard's operations centre copes with 1.4 million calls a year, and the automatic distribution system for 999 messages is capable of handling 400 calls simultaneously. That requires millions of miles of cabling housed underneath the raised flooring to the entire fifth floor. He switched on the Mag-Lite torch and began to crawl under the floorboards. About ten yards ahead he could see the cabling leading to the mainframes in the information room. He quickly identified the route to the multiplexer port interchange by its characteristic red-rubber-clad, heavy-duty wires. He'd been in the building for eleven minutes by the time his tiny modem was in place between Toby's terminal and PNC2. The sweat began to roll down his face as he crawled back along the duct. He emerged with a smile from the depths. The girl was still in the process of converting her fingers into gothic talons. He told her that they should be back on line in ten minutes. He had six to get back to the van.

Deborah Barnes watched the columns of data flood down the screen. There was too much for anyone to comprehend. Her nervousness returned. The intercom buzzed into life: it was Chief Inspector Lee.

'In my office, now,' he shouted.

'Can't this wait?'

'Now, Barnes.'

Jack had counted forty-six nipples in the newspaper, started the crossword and read his horoscope three times. Not a good day for love liaisons, but everything was set for an unexpected competition win. As he hadn't entered any he went back to eight across.

Inside Lee's office, Leone looked as stern as her surname suggested. Lee was looking equally grim. The plan called for Leone to be in Lee's office at precisely 9 a.m. to get Barnes away from the screen.

'Are you positive that Mr Sloane has been denied access improperly?'

'He's sure, but before I lodge an official complaint with the Commissioner I want to see if there's another way around this.'

'I appreciate your attitude.'

There was a knock at the door.

Toby could feel his breath coming in short, ragged bursts. He had to control it. He would need to have expelled all air from his body, to be absolutely still, when the moment arrived. It wasn't even that, he thought ironically, not even a moment; much, much less. The liquid-crystal face of the watch was a blur of movement. He breathed out all the air in his lungs and pressed the command.

With thirty seconds to spare, George frantically positioned himself at the terminal inside the van.

'Let's go, Jack,' he shouted. The engine gunned and they were passing the gate as George hit the modem send. Jack could hear the tinny pitch of the message. Christ, had they got it right?'

The WPC in the Information Room heard a faint echo in her earpiece. She looked at the screen, puzzled at the curious sound effect. She swivelled in her chair to speak to Barnes, who was now absent. There was no one to give her advice on this. It was something her months of training had never dealt with. She watched the screen avidly for the request. It appeared a few seconds later: another enquiry about car registrations. She breathed a sigh of relief – it must have been a glitch in the HOLMES system. She'd mention it later to her boss.

'That is not right, sir,' Barnes replied angrily to the allegation put to her by Lee. 'Every request pertinent to the Speakman case has been replied to positively. I have the complete log of all Mr Sloane's enquiries.' She glared at Lee for forcing the lies from her mouth.

Not quite all, thought Leone, but has it worked?

'Has it worked, George?' Jack asked. They were parked 200 yards along the road from Scotland Yard.

He could see that the dark eyes of Sloane's brother were screwed shut; he was listening for a corresponding high-pitched fuzz of sound. He held up a hand to quieten Jack.

Jack scanned the pavement; this was terrible. It was only a few seconds but it felt like minutes, hours. The silence was unbearable. Then he heard it: the shrill tone of a response.

'Come to Poppa,' George said quietly. 'Come here and be a good girl.'

Abruptly the noise came to an end. Jack spun round to watch George key in another command to the terminal in the van.

'What are you doing?'

'Sending it where they can't trace it.'

'Have we got it?'

A huge grin spread across his companion's face. 'I don't know what we've got but we've got it. Jack, get out of the overalls and make your way home.'

'Why?'

'Thanks for your help; couldn't have done it without you, but we all have our own agendas.'

'George!'

He watched as the West Indian keyed in a new destination number to the keyboard. 'Inside that building is a list of all the informants and police undercover operatives in the ALF. Go home, Jack, this is my show now.'

'Does your brother know about this?'

'Everything is a trade-off. Bye, Jack.'

'So, Miss Stern, you accept that I will personally investigate this matter?' Leone nodded. 'If I believe that there has been deliberate obstruction, those responsible will be punished and the information furnished to Mr Sloane.' He was a superb liar, Leone thought.

'I hope we'll be able to clear this up, Chief Inspector.'

Deborah Barnes stared icily at the solicitor: she had backed down too suddenly. 'Sir, if I might be excused.'

Her superior nodded grimly.

'Miss Stern.'

'Inspector Barnes.'

She saw a look of relief in the female lawyer's eyes; relief and hope. What was going on?

She sprinted back to the computer room for an update from the WPC, who was told to take a coffee break. After she had left, the inspector keyed in the access codes to the hidden files; he'd got in. She had no idea how, but he had. She threw back her head and laughed: she had planned to lead him to them anyway.

CHAPTER TWENTY-FIVE

They had arranged to meet at Toby's flat in Maida Vale at the end of his normal working hours at Scotland Yard. He had found it difficult to concentrate on his work, but felt an early departure might well cause the ever-present Inspector Barnes to be suspicious. As it was, she had been strangely pleasant when their paths had crossed at lunchtime, going so far as to ask him, with a secret smile, if he was getting everything he needed. It had been the briefest of meetings but left him feeling uneasy.

By 8 p.m. Jack and Leone had arrived. She was surprised by the general untidiness of Sloane's apartment. Small laminated wood bookshelves took up every inch of available space in the main living room. In contrast, the books they held were worth more than the contents of the flat itself. The paintwork was badly chipped and two futon sofas squatted close to the thin carpet, which was covered in pink, ribbon-bound briefs. Without any formal greeting or conversation Toby sat at the computer terminal clutching a floppy disk.

'It went to a friend's computer shop,' he said. 'He copied it, then I watched him clear the data from his screen. If they get a trace to him he'll deny any knowledge of the transmission.'

'What have we got, Toby?' Leone asked as she pulled up one of the director's chairs to the left of him. Jack did the same to the right. All three could now see the blank screen.

'I nearly had a peek ten minutes ago, but I thought we all deserved to see it together.'

'George not coming?' Jack asked.

Toby was busy logging on to the PC's A-drive and inserting the bootleg disk. As it whirred in response to the keyboard commands he eventually replied, 'This isn't his game. He's playing another by now.'

Jack had considered telling Toby of George's own plan with the modem link-up but reckoned that it was better left unsaid. A list appeared on the screen marked: 'Speakman. Evidence. Unused. Category one.'

'What does the category mean?' Jack asked.

'They have so much information on the investigation that they would have to catalogue it according to its status,' Toby whispered, as if Inpector Barnes was still watching his every move. 'They tried so hard to hide this stuff that category one must mean this is the evidence most damning to the prosecution's case.'

'Let's hope so,' Leone commented sincerely. She still felt uneasy about what they were doing, but she was now so far down the road that turning back was as dangerous as continuing.

'Let's see what we have.'

There was a list of three names on the menu of available topics. They read, 'Professor Sven Trondl, Doctor Ian Coombs, Patricia Barraclough'.

'Are any of these names familiar to you, Toby?'

He narrowed his eyes for a moment or two, then pushed his glasses back up to the bridge of his nose. 'I don't know the medicos but I think I've heard the third name before: I'm not sure where. It'll come. Let's see what Prof Trondl has to say on the matter.'

He clicked the mouse over the name. A document appeared before them.

'Jesus,' Toby exhaled. Jack and Leone looked to the heading of the work.

FBI
Killer's Psychological Profile

'Is it surprising that Scotland Yard should work with the FBI?' Jack asked.

'Very unusual,' Toby answered, 'but sometimes they use them to crime-fingerprint, as they call it. So far as we know, there's nothing stateside to bring them on board. Let's read on.'

Killer's name/chosen alias/nom de plume/designated Operation Name:
UK: 'King Arthur'.

Victims:
In UK operation, seven (names and ages annexed to end of profile).

Modus Operandi:
All victims in UK abducted without eye-witnesses (however, see statement 5612/a). All subjected to sexual assault. No semen samples found, except UK case number 1; Colleen Bridges.

'My God, that's count one in Speakman's case,' Leone shouted. 'Toby, have you ever seen any reference to a semen sample in the papers?'

'You know I haven't. When they took the hair sample from Speakman I was looking for a cross-match; there wasn't one.'

Jack was puzzled. 'Does that mean that they couldn't match it to them?'

'If they could,' Toby said, 'then we would have heard about it a long time ago; it would have been the final padlock of the case. I imagine that's what Dr Ian Coombs is going to tell us about.'

After assault, victims bound in an identical manner (see sketch at back of profile). All had eyeballs forced from sockets: likely use of double thumb pressure to achieve this end. All girls still alive and conscious when mutilation occurred. Then taken while still alive to stretch of water, weighted down and sunk.

This was the first time that Jack had been confronted with the bare method the murderer used: he felt sick.

Profile:
Having read all the available data in the case I have formulated various opinions of the killer. I have also utilised the FBI profiling register of known offenders and offences in reaching these conclusions.

General:
The killer is a white Caucasian male, in the 30- to 40-year-old bracket. He is physically strong (see weight and strength

ratios of victims). He works alone. The sophistication of the stalkings and abductions illustrates that he is intelligent. The gaps between the killings indicate that there is no pattern to the murders. He does not, for example, react to any date, month, or lunar phase. He is therefore extremely controlled and only strikes when he feels that the time and circumstances are right: i.e. he dictates what will happen; it is not dictated by his psyche.

'This doesn't sound like Trevor Speakman,' Toby commented. 'If it did, we would have had it rammed down our throats by the prosecution.'

'He looked strong enough to me when I saw him in court,' Jack commented, waiting to see how the lawyers would react to this challenge.

'It's the only part that does fit, Jack. Toby and I have met him: he's no actor – what we saw was a frightened man with a limited IQ drugged up to the eyeballs.'

'Perhaps he's such a good actor that it isn't apparent he's acting. Can't schizophrenics convince themselves that they haven't done it?'

They all knew it was a good question and one that Sedgewick had continually used.

'Perhaps the Prof can help us out on that one.'

They watched as the screen rolled to:

Specifics:

1. The targets. The age groups and sex of the victims indicate a hatred of girls of this age. There may be an adolescent trauma causing him to fix on this age group as deserving of punishment and pain.

2. The bindings. These are of a particular type as used by sailors and divers.

Leone's and Toby's minds retrieved the fact that Speakman was an experienced deep-sea diver, but neither of them spoke.

The hands of all were bound in front of them almost as in supplication or prayer. Again, there is some deep reason why this is important to the killer. He may have been bound himself

192

in a similar manner or forced into some act that the binding represents.

3. The blindings. This is an important part of the make-up of the murderer. He does not wish his victims to see him; that is why their eyeballs are removed before the end. There is some shame (perhaps some rare insight), either as to his physical appearance or by virtue of what he is doing, that causes him to mutilate his victims in this way. What is of interest is that the sexual abuse occurs before they are blinded, so it may be that he does not reveal himself fully to them until the moment of the blindings. The killer may possess some physical deformity that is hidden from the casual observer; for example by clothing, an eye patch or some form of prosthesis. Discover what it is he is hiding and you will discover the killer himself.

4. The water. This is an important symbol to the killer. He could have disposed of the bodies in any number of places, but the choice of the water has remained constant throughout. He may believe that water will cleanse the souls of the departed, that it will clean him eventually, but he also hates it. The girls' bodies are almost offerings to a hostile entity: a sacrifice that will protect him and give him more power. He fears the water: the water has hurt him and he does not want to be hurt by it again.

'Speakman had a bad diving accident,' Toby said darkly.

'That's true,' Leone countered, 'but this professor reckons that it was a formative experience, not a latent one. Look.' Leone pointed to where she had been reading ahead.

It seems apparent that all these symbols are related to a massive childhood/adolescent trauma that has led him to kill. He would be diagnosed as a psychopath with an overwhelming power drive. He is likely, because of the intelligence and cunning he has exhibited, to be a successful man in his chosen field. In short, he is one of the most dangerous serial killers the public could ever encounter.

Professor Sven Trondl, 15 February, 1996.

'Look at the date, Toby,' Leone said quickly.

'Why?' Jack asked.

193

'It was well after Speakman's arrest. They've known all along that they've got the wrong man, but have gone too far down the line to stop it.'

But Jack's attention had been wrenched away by something else. As the screen pushed past the annexes to the profile, a black and white photograph appeared before his eyes. It showed a young girl bound with ropes, praying to a deaf God with empty sockets where her eyes should have been. He felt the shudders begin in his stomach: his arms began to tremble, his eyelids clicked shut. It was the same knot as he had remembered the other night.

'Jack, Jack, are you all right? What the hell's wrong with you?' Leone asked. She watched as he pitched backwards off the chair and lay still on the threadbare carpet of Toby's flat.

'It's him,' a wretched voice pronounced. 'Him.'

He passed out.

CHAPTER TWENTY-SIX

La Saux had been unable to move his legs for days. He could feel the sores on his buttocks and wrists. They had split on what he assumed to be his third day in this terrible place. It was difficult to gauge the passage of time; his only clock was the pain he felt. His injuries felt inflamed if not gangrenous. His genitals were horribly swollen by the corrosive fluids his captor had calmly reintroduced into his quivering body.

That was the real terror of it all: how dispassionate his torturer was when conducting their 'chats', as he referred to them. The man's voice betrayed no passion or emotion. There was no evidence, either, of any obvious enjoyment at what he was doing. Merely a patient, world-weariness at the necessity of the situation.

At least that fucking madman had taken the needles away from his neck, so that he could slump his head to the side in a vain attempt to sleep. There had been little of that during his period in the cottage; at least he assumed it was a cottage. He could just make out darkened beams across the low ceiling of the room where he was held. His internal organs felt inflamed beyond endurance, yet still he remained conscious when the questioning recommenced.

The glucose bags continued to give him the strength to endure, but did he want to endure? His captor had detailed what each new batch of catheter additive contained before he forced the contents back inside his screaming urethra. He had taken to bluffing, telling La Saux that this was the one that would take him, this was the potion with the fatal brew. On the last occasion Victor had scrunched his face and excreted into his massively soiled underwear as the pressure was brought to bear, when, instead of the expected nail-sharp agony, he experienced a warm soothing balm throughout his entire genitalia.

'You've been a good boy. What you told me about the Internet

195

proved to be correct. This is your reward: it's a painkiller. Its effect will enable you to clear your mind of any tricks or bluffs you might attempt to pull. I know when people are telling the truth. That is my occupation: I am a professional lie-detector.'

His tormentor had waited until he slept, then cleaned away the detritus of his body and his fear. La Saux was grateful for the restoration of some dignity; it also indicated that his ordeal might be coming to an end.

That had been many hours ago. Now night was falling again. The paltry light from the early-winter sun turned to darkness as he waited for the man to return. He was about to drift back into another nightmarish sleep when the door opened slowly and light footsteps clicked across what he took to be a rough stone floor. He closed his eyes quickly, pretending sleep.

'Ah, to sleep, perchance to dream, Victor; but then you are not asleep at all, are you? Who could sleep through such an ordeal? Aren't your dreams of what is to come much worse than that you have experienced already?' There was a pause, then a disappointed sigh. 'Victor, Victor. Very well, while you sleep I shall bring you up to date with my needs.'

La Saux heard the familiar squelch of soft leather as his tormentor sat down behind him. 'I am not by my nature a very trusting man. Some might even say that I possess more than a tincture of cynicism: I have too much self-awareness to disagree with that opinion; at least with you, my confidant. For that is what you are: my mentor, and I your *tor*mentor. Strange commodity, words, don't you agree, Victor? How two very different words can so aptly fit a burgeoning relationship such as ours. But, then again, pictures were always your interest, were they not?'

He stopped as if hearing a response. 'No, no, dear friend Victor, save your energy; you will need it. Now, where was I? Oh, yes, my sad lack of trust.'

La Saux's muscles, cramping with terror as the dark man continued his soliloquy, begged to be moved into another position. He ground his teeth and willed them to remain still.

'Do you dream, Victor? I wonder, what does a pornographer dream of? What deliciously forbidden treats inspire your passions? Surely something unconnected to your work – something very different indeed. I have it: a beautiful child playing carelessly with its parents, a butterfly, perhaps, or a spring morning in the forest. Your tastes must be so jaded with familiarity, like a fat boy in a chocolate factory who pukes away his passion for that delicacy. I understand, Victor, I truly do. I have had my own "hobby" for some years now. Some say it's more of a compulsion; they may be right. Still, I have had to put away my tools for the moment. We can't have people getting the wrong idea, can we? There are also matters of High State to which I must attend.' He paused once more as if hearing further conversation. 'No, no, sweet Victor, those do not concern you, though I must say you do have a persuasive tongue, at least for the moment.'

Le Saux retched at the threat; the man continued. 'There are one or two loose ends to dispose of.'

'Is that all I am to you, a loose end?' La Saux's voice was thick and clogged with lack of use: its only exercise these days was screaming at the pain of his torture.

'Your business enterprise has brought you into conflict with something that you are incapable of understanding. You have rendered yourself a loose end by its inception.'

'But I didn't know.' He realised that his voice contained the whining edge of self-pity that he loathed in his own clients as he squeezed the last of their money from the family bank account.

'You say, "I didn't know". It is not a state of knowledge that matters: it is merely a state of being. Call it luck, fate, kismet, destiny or *Rota fortuna*: whatever the desired description, it is because it is.'

'I didn't know who you were.'

His captor laughed at the response.

'If I hadn't got to you first, then I have every confidence that you would have ruined my existence, and my future, which, unlike yours, looks very rosy indeed.'

La Saux fought back the sobs that began to tug at his chest, then battled to control his breathing.

'Very manly of you, that,' said the voice over his shoulder. 'Quite impressive in the circumstances. I doubt that I would exhibit such profound courage, but then again I know the end of your story; you can get to experience it.'

'Isn't there any way we could come to some arrangement? I am a very wealthy man.'

'So am I.'

'Don't you want to be richer?'

'I am rich enough.'

'Then what about power and influence?' La Saux was attempting to find the dark man's weak spot. His life had been spent in pursuit of that ever-present desire which every human being possessed.

'Those too I possess and will soon have more.'

'My files.'

'Continue.'

'My clients' files.'

'What: paedophilic bank managers from Esher? Their sell-by date must be well past.'

'There are others: politicians, lawyers, journalists, even a Cabinet minister.'

'Your life expectancy is increasing.'

'You can have them all, you will know what to do with them: I just want to live.'

He heard the man exhale slowly. 'It's strange: there you were a few days ago with the prospect of the biggest deal of your life begging you to make it, and here you are now, with me, willing to give it all away just to live.'

'Yes!'

'So you do not want to be partners? You will hand everything over, just like that?'

'Yes, for God's sake, yes,' La Saux screamed.

'Very well.'

'What? You mean you're going to let me go?' He was filled with a childlike expectancy and sweetness as he felt the bonds at his wrist being loosened.

'It would seem such a waste otherwise. Where are the files kept?'

'In my safe.'

'You mean the one in your home? Under the floorboards with your security bonds?'

'What?'

'Oh dear, are those the files you meant? I thought you had others. No: I have those files already, and I took the software and video, by the way.' The wrist bond was pulled sharply against his skin. 'Do you know the secret of good torture?'

'I don't—'

'Timing. Now, in this next and indeed final catheter bag, which I am delighted to see you have filled to the brim, I have strychnine.

Answer my next question yes or no and be very, very truthful. Have you made any copies of the merchandise?'

'No, I swear it, there are no copies. I didn't want to take the risk of a rogue copy being touted around: please, please believe me.'

'But I do believe you, Victor. Now, finally I do, truly. Honestly, I believe you.'

The man moved from behind him. He still wore the black leather mask, though through the ragged zip he was smiling. La Saux saw him reach up to remove the covering from his face.

'Don't, please. If I see you, you will have to kill me.'

'But you have seen me many times before, Victor: me and the others.'

The mask was removed with a flourish: La Saux had seen the face on the tape a hundred times before. The man shook his head slowly from side to side.

'Not knowledge, just being: just being at the wrong place at the wrong time.'

As Victor La Saux screamed, the contents of the bag were squeezed before his eyes.

Two minutes later as the convulsions stopped, as his last ragged breath was leaving his body, he had a vision: not a vision of Christ or the Madonna, not an insight into the hereafter, but a vision of a large boxed crate bound for Amsterdam.

'Fuck you, too,' he whispered, and died.

CHAPTER TWENTY-SEVEN

He was naked, in a strange bed, in a strange place. Jack could feel the weight of the duvet across his chest and legs. He needed to pee, but more importantly he needed to know where he was.

The room was neatly proportioned, with matching pine furniture. A large, floral-print two-seater sofa sat opposite him, close to the wall; on the table before it a cafetière issued steam from its curled lip. He had a sudden longing to hear his old friend Coffee Buddy. Two cups sat before it; one was half full. What the hell happened last night?

Jack threw his memory back to the meeting at the young barrister's flat. The last thing he could remember was a wave of nausea when he had seen something on the computer screen: after that, nothing.

His clothes had been neatly folded on a Windsor nursing chair; he was embarrassed to see his boxer shorts perched on top. Something told him that this wasn't Toby Sloane's apartment. If it wasn't, then it must have been Leone who had undressed him and put him to bed. That thought caused conflicting emotions to surface. He had to admit that in idle moments he had imagined them sharing a bed but this wasn't the scenario of his choice.

He decided to dress, then felt a pain at the back of his head. On examining the area he discovered an egg-sized lump and a little matted blood. Shaking away the vestige of pain, he extended one leg out from under the duvet as the door opened.

'You stay right there, Jack Forth.' Leone entered the room wearing leggings and a baggy Aran-knit sweater.

He quickly pulled his bare leg back under the security of the quilt and pulled its top edge higher over his chest. Leone half smiled; he returned a puzzled half grin.

'What happened?'

'You tell me,' Leone said kindly. She sat on the sofa and sipped from the cheerful coffee cup on the table.

'My head?'

'You bumped it as you fell.' She could see from Jack's face that he was puzzled. 'Have you ever suffered from fits or seizures?'

'No, I—'

'You did last night; at least that's what I think it was. Coffee?'

He nodded. 'Describe it.'

Leone filled the cup, raised the jug of cream. He shrugged; she brought it to him black and sweet.

'When the sketch came up on the screen you went down. We were both stunned at first. You were muttering – no, that's the wrong word – you were saying miserably, "It's him". You repeated it a couple of times then passed out. Do you remember any of this?' He could only shake his head.

'We put you on your side, expecting some convulsions or something. Toby pushed a pencil in your mouth so you wouldn't swallow your tongue. I was about to call an ambulance when you came back to semiconsciousness a minute or two later. It was as if you were with us but weren't really. Is this helping at all?'

Jack sipped the sugar-laden caffeine. 'Not one bit,' he replied honestly.

'Then things got really weird. You're not some secret opium fiend, are you?'

'Only on my days off. Tell me what happened.'

'OK. You grabbed the pencil from your mouth, looked at it, then smiled, took a piece of paper from Toby's desk and began to draw furiously.'

'What did I sketch?'

Leone removed a single piece of paper from a file that had lain unseen on the couch hidden by the table. She walked over to the bed and sat beside him. Jack shuffled uncomfortably aside to allow her more room and she laid the picture flat on his knees. Jack looked down.

The scene depicted was of the terrace of a heaving taverna. There were several tables all fully occupied by large angry men with elaborate moustaches, wearing peasant dress. The table tops were covered with empty ouzo bottles. Judging by the sizes of the figures, the perspective was that of someone sitting down, or small in comparison to the rest of the picture's occupants. In the corner, an angry scene was in the throes of enactment: a large-bellied man with a grimy apron had his finger raised in a threatening gesture towards someone who was out of the picture. The man – he looked like the owner or cook – had a face of fury. All the others ignored the occurrence as if it were a regular event, or they had something much more important on their minds. Jack scanned the picture further, searching for more detail. He saw an olive-skinned girl staring sadly at the angry scene, her eyes large and perfectly almond-shaped.

Jack was confused. He could tell by the familiar contours and detail that it was his work, but had no recollection of the drawing or its subject matter.

'Does it ring any artistic bells?'

'The only bells I have are the ones from the bump on my head.'

'It'll come back.'

'That's just the problem: I think that's what's happening.'

Leone looked to him for an explanation. Jack spent the next twenty minutes detailing the breakdown he had suffered in Cyprus shortly before the Turkish invasion in 1974. She looked saddened when he described the effects on his life thereafter.

'But more than that I still don't know.'

Leone nodded sympathetically. 'This Helena Dwyer, your shrink . . .'

'Therapist,' he reminded her with a smile.

'A spade isn't a "gardening implement" where I come from. Anyway, do you reckon she could help with this?'

'I think I'd better find out; it could be important.'

Jack's memory of the earlier part of the night began to return. 'What about the other two statements?'

'Toby rang first thing. He was right about Dr Coombs' evidence: he's a DNA man. The samples they found in the first victim were tested against Speakman's: there's absolutely no match. In fact, because of his blood group he can be positively excluded from involvement; at least on the sexual assault.'

Jack was genuinely puzzled. 'But doesn't that mean the prosecution would have to let him off that count?'

'No, it makes it harder to get a conviction, that's all. Look, all they have to do is say that Speakman provided the girl for others, then disposed of the body. Once the jury hear the horrors of the other cases they'll be more than ready to accept that scenario.'

'That isn't fair.'

Leone paused and took a further sip from the cup. 'Who said the law is about fairness?'

'What can you do with it, then?'

'It gives us an opening that count one is the weakest of all the lot. If we can cast doubt on that then there is a chance that the others may not succeed.'

'You don't seem very confident.'

'To be honest, Jack, I'm not. What we really need . . . no, this sounds silly.'

'Go ahead,' he said encouragingly.

'Look, the odds are still so stacked against Speakman that we don't just have to prove that he didn't do it: we have to prove who did.'

Jack whistled aloud.

'Told you it was stupid,' she said.

'No, not stupid – just a tall order. Where do we start?'

'We?'

'Much as I would like to spend all day in your bed, I want to help. By the way, did you . . . ?' He nodded to the pile of clothing.

'Yep. You're not the first bloke in a state I've had to put in the sack: though they are normally under the influence of too many tubes rather than too much weirdness.'

He grinned at the candid solicitor.

'But where we start, Jack Forth, is by you getting dressed and confirming to your daughter that you are all right and that I haven't sold you into the white slave trade.'

'Hollie?' Jack began to pull the duvet back.

'She's fine. Sounded quite pleased, really. We had a little chat: women's stuff; you know how it is. In answer to your question, we start with the third statement.'

Jack recalled the name. 'Patricia Barraclough.'

'Spot on. Do you remember in the FBI profile a reference number of the only witness to an abduction?'

Jack did.

'Well, the good professor was referring to her. Her statement was with the other stuff; we'd never have found it otherwise. We need to speak to her.'

Jack decided the time for modesty was past. He climbed out of the bed and walked languidly to his clothing. Leone grinned, aware of his decision.

'Where can we find her?'

Leone looked him full in the face as he drew his Levi's up around his slender waist.

'That's the problem. Five years ago she was a hooker working out of King's Cross. God only knows where she is now; but I've got a private investigator on it.'

CHAPTER TWENTY-EIGHT

A t forty-two, Tony Jacobson was already looking back on the best years of his life. His dismissal from the vice squad section of the Metropolitan Police a year before was, he had no doubt, politically motivated. The new chief had swept into power on a platform of cleanliness. It wasn't the streets he was concerned with wiping free of the grime and graft of the underclasses, it was the Met itself. The vice and drug squads were the first to suffer.

He wasn't the only one to have had first go at a new girl around the red light areas; it was a perk of the job. Many of the others had also accepted gifts from the girls, but they were handed over freely as grateful thanks for the fatherly advice he gave them so readily. When he was kicked out, without either a pension or a reference, the only job open to him was that of a private detective.

He had embraced the opportunity as he used to embrace the girls themselves. Whilst he didn't have the authority a warrant card granted to any useless undergraduate entrant to the Met, he felt he possessed a natural air of confidence. Besides, the girls still respected him, he knew that; they had to or risk a telling off.

The girls, his girls, knew everything that was going off or down. His sideline as a paid police informant helped to supplement a gradually growing business. The call from the Aussie woman solicitor was a little piece of sunshine in his newfound existence. He had been delighted to brag about his contacts in the world of prostitution, pointing to an excellent police record as evidence of his trustworthiness: thankfully the stupid bitch hadn't asked for any proof of that.

His brief, for which a handsome fee had been agreed, was to locate the whereabouts of one Patricia Barraclough, or 'Fat Patty' as she was known in the game. He'd known her for years. She was, as her nickname suggested, gross beyond obesity; her other, less kindly, name was the 'Elephant Woman'. Still, Fat Patty had a heart all right; it was made of the hardest substance known to man. All he had to do was track her down. That, as they said in the Met, was a piece of piss. As the years and breakfast fry-ups had taken their toll, she'd become repulsive to all but the most perverse punters. Instead, she ran a 'take-away' hooker service for a sharp dude, with an imported Chevrolet, known as 'Clive of Islington'. Her natural nose for hard business and soft targets had come to the fore once she had taken up the business of management.

Jacobson had asked his client what it was she wanted 'Miss Barraclough' for: her response had been fucking rude, to say the very least. Still, that was briefs for you. Apparently she'd shopped around a little before tinkling his bell; there was a lot of snobbery, even in his own sleazy world. Still, she had been directed to the best and that was what he was, or would be. He had decided not to warn 'Fat Patty' of his arrival; she might misinterpret his interest as another shakedown.

Standing at the corner of Islington High Street, Jacobson watched the premises with care. He watched the 'drive-in' queue ebb and flow two or three times; they were making good money here. It was less risky than a punter driving the roads, cruising for some quick pleasure. The routine was simple: at one door the client was handed a brochure, at the next he made his selection – according to availability, of course – and at the next the escort was waiting. Lovely and clean. Jacobson admired the hell out of it: this way no irate citizens complained to the Met about kerb crawling. There were no innocents to corrupt; everyone in this game was corrupted beyond redemption.

In the best Sam Spade tradition he wore the collar of his Nike tracksuit top up around his neck; it helped to cut the chill of the London fog. Jacobson waited until he saw Clive's car drive away for another round of takings collection, then made his way over to the distribution booth. A young West Indian, tall beyond his years, was quick to notice the approach on foot. He wore the badge of the young blood – no-lace pump-up trainers, ludicrously baggy trousers and a tight Lycra cycling top that strained against the musculature of his vast upper arms, exposed despite the weather. He looked the portly detective up and down; it didn't take very long.

'You're scruffy enough to be from the vice squad. Clive paid you fuckers off last week.'

Interesting, thought Jacobson, and heartwarming to know that nothing had changed in his absence.

'Just checking hygiene standards.'

'Then check your own, scumbag.' The black youth giggled, his voice strangely high-pitched. Jacobson put it down to the nut-shrivelling effect of anabolic steroids.

'Cut the crap, Denzil, just tell Fat Patty that Jacobson is here.'

'You must be desperate.' He looked down at the ex-policeman. 'Shit, Jacobson, so must she.'

Jacobson punched him in the windpipe with two telling blows. The young Negro took some time to fall: he was held up only by his own astonishment.

'They call me *Mister* Jacobson,' he whispered to the gasping youth.

Inside, the intercom operated like an alternative McDonald's. As their names were called, girls appeared with a car registration and a name for their customer. Again, Jacobson was impressed. Then he saw her in the corner of the surprisingly clean interior of the premises: Fat Patty was dressed more smartly than he had ever seen her in her previous career. The bulging miniskirt was replaced with a dark-grey pyjama suit, panda make-up with an even blusher. She noticed him, frowned, then beckoned him over. He almost collided with a stunning, long-legged Scandinavian who was following her despatcher's orders to the door.

'You on foot, Jake?' She glanced down to the cheap Taiwanese training shoes on his feet, '''Cos we don't do carry-outs.'

He smiled appreciatively. 'How are you keeping, Pat?'

'I hear you're a snoop, now.' Her jowls quivered as she built herself up to a gag. 'No, in the States they call them "private dicks": that was one thing yours never was.' Her fat wobbled as she dragged the laugh out.

'I'm here on business; someone wants to meet you.'

Through the gross accumulation of flesh around her upper cheeks he almost saw her eyes narrow.

'I've been out of that side for a while now; can't say I miss it.'

Jacobson pulled a wooden chair up as close as he could. 'This is different – a solicitor.'

'I've had hundreds of them.'

'Pat, I'm serious: a female solicitor who wants to talk to you.'

Another chit was passed to her; she checked the noticeboard for availability. 'Send Trudy,' she shouted to the runner. 'He'll never know the difference.'

She returned her attention to Jacobson. 'Is it about Colleen?'

'She wouldn't say, but you and I both know that King Arthur's trial's due soon. I don't think it can be about anything else, do you?'

'I told the police everything I knew years ago; there's nothing to add.'

'She's not from the CPS, she's from the firm that's defending him: I checked her out with some mates in the force.'

The huge woman attempted to jump to her feet in rage. Jacobson lent her a hand, but the impact was lost.

'I know how close you were to Colleen, but the problem is this: she told me that if you didn't agree to meet, she'd get a witness summons for your attendance at the trial. If you don't attend you'll be dragged before the judge for contempt, then locked up. Pat, who'll run the business then?'

'Anybody,' she replied sadly.

'Exactly, and you lose a nice little number on your bum rather than on your back.'

'What's in it for you?'

'I have a finder's fee, that's all; you get a hundred just for your trouble. It's up to you; whatever you say.'

'I work antisocial hours; a hundred and fifty, cash. I come off shift at four a.m. You know where I live: tell them to get there at five-thirty.'

'Still the same gaff at the Elephant and Castle?'

'That's the one. I don't want you there.'

'Pat—'

'No. Too many people know who you are and what you are. I don't want to be associated with a grass.'

Jacobson looked around the brothel. 'What about here?'

'This is different; this is business.' She raised her voice alarmingly. 'Now piss off, there's no freebies for ex-coppers in this place.'

Jacobson played along with the explosion, even feeling a kick up the backside from her as he scuttled away.

Within twenty minutes he had relayed all the information to Leone Stern. He outlined the address and the time of the meeting with 'Fat Patty' Barraclough.

Jacobson smiled as he returned to the seedy offices he also called home; that was a good night's work.

'King Arthur' thought the same. The tap on Leone Stern's telephone had succeeded beyond his wildest dreams; and, when he dreamt, the dreams were beyond the ordinary without exception. The surveillance equipment had been a precaution. It had transmuted into a hotline of ready information. So simple, yet so effective – as all the truly great things were. It had cost him no more than £20 for the state-of-the-art brochure on surveillance equipment and ready cash to purchase the hardwear. Now he had a meeting to attend.

The solicitor reached for an *A–Z of Greater London* and with little difficulty located the home of 'Fat Patty', the Lady of the Night. Her demeaning sobriquet did little to whet his keenly honed appetite. She would be old, used and wattled, not like his 'others'. She would carry the fleshy baggage of time in rippling pasty flesh; he would just have to use his imagination, and that had never been a significant problem.

CHAPTER TWENTY-NINE

It was 5.30 a.m. and the night lay like a tarpaulin over the South London sky. Heavy drizzle forced the windscreen wipers on Leone's hired BMW into overtime. She and Jack were both dressed against the early-morning chill.

'Are you sure you're up to this?' she asked him as he directed her with the aid of the *London A–Z* around Southwark to their rendezvous with Pat Barraclough.

'Still got a slight headache; nothing to worry about.'

Leone indicated to turn right at the huge roundabout around the Elephant and Castle.

'It's not the headache I'm worried about: have you had another episode?'

He knew what she was referring to. 'No.' He wanted to move away from the subject. 'Hollie said thanks for letting her know where I was. She told me I drink too much.'

'Wish it was that easy,' Leone muttered. 'Left or right here?'

'Two lefts then a right. The tower block should be straight in front.' Leone began to follow his instructions. 'How do you know you can trust this Jacobson character?'

'I don't, but the same pal who gave me the inside track on Berkeley reckoned that if anyone could find her, he could.'

The traffic was scant as they proceeded. The streets and pavements reflected the night lighting in hazy puddles of indifference.

'You never told me what her statement said.'

Leone shifted down to second gear as she navigated another corner. 'Look in my handbag on the back seat; Toby faxed a copy through to me earlier.'

'It's too dark to see in here; précis it for me.'

It was an activity Leone was well used to. The proper presentation of a case was just that: a concentration of the important

213

facts, omitting the nonsense a legal case attracted like a powerful magnet.

'Trondl, the professor, was right. So far as we know there were no other witnesses to an abduction. What she saw didn't amount to an abduction at the time, but she was the last person to see Colleen alive. The two of them normally worked out of King's Cross; there's an area at the back of the station that's a renowned pick-up spot. The weather was bad that night, similar to tonight in fact. Colleen had only come from Northern Ireland a few weeks before. Pat was keeping an eye on her until she could look after herself; she was only fourteen years old.'

'Christ,' Jack muttered bitterly.

'There's a lot, too many, who are even younger. There weren't many punters about so they decided to call it a night and wander up to the West End for a few drinks. A taxi driver logged their fare at about one a.m. He dropped them at Leicester Square. They had a couple of cocktails in a couple of clubs, then decided the night was a literal washout.'

Jack could see that they were approaching a dark, looming tower block. 'This must be it.' Leone pulled the car up to the pavement in front of the grim, defiant edifice.

'No,' Jack said. 'It's never good practice to park too close to a target. Stick it out of sight down one of those side streets.'

'Why?'

'Just that old habits die hard, I guess. Indulge me. Carry on with her account.'

'They had said goodnight; as they lived in different parts of the city, their paths home took them in different directions. It was about two-forty-five a.m. Pat remembers the sound of a car's wheels on the wet roads. It was driving slowly. She heard it stop and knew it must have been near Colleen. She was right. Pat watched from the corner as Colleen leaned into the open window on the front passenger side. The car was facing away from her. She saw it was a very expensive make: a Bentley, Daimler, something like that. It was too dark to make out the registration at that distance but she could see that there were a number of heads, through the back window, because they were illuminated when one of them – it must have been the front seat passenger – lit a cigarette for Colleen. Pat said that she was leaning right into the car with her backside stuck out in best hooking pose.'

'Did they grab her?' Jack asked, looking at his watch.

'No, that's the thing: she was a working girl; she got in voluntarily.'

'I thought you said it was an abduction.'

'That's because she was never seen alive again.'

'So it could have been just another client.'

'That's possible, but if it was so why didn't they come forward when her body was discovered?'

'Embarrassment? They were probably all married.'

'True, but if that were all, why did the police hide Barraclough's statement?' It was an excellent question. 'What her statement did say was that she had a partial recollection of the reg number – it looked like a personalised one – and a car colour: British racing green.'

Jack pulled on his gloves; it would soon be time to move. 'Then why hide her statement?'

Leone looked dead ahead before replying, 'I think she was either paid off or the police managed to trace the owner of the car and have protected him ever since.'

'Shit. Would they do that?'

'Not normally, but it depends who he is. That's what we need to find out from her: how the police dealt with her and whether she was warned off or paid off. Come on, I think we'd better make a move.'

'We're ten minutes early.'

'Good. Let's try and keep her off balance.'

Leone locked the car and activated the alarm. She zipped her dark-blue padded jacket up to the neck. The drizzle had hardened to needle-sharp rain. Jack was wearing a black Berghaus climbing jerkin nipped to the waist, and inky leggings, tucked neatly into soft-soled training shoes.

'You look like you're about to storm the Iranian Embassy.'

'I'm not allowed to talk about that operation,' he whispered, his jaw clenched to Eastwood toughness. It was only when he winked that Leone was sure he was joking.

They entered via a small shattered glass door in the centre of the frontage. Two light bulbs encased in wire mesh cast the foyer in a sickly pale yellow light. It was just after ten minutes to four when they stood in the dank, creaking lift on their way to the sixth floor. Neither of them felt like talking. As soon as they had entered the building its atmosphere sucked any animation or humour from their bodies. The interior of the elevator was daubed with obscene drawings and threatening graffiti.

'Nice place,' Leone said to herself.

'Some people don't have any choice,' Jack replied, annoyed.

She hadn't realised she had spoken aloud. 'Sorry.'

'I'm nervous too,' he offered.

The dull ping and the grimy digital board told them they had arrived. In contrast to the lift, which at least had the benefit of some dubious lighting, the hallway of the sixth floor was pitch dark. Jack reached into an inside pocket, removed a small but powerful flashlight and flicked it on.

'Boy Scout?'

'Soldier,' he whispered.

'Same thing.'

Jack trained the narrow beam up to the ceiling. The light bulb had been removed.

'I'd prefer it if it were smashed.'

'What?'

'Keep your voice down. Look,' he breathed into her ear, 'the screws on the mesh haven't been put back in properly. I don't like this; you stay here.'

'In the dark? No way.'

Jack switched the beam to a wider distribution and used it to scout the corridor.

'Now let's make this quick. I want you to stay here and keep watch. Be prepared to move quickly.'

This time Leone didn't argue. There was something surreal about the whole thing. Jack moved on hushed feet to number 63. He knocked quietly on the door. He wasn't surprised to see it swing open. He didn't need to see the blood, he could smell it: thick and coppery, it assailed his nostrils like deathly ammonia.

The flashlight picked out the cheap furniture in the room. He spotted the first splatters of drying red on the cheerful, floral wallpaper. He found her in the bathroom, her vast shape all but filling the tiny space. Her shoulders and head were dipped into the water, which had been transformed to a deep crimson by the massive blood loss. He noticed her hands were bound behind her. Jack knew she was dead; it was futile to even attempt to take her pulse. He needed to see her eyes, if there were eyes to see.

He leaned forward and with real effort began to pull her back, expecting the worst, anticipating the horror of empty eye sockets, but she was wearing dark glasses. The sick bastard had sellotaped the arms of them to her ears, but the message was clear: it was a calling card.

Jack's mind was speeding ahead. This was the work of the real King Arthur. He had left the glasses to signify blindness. He couldn't commit an identical murder or the police would know they had the wrong man. That was when he heard the police sirens approaching rapidly up the road. Jack dropped the dead woman's head back into the bathwater and stumbled back. Leone's face was thrown into confused relief by the flashlight beam.

'It's a fucking set-up,' he hissed. 'Down the stairs slowly; don't make any noise. They'll come in the back and the front. They'll expect us to run into their arms. Walk behind me and make no noise at all.'

He began to make his way down the stairways, the flashlight extinguished but still held firmly in his right hand. Leone disobeyed him at once.

'Jack, why don't we stay and tell them what happened?'

'We can't afford to. The killer's set this up beautifully. He'll have left some evidence to tie whoever is caught to the murder, I can feel it. Now for God's sake be quiet.'

They saw the dancing flashlights flicker across their route and heard the thunder of men's feet approaching their position. Jack was frantically looking for a hiding place; their paths were going to meet at any moment if he didn't find one. To his immediate right he saw a cleaner's cupboard. 'Thank God.' The lock was in poor condition. The police were approaching fast. Now the men's voices, harsh whispers, could be heard; they could only be one or two landings away. The lights were growing clearer with every step. He fished in his pockets and found a Yale key. They were almost on the same landing. He wiggled the rusted mechanism back and forward. The lights were almost on them; no more than brief feet away, just around the corner. It ground, then clicked. Jack grabbed Leone by the arm and threw her in. He sat on top of her in the confined space and quietly shut the door. How they had missed them Leone would never know. Jack listened intently. The clatter of boots receded.

'We've got to move quickly now,' he urged. 'As soon as they find the flat's deserted, they'll start a thorough search.'

Jack led the way down the last two floors. He saw the two empty police cars, doors flung wide open, parked sideways across the road. They must have had a really hot tip to go in like that.

'We've been lucky,' he whispered. They inched away from the building through the shadows and into a darkened street.

The battery of the image intensifier hummed, barely in the range of his hearing. The laser picked them out as they shuffled away from the scene of his trap. He was more than a little annoyed. The flats were now alive, alerted by the police sirens. Inhabitants leaned over balconies, straining to see what it was all about, when only he knew. Forth and Stern must now suspect that something was more than a little amiss, but they had wisely decided against sharing that suspicion with the good officers of the Metropolitan Police. A wise move, and the wisdom came from the most unlikely of sources. Stern was bright enough, but not intuitive. The man must be instinctive, a quick thinker; that conclusion was both refreshing and frustrating at the same moment. Still, it made the sport more interesting.

He shrugged away his annoyance. What was, was: it was how one reacted that made the outcome more pleasing. Anger was for lower life forms whilst rational thought was a spiritual evolution. He had reached his present state of enlightenment long ago and refused to devolve to the swamp again.

It was time to decamp. When the police failed to find the suspects he had promised them over the telephone minutes before, they would search the area. It wouldn't do to be stopped and questioned by them, not again. The memory gave him a delicious shiver. It had been two years before. He had been somewhat sloppy. His Range Rover had been seen at one of the 'showing' points. It was some time after that they had courteously approached him, but he remembered the dark thrill of their grovelling questions and his crisp answers to them. He had never used the Range Rover again, at least not for the 'showings'.

But his work was not yet over for the evening. There was another who knew about the proposed meeting that night.

He melted easily into the darkness, as he always did.

'You were right about parking the car where we did.' Her voice was high and jittery.

'Are you OK to drive, Leone? I'll do it if you're shook up.'

She steered the vehicle across Tower Bridge. 'How can you be so bloody cool? For God's sake, a woman's been murdered because of us.'

Jack thought for a moment before replying. 'No, you're wrong. She was killed because of what she knew, or could tell us. What worries me is, how did the killer know about the meeting?'

'Jacobson?'

'Let's find out. Do you have an address?'

'God knows what we might find there,' Leone said bitterly.

'Let's telephone Jacobson first,' Jack said. Leone was relieved at the suggestion, and also the fact that she hadn't gone into Pat's flat with him.

'Tell me how she was killed.'

Jack shook his head. 'Later, when you're ready. I've got to deal with it myself first. There is one thing I am sure about: Trevor Speakman is not King Arthur. The real killer was in that flat minutes before we arrived. He was probably watching the whole thing from outside. He'll be furious when we don't come down the lift in handcuffs.'

Leone shivered. She began to speak.

'No, later. I'll tell you everything. First we'll ring Jacobson.'

She offered the use of her mobile phone. Jack refused. 'Too easy to trace. Stop at the next phone box.'

The telephone rang for several minutes before a bleary voice answered it. 'Jacobson, and it's too early.'

'Did you tell anyone about the meeting with Pat Barraclough?'

'Who the fu—?'

'Answer; your life depends on it. She's dead.' Jack could hear the confusion at the other end of the call.

'No, I mean of course not.'

'If you're telling the truth, then your own life is in real danger.'

'What's this—?'

'Shut up,' Jack screamed. 'Don't stop for anything; get out of there now. Take this down.' Jack gave his home number. 'If you go to the police you will still be in danger. Do you understand? Now, get out.'

Jack returned to the BMW.

'Was he there?'

'Yes, and I believed him. Why would he tell anyone else about this?'

Leone shrugged. 'You didn't, I didn't and Jacobson didn't. Then who did? There isn't anyone else.'

'I know,' he mumbled bleakly. 'You made the call from your flat?' She nodded. 'I hate to say it but I think King Arthur's been listening to every word you've said in there.'

Her foot hit the brakes instantly. Thankfully there were no other road users around. Her head rested against the steering wheel; it had been a tough morning and it was only 6 a.m.

'Get in the back. I'll drive.'

She climbed between the seats without argument. 'Where are we going?'

'To meet my parents; at least you'll be safe there.'

Jack Forth had never been more wrong in his life.

CHAPTER THIRTY

The brass alarm clock she had set a bare two hours before clanged through a shallow sleep. She knew it was going to sound before it did so and was wishing the moment away for all she was worth. Her dreams had been of a faceless woman walking the streets carrying a sack full of eyes: perhaps waking wasn't such a bad thing after all.

Jack had led her through the front door of his parents' home as the dawn light was beginning to break over the elm trees nearby. Patricia Barraclough would never see another sunrise. Had she been responsible for the woman's death? It was a question she would always ask herself, but deep inside she was afraid of the answer.

It was 9.15 a.m. The flight from the tower block seemed as if it had taken place months ago in another land, another world; she didn't really know. Things felt fuzzy, yet sharp around the edges. Inside she was raw with shock at the speed of events. What was worse, she had only three and a half hours before she was due to meet Toby and Jeffrey Sedgewick QC for a conference with Trevor Speakman.

Jack had shown her to what was obviously his old room at his parents' home. The walls were plastered with intricate ink drawings of fabulous architecture; they were not prints. They had been hand-drawn by the young Jack Forth before he was robbed of his gift. Each of them had a tag affixed, dating and naming the buildings in the detailed sketch, though many were sufficiently well known not to require a label. It was the dates of the drawings that amazed her – they ranged between a slightly smudged rendition of the Houses of Parliament (Jack aged six, 1967) to a fabulously accurate portrayal of the Acropolis in all its crumbling beauty (Jack, thirteen, 1974). That must have been shortly before his breakdown, she remembered.

The room was small and comfortable. It felt warm in the way a close family can imbue a house with their own happiness. Jack's distressing adolescence precluded him from much participation in that. Leone could only conclude that his parents were wonderful people. The long rugby shirt he had lent her to sleep in seemed to smell of him, but she was sure that was just her imagination. He was a strange man – brave, resourceful and strange.

She turned to look out of the window, then suddenly began to tremble as she remembered Jack's words from a scant few hours before. He had to be right. There was no other way, unless Jacobson was lying, for the killer to know what was going to happen. She had to rule out coincidence. It was terrifying, but it did mean that they were on the right track, despite the costs that were being measured in human life. Leone believed that discovery of the ownership of the green car that picked Colleen up was the next link in their investigation. They needed Toby's expertise on the HOLMES system to track it down: it had to be in there somewhere. As yet, the barrister knew nothing about recent events; Jack had persuaded her that the less he knew about the murder the less chance he would have to be compromised by it. She had lost all ability to calculate her own position. The delayed shock began to kick in and a tear rolled down her cheek.

There was a timid knock at the door. 'Are you awake, Leone?'

'Sure. Come on in, Hollie.' She recovered, wiping the duvet across her face.

Jack's daughter walked in with a huge grin and a breakfast tray in her hands. 'Grandma thought you might be hungry.'

She wore a grey school uniform that she probably hated, and pigtails that she probably hated more. Leone could see where the hair was growing back after the swimming accident.

'There's cereal, some toast, juice and coffee; isn't that what Australians drink?'

'No, we drink too much beer, but this will be fine for now.'

Hollie beamed at her, delighted to be involved in such adult kidding. 'Dad said it was a late night.'

'Work.'

'That's what he said.' The little girl's eyebrows were raised in amusement.

'How old did you say you were?'

She handed Leone the tray. 'I didn't. Dad always says I'm a thirty-five-year-old midget.'

'I can see why.' Leone smiled, then felt an unfamiliar wave of belonging.

Hollie sat down on the bed. 'You like him, don't you? I can tell. He likes you too. He gets all flustered when I ask about you. It's great fun. He did the same with Grandma at breakfast. Grandpop just raised his eyebrows at her; it's his way of telling her to be quiet.'

Leone raised her own eyebrows meaningfully.

'Oops, sorry: I talk too much when I get excited.'

Leone moved her eyebrows up and down furiously. Hollie began to giggle.

'Grandpop has to do that sometimes.'

'I'd better get dressed.'

Jack's daughter looked disappointedly at the breakfast tray.

'I thought I could come downstairs and have breakfast down there. It's about time your grandparents met their house guest.'

'Cool.' The expression sounded alien in an English accent; Leone marked it down to *Baywatch*. 'But Grandpop's taken Monty for a walk.'

'Monty?'

'After the Second World War Field Marshal, because he's a small, stubborn, wire-haired beast who won't do what he's told.'

'I see,' replied Leone, though she didn't.

'Mummy used to wear that,' Hollie said pointing at the rugby shirt.

'I'm sorry, I didn't—'

'I never knew her but Daddy tells me all about her. He says that just because I can't remember her doesn't mean I can't know her now.'

'You don't mind?'

The little girl looked at her squarely for a moment, just like her father did. 'No, you're cool. If Dad doesn't mind that means Mummy wouldn't either. Oh yes, I heard Daddy talking on the phone. He's seeing the woman from the loony bin this afternoon. You'd better watch her, I think she fancies him.' The juvenile cyclone was more than Leone could take in. 'I'm off to school. See you soon.'

Hollie Forth jumped off the bed and swept out of the room. Leone dressed and made her way downstairs. She could hear conversation emanating from a room that proved to be the kitchen.

'I can tell, Jack, something is worrying you. Is it anything you can tell me about?' The voice was gentle.

'I'm sorry, Mum. I'll tell you one day when it's all over, but for now just trust me. I'm more worried about Leone.' The concern in his voice made Leone tingle again.

She made her entrance, carrying the breakfast tray. 'Did I hear my name mentioned?'

Jack's mother stood immediately, smiled warmly, then took the tray from her. 'The coffee will be cold by now. Have a seat, Leone. I'm Jean. He's trouble, but well worth the effort.' She was still a good-looking woman with soft, green, Irish eyes, raven hair streaked with an auburn tint and whispers of grey unselfconsciously tumbling across her shoulders.

'Mother!'

She ignored Jack's exclamation. 'Did you sleep well, my dear? The bed's a little lumpy.'

'Fine, really. I'm grateful to you for putting me up for the night.'

Jean's tea towel was already drying another cup for her to use. It was soon filled with fresh coffee and placed on the table.

'Not just for the night. Graham – that's Jack's father – and I want you to stay here as long as you wish. No questions asked.'

'Thanks.'

'Now then, help yourself to anything you want. Jack, I'm going to see Mrs Ives; something desperately important's happened.' She kissed her son goodbye, then as naturally repeated the action to Leone's cheek.

Once she had left, Leone spoke. 'Who's your father, Cary Grant? They're all so charming.'

Jack looked down into his own cup. 'I know; I haven't been easy for them to cope with. We need to talk.'

'When are you seeing the woman from the loony bin?'

Jack looked up, startled.

'Hollie,' Leone explained with a smile. 'Quite flattering, really; she told me about the other woman in your life, kind of a warning. Should I be worried?'

He grinned appreciatively. 'Three o'clock. I think I'm ready for it. That blackout the other night helped; last night convinced me.'

'What do you mean?'

Jack chewed on his bottom lip where the stubble pushed up from the skin. 'It sounds screwy, but it's just that I feel I know King Arthur. Well, perhaps not *know* him, but that we have met somewhere, sometime . . .' His voice trailed off. Leone looked for signs that he might be experiencing another seizure. 'It's just that everything that's happened seems to force me towards him: the paintings, you. Jesus, I wish I could fucking understand.'

'Jack?'

'Yes? Sorry: it's like a vague memory of something. The drawing of the taverna is part of it, I know it is; that's why I have to find out.'

'What about last night?'

'It's in the papers and the breakfast TV news; she was tortured and drowned. It was him.' He knew, as he said the words and delivered them with such finality of conviction, that he was right.

'What are we going to do?'

'Firstly, I'm going to track down George Sloane. He knows what he's doing in the technology department. We'll go to your flat and search it thoroughly. If there are bugging devices there then we'll leave them in place. Perhaps we can use them to trap him. I'll get some clothes for your conference with Speakman. You have to continue as normal; you still have an innocent client on your books.'

Jack tracked down Toby's brother with the barrister's assistance. They met outside Leone's home. George had a toothy grin and held a holdall with a bulky item inside.

'You've done this before.'

The West Indian smiled even more broadly. 'You don't want to know, Jack.'

'Perhaps not.'

Jack held the door open. George walked in with a finger over his pursed lips. From within the holdall he produced a matt black box with four dials on the left-hand side. It had a separate joystick and appeared to be battery powered. Jack could see the item was called a 'Broom, Non-linear Junction Protector', and he presumed it to be a countersurveillance device.

He watched, fascinated, as George discovered three separate

bugging devices in the apartment. As each was discovered Jack indicated with a nod of his head that it should be left in its original place. After the work was done, Jack gathered a change of clothes for Leone. They left the flat without comment.

Outside, Jack turned to thank George, whose face was wearing a pronounced frown.

'Think you got the lot?'

'I hope so, man, but he's good. The sweep I did would have found most of the ones I know of on the market, but new gear is appearing all the time.'

'Safer to presume there might be others?'

'I'd say so,' George replied. 'But this is very heavy-duty action, Jack. Are you up to it?'

Try as he might, Jack Forth found the question impossible to answer.

CHAPTER THIRTY-ONE

Leone was five minutes late for the prison appointment with the barristers and Speakman; her mind was whirling. Jack had returned from her home, his face grim with thought. He had chosen a smart, black wool dress and court shoes, and carried a small Selfridge's bag containing some underwear and a pair of tights for her quick change. It wasn't the idea of his roaming through her apartment that concerned her, it was whether the killer of Pat Barraclough had done so as well. Jack's face said it all.

At first, all he would say was that she was staying with his parents until further notice. She had managed to drag the truth from him, grain by grain. Why was he so stubborn? When he had told her of the phone bug and the two others they had found, she gagged on the thought of what that meant; *he* had been there. He had been there and heard every word she had said and listened to everything she had done, whoever *he* was. But Leone Stern wouldn't cry – the time for tears was over.

They had arranged to meet at the end of the day's business. Jack was so concerned for her that the prospect of revisiting his bleakest point through hypnotherapy seemed to have receded in importance.

Toby and Sedgewick were waiting inside the security doors for her arrival. As she negotiated the regulation searches by the prison guards, Toby raised one hand in greeting; Sedgewick was staring into space. The only point of flamboyance about his person was a pink Liberty handkerchief that hung foppishly from his front breast pocket. In the seventies he had been the foremost advocate of his generation, until his wife's death led him to another companion: alcohol. His intake was prodigious. Many stories circulated around the Temple concerning stand-up rows with High Court and circuit judges. These were always launched after the luncheon adjournment.

Leone approached. 'Mr Sedgewick, Toby, I'm sorry I'm late.'

'That's quite all right, my dear. Mr Speakman isn't going anywhere in a hurry. Now, how long is this conference scheduled for?'

Toby spoke. 'I mentioned it a little earlier, Mr Sedgewick: we're booked in for the rest of the day.'

Sedgewick pursed his lips and nodded sagely for a few seconds. 'Of course you did. All day, you say?' He checked the gold fob watch in his waistcoat pocket. 'I have an hour and a half before another appointment. I'm sure that between us we can glean sufficient of the case from the defendant not to delay us overlong.'

Leone's and Toby's eyes met in a mutual lack of surprise. She would be amazed if Sedgewick lasted that long.

'Any news of a surprise alibi witness leaping out of the woodwork?' he said sarcastically. It was clear that he was still refusing to accept that Speakman might be innocent.

'Not as yet, Mr Sedgewick. We're working on that angle.'

They had agreed to withhold the findings from their illicit search of the HOLMES system until they knew what they really had on their hands and, given Sedgewick's attitude, he could go public with their methods of entry.

'The outlook hasn't got any brighter for Speakman since our first meeting, don't you agree, Miss Stern?'

Leone shrugged. If she disagreed with the QC an explanation might be called for and she wasn't in a position to explain what had occurred over the last few days.

'I believe it looks very bleak indeed,' Sedgewick went on. 'Haven't seen one like this in years: not since the Birmingham Strangler tried to deny his guilt; that didn't work either.'

'Didn't he claim he was insane rather than innocent?'

Sedgewick smiled kindly as if she were a first-year law student asking how you can defend someone you know to be guilty. 'It means the same thing to the baying public. They don't just want a pound of flesh, they require the blood that goes with it. Fact of legal life, Miss Stern; that and a solicitor promising that the cheque is in the post. No personal offence intended.'

'And none taken, Mr Sedgewick.'

'I've spoken to the pros. There are still no deals on offer. Can't say I blame them but I hope they'll soften the nearer we get to the trial date.' He spoke in a rich, lightly amused, middle-class burr. It had once been a much-admired presentation device; now it was more commonly heard ordering another large Scotch.

'I doubt that Mr Speakman would bargain with the prosecution anyway,' Toby interjected.

'Of course, of course, and he is entitled to put the Crown to proof on everything they allege; that is his right. If he chooses to exercise it then he's entitled to the best representation available.'

Leone could not agree more and lamented the unsuitability of the person who was to fill that role.

'Shall we proceed?'

Sedgewick began to lead the way. Toby fell in alongside Leone. 'He said in the cab that he's going to put pressure on Speakman to plead guilty,' Toby muttered out of the side of his mouth.

'Did you disagree with him?'

'I tried. It was pretty pointless. He just listened politely, nodded and said, "Of course; of course". I gave up after that.'

'Any news on the green car?'

'I went to the Yard first thing and set a search program. I'll know more this afternoon.'

'But we're scheduled to be here all day.'

Toby looked ahead to the whistling QC. 'That I very much doubt.'

Speakman was standing at the far side of the melamine-topped table. He stared at her, and only her, his eyes begging for some small morsel of hope; as yet she felt unable to grant him that gift. They still didn't know enough to be confident. Speakman appeared to understand and dropped his gaze to the table's grey top. His face seemed more defined than she could remember: sunken cheeks and tight, yellowish skin. The prison overalls sagged around his stomach. She noticed that his hands were trembling and swollen, plump like a baby's, the nails grown beyond their fingers' ends. They were locked in with him.

Leone forced a false cheerfulness into her voice. 'Trevor, it's good to see you again. You know Mr Sloane.' Toby nodded curtly, not one for social niceties. 'And Mr Sedgewick, of course.' She thought the best way to deal with this was to ignore the previous meeting at the pre-trial review conference.

The QC beamed a sharky grin at her and his client. 'Mr Speakman, please sit.'

The defendant waited until the others sat first, then slumped into the waiting chair.

'We got off to a bad start but please remember that I am here to represent your interest. I can only fulfil that obligation, however, if we can trust each other. I for my part believe everything you tell me; you for yours must believe everything I tell you, however unpalatable that may be.'

Speakman was obviously thrown by the lengthy word.

'He means unpleasant or hard,' Leone said. Sedgewick glanced sideways at her, raised one eyebrow slowly, then returned his attention to Speakman. The inference was clear to her: shut up, Leone – if I want your help I will ask for it.

'Trust, Mr Speakman,' he continued, 'is a rare commodity in this day and age. You, I have no doubt, will tell me things that I will have difficulty believing, but believe them I will. I will ask or advise you to do things that you will not believe but I hope you will do them. I have spent forty years practising as a professional advocate to bring me to your door; that must be worth some measure of trust.'

Speakman looked bamboozled by the speech, which Leone surmised was its intention.

'Now, let us pretend that I know nothing about this case. Tell me in your own words what has occurred to bring you to this position.'

He settled back comfortably in his chair, hands linked across his inflated stomach. For the next hour, after some hesitation, Speakman went shakily through the story of his life. Sedgewick nodded encouragingly at wholly inappropriate times and never took one note of anything that was said. Toby scribbled away, though there was nothing new in the lengthy, disjointed disclosure. On several occasions Leone attempted to move the matter along to something that was pertinent to the defence case, but Sedgewick repeated the sideways glance and raised eyebrow. Eventually she was rendered impotently silent.

Speakman began to complain about his treatment inside the prison when Sedgewick's fob watch pealed the stroke of one.

'Fascinating,' he said quietly. 'I imagine you feel much better for getting all that off your chest.'

Amazingly Speakman smiled shyly and spoke. 'I do, Mr Sedgewick; this is the first proper conversation I've had in months. Thank you.'

Sedgewick nodded again. 'I trust that reliving your ordeal has taught you something; given you a valuable insight into your predicament.'

'I don't understand, sir.' Speakman was looking from face to face. Toby was staring at the floor; Leone was glaring at the QC, waiting for the killer blow.

'It must have shown you how hopeless things really are.' Speakman rocked back, as if he had been kicked in the face. 'I want you to think about that on the run-up to your appearance in court.'

Leone noted he refrained from using the word 'trial', as if it were some obscene oath.

'Trust, Mr Speakman: you promised when we began that you would trust me. I'm grateful you feel able to do so. It's quite, quite hopeless. Better you know now than later; gives us a chance to prepare a proper mitigation.' Sedgewick was attempting to ride roughshod over the client's instructions.

The defendant was staring open-mouthed at Leone; she had to do something. 'Mr Sedgewick: Mr Sloane, Trevor and I covered that point at the first conference. I understand you were indisposed.'

'Flu.'

'Of course; of course.' Leone thrust his own expression back in his face, but so politely that he could not be seen to take offence from it. 'Mr Speakman was adamant then that he was not guilty of the charges; he reiterated his plea before Justice Singleton. I don't suppose that has changed, has it?' She glanced at their client, who was furiously attempting to understand the power struggle that was taking place before his bewildered eyes. He shook his head.

Leone could see that the QC's face was losing its grey pallor and reddening around the cheeks. 'I only mention this, Mr Sedgewick, because you didn't have the benefit of the first conference and everyone was a little bit on edge at the plea directions hearing.' She sounded so reasonable, so helpful.

Sedgewick smiled icily. 'And I am grateful.' He swivelled his attention to Toby. 'Sloane, I am a little disappointed in you. As it is, I now have to leave at a crucial point. Mr Speakman, as you can see, I am fully in control of this situation. Rest assured that all my abilities will be at your disposal during the case.'

'Trial,' Leone reminded him, going just too far.

'Of course; of course,' he responded through lightly clenched teeth. 'Please continue in my absence. Good day to you all.' The angry lawyer mustered what dignity he could from the scene and departed.

Toby's face was stern, though his eyes were laughing. Speakman looked bemused by the entire episode.

His concentration lapsed after a further hour of digging in his memory for potential witnesses. Eventually, his tiredness apparent, they concluded the conference with promises to the confused prisoner that they would keep trying.

Outside the prison, Toby exploded into a fit of giggles. 'Fantastic, bloody fantastic.'

She'd barely seen him smile before and here he was outside a maximum-security prison braying with laughter to the passing world. Leone began to laugh too.

'Did you see his face when you led Speakman away from a guilty plea? He was so angry I thought he was going to have a thromby.'

'You didn't mind getting it in the neck?'

'Not a bit of it. I would volunteer to be spanked by the Bar council in my Inn of Court to see that again. I bet the old single malt's taking a hammering by now.' Their laughter began to subside.

'Seriously, Toby.' He straightened his face, then snorted through his nose and began to giggle again. 'Stop it!' Leone was going the same way. 'This is serious.'

'I'm OK. Wait till I get back to chambers with this one.'

'Where are you going now?'

Her question straightened his face completely; there was work to be done. 'Back to the Yard to pick up on the green car trace. It's early days, but worth a look. What about you?'

'The office; I'm expecting a call from Jack.'

'Is he all right after the incident the other night?'

She couldn't say. Leone didn't know what Jack was going through right now; she wished that she did.

CHAPTER THIRTY-TWO

J ack was apprehensive. He didn't want to go back and visit a terrible time in his past, but felt robbed by circumstances of choice in the matter. As the key entered the front door of his flat he wondered how changed he would be by the experience ahead. But he was being cowardly and selfish. There were others involved now. Leone's home was bugged, Jacobson was probably in danger and Pat Barraclough was dead.

Should he go to the police – at least try to explain? Taylor, Berkeley, Boatman, Barraclough and half-remembered schooldays. But he couldn't explain. The blood on his hands was only there because he had lifted her out of the water; would they accept that? Jack had doubted it at the time of their escape and retained that doubt. Had *he* been a police officer attending the scene of the murder, any sorry account so close to a butchered woman would have caused him to smile grimly and comment, 'Save it for the jury.' No, such a course would have taken him out of this game, and time was pressing on Speakman.

Jack moved cautiously into the hallway of his home. His recent experience had left him jittery, on edge, ready; for what, he didn't know. The low autumn sunshine lent some mean light to the front room as he gently pushed the door open. The place looked untouched. Then again, Leone's place must have appeared that way to her. Whoever they were up against was very professional, careful – deadly. Jack shook away his paranoia. He cast his mind back, tried to decide whether he had ever told Leone where he lived, and was relieved to recall that he never had. Unless he had been followed home by the killer there was no other way that he, or she, could know of his address.

Jack moved through to the kitchen and switched Coffee Buddy into life. It was then that the red light on his elderly answering machine caught his wandering eye. There were two messages:

233

one from Tom Leath, asking him to get in touch about a dinner appointment; the other was Jacobson.

'I don't know who you are, Mr Forth, or what your game is, but you were right about Pat. Horrible. I liked her. I'd go to the police about this if you hadn't saved me. I'll explain later what happened. I don't want to talk any more on a tape; too dangerous. Take down this number.' Jack followed the instructions. 'It's eleven a.m. now. I'll be here until two. After that I'll have to contact my old colleagues if you don't ring me.'

Jack checked his watch; he had a bare five minutes to call the private detective. He didn't bother to listen to any more but rang the number instead. After a nervous few minutes the steward at the police club put Jacobson on.

Jack muttered his surname. 'Why there?' he asked.

'Safest place I could think of, apart from the Yard itself. You and Stern got me into this, but I guess I owe you, Forth. I want to meet now, here; nowhere else.'

'I have another appointment,' Jack explained.

'Cancel it. I'm indebted to you now; I might not be this time tomorrow.' The line went dead.

Jack again had no choice. If Jacobson told the police what he knew, that would lead to Leone and then to himself. He didn't want to have to explain why they had run away.

He left a message on Helena Dwyer's answerphone cancelling their appointment. He didn't know whether to feel relieved or disappointed; he only knew that he needed to speak to Jacobson. The past would have to remain buried for a little longer.

Forty minutes later a suspicious-eyed steward demanded identification before directing him to a corner table in a crowded, smoke-clogged room. Knots of tall, overweight men and petite, hard-faced women with blonde, black-rooted hair glanced at him before dismissing any danger and continuing their tales of law enforcement in the city.

The man sitting alone could only be Jacobson. He had his back to the wall, commanding a viewpoint that covered the entire room. The man was clearly on edge. Jack would have to deal with the situation carefully. Before the investigator sat several empty whisky tumblers forming an orderly row. His chubby face was unshaven and watchful; a crumpled tracksuit completed the unimpressive display.

'Forth?' Jack nodded. Jacobson looked down to a chair; Jack sat in it. 'Drink?'

'Too early.'

Jacobson smiled at the light rebuke and downed a double tot of the amber liquid. 'Not for me.' He raised his glass in the direction of the bar. A knowing steward turned once more to the optics lined up on the wall. 'Nerves aren't too good this morning. I'm glad you woke me up with your call.'

'What happened?'

'Shit, when I think . . .' Jacobson stared into the distance, shaking his head at his early-morning experience.

'Tell me!' Jack didn't have time for this performance; his demand brought the detective's eyes around to his.

'This is my territory: don't push it.'

Jack raised the palms of his hands up to chest level. The man was under stress; he didn't need to be pushed.

Another measure of whisky was provided by the barman, who whispered, 'Everything all right, Jake?' He pursed his lips and glanced meanly at Jack.

'It's fine, Tommy. Have a drink on me; stick it on the slate.'

Jacobson waited until he had returned to the other side of the bar. 'I didn't know whether to take you seriously or not, but there was something in your voice . . .' He eyed Jack curiously. 'I got straight out of the office. There's an alleyway at the front; I watched from there.'

Jack was now very interested. He leaned forward. 'Did you see him?'

Jacobson took a sip from the glass. 'No. The only thing I saw was the smoke. He must have got in the back – there's a fire escape. By the time I got to the foot of the building the windows exploded with the heat. I've lost everything.'

Jack nodded sympathetically. 'No insurance?'

'Couldn't afford the premium on a fire trap like that. By the time I switched around to the back entrance he was long gone but I could smell the petrol; he used plenty of it.'

'He?'

'Educated guess; women rarely play around with fire. Our "torch" had done a good job. There was a shoring beam wedged against the door; he didn't want me to have an easy escape. Shit, when I think . . . barbecued bailiff.' He smiled grimly. 'I rang the fire brigade. It's office space so I just banged on a few doors in case there was any illicit screwing; no one was home. Why did he do it? I mean, just what the hell is going on here? It's all over the club about Pat's murder – poor cow, spent half her life avoiding water then ends up drowning in the stuff – then he tries to fry me alive.'

Jack watched the increasingly panicked man carefully; did he dare to take a risk? 'Have you told anyone about this? Any of your mates on the force?'

'Not *yet*.' He stressed the last word.

'So you intend to?'

'Convince me why I shouldn't. There's a murdering bastard out there. He'll know by now that he didn't give me a warm bed for the night; he could try again.'

'No,' Jack corrected, 'he *will* try again.'

'Why? I mean, what the fuck have I done to him? Who the fuck are we dealing with here?'

'You spoke to Pat Barraclough: she could have told you something that he doesn't want to become common knowledge.'

'She didn't tell me anything that I didn't know already.'

'But he doesn't know that: he might suspect it, but can't afford to take the risk.'

Jacobson downed the remainder of his drink and banged the glass down on the scarred table top. 'At the risk of repeating myself, I ask again: who is he?'

Jack knew this moment had to come. Someone had tried to burn the worried private investigator alive. The important question he would ask would be, who? But would he believe him? Jack had to make it good.

'King Arthur.'

Jacobson's eyes narrowed to small slits, his round face puzzled. 'But Speakman—'

'I'm not talking about Speakman. I'm talking about King Arthur – the *real* King Arthur.'

'This is bullshit.'

Jack shook his head slowly. 'No, it's incredible, but bullshit it is not. Let me convince you. When I'm finished – and if you're not convinced – then go to the police, though I doubt they can protect you in the long term.'

Jack spent the next three-quarters of an hour outlining what they had learned during the past few weeks, but was careful not to allow Jacobson to become too intimate with all the details. The ex-policeman forgot about his need for strong drink as the tale unfolded. Jacobson whistled as Jack described his escape from the scene of the prostitute's murder, although he was careful not to mention Leone's presence. He needed the detective's help.

'Any idea who it could be?' Jacobson asked.

'If I had I wouldn't be sitting here. You still haven't given me your answer.'

Jacobson stared intently into Jack's face before flashing a quick smile. 'I'll need some money.'

'Same rates as before.'

The detective winked. 'Double: danger money.'

'We're all in danger.'

'That's your problem. For me this is business, not a *Rough Justice* programme. Now, are the rates agreed?'

Jack decided not to quibble further: Jacobson wasn't going to the police with what he knew – at least not for the moment.

'Where do I start, boss?'

'Ever been to Oxford?'

'The football ground, yes; the university, well my grades from Hendon Police College weren't quite good enough.'

'Back to school, then. I want you to investigate whether there's any connection between Jonathan Berkeley and these people. I don't know what you're looking for, but you strike me as a man with a nose for shady business. Take these details down.' Jack gave the name of Berkeley and his college year taken from the newspaper, then handed Jacobson a list of all forty-three partners at TWC: without exception they were Oxford graduates. He figured whoever was controlling Boatman and the firm's personnel records must be on that list because of restricted access to the archive vaults at the offices of TWC. They could only hope, however, that some connection could be found with Berkeley during his formative years at university. It wasn't much, but it was all they had. Jack just hoped it would be good enough.

CHAPTER THIRTY-THREE

A t 4 p.m. Toby was back in the Central Communication Complex at Scotland Yard. He was on the telephone. 'Any cheques in?' he asked the fees clerk at his chambers. It was a daily enquiry asked by every barrister across the country; the answer was almost always the same.

'Not today. The Crown Court have stopped paying defence's fees again; they reckon there's only one clerk with authority to sign the payment slips and he's on extended leave.'

'Probably in the West Indies with the Lord Chancellor,' Toby replied acidly. It was always a source of irritation: the public regularly read of the high-flying commercial silks or libel specialists who earned the equivalent of a pools win on each case; they never heard of the meagre payment for a scruffy burglary at Snaresbrook on a wet Wednesday in January.

'Anything in my pigeonhole of interest?'

'Just brown envelopes from the Inland Revenue, but the good news is that the VAT inspector's making a flying visit tomorrow and wants all your records.'

'Terrific. One thing you could do, Colin.'

The clerk listened. He was used to members of chambers attempting yet another futile scam to get hold of fees to which they were already entitled.

'Get me an interim payment on the Speakman case, will you? A man cannot live on computer bytes alone.'

Toby returned his attention to the screen before him, the remnants of a sad ham sandwich daring him to take another bite from its soggy bulk. He felt tired – tired, fed up and frustrated. He and Leone had decided to concentrate on the green car mentioned in Pat Barraclough's statement. He had read the news of the woman's murder in the morning edition of the *Guardian* – true to form the paper had spelled her name incorrectly – after the conference with Sedgewick and Speakman. Leone hadn't said a word about it: either she didn't know or she wasn't talking. It was too huge a coincidence to ignore. The day after they accessed the information and discovered her existence it was snuffed out. Someone must be trying to stop them. That told him they were on the right track; but the track of whom and what?

There were ten thousand green cars, at least, sighted during the enquiry; he had set a program to collate them all into one file. What he had to do then was examine how each of the sightings had been followed up by the detectives investigating the case. That procedure was known as TIE: trace, interview and exclude. Once a piece of information like this comes into the incident desk during a murder enquiry it has to be pursued. Assuming that the police had managed to track down the owners of those vehicles to eliminate them from the enquiry, it meant that he would have to look at ten thousand TIE statements, compiled by the officers who had conducted the interviews. There was no other way of tracking down the car.

It was going to be a very long night with no guarantee of success. He had thought about restricting the search program to those cars sighted during the Colleen Bridges investigation but, again, there was no way he could trust the prosecution. If, as he suspected, there was something the Crown didn't want him to find, they could have hidden the TIE statement anywhere in the system.

He could not afford to be slipshod in his search, but it was taking up time that they didn't have. As the hard disk whirred, he read through the rest of the newspaper. One full-page private advertisement caught his attention. It listed a hundred names in bold print: he didn't recognise any of them. His eyes swept to the small print at the foot of the page, which read: 'All these named are police informants inside the ALF'.

Toby smiled broadly. It was nice to see his brother's handiwork in the nationals. George had been too ready to help, somehow. It was no surprise that he'd had his own hidden agenda, and Toby was sure that this outing list was the result of another modem call on the HOLMES system. Jack must have known but had chosen not to say anything to him. Leone was right: Forth was a man they could trust, though the incident in the flat had been extremely odd.

The sound of a door opening caused him to close the paper over the item. Inspector Barnes risked a half smile before closing the door. He turned back to the console and flicked on the screensaver to hide the program from her, though it was a futile gesture: the operator at the corresponding screen in the information room knew what he was doing right down to the pixel.

'Have you everything you need?'

He gestured with his hand to the remains of his lunch: 'Good food'; he raised the tepid coffee to his nose and savoured its aroma: 'Great drink'; then he swivelled his chair back to her and dropped his voice to a whisper: 'Excellent company. What can I do for you?'

She turned her head slightly to one side, then folded her arms across her chest. 'It doesn't have to be like this, you know.'

'Like what?' Though he knew what she meant.

'So you don't like the police. I don't like a lot of them myself.'

'It's not a glee club; what did you expect?'

She smiled thinly and shrugged. 'I'm not complaining, just stating a fact. We want the same thing, you know.'

Toby was intrigued by her will to continue the discussion. 'Which is?'

'Safe streets; killers in their rightful place.'

'I take it you mean prison rather than the gibbet.'

'Whatever the law says is the right punishment is fine by me.'

'So you don't want to venture an opinion?'

'I'm a senior police officer: I'm not allowed one.'

Toby was beginning to see the drift of her complaint – he pursued it. 'A senior police woman, you mean?'

'Quite.'

Toby nodded in understanding. 'It's the same at the Bar. Women have to be twice as good as their male counterparts just to be on equal terms. Then if they don't act like good little girls—'

She waved her hand dismissively. 'It doesn't matter. I'm a big girl.'

Toby gave her a wry grin. 'OK, so you're a member of the human race; welcome. Why are you here?'

'I don't really know myself. Look, I know what you're looking for and I know what you've found already.'

He didn't like the way the conversation was turning. 'Meaning?'

241

'You know what I mean. It doesn't need to be spelled out, does it?'

Toby coughed lightly. 'No, I don't suppose it does. Who are you attempting to compromise; me or yourself? It has to be one or the other.'

Barnes considered the irrefutable logic of his assessment. 'Neither, though that may be the effect. You were very lucky to get away with it, but you did; that's a fact. The point is, you should have had the information anyway.' Toby eyed her carefully, tracing the contours of her bony body for any signs that she was taping the conversation. She followed his gaze and his line of thought. 'No, I'm not recording this; neither is anyone listening.'

'And I have your word on that?' His voice was touched with the experience of cross-examining too many eager constables in too many cases where a conviction was more important than a fair trial.

'Very well. I know about the three files that were dragged out of PNC2. I've known since the moment it happened and I've done nothing whatsoever about it since.' She fixed him with a harsh stare. 'That compromising enough for you?'

'Not quite: you could be here as an *agent provocateur*. This could be an attempt at entrapment. You know the law as well as I do: even if I were tricked into a crime or a confession, it wouldn't make me any less guilty.'

'I'm not asking you to confess to one crime or commit another.'

'Another?' he said quickly, wishing to distance himself from any allegation. 'That sounds as though you're alleging that I've already committed one in the past.'

She shook her head in obvious exasperation. 'Christ, you lawyers: don't you ever relax your guard?'

Toby smirked, then realised it was an unattractive trait. 'I'm not a lawyer, I'm a barrister, and the answer is no. Show me an advocate who isn't suspicious of the police and I'll show you an employee of the Crown Prosecution Service.'

'Point taken,' she admitted. All too often the zeal of a Crown prosecutor had overshadowed her own interest in a case: more Witchfinder General than seeker of the truth.

'What I want to know, Ms Barnes . . .'

'"Miss" will suffice.'

'. . . is why you're doing this. I am briefed to represent Speakman in his defence and will do whatever it takes to save him from a conviction. You are here to do the opposite.'

She placed her hands on her hips. He supposed it was meant to make her appear intimidating: it almost worked. 'That's where you're wrong. I believe that if Speakman has murdered then he should be convicted and punished, but he has the right to a fair trial. You don't remember me, do you?'

'Should I?'

'We met seven years ago. I was a constable and you were still hacking around the magistrates' courts trying to get a practice. It was a supplying drugs case where the evidence was weak. I watched you destroy my shift sergeant in cross-examination. He lied through his back teeth and you exposed him. He retired after that case and I swore that I would never go down the same route. I learned more about justice from watching that case than I ever could have from training school or listening to the old-timers. It's not about winning and losing, it's about the truth.'

Toby rose slowly from his seat and walked around the room. 'That was a very stirring speech.' He continued to pace. 'Never heard it from a police officer before: no, that is a definite first.'

'What do I have to do to convince you?'

He stopped abruptly. 'Tell me what you stand to lose.'

Inspector Barnes let her arms slip from her hips to her sides. 'When I joined up I believed I could make a difference, could forge a career for myself. This is as high as I go. It's not official, that would be too honest: no, it's little sideways moves until I retire. But I never broke the rules, you see. Bent them a little from time to time; it's the only way anything is achieved. I always thought that the system was fair; had to be fair to continue to work. I've watched you, monitored all your moves, but you shouldn't have to scratch around for the information: it's yours by right. They're taking me off HOLMES once a replacement can be found. I have a little something on my boss that will ensure I don't suffer demotion. I want to do something right before I go.'

Toby was impressed with the passionate sadness of the woman's speech. 'Which is what?' The edge of sarcasm was now absent from his voice.

'You want to know who owned the green car that Pat Barraclough saw the night of the first abduction.'

243

Toby's eyebrows rose. 'You know?'

She nodded firmly then moved towards the computer. Inspector Barnes flipped the screensaver off, keyed in several commands and waited patiently for the matrix to conjure up a name. Toby hovered by her shoulder in anticipation.

'Be prepared for a shock.'

When the name appeared, Toby Sloane wasn't shocked: he was stunned.

'You wouldn't have found it otherwise, Mr Sloane: like many aspects of this case it's been buried under a landslide of irrelevant documents. Good luck: you're on your own.'

He was still too blitzed by the revelation to speak, and was unaware of the policewoman's exit from the room.

He snatched the phone from its cradle and telephoned the home number of Leone Stern. They needed to talk, they needed to know what to do next; it was too big for one person. There was no reply. He decided against leaving a recorded message on her answerphone. Instead he attempted to call her at the office, but her secretary had no idea where she was.

'Shit, Leone,' he muttered, 'where the hell are you?'

CHAPTER THIRTY-FOUR

Jacobson's train took almost an hour to complete the journey to Oxford. The late-autumn chill had bitten through the train's ineffective heating system and caused the inside of the windows to steam over. Jacobson didn't care. He didn't want to see the outside world trundling past. Twee countryside and autumnal peace were not his kind of thing at all. Give him a decent boozer and a game of cards: that was his peace, his personal bliss. Still, he had 200 quid in his wallet and a job to do. He was sure he could spin the task out until the money was gone. The return ticket ensured he would get home.

Home. That was a joke. The office was reduced to crumbling ashes; his clothes had gone up too. If it hadn't been for his mum hanging onto some of his old gear he would have been wearing a tracksuit again. As it was, fashion had come full circle and the flared trousers and tie-dye top from his days of 'love and peace' were now strangely in vogue. He decided to flog them down at the market stall his cousin ran when he got back to London.

Forth had clued him in on what he knew about Berkeley, which wasn't very much, a lot of supposition really. Nevertheless, Jacobson had made a couple of calls before he'd jumped on the train that morning. It appeared they were on the right track; the banker had been very bent.

He crossed his legs at the ankle and slapped them down on the seat opposite; they couldn't be far from Oxford now. He'd told Forth the truth about the place: he'd only been to football matches there. He hadn't told him in what capacity. Things had been pretty smart then: not long out of police training college, then seconded to an infiltration unit of the anti-hooligan squad. His accent and background provided the perfect cover as a Millwall fan on the rampage at an away game. To be honest, he'd quite enjoyed the violence; nothing too savage. Then a fifteen-year-old got stabbed

245

in the back at the Oxford United ground. He'd got involved and the cover was blown. The Millwall fan was still inside; at least, he hoped he was.

That had been his last trip here. He knew a few Oxford graduates, though. They minced into the Met on the graduate entry scheme and spent about half an hour on the beat as a PC before being spirited away to Bramshill Training College for a glowing, brown-tonguing career.

The guidebook he'd picked up at the station bookshop spoke of the soaring beauty of the place. The Bodleian Library, Christchurch and the Isis, the sense of history, of timelessness; it was all bollocks to him. He needed to find the bloke who had tried to fry him and butchered Fat Patty. If what he was doing could help then he was all for it: besides, this was an all-expenses-paid holiday and it would be safe.

An annoyingly cheerful guard announced that the train would be arriving, 'in our beautiful city of Oxford in two minutes.'

Jacobson slung his sports holdall over his shoulder and slouched along the carriage aisle as the train reached his destination. Students – Christ, you could spot them a universe away: peachy complexions and exaggerated farewells, cashmere sweaters with designer holes at the elbows for that evaporated-family-fortune look, and bikes, bikes everywhere. They wouldn't last a nanosecond in London with the traffic and the mountain-bike thieves.

As he made his way to the Tourist Information Centre, the prettiness of the late-blooming flowers and the grandeur of the architecture settled a gloom on his mood: he needed a drink, but a map from the Information Centre would be required to formulate his strategy.

After queueing for fifteen minutes behind a group of confused Italians he eventually paid for his guide and carried it to the nearest boozer. The decor was disgraceful: bare bulbs peeped from the ceiling, the air was choked with smoke and thronged with unshaven men playing pool and drinking hard, even at that time of day. Jacobson sighed with relief. This was more like it – he felt at home. The barman who took his order for a pint of premium-strength lager and a large Scotch was acceptably surly, though lacked the real edge of menace that a Cockney in his job would bring to the task. Jacobson thought the touch of slopping some of the pint over the filthy counter helped a little. Two hundred quid would go a long way in this place.

'You got any accommodation?'

The whey-faced landlord wiped a glass with a filthy cloth. 'It's cash up front, fifteen quid a night, no breakfast, no women unless you sort it out through me.'

'You're on.'

Jacobson always separated any rolls of cash into smaller caches – that way, no jealous drinkers would hit on him for a pint or try to roll him when the pubs shut. He selected three five-pound notes from some loose change and placed them in the puddle his spilled beer had created.

'I don't like hippies,' the man warned as he shook off the excess liquid from the cash.

'Me neither,' said Jacobson enigmatically, mindful of how he was dressed. He grinned to himself as the landlord scratched his simian forehead in genuine puzzlement. This would do; this would do nicely.

After a couple of drinks he was feeling nicely refreshed, and able to study the geography of the place. Most of the colleges were neatly positioned in a roughly central area. It looked as though the city had grown round them, rather than the reverse. He pinpointed the one he would concentrate on and was delighted to see there were over half a dozen pubs within staggering distance of it. He was feeling much better. Tony Jacobson raised a glass to Mr Jack Forth and Miss Leone Stern. They'd made him feel like a proper copper again. There was nothing like a clear new day to start a job; tomorrow would do nicely.

'Toby, you can't be serious.' But she could see by his face, across the snack bar's table, that he was. He looked suddenly older, weighed down with the seriousness of what he had recently learned. He had eventually tracked her down in the library of Teal, Windle and Crichton and the timbre of his voice had soon convinced her that the news he had to impart was too important to deliver over the telephone. Besides which, after Jack's discovery of the bugs in her flat, she didn't feel happy about talking anywhere that wasn't face to face and wasn't private.

'Here, I took a copy of the report.' He produced the document solemnly, as if it were a tablet of stone.

Leone read how senior officers had interviewed the car's owner some months after the event and how, through the TIE procedure, he had been eliminated from the enquiries. On the night of Colleen Bridges' disappearance the car had been garaged, according to the statement. 'It could be the truth. Pat Barraclough . . .' She dropped her voice to a low murmur as Toby looked around the quiet snack bar nervously. 'She didn't know the full registration number of the vehicle. It just needs to be one digit out to be completely misleading.'

'That's what I thought, so I clicked onto a reference number at the foot of the page.' He pointed to it; it meant nothing to her. 'What came up was the original witness statement made by Pat Barraclough.'

'We already have that,' Leone said, 'don't we?'

'No. What we have is a doctored version – the one that makes no mention of a full and accurate registration number and make of car. She must have been warned off or paid off. The owner certainly has enough money and influence to do that.'

Leone knew he was right. The name had stood out when she saw it on the document. He was one of the richest men in the country. But more than that, Sir Colin Bigg was the owner of TWC's largest client – Bigg Truck Haulage, Speakman's employers.

'If,' Toby began, 'it was a genuine error, why was the statement doctored?'

'That's not what really bothers me. What bothers me is why the maker of this statement is now lying on a mortuary slab,' Leone replied.

'We have to go to the police with this,' he said forcefully.

'Think, Toby. It must have been the police who altered the statement. Do you think for one moment that once we raise the issue we'll ever see it again?'

'But I have a copy.'

'And how did you come by that copy?'

His mind switched to Inspector Barnes. 'I'd rather not say.'

'Exactly my point. They'd explain it away at a stroke, then go for your throat on all the information we've stolen from PNC2.' He nodded miserably, all too aware that what she said was the truth. 'Jack always said there was a connection between the Speakman case and the death of Berkeley.'

Toby looked up over the cup of decaffeinated coffee these places presumed to call a drink. 'What do you mean?' She had to let him know everything. 'I always wondered what TWC were doing with a criminal case: I thought they'd stopped doing that sort of thing.'

'They did. Any crime has been delegated to small firms in the area where the offence takes place.'

'Is he being protected by the firm?'

'You'll get paid, don't worry.'

'I couldn't care less; I'm in for the ride now.'

She couldn't help but smile. 'Someone's protecting something. Certainly the police are involved, or were when the statement was changed, but they wouldn't have any access to my firm. You have to remember that Bigg is a massive subscriber to Tory Party fundraising, a friend of the PM. There may be several agendas, not just one.'

Toby grimaced as he swallowed the remainder of his drink. 'We have to be on solid ground with this; it's no use steaming into a leading businessman's office and accusing him of God knows what.'

'You're right, Toby. There is one thing I am desperately interested in, though.'

'Go on.'

'In Pat's statement, the one we discovered, do you remember what she said about the figures in the car?'

'I see what you're getting at.'

'What we need to know is, who else was in the car the night that Colleen was murdered?'

'One person was certainly there.'

'Who?'

'You don't think Sir Colin would drive his own Bentley, do you?'

'The chauffeur, right?'

'Got it. Find him and we've got the link.'

CHAPTER THIRTY-FIVE

Jacobson's room smelled of all the people who had been there before him. The dirt and the lack of caring hung in the chipboard wardrobe, crawled across the smudged shaving mirror and slumbered in the dank mattress of the single creaking bed. It was mid-evening. His cheap digital watch flashed a red reminder that he had things to do. Before the whisky had forced him to an early nap, he had spent some of Forth's money on a second-hand tweed suit from a nearly-new shop in a back lane from the Cornmarket. A pair of clumpy brown brogues helped the ensemble; a white collarless shirt, some tarnished brass studs and a frayed striped tie finished the outfit. It lay slumped across an orange plastic chair by the grim light of a low-wattage lamp.

He stretched. Nightfall was approaching quickly. He reviewed his objective. Bars were the place to find things: people, loose talk and secrets. Approach a man in the middle of the day, when the sun shone and its light illuminated his life, and the result would be negative; but get him in a bar, when the night was closing in and his gut was full of strong drink, then the truth crawled out for breath. Students were good drinkers, but so were lecturers, or 'dons' as they were known in this curious place. He decided to target the pubs surrounding the college to watch and listen; get the lie of the academic land. If he got a result he would use the forged warrant card in his wallet to push further ahead, but first he was going to check with the college porter.

He rose from the musty confines of the thin cream sheets and candlewick bedspread, splashed a little tepid water on his face, dressed and left to begin his pursuit, foregoing his earlier resolve not to start work until tomorrow. Downstairs, the barman noted his change of clothing with little approval as Jacobson pushed through the thick air of the dingy pub and into the night.

Outside, the cold had snapped closer, forcing his hands into the pockets of the newly purchased jacket. He had a good memory for routes and directions. Firstly he identified the dark, forbidding exterior of the college itself; it looked like a place where gargoyles would feel at home. Students milled around its entrance, scarves wound tight around slim necks, clutching cases, holdalls and their dreams. A dark custodian sat in an office to the right of the front gate. His gaunt features scanned the movement outside his domain; he must be the college porter. Nothing moved in or out without his knowledge and permission. The man appeared to be in his early fifties, smartly turned out in black jacket, waistcoat and sombre tie. He nodded curtly as Jacobson approached the open door.

'Good evening,' Jacobson offered.

'Sir,' the man replied crisply but without respect.

'You'll be the porter?'

'Sir.' His tone remained the same.

'I mean the man who counts around here.'

'Some say that, sir, I just do my job. May I ask what it is you want?'

'Information.'

'Are you from the newspapers? I don't talk to the newspapers.'

Jacobson realised he would have to use the bogus warrant card earlier than he had expected. He produced it at a reasonable distance and in bad light. 'Metropolitan Police: DI Denny.' Jacobson spoke in a firm, loud voice.

The porter moved quickly to the door, ushered him through, then closed it quietly behind him. 'Cup of tea, Inspector?'

Jacobson rubbed his hands together against the nip of the night. 'Something a little more warming might be appreciated.'

The porter gave a knowing nod, then reached into a drawer below eye level. Jacobson heard the delicious gurgle of a spirit bottle giving up its contents to a tin cup, which was produced and handed to him.

'Appreciated.' He raised it towards its provider.

'What is this about, sir? We don't often see Met officers around here.'

'I didn't get your name.'

'Briggs, sir. The gentlemen here call me Basher, though I don't know why.'

Jacobson glanced at the porter's hugely knuckled hands and

could hazard a guess. 'How long have you held this job, Mr Briggs?'

'Not "Mr", sir; Briggs is my name and I'm proud to be called by it. Chief Porter, ten years come Christmas.'

It was the period before that Jacobson was concerned with. 'What about before that?' He took a nip from the blended whisky in the cup.

'Assistant Porter for fifteen years after serving with the Durham Light Infantry for twelve.'

That explained a lot.

'RSM?'

'Colour RSM,' Briggs corrected him proudly.

'I'm trying to trace a couple of old boys.' Briggs's face darkened. 'No scandal, I promise; purely routine.'

'Who are the gentlemen?'

Jacobson gave a few names he'd memorised from the list. At the mention of Berkeley, Briggs's face hardened.

'I read about Mr Berkeley in the newspaper. Terrible shame, an accident like that. It was an accident, wasn't it, sir?'

'Of course it was. You haven't heard any different, have you?'

'Just making things clear so far as the college is concerned.'

'Understood, Briggs.' He waited for further details.

'As I say, I was the assistant porter at the time. Mr Ashurst was in charge then; he dealt with discipline.'

'Is there much call for discipline in a place like this?'

'Not so much now; most of the students are here to study. It wasn't always like that.'

'How was it, then?'

Briggs looked bathed in nostalgia. 'Different, that's all; different.'

Jacobson had to get him back on the right track. 'Do you remember Mr Berkeley's friends; anyone he hung around with?'

'He had his fair share of the boys, if you know what I mean, but he did have an older bloke that he was friendly with.'

'Can you remember his name? Did I mention it?'

The porter shook his head. 'Nah, I can only remember him as a cool one. An orphan, if I remember rightly; a bit older than Mr Berkeley; a postgraduate. Not the same breeding but clever enough. They were in the same boat, I'm sure.'

'Sorry?'

'The college boat – a coxed four. Mr Berkeley was cox, his mate was stroke; I don't recall the other crew members. I always thought it was odd the two were friends. Still, there's nothing queer as—'

'Undergraduates?'

The quip caused the porter to stop in his flow. 'Folk,' he said suspiciously. 'You haven't told me what this is about, sir.'

Jacobson saw off the remaining drink in his cup. 'I'm afraid I'm as much in the dark as you; just following orders. You'll remember what that's like.'

Briggs moved towards the door. 'If that will be all, Inspector?' He began to open it. Jacobson felt the rush of cool air begin to sprint across the cosy haven.

'Mr Ashurst; what happened to him?'

'Sad tale. Dismissed for thieving just before I took over.' He pulled open the door to its full extent and gestured with his arm for Jacobson to leave.

'Is he still alive?'

Briggs shook his head. 'Barely, he's drinking himself to death. Couldn't bring himself to leave Oxford, though; loved the life too much.'

Jacobson decided to follow the sweep of the porter's arm to the outside world; if he became more suspicious, the local force wouldn't be too impressed with his impersonation of a police officer. 'Where will I find him?'

Briggs stared hard as if making an important decision. 'I suppose it will be company for the poor old sod. He'll be where he is every night: along at the White Hart on St Aldates.' Jacobson could remember its location from his study of the tourist map. 'Don't take anything he says seriously; a very bitter man.' Briggs looked him hard in the face. 'It wouldn't be a good idea to tell him you've been talking to me.'

Jacobson didn't need to enquire any further; he could guess the complete scenario. He felt the porter's cool stare gouging into his back as he walked away.

The White Hart was a brisk five minutes' walk away. Jacobson covered the distance at speed. Cheap Scotch didn't agree with his body's needs and the old, new shoes were beginning to blister his ankle. He wanted to slip them off as soon as possible.

It was a quiet public house. Small knots of drinkers around dark oak tables talked in low voices as if in a cathedral or a church. Jacobson decided the mood would have to be low and relaxed, or he would stand out like a controversial author after a fatwa.

It took a few seconds for the quiet barmaid with downcast eyes to provide him with his liquid need, and he sipped it thoughtfully as he scanned the pub for Ashurst. He kicked himself mentally for not forcing a description of the ex-porter from Briggs, then accepted that another five minutes might have meant a disaster.

It was a man's bar: no fruit machines, no gimmicks, no fuss or flowers, brass rails or vacant promises of karaoke evenings or pub quizzes. The ceiling was dark and low; ancient beams snaked across like thick arteries. Walls were thickly plastered and unadorned. In one corner sat a bulky man staring into a flaming fire. Before him on a squat table sat an empty pint and a tumbler with a splash of rum remaining. Jacobson could spot a drunk at fifty yards. The broken capillaries on his nose glowed crimson in the firelight: rum, all right, and bitter, best bitter.

Jacobson ordered the drinks and placed them before the gazing man who neither moved nor acknowledged Jacobson's presence.

'Whatever you're selling, I'm not buying,' he whispered in a thick, Cotswolds accent.

'You haven't changed, Mr Ashurst,' Jacobson chanced. The man turned his head to look at the drinks' purchaser. His eyes had the rheumy glaze of the perpetually half drunk.

'I don't recognise you.'

Jacobson didn't suppose a rummy's memory would be particularly good. 'Not surprising: must be twenty years.' He sat on the chair opposite. 'I don't expect you to remember me, but I remember you. Who in Oxford doesn't know Ashurst? This is the first time I've been back since I got the sack from Merton.' Jacobson remembered the name of the college from the guidebook.

'You too?' Ashurst asked, before returning his attention to the searing flames.

'A misunderstanding,' Jacobson explained.

'Mine wasn't: it was set up,' he continued absentmindedly, as if the story was boring to its participant.

Jacobson decided to risk another guess. 'That bastard Briggs; we all heard about it.'

Ashurst picked up the rum glass and downed it in one. 'You're well informed. The bastard was after my job from the start – saw his opportunity then took it. Anyway, what's it to you after all these years?'

Jacobson joined in the fire-watching; it seemed the right thing to do. He swigged his own drink down. 'I've done all right for myself down the years.'

The ancient ex-porter looked at Jacobson's clothing. 'It's a hand-made suit, but it wasn't made for you.'

'Well spotted,' he admitted. Ashurst might be an alcoholic, but he was a mental street-fighter. 'I'm a private investigator.' It was the first truthful comment he had made all night.

'And this is a disguise, I suppose,' Ashurst finished for him.

'Something like that.'

It was a stand-off. Jacobson waited to see what the bitter man would say next.

'If you want any dirt on the college and you can pay me you can have it. I don't owe those shits anything. You certainly don't know me and if we had ever met then I would remember you, drunk or not. Now, fifty quid in my hand says if it happened I know about it, and you buy all the drinks.'

Jacobson grinned until his face was sore. This man would have been awesome in his day. Briggs must have pulled a very, very clever stunt to take him out. He removed the fifty pounds from two separate hiding places in the suit. After he bought another round of drinks, Jacobson outlined the objects of his search.

Ashurst nodded gravely. 'The Berkeleys have always been thieves – generations of them. Difference was, they got away with it; that little wanker got caught with his hand in the safety deposit box. He was weak – weak and stupid. The other one, Crichton, now he was a dark one. Very bright, too: he got a research grant to study in another country – can't remember where.'

'Go on,' Jacobson encouraged.

'Berkeley was connected, Crichton wasn't. He soon put that right: even got the weed onto the college boat. Little Berkeley was very proud of it: always referred to the two of them as the "boatmen".' Jacobson made a mental note of the name. 'He was an aloof one, Crichton. Liked the dons, though – one in particular, but the name's gone for now. Anyway, the thing I always remember was that he would row like fury on the Isis. I remember watching him row, like he hated the water or something – really slashed into it. He could pull that boat along on his own, but he was always careful how he got out of the boat at the end of a race. Right up to the side it had to be; right on the river bank.'

Jacobson was starting to believe that Ashurst was rambling until he continued in a very quiet voice. 'Then there was that incident with the girl.' He leaned forward, rum glass in hand. 'I never found out what the full story was, and I knew everything. The Master kept a tight lid on it. Bad though – that's the acid test, you see: the less you hear, the worse it must have been. I never found out which of them it was, but the girl was paid to keep her mouth shut. She was a local tart who liked some well-bred dick. Got more than she bargained for that night.'

This was the stuff that Jacobson wanted to hear. He didn't know whether it would help Forth, but it would keep the money coming. 'What happened?'

'Another twenty quid?'

'After, if I think it's worth it.'

Ashurst looked slyly at his drink. The barmaid had the refills ready on the bar.

'Make it good,' Jacobson warned, placing them on the now cramped table.

'She almost drowned – that is, one of them almost drowned with her in the Isis. If a couple of the other undergrads hadn't been swimming naked she would have died.'

Jacobson's mind flashed back to all that Forth had told him about King Arthur, and imagined the watery death of Fat Patty, but Berkeley had been dead for two weeks by then.

'Which one was it?'

'Does it matter? It's history, like me. No one ever said, not even the girl. You could ask her, though.'

The call for last orders rang throughout the hushed quiet of the pub.

'Where is she?'

'That twenty quid?' Jacobson fished in a trouser pocket. 'It's now thirty,' Ashurst added. Jacobson slammed the money down on the table. Ashurst scribbled down an address on the back of a beer mat and handed it over. 'She's still a tart; used her myself a few years ago. Even tried to ask her about that night. She'd never say a word, though, not a word. I never tried offering her money. One for the road?'

Jacobson told the wily ex-porter it was his round. Ashurst flashed a smile. 'No. I think I've had enough for now.'

Jacobson made for the telephone box to call Jack Forth at home. There was no reply. He checked his battered diary for the number Leone Stern had given him as a contact when he had attempted to find Fat Patty. This time the answerphone cut in. After the bleeps he left a message.

'Miss Stern, it's Jacobson. I'm in Oxford following the connection Jack put me onto. They called themselves the "boatmen": I don't know if that means anything to you. I've got a contact on a girl who was attacked by one of them years ago, nearly drowned. One of them sounds like our man. Look, I'm running out of money. I'll call tomorrow.'

CHAPTER THIRTY-SIX

J ack parked his father's Volvo in the multi-storey car park in the centre of Oxford. The contrast between the bright winter sun and the gloom of the enclosed parking area caused him to rub tired eyes as he placed the ticket on the side window. Jacobson had left two messages on his answerphone, the second giving directions to the bed-and-breakfast accommodation where he was lodging. Jack needed more details from the PI. The information the brief messages held indicated that they were on the right track, but he didn't know where that track would lead them.

Oxford was a city with a split personality. The splendour of the colleges and ancient churches stood out like roses among the thorns of the concrete 1960s and gaudy 1980s architecture. It didn't take an artist to notice the stark contrast between what it had once been and what it had become. The streets throbbed with tourists willing to ignore the squat grey squalor of the city's architectural poor relations. They paid attention only to those items that the tourist maps and guidebooks designated 'places of interest'.

Jack followed Jacobson's instructions until the decaying pub sign confirmed that he had arrived. Jack knocked, then hammered, on the front door until a stout middle-aged woman in a headscarf and slippers peered around it.

'He's not up yet,' she said quickly. 'The pub doesn't open until eleven; come back then.'

Jack believed she was referring to the landlord. 'It's one of your guests I want to see.'

'I'm just the cleaner. I don't know anything about that. But there's a back door that the guests use.'

The door was firmly shut in his face. He scouted down the squalid alleyway past crates of empty beer bottles until he found a blistered green door. It was open – he entered the dark hallway. There was no natural light in the place. Jack found the wobbling handrail and made his way up to the first landing, stepping over two filthy mattresses in the passage.

'Jacobson?' His voice bounced back off the slate-grey walls into his own ears. He knocked gingerly on the battered doors to the two rooms but there was no reply. Jack negotiated the next set of stairs asking the ammonia-soaked air the same question. 'Jacobson? It's Jack Forth.'

He continued the search up to the top floor, where a single beige door marked '11' stood half open. Jack repeated himself again. He heard a groan. He pushed open the door until it banged against a rubber stopper and catapulted back into his waiting hand. Jack looked around the room; it was grim. His eyes swept to a hunched figure in the bed, but there was no movement. Treading lightly he walked inside. 'Jacobson?'

The figure in the bed flopped over to face him. It was Jacobson all right, but his face was badly swollen and one of his eyes was inky black.

'Christ, what happened?'

A single bloodshot eye opened slowly then painfully shut itself again.

'Never argue with a Scot about football, Mr Forth, they can be very persuasive.' Jacobson ran his fingers over his face, prodding gently at the areas of damage.

'So you were fighting in a pub with a pissed Scotsman?'

Jacobson sighed. 'It was a disagreement, that's all.'

Jack bent down to inspect the damage. 'It looks as though you lost the debate. Are you really all right?'

Jacobson strained to sit upright. 'Nothing permanent. Ribs are a bit sore.'

'Did you inform the police?' Jack asked, then regretted the question when he saw the ironic smirk on Jacobson's face.

Jacobson reached to the small bedside table, lit up a cigarette, then inhaled the smoke gratefully. 'Forget about it, Mr Forth; my business. It won't get in the way of the investigation.'

Jack glanced around the grime of the room and smiled at the grandiose title the PI had given his task. He noticed a tiny electric kettle plugged into a lethally wired socket at the foot of the wall by the window. He busied himself making two black coffees as Jacobson repeated all that he had learned the night before.

'I went to the address Ashurst gave me. The place was boarded up; looks as though it's been derelict for some time.'

Jack handed a chipped mug to the supine man and watched in fascination as a large tot of whisky was poured from a bottle under the bed into the dark brew. Jacobson almost offered him the bottle, then appeared to think better of the gesture. 'Perhaps a little later,' he muttered.

Jack sat on a creaking chair in the gloom-infected room. 'What next?'

Jacobson sipped his Irish coffee. 'When I got back here there was a lock-in. I made my peace with the landlord.' Jack didn't want to know why war had broken out in the first place. 'He knows a lot of the scrubbers around here – knows her as well but didn't have an address. He does know the pubs she looks for trade in, though. That's my job for the day.'

'What's mine? I mean there must be some reason you asked me to come here.'

Jacobson nodded. 'Horses for courses, Mr Forth.'

'My name's Jack.' Jacobson nodded again. 'Where do you see this particular horse running today?' Jack asked.

'We need to know some more about Berkeley and Crichton. It seems pretty clear to me that the kind of circles these men ran in wouldn't have too much time for an ex-copper with a taste for drink, and these war wounds might get me into a decent pub but not a posh college.'

Jack could understand the logic of the situation. 'Do we need to visit the college at all?'

'I don't know, to be honest with you, but we need some more background information from some source. I should be able to find out what happened in the river that night from the scrubber, but that isn't enough. It was years ago. You need to discover more about this Crichton bloke.'

Jack considered the proposition; it made sense. He couldn't concentrate on his own life until all these things were resolved. If he refused then he would be just running away again; he'd done enough of that for one lifetime.

'Where should I start?'

Jacobson swung his legs out from under the bedspread and stretched his arms to shake off the stiffness of his beating, almost spilling some of the drink from his mug. 'I once worked for a real copper, a DCI called Boardman; retired now. He used to say, "Dig deep, until you hit bedrock, then dig deeper."' Jack looked puzzled. 'I didn't understand it myself then, but what he meant was, "The darker the secret, the deeper it's buried". Go back to the start. Find out who Crichton is, what his story is, who his parents were, that kind of thing. If you dig that out, you'll find his secret.'

'What if he doesn't have one?'

Jacobson pulled his newly purchased tweed trousers over his gut and fastened the button. 'We all do, Jack. I know I do, long may they remain buried: I dare say you do too.'

Jack didn't answer because he still didn't know the truth – not until he went into deep hypnosis again. He pulled open the thin draylon curtains as Jacobson continued, 'No. If this bloke is Arthur, then he's got tons of rubble covering his tracks.' He passed a drink-stained guidebook to Jack Forth. 'There's a smart library here called . . .'

'The Bodleian,' Jack concluded for him. 'OK, I'll start there. And you?'

Jacobson grimaced as he buttoned the cream shirt up to the neck. 'I'll do some digging of my own. The scrubbers won't be out hunting until night time. I'll find her then. Why don't we meet up for a pint at about ten o'clock? We should both know a little bit more by then.'

'Not back here,' Jack responded.

'As I said, Jack, horses for courses. OK, but it can't be anywhere too plush or I won't get in looking like this.' Looking the curious figure up and down, Jack could not disagree. 'There's a pub called the White Hart just off Carfax. I'll be in there, hopefully with company.'

'You could do with some new clothes, Jake.' He watched as Jacobson pulled the frayed tie up snugly around his neck, then threw an ill-fitting jacket around his shoulders.

'These are new.' He turned and winked with difficulty at Jack Forth's wide smile. 'New to me, anyway. Did you come in the back way?' Jack nodded. 'Fine, then leave the same way.'

'No more arguments about football, OK?'

Jacobson grinned as he walked towards the door. 'Jack? When my mother dies, you get the job. Ten tonight. Be lucky.'

It took Jack half an hour to walk to the library, taking a detour to Crichton's college. He flashed his press pass, saying he was doing a sketch for *Vogue*, and he was able to check the scrolls of former college members who had successfully negotiated the dangerous climb from undergraduate to graduate. The rich oak scroll bore Crichton's name and that of Berkeley in gold leaf, though in different columns. Crichton's date of birth would now be vital in Jack's search for the past of the enigmatic figure.

Once at the library, Jack studied a plan of the building, then made his way to the reading room, where a small booth was vacant. The college yearbook confirmed the Berkeley/Crichton connection: the fact that they had graduated at the same time from the same college, the level of degree each man had attained. Other than that there was little the college record could show him about the past of Rex Crichton apart from his date of birth. Jack was, however, particularly riveted to the articles that dealt with the future placements of the proud graduates. Berkeley, true to form, was to enter the family banking business, but congratulations were offered by the compiler of the yearbook to Crichton himself. He noted the extract:

Crichton, Rex Frazer LLB (Oxon) leaves for the USA to further his legal studies after the summer vacation. Winner of the Oliver Wendell Holmes prize for Jurisprudence, Mr Crichton begins a doctorate in Conflict of Laws at Yale University. He intends to attempt a solo crossing of the Atlantic in June in aid of the Barnardo's Charity. Congratulations go to him and his family for this noteworthy achievement.

There was something important here, Jack knew it. Jacobson had outlined his conversation with Ashurst, the disgraced porter, who had a vague recollection that Crichton had moved abroad to study. But there was something more. Jack threw his mind back, attempting to retrieve the wisp of a memory. He closed his eyes in an effort to relax enough to remember. There was something he didn't want to force from his reluctant memory; if it was there it would come, he didn't want to tie himself in knots.

Frantically, Jack leafed through the college year books until he reached 1978, three years after the announcement of Crichton's departure across the seas. There he was. At least there his name was:

Dr Rex Crichton was guest of honour in hall at the start of the Michaelmas term. He successfully completed his solo crossing of the Atlantic earlier in the year and will present a cheque to the local representative of Dr Barnardo's for over £30,000. The doctor, a former member of the college, was granted his degree by the University of Yale earlier this year. He turned down a prestigious post as Jurisprudence lecturer to return to England and take up private practice. He has subsequently qualified as a solicitor. We wish him well in his chosen future and hope that he will return as our valued guest when he is not practising law at the sharp end.

He knew from Leone that Crichton then took the firm of Teal and Windle by the scruff of the neck and thrust it vigorously into the booming eighties. All that was Leone's province. He wanted to concentrate on what had shaped this man into what he was. Jacobson was right: find the secret and you found the key to the man or the beast. But where did he look? There were thousands of books in this vast place; would any one of them give him the key to the past? Jacobson had suggested that he dig around in Crichton's family history. He wasn't a genealogist; he had never attempted to plot a family tree. Where did he start? The librarian was helpful. He suggested that, if the subject of the research was well known, then *Who's Who* would be a good place to start. If the subject was a member of the aristocracy then *Debrett's* or *Burke's Peerage* might aid his task. Jack found copies of all the heavy books.

Though the name Crichton appeared in the register of the gentry, none of their progeny held the Christian names Rex Frazer. Jack wasn't surprised. Crichton seemed to have too much spine to belong in those tomes. He turned instead to *Who's Who* for guidance. The senior solicitor featured because he held the office of Recorder, another name for a part-time judge. It gave his date of birth and his birth place as Exeter. Jack shuddered as he recalled that the dead girls' bodies formed a circle around that city, but then the police were looking for a savage killer, not a senior solicitor in a city firm. Jack was now more sure than ever that Crichton was the killer, but what evidence did they have of that? The police and the public had Speakman. They didn't need anyone else. Jack needed something concrete to nail Crichton with, but how did you drive an iron spike through vapour?

CHAPTER THIRTY-SEVEN

He replaced the receiver carefully; more carefully than his rage should have allowed. The day had started so well: an invitation to another garden party at the palace was a poor second to his final letter of confirmation from the Permanent Secretary to the Lord Chancellor, confirming the day of his appointment to the High Court bench.

Mr Justice Crichton. He had rolled the words around his tongue, delighting in the crispness of the vowels and the rightness of his recognition, as he showered, rubbing a rough pumice stone over the scar tissue that looked like rivulets on his torso and groin. It stood pink and prominent against the unblemished alabaster of the rest of his body. He had sought his own rebirth by years of effort; the letter promised the heady excellence of complete, unequivocal acceptance. And then the phone call.

It had been some time since he had spoken to the odious Sir Colin Bigg. When they had parted after the celebration that began in the Explorer's Club five years ago their paths had crossed only on the most pressing of business. Even then, Bigg's eyes were silently accusing, though he did not have the vision or courage to wish to know the truth about that night and beyond. But today the uncouth market trader's voice had been quivering in panic.

Crichton threw his mind back to the girl, the first English girl – or was she Irish? He couldn't remember: silent tears of pain and fear possessed no accent, no inflection to mark one of the enlightened's passage into true knowledge. Berkeley's apartment; the girl dancing in grimy underwear, grinding out a pelvic thrust to excite the gross haulier, the grinning banker and the other one; all stripped naked, fondling her as she passed, and their own erections as she continued to dance. Thin ribs and pale, hairless legs as he, Rex, king and chancellor, judge and jury, confessioner and executioner, warmly welcomed the girl's true wish.

With every act of her body in that darkened room for sex, she had volunteered to know, to see beyond and experience the one great truth. He could not disappoint her. How could he deny her, or any of them, the right to that which she was entitled from the moment she was born? The tenements bred them; the bright lights of teeming cities flashed a neon WELCOME to their tired little bodies – used bodies and soiled minds.

Before he killed them he examined them for flaws, defects, moles, birthmarks and scars. Oh yes, always for scars, for *they* were a living chronicle of a body's existence, its awareness, its ripeness. He had paid for beautifully scarred girls from Bogota to Saigon, but they failed to match up. When they had seen him, viewed him in rigid fascination as he took what they truly wanted to give so freely, they saw his own skin's chronicle of existence. As he squeezed the sockets to freeze that last vision into their souls he knew that they loved his imperfect perfection and adored the tarnished beauty of his skin.

How could he know that the weak fool Berkeley had videoed the entire episode in the apartment? The girl, Colleen, had to make that journey in any event; the chosen did not only choose themselves, circumstances played their part. It was all part of the vast wheel that ground each day into segments, and each life into dust.

Now Bigg was panicking at the thought of Leone Stern's insistent telephone calls. The girl had to be taught a lesson: a hard lesson, one that would leave her time to contemplate the futility of struggle. Besides, she was too close now. His own slack rein on her activities had proved ineffective. Things had to be done, attended to, put to rights.

What scars do you carry, my lovely, strong Leone? Are they all inside? Etched upon your body by a dead client, sterile affairs and a killer father? If that is all, then there is room for more; there is always room for more.

Rex Crichton studied the address of the man Jack Forth; her lover, the man he had followed home from their restaurant meeting. Solicitors sometimes made house calls too.

CHAPTER THIRTY-EIGHT

Jacobson was late: by Jack's watch half an hour late already. The mood in the pub was low and slow. Drinkers talked through the quiet background jingle of country folk music. Jack nursed a tonic water with ice and lemon. He could have murdered a real drink, but there was too much to do. He needed a clear head. He heard the swing door open and a high-pitched laugh. He turned to the incongruous noise, along with all the others in the drinking hole. There she was with a grinning Jacobson behind her. A thin pink raincoat barely failed to stop beyond a bobbled black micro-miniskirt. Her eyes were panda black. Thin, rickety legs stretched towards scuffed high heels: that would be her, all right. Jacobson moved towards a man who was sitting staring into the crimson flames of a well-stoked fire. He whispered to the stranger, who turned to look at Jacobson's escort, nodded, drank his measure of what looked like rum, then left.

Jacobson approached her from behind, took her by the arm and led her towards the fire. Her eyes were set deep into grey hollows. This was a woman who had seen too much, done too much, had too much done to her. Her murky past was etched across her walk, her dress and the lankness of her hair. No thick make-up could hide those memories. No amount of nail varnish could cloak the hundreds of backs they had clawed in fake passion. Jacobson guided her to a seat next to Jack's.

'Janey, this is my very good friend Jim.'

The woman looked into Jack's face and almost smiled. He caught a glimpse of the ruined teeth that denied her the freedom to indulge that response. Involuntarily, he looked away.

'You're not a dentist, are you?' The voice still had a remnant of Scouse; the pronunciation through the nasal passage rather than the mouth.

'No,' he answered.

'Some people have a thing about my teeth.'

'Not me.'

She turned to Jacobson who was watching the encounter with wry amusement. 'Well, get us a frigging drink then, Terry.'

Jacobson winked at the reference to the false name. 'Certainly, Princess: Pernod and Babycham again?'

'With a dash of blackcurrant.' She turned back to Jack. 'Get your good-looking friend one as well; he looks uncomfortable.'

She was right. When he had been in the forces, he envied the troops their easy way with prostitutes. He always felt he reminded them of what they really were, when all they wanted to do was pretend that they weren't for a while.

'No, I'm fine. Got to get back to London tonight; driving.'

'You've come a long way for a shag, love.'

'I haven't . . .'

'It's extra for two of you at once.'

'Hasn't . . . ?' He hesitated, then remembered. 'Hasn't Terry told you what we want?'

'Kinky is very expensive; depends on what it is you want.' She was matter-of-fact as she spoke. Jack reminded himself that this was a business: if she didn't do it she didn't eat. 'Where's Terry with the booze?'

Jacobson was there at her shoulder with three drinks. He placed them down on the table. Jack's was a low-alcohol lager.

'You're late, Terry,' he remarked.

'His name's not Terry and yours isn't Jim, but don't worry, it's all part of the game.' Janey took a full gulp of the purple, fizzing liquid. 'You didn't get me any ice.'

'On a night like this?' Jack asked.

'It's not right without ice. I like things to be right.' She passed the drink back to Jacobson. 'Put another one in there. Got to keep the cold out.'

Janey pulled the garish coat around her sparrow shoulders. Jack could see a black brassiere through the crocheted material. Janey followed his eyes and parted her coat again.

'Peeper, are you?'

Jack felt his face flush. 'No.'

'Then what are you? S an' M? Schoolgirl seducer? Golden showers? Fist fucker?'

'Artist,' he said to shut her up. She must have been drinking

270

earlier and her voice was starting to carry. She put her hand across her mouth as she laughed, then controlled herself when she noticed the grim look on his face.

'Sorry, but that would be a first, someone paying to paint me.'

'Be quiet,' Jacobson hissed, placing her iced drink down.

'No,' Jack continued. 'I want to pay you to talk.'

'There are phone lines for that.'

'Not for what we want to know.'

Her face lost all trace of its recent laughter. 'I don't know anything that's worth paying for, but if there's money involved I'll be glad to make it up.'

'You won't have to invent what we want,' Jacobson said, his voice a low whisper. 'You might want to forget it, but Jim will make it worth your while to remember.'

Janey's voice was tinged with creeping worry. 'Are you from Vice?'

'No, Janey, we are not. You're right, my name's not Jim: it's Jack, and I'm not a policeman.'

She turned to Jacobson. 'You are, though, or were: can always tell – cockier than a pimp.'

Jacobson shrugged. 'A long time ago.'

She seemed to measure the two of them, turning over in her mind the options available. 'All right. Money up front. Thirty, no, fifty quid for starters.'

Jacobson let out a low whistle, then spoke. 'It had better be good, Janey.'

She ignored the implicit threat. 'Ask away, Jack.'

'Years ago you were involved in an incident with a couple of students.'

'Jack, love, there's been hundreds of incidents and thousands of students.'

'Not one who tried to murder you!'

The drink in her hand almost dropped from her grip, spilling her precious ice onto the dark carpeting between her seat and the table. Jack could see that her pupils had opened wide. She swallowed hard.

'We know all about it, Janey,' Jacobson continued, 'know you were there, know what happened, know how lucky you were to survive.'

'I knew this would happen one day.' Janey's voice was pitifully quiet. 'I still can't go swimming, you know. Can't even take my little girl to the baths.'

Jack was surprised. He'd never thought of prostitutes having families, feelings, lives – just open, negotiable bodies. He felt ashamed for his narrowness of vision.

'Can't even take a bath; I always have to shower. I—'

'It's all right, Janey,' Jack said softly, 'but we need your help with this. Others need protection from him.'

'But he's inside: Speakman, I mean. He's inside.'

'You know what we're talking about, Janey, and you know it wasn't Speakman.'

Jack's mind was racing. She had made the connection so quickly – too quickly for them to be mistaken.

'I hoped I was wrong.'

'Tell us about it.'

She ignored Jacobson's demand. 'I knew I wasn't wrong: those poor little girls. I thought he'd come for mine one day if I didn't keep my mouth shut. Jesus, he still might.'

'It was two of them, wasn't it? Two of them at first, then one of them tried to kill you. Which one was it?'

Her face switched between the two waiting faces, her eyes beginning to fill with tears. 'Don't you understand? He's out there, still out there. He knows who I am. If you can find me, so can he.'

'Janey, tell us which one it was.'

'Please,' she whispered.

'Was it Berkeley or Crichton?'

'I don't understand.'

'The big one or the small one?'

'My daughter!'

'Which one?' Jack pushed.

'What about my daughter?'

'What about the ones who died: they were somebody's daughters too, or doesn't that matter?'

'He'll kill us.'

'Keep your voice down, Janey,' Jacobson warned, 'or I'll kill you myself.'

'Shut up, Terry,' Jack whispered. 'Look, Janey, if we catch him then he can't harm either of you.'

'They haven't caught him yet: they won't, can't, he's pure evil.'

272

'Who is, Janey?' Jack pressed. 'Who's pure evil?'

'The big one,' she shouted. 'The one with all the huge fucking scars on his body; the one I laughed at; the one who tried to squeeze my eyeballs out.'

'That's enough,' a voice shouted from behind the bar. Jack turned his head to the red face of the landlord who was making his way over to them. 'Get out, the three of you.'

Janey was on her feet first and out of the door. Jacobson moved towards the approaching man, then thought better of it and walked out too. Jack followed and felt a push to his back. Outside, Jacobson stared at a pair of car tail-lights receding into the dark distance, the white taxi sign glowing on the vehicle's roof.

'Shit, we'll never find her again – not in time, anyway.'

'We don't need to – she's given us what we needed.'

'It's not evidence,' Jacobson said, pulling up his collar against the night's chill.

'But it's confirmation. It means we're on the right track and we know his weakness now.'

Jacobson turned to flag down a taxi. 'I can't see any chinks in his armour from where I am,' he muttered over his shoulder as the cab pulled up.

'His body is his weakness; his scars. We need to find out how he got them. If we do, then we have a way into him.'

'I'm going for a drink, Jack. I need to think. You?'

'Back home, like I said. When are you coming back?'

'I'll be in touch. By the way, you didn't give Janey her money. Hand it over; I'll see she gets it.'

'No. It was good for her soul to do it for nothing. What about you?' The taxi beeped its horn.

'I haven't got a soul, but I'm gonna hunt this bastard down. Later.' Jacobson swung himself into the cab, closed the door. As it moved away, Jack felt the chill of the cold himself. It would be a long night. It was time to return to London.

As he picked his way through the streets to his father's car, he mulled the story over. How did Crichton get the scars? That was the key to his hatred. The FBI profiling had made it clear that some childhood trauma had shaped him: what that was he could only guess, but soon, he swore, he would know.

CHAPTER THIRTY-NINE

A single warm light from the lounge split the darkness as Jack negotiated the drive of his parents' home. The journey had allowed him a chance to think. He dimmed the lights and locked the car door as exhaled breath became visible vapour in the cold night air. The street was quiet. Jack gently padded to the front door, inserted his key and entered.

Leone had taken his call from Oxford before his departure. All the others were asleep. She had insisted on waiting up; he hadn't argued. He opened the door to the lounge, where Leone had fallen asleep over a bulky file on the sofa, her long legs encased in a pair of tight tracksuit bottoms: a baggy grey sweatshirt lessened the impressive span of her swimmer's shoulders. She woke with a start, stared wildly around the room for a second, then settled a warm weary smile on him.

'Jack.' Her voice was low and thick with sleep. 'You don't know how good it is to see you.'

'It took longer than I thought.' Leone waved a dismissive hand. 'Hollie OK?'

'She wanted to stay up but her grandma appealed to her vanity – said she'd look prettier in the morning.'

Jack nodded thoughtfully. His mother always knew the way to the heart of a matter. The only time she had failed had been during his breakdown. At least, she called it failure; he called it caring. 'What about you?'

Leone stretched her arms high above her shoulders, turned her head sideways and yawned like a great cat. Jack noticed her sharp teeth in the semi-light of the room. She looked feral, untamed, untameable. 'I never look good in the morning.'

Jack knew he would love to find out. She flicked a quizzical glance in his direction, as if reading his mind. He dropped his eyes and removed his jacket.

'Want a drink? Dad's got some terrific malts.'

'I know; that's why I fell asleep.'

Jack grinned knowingly. His old man was a charming dark horse; he'd never have won Jack's mother otherwise. 'Have you told them anything?'

'They haven't asked. Apart from Hollie; she never stops.'

'She has a lively mind.'

'And imagination,' Leone added. 'Thinks we're going steady. Quaint, huh?'

Jack poured two large measures of the fifteen-year-old Laphroaig into chunky tumblers and handed one to Leone. 'Are we?' he asked, sitting down next to her.

As she tasted the peaty drink, a small drop spilled from her thick lower lip. Instinctively, he reached out a finger to halt its progress. Before he reached the flowing liquid he withdrew his hand quickly, but Leone took it in hers and guided the searching finger back to its destination. Jack smoothed the malt back up its path towards her parted mouth as Leone gently took his finger in her lips and kissed off the whisky. Her eyes were closed and while the moment was brief it was charged with sexual static. He withdrew his finger gently. Leone opened her eyes.

'I'm sorry, I'm not ready for this – not here, not now,' he said.

Her eyes flashed with a momentary anger, then calmed with understanding. 'It's all right.' Her voice was soft as clouds. 'I'm a patient girl.' Leone took his hand in hers. 'Now, tell me about Oxford.'

The next two hours were spent with regularly replenished glasses, as each lived the other's experiences of the last twenty-four hours. Jack listened intently as Leone described her search for Sir Colin Bigg's chauffeur.

'Toby thought it best that we stayed well clear of Bigg Truck in our enquiries so as not to alert Sir Colin. We figured that the car he owned in 1990 would have to be serviced locally at an approved Bentley dealership. In fact, there's only one garage, called Emmins of Exeter. Sure enough, it was regularly tuned and tweaked there. The mechanics put us onto him.'

'What's his name?'

'Brian Stafford. He was sacked three weeks after the night of Colleen Bridges' disappearance when Sir Colin moved abroad for six months.'

276

'Will he give a statement?'

'He's swearing it tomorrow. This guy is amazing: a former military policeman and a real hamster as far as records go. He's got diaries going back decades but, most importantly, he confirms that he was on duty on the fourteenth of September 1990. Sir Colin lied to the police: the car wasn't in Exeter, it was in London picking up Sir Colin and two friends. Stafford remembers they went to a club called the Explorer's and he didn't take much persuading to tell us that they picked up a girl later that night!'

'Colleen Bridges.'

'Who else? We're really getting somewhere now, Jack.'

'Can he identify anyone in the car?'

'Unfortunately not, but he does confirm that when they came out of the club they had another man with them. He dropped them all at an address in Knightsbridge after picking up the girl and waited for Sir Colin for about two hours. That makes four people in the car who had contact with the victim and four semen samples.'

'Why did Sir Colin lie about the car?'

'Obviously because he didn't want to be connected with the investigation. Stafford reckons they were celebrating some big win on the stockmarket that night and were all seriously drunk. My guess is that it was probably the Boatman scam.'

'There's still a lot of pieces to fit together.'

'I agree, but the inference is so strong. Think about it: Bigg is Speakman's employer, who's withholding important evidence from the police. Jonathan Berkeley is, or should I say was, up to his neck inside Bigg's deals. Crichton must have been there, and the fourth man could literally be anyone . . .' Leone was racing away.

'Wait till you hear about Oxford,' Jack interrupted. 'Remember: step by step.' Leone squirmed as Jack recounted the last words Janey had said before escaping from the White Hart.

'We need a sworn deposition from her, Jack.'

'She was terrified. I think she's been terrified since the night it happened.'

'Then she'd make a great witness for the defence.'

'Even if she were willing to testify, what good would her account of an incident years ago do?'

Leone's face hardened as it adopted her public lawyer's persona – the face Jack had seen her wear in the magistrates' court. 'It's called similar-fact evidence and, while that's a legal term, for once it's grounded in common sense.'

'Go on.'

'In Speakman's case the prosecution are saying that if you're sure he's guilty of one then, because the other killings are so similar in their circumstances, you can be sure that he's guilty of the others.'

'Like the Yorkshire Ripper trial.'

'A bit. But if we can show that an attempted murder took place in identical circumstances, and we can put Crichton there and at the scene of the first murder, it goes a long way to establish Speakman's innocence.'

Jack considered the information. 'What about the other murders?'

'They're all based on the same facts; there's no real direct evidence.'

'Apart from the drugged girl in Speakman's lorry.'

'Crichton put her there.'

'What?'

'It's the only credible explanation. Crichton is our man; everything points to it. The whole case has been a set-up from the start.'

'That's a lot of long-term planning,' he said.

'He had a lot to lose.'

'But how would he know where Speakman was when the girl was abducted?'

'Good point. Crichton and Bigg have been as thick as stockbrokers for years. The Bigg Truck Company is computerised: the data files will hold records of all the drivers' deliveries, when they were picked up, by whom, and when and where they were delivered. All Crichton had to do was select any spot on those routes that Speakman took at a specific time, then bingo! A thick patsy without an alibi.'

'But you can't know that Crichton had access to that.'

'We have to assume it.'

Jack shook his head wearily. 'It's a huge assumption.'

'It's the only one we have; without it, Speakman will go down the steps forever.' Leone's earlier tiredness was swept away with the passion of her logic.

'All right, let's accept that Janey gives us a deposition. How are we going to tie in the night at the Explorer's Club? Bigg's chauffeur could be disbelieved.'

'We need DNA samples from them.'

'We'll never get them. What are you suggesting, that we exhume a couple of bodies and then tie Crichton and Bigg down while we extract some tissue?'

Leone shook her head. 'No. Before a DNA match is made we try simple blood grouping. I'm going to issue *Subpoenas duces tecum* – it means for documents – on Berkeley. A judge will decide whether we can have them or not. If his blood groupings don't match, then he's excluded. The chauffeur's agreed already.'

'What if they do?'

'Then we look further and try harder.'

'Is a blood sample sufficient?'

'Yes, why?'

'I've still got Berkeley's bloodstains all over my jacket – I just put it in a plastic bag in the wardrobe.'

Leone's face lit up with a ferocious smile. 'Brilliant, Jack. You see, we can do this.'

Jack rose from the sofa and stretched his stiff legs. 'That still leaves the others.'

Leone's animation slumped as her head rested on the sofa's soft back. 'I know.' Her eyes were closed; she rubbed them with balled fists.

'What about Toby?'

'He knows everything,' she said without opening her eyes again. 'He's using HOLMES to run a check on Crichton – well, any cars registered to him that might have been spotted near the abduction or murder points.'

'He's too clever to make mistakes.'

'Everyone makes mistakes. Even the Yorkshire Ripper did. He was picked up because his car had false plates on: it was only when the car was searched that the hammer and screwdriver were discovered. He'd been interviewed nine times in the investigation.'

'I didn't know that.'

'It was one of the reasons that the HOLMES system came into existence. Toby's also searching for hire cars that might have been rented in his name, that might have been seen there. He had to move the victims somehow.'

It was a harrowing thought. The girls would still have been alive at this stage. What awful fear must have charged blindly through their terrified minds? Jack shivered. 'Where does this leave you?'

'In what regard?'

'Well, let me put it this way,' he replied grimly, 'you are defending an innocent man for multiple murder and you believe that the real killer is your boss. It's hardly a mistletoe scene at the firm's Christmas party.' She closed her eyes again.

He looked at her and something inside her connected with him. 'It doesn't make sense, though, Leone. Why did he choose you in the first place if he wanted the defence to fail?'

She snapped open her eyes at last and raised one eyebrow. 'I'll take that as a compliment from you but not from Crichton: no, he wanted the job done by someone he thought he could control. If the defence was too inept then the Court of Appeal might overturn the conviction. That was a possibility – though an unlikely one, knowing the Court of Appeal.'

Jack decided to push ahead. He didn't want any secrets to keep them apart. 'Control?'

She slumped back and crossed her legs. It was supposed to make her appear relaxed, but her face was taut as she replied. 'There was a client – hell, no, a kid, a child – on remand in an adult prison. He was desperate. I was late for a bail application so it was refused. He hung himself. End of life, end of case, end of story.'

Jack could see otherwise. The memory still lived with her and always would. It explained her devotion to the present case.

'There was an inquest – the normal hand-wringing. The coroner exonerated the firm from all blame; the dead boy's mother spat in my face and called me a murderer.'

Jack sat back down on the sofa and reached for her hand. She pulled it away. He took it gently and felt her trembling through its warmth.

'Can't carry the guilt baggage of the world, Leone.'

'Just my own, but thanks anyway. That's how I see my selection in the firm for the Speakman case: I fucked up badly and the firm supported me, now I'm supposed to be a good and grateful girl. Besides, Rex Crichton probably knows about my father.'

Silence descended. They were separated by the insistent past.

'It's late, Leone.'

'Let's sleep here. Just hold me, that's all.'

They stretched out on the sofa, her head on his shoulder, his arms around her, her legs twined around his.

'Well that's the Stern plan for a triumphant acquittal,' she whispered.

Jack loved the comfort of her body against his. It had been a very long time, too long, since he had shared that innocent warmth of another, but his mind was beginning to throb. 'I need to know Crichton's secret. I need to know what it is that drives him, compels him to do what he does. I think we're alike in some respects.'

'Bullshit.'

'No, I mean it. He sees things with enormous clarity, just as I used to. He sees the vast canvas before him and isn't afraid to daub it with his own marks. I've lost that courage.'

'You admire him.'

'No. I respect his intelligence: it's something preternatural, ancient, beyond morality. There is one thing you might not have considered.'

'What's that?' she replied sleepily.

'He's stopped killing girls. He had to, or the police would know they had the wrong man. That means he has what he's always wanted, or is very close to his day of triumph.'

Leone's deep breaths told him that the exhausted woman was now sleeping, but Jack knew he was right. Crichton had stopped and, if Speakman was to remain in prison, he would never again be able to murder in his chosen fashion. What is your secret, Rex? What made you like this? Or were you just a bad seed, rotten from the first so as to be beyond the understanding of this world? Jack felt his own mind begin to loosen its hold on insistent reality and sink into the warm bath of sleep.

CHAPTER FORTY

Thick banks of fog had slowed the traffic to a cautious crawl. Jack's headlights attempted with little success to cut the hazy scene into compartments of vision. He had sucked on a host of tiny mints as he inched his way to Exeter town centre. It was late morning, though it looked like midnight. The earlier part of the day had felt unreal.

Hollie had woken them from their entwined sleep on the sofa; he had been flustered. Leone had grinned conspiratorially at his daughter, who had shrugged her shoulders and said, 'Kids'. Leone had set off for work without reference to the night before. Jack was too confused to raise what had nearly happened. His mother and father glided through breakfast with quiet approval of what they believed was happening to his life, whilst Hollie talked incessantly of her day ahead at school. He had been silent. His eyes attempted to find Leone's to reach an understanding but she too was concentrating on the day ahead.

When they had all departed, each to their separate functions and duties, he had looked long and hard at the picture of his wife on top of the television. He had attempted to find some words or thoughts to describe to her image how he felt about Leone, then stopped when he realised he was merely experiencing guilt. A morning run and a soothing shower helped him to stockpile his emotions on the growing mound called 'later'.

Several phone calls into the day, Jack believed he had sufficient information to seek the real Rex Crichton. Using a battered copy of the *Writers' & Artists' Yearbook*, he had tracked down a magazine, *The Local Historian*, that specialised in methods of research, sources and background material, helpful to regional but particularly family historians. The editor, Dr Bonney, had, on his enthusiastic agreement to take the publication for the next year, given him a sufficient grounding in research to make a start. She

283

knew something of the Exeter area in general, and of the university library in particular.

'You will find back copies of local papers, Mr Forth, mostly on microfiche. They will drive you goggle-eyed, but if you look long enough you'll find what you want. All births, deaths and marriages should be recorded.'

'What about parish records?' he had asked.

'Yes, but which parish?' she had replied fondly, in obvious reminiscence of similar searches. 'The newspapers should identify any church – that should lead you to the records – but you will have to be patient: these things take time.'

Jack had thanked the historian for her help, but was conscious that time was a scarce commodity. He followed her directions through the labyrinth of another city bastardised by 1960s grey concrete, until he found relief in the grounds of the university. Inside the library, he was shown to a booth, where he began his arduous search for the Crichton family history. The local papers had been saved from oblivion for the last thirty years on this system. That would not allow him to find the details of Crichton's parents' wedding, nor of his birth. He didn't know what he was really searching for, but felt certain that the young Rex would have made himself known in some way to the world; he had certainly done so since. Jack was conscious that any laxity on his part might lead to his overlooking a vital piece of information. He began at the beginning: in the words of the song, it was 'a very good place to start'.

It was mind-numbing work. After three hours his head was churning with church fêtes, jumble sales, deaths and births: all the minutiae that chronicled the day-to-day business of an English city. It was a sobering trawl through the lives of others. One day he too would figure in a brief newspaper announcement of his passing. He shrugged the thought away. There really wasn't time for this morbidity.

After a depressing lunchtime sandwich in the refectory, Jack resumed his labours. In the library the morning's students had been replaced by a fresh-faced batch of information seekers. His fingers were sore with clicking the plastic continuation button. He had slipped his suede boots off and stretched and he curled his toes to break the tedium of the operation. It was just after 4 p.m. that an article grabbed him by the eyeballs.

LOCAL WOMAN IN DROWNING TRAGEDY

Jack sat upright when he read the name of the victim, Eleanor Crichton. He read on. The article reported that a married twenty-eight-year-old woman's body had been recovered from the River Otter by the police, that the circumstances were not suspicious and that the coroner had been informed. It went on to report that her husband, James, was comforting their ten-year-old son, Rex, who was in the children's wing of the hospital, though this was unconnected to the drowning.

'More bloody water,' Jack muttered, as his aching finger clicked swiftly through the pages to the inevitable coroner's inquest. He found it in an issue two months later. The hearing had been relatively straightforward.

James had given evidence that his wife had been severely depressed for a month after an accident to their son, Rex, in which he had been badly injured. He had gone on to testify that she had taken to drinking heavily, whilst their son underwent painful surgery. She had refused to visit the hospital.

On the day of her death, his wife had seemed better in herself. There were no witnesses and no note.

Jack concentrated hard. There was something from this information that linked up with the account Janey had given to him and Jacobson in the pub in Oxford. It was the surgery. Hadn't she told them that before Crichton had tried to drown her she had seen horrific scarring on his body? If that was right then this could be the source of that scarring. But it went further than that. Jacobson had spoken to the college porter, who had said that, when Crichton rowed, it was as if he hated the water, he slashed into it with such fury. Had he been scalded? Would that account for the terrible injuries Janey had laughed at which had almost cost her her life? Or was it the manner of his mother's death that made him hate the water as much as he did?

There had to be more than this. The young Rex had to have been affected in some way by all this. It couldn't have lain dormant for all those years. Jack wanted to know what happened to Crichton's father. With any luck he might still be alive and traceable.

An item in the same paper one year later dashed his hopes and enthusiasm. It was reported that James Crichton had perished in a fire at the family home, a small cottage on Exmoor. The coroner recorded a finding of accidental death. Rex was orphaned at eleven years of age. Jack almost felt some sympathy for the young child, then reminded himself that the boy had become a man and that man had taken the lives of seven innocent girls. All this background was not an excuse, but it was a partial explanation. Jack needed to know what happened to Rex after that. Was he cared for by family? Or placed in an orphanage? Something had to have taken him and shaped him into what he had become.

The rest of his search was fruitless until an article from three years before demanded his attention. It outlined a trust founded by Rex Crichton, a London solicitor, to a Barnardo's-run school. So, the orphan had found his place and gone on to make a name in the world. What Jack noted from the article was that Rex had been resident at the school for only two years before being fostered. He also took details of the whereabouts of the establishment itself. That would be his next port of call.

As he shuffled away his papers, Jack knew he was getting closer to Crichton, but the more he discovered the less he really knew. On the face of it, the solicitor had combated overwhelming odds to secure his present position, but in doing so had murdered seven times at least. How do you hide your fury, Rex? Where do you keep it when normality demands your attention? Or is it ever present, like your scars, cloaked by a thin veneer of civilisation?

There was more, much more, but Jack didn't want to understand the psychopathology of a killer: he wanted to stop him, catch him, punish him. But that, as the saying went, was much easier said than done.

An hour later Jack was shown into the oak-panelled office of the school's headmaster. *The A–Z of Exeter* had provided him with its whereabouts and a well-chosen lie had allowed him past the receptionist. The head stood to greet him. This in itself was not a simple task. The man appeared hewn from the same wood as that which hugged the walls, and around the same time as it was felled. His face was as wrinkled as his tweed suit, but the eyes lied about his age.

'Mr Forth, welcome. It isn't often we have journalists visit us. Which paper did you say you were from?'

Jack felt his hand taken in a bear grip. 'I didn't: freelance.'

The intelligent brown eyes searched his own for sincerity: head-masters were experts at this. Jack almost dropped his gaze but he fought the compulsion successfully.

'Please have a seat. I've ordered some coffee.'

They both sat: Mr Peterson in a huge leather Carver, Jack in a straight-back that forced him to sit upright.

'So you're interested in one of our old boys?'

Jack nodded before replying, 'Not just one in particular: any who have gone on to achieve distinction in the world.'

Peterson sucked his teeth. 'With the disadvantages these children have, to live a normal life is distinction.'

'Of course . . .'

'But that wouldn't sell your piece to the press, would it?'

'The point can still be made, Mr Peterson.'

The old man appeared a little more satisfied.

'That would be appreciated by all here. Could you explain a little more about your project?'

Jack swallowed lightly before beginning his pitch. 'Everyone knows about the success of Barnardo's boys such as Bruce Oldfield, the designer, or Leslie Thomas, the novelist, but I'm researching less famous boys who still contribute hugely to the community by their works.'

'That's why you are looking into Crichton's history in particular?'

Jack noted the use of the solicitor's surname in the reference, also an inflection in the teacher's voice that smacked of personal recollection.

'I know that his early life was wrecked by tragedy and his later life wreathed in success. Did you know him?'

Peterson had switched his gaze away from Jack and it now rested on the portrait of a small Jack Russell terrier. 'If you know that then you also know that Crichton has been generous to the school.'

'I read about the trust, if that's what you mean.'

Peterson appeared thoughtful, if not vexed, like a commuter halted in the crossword by a consummately cryptic clue. 'I am long overdue my retirement, Mr Forth. Duty and a love of this school and all it represents have kept me here too long.'

'But you knew him?'

'I met him, Mr Forth, but as for knowing him . . .' Peterson's voice trailed off again, lost in the long tunnel of memory.

'What kind of pupil was he?'

'Scholastically?'

Jack nodded.

'Brilliant – one of the most gifted boys we have ever had pass through our doors.'

'Easy to teach?'

'He knew more than many lecturers, I believe, myself included.'

'Naturally gifted, then?'

Peterson looked to Jack's hands. 'For a journalist, you do not appear to make many notes.'

Jack realised the pad he'd bought in the paper shop was virtually unused. 'I have a very good memory.'

The headmaster stared once more into his eyes, seeming to search for the truth behind his visit. 'Though you are not a good liar.'

Jack felt himself blush. This was a good and decent man and he felt guilty about the deceit.

'I know boys, Mr Forth. I can see their hearts in their eyes and anticipate the men they will become.'

'Did that happen with Crichton?'

Peterson continued to stare. Jack looked back without flinching. Eventually the teacher replied, 'Your question tells me more about your search than your introduction did. Your eyes tell me that you are an honest man. I have lived by my judgement, I shall be guided by it now. If I tell you of the past, Crichton's years here, will it ever appear in print?'

Jack placed the pad on the walnut desk and waited.

'I thought not. I cannot afford to have what we have all worked so hard for tarnished by adverse publicity.'

'If it is, it will not have been engineered by me.'

They were interrupted by the appearance of a coffee tray, brought in by his receptionist. As she left, Peterson asked her to ensure they were not disturbed. She closed the door quietly.

'You asked me if I saw the heart of Crichton through his eyes.'

Jack nodded, he didn't want unnecessary conversation to interrupt the narrative's flow.

'The answer is no, I couldn't see anything: there was nothing to see. I have experienced the selfish and the weak, the greedy and the good. These things were there to see, if one knew where to look, but the terrifying thing about him was the absence of any of these things.

There was an age about him, a knowingness that far surpassed his years or my understanding.' He paused in his discourse.

'Please continue, Mr Peterson.'

'I always suspected that one day someone would come to ask about him. I hoped that by then I would have retired or be dead: that, it appears, is not my lot.'

'He was here for two years.'

'It seemed much longer, Mr Forth, believe me. His departure was almost greeted with a school holiday: it certainly felt like that after he was fostered.'

'What did he do that was so awful? I really need to know. There is very good reason for you to share it with me.'

'I'm sure there is.' Peterson's voice had hardened as he spoke. 'The staff feared him almost as much as the other children did. When he arrived after the death of his father, our hearts went out to a victim of such tragedy. He accepted no kindness and refused any effort to discuss his feelings. It was as if he had none. This in itself is not unusual in a child who had been through such trauma, but he seemed to thrive on it. As I said, his schoolwork was outstanding. He read far ahead of any syllabus we provided, seemed consumed by the work. We allowed him to go his own way, though hoped that he would emerge from this cocoon of concentration and coldness.'

'And?' Jack asked, certain he was approaching some promise of the truth.

'And we were entirely wrong, Mr Forth. He was not created by his tragedy. I believe with all my soul that he created the tragedy himself.'

'Mr Peterson, I've read about the deaths of his parents. You're not saying he was responsible for those, are you? I mean, my God, did he ever admit it?'

The headmaster shook his head sadly. 'He didn't have to, Mr Forth, it was there in him from the start. I know that sounds like the senile chattering of an old man, but it is not. Tell me,' he said firmly, 'have you ever heard the theory of the "Bad Seed"?' Jack shook his head 'Many sociologists believe that we are all a product of our genes and our environment, that they make us the people we are.'

'It makes sense.'

Peterson continued, 'To me also, until Crichton. The bad seed stands outside that belief. Basically, it postulates that some people

289

are just born bad, that they are evil freaks without conscience or feelings.'

Jack was conscious that he was hearing an accurate description of King Arthur. 'OK, Mr Peterson, why should that apply to Crichton? You said he'd never admitted involvement with his parents' deaths.'

The ancient teacher appeared reluctant to proceed.

'Please, it's life or death. I don't use those words lightly.'

'Very well. It was what occurred here that convinced me.'

'Such as?' Jack needed to push. He knew he was close to some insight that might help them to stop the killer.

'Things began in a small way, as these things do: incidents of bullying that became acts of cruelty. None of the children were willing to tell us what really happened, though: it was always "an accident". That couldn't explain cigarette burns to a young boy's stomach. The police were called in on several occasions but it always came to nothing. Then we began to find the animals, or what was left of them.'

Jack could see that Peterson was becoming more angry as he spoke.

'Squirrels vivisected, rabbits from the classrooms of the younger children drawn and quartered, Mr Forth: it was horrible. All of the children – I shall rephrase that – *almost* all of the children were deeply upset by the occurrences.'

'I take it Crichton wasn't.'

'Precisely. I was enraged by the senseless butchery and accused him, here in this very office. He didn't even laugh in my face, just nodded his head as if he had been forced to make a decision. The next day I found my Jack Russell, Chips, nailed to the door of my quarters. There was no evidence, but I knew, and he knew I knew.'

'Take it easy, Mr Peterson, please.'

The old man's gnarled face was reddening by the second.

'Then the fires. We were lucky that none of the staff or children was killed. Crichton was fostered and it all stopped.'

'Who would take him with a track record like that?'

Peterson's voice dropped to a low whisper. 'To my shame, I wrote a glowing report, the best I ever gave one of our boys. I was willing to do anything to rid the school of him. An army family had lost their only son to a brain tumour. I believe Crichton was as pleased

290

as the rest of us to have new opportunities at his disposal. When they visited, he was charm personified. They were convinced, he left, we breathed again.'

Jack paused. This was a huge amount of information to take in and he needed to test the truth of it: the teacher could be senile. 'Why have you chosen to tell me all this?'

There was a moment, just the briefest hesitation, during which Peterson dropped his head. 'Because I always believed that I handed the evil on to somebody else, that I failed. I knew this day would come, Mr Forth. I don't want to know anything from you, just the promise that what I tell you will be put to good use.'

There was one question that Jack now needed the answer to, although he suspected that part of him already knew it. 'The army family, where were they stationed?'

Peterson looked quizzically at him. 'Cyprus. Do you know the island?'

CHAPTER FORTY-ONE

The muted music in Helena Dwyer's waiting room was intended to calm, but had the opposite effect. Vivaldi's baroque 'n' roll always set Jack's teeth on edge. Helena had agreed to see him immediately, explaining, in her soothing tones, that she had other patients but would make time.

'Are you sure you're ready, Jack?' she had asked over the telephone. It was a question to which he would not know the answer until they began the session. His fingers drummed on the table top. The receptionist raised a savagely plucked eyebrow in his direction. He paused the beat momentarily, then plunged into a long, finger drum roll, at which she pursed her lips slightly and continued to type another report on another blighted life.

Was he ready? Would he ever be really ready to face what it was his mind was protecting him from? He tried to clear it of fear. It had worked before. In the Gulf, where the alien sand forced the invader to dream of water, he had dreamed of Fiona; his memories of water were too terrifying to be released untrammelled in the secret state of his memory. But the dreams had still come, increasing in ferocity, blinding in detail, until the moment he woke and they slunk away like old, lonely men caught masturbating in a porn cinema. As the focus of the dreams moved from shadows to blurred light, buttery around the lens's rim, he had managed to remember a little more each time; just a snapshot or a smell, but sufficient to build a dossier of half evidence.

It was that which had led him eventually to Helena Dwyer. The session about Fiona's death had been a big breakthrough. It had forced him forward, to the belief that there was a future. Even if everyone's fate was the same in the end, he believed that the measure of a life was not how you died but how you lived. All the business with Speakman and Leone had come so white hot on the heels of that memory that it was only really now that he could find any peace in it. But there were darker things ahead. He could smell them on the staleness of his breath and had half snatched at them over the last few weeks.

He shared a secret with Crichton, something that bound them in the past and in the future. The water had scalded the solicitor into deformity and then claimed his parents, but there was something more than that.

An intercom buzzed, jarring him away from his thoughts. Before the receptionist spoke he was up on his feet. Helena was patting the shoulder of a young girl, her face marred by a huge purple birthmark; she was smiling. Jack waited patiently until she had left and Helena turned her attention to him. She nodded, a warm smile on her face.

'No calls, Diana, not even if Freud returns from the grave to tell me I was right about him all along. Come on, Jack, we've got a lot to talk about.'

Inside her office, the lights were dulled to a creamy glow. He could smell fresh flowers – hyacinths. They were carefully arranged in a Lalique vase. She followed his eyes to them.

'I know,' she said, her voice an amused whisper, 'I should have just stuffed them in. It's the control fiend in me.'

Helena indicated that he should sit in the deep leather bucket chair that forced his shoulders to relax and his legs to rest, straight, in front of him. It seemed only natural to cross them at the ankles.

'I'm glad you've come. When you cancelled the last appointment I was concerned, but not worried. I know we're getting there. Do you feel that way? Do you feel we're making progress?'

It was her way. Always the common bond of work, achievement and caring. When he had first begun these sessions he had been hostile to the transparency of her technique. Time and trust had shown him that her ways worked because she did care and was eternally patient.

'Sometimes. Other times I'm afraid to keep searching. I feel that leaving well enough alone is the safest course.'

The gaps between his answers and her next question always seemed lengthy.

'What about today?'

'I can't afford to wait any longer. Things have happened, to me and to others, that have forced my decision.'

She nodded slowly. 'Is this to do with the sketch you showed me last time? Is it the same business: the trial of King Arthur?'

It was his turn to nod his head.

'What made you decide, Jack? Don't feel compelled to tell me: it's none of my business, but it would help me.'

'I have responsibilities to others.'

'Are you sure what you feel isn't merely that impostor, guilt?'

He was quick to respond. 'No, they're different things. Guilt is how we feel when we haven't done enough, but could have. Responsibility is doing the right thing, even if it isn't good enough.'

Helena closed her eyes as she worked through his words in her head. 'You've learned a great deal very quickly, Jack. You should be very proud.'

'No, just determined to see this whole thing through to the end.'

'And if the end is bitter?'

'If it is, it is, but I will have done everything I can do to avoid that.'

'But how will you feel?'

It was the most direct question she had ever asked him. In the past she had never once demanded an appraisal on his future state of mind.

'Sad, upset, angry, but not guilty; not that ever again.'

He had been staring at the hyacinths as he spoke, noting the intricacies of the variegated leaves and many-headed lilac flowers.

'You have met someone, Jack, I can tell.' He blinked at her smiling face. 'Is it the lawyer?' Jack pursed his lips. 'I know I'm being a little unprofessional by forcing the pace, but you seem so strong. Has she given you strength?'

Jack hadn't had a chance to think about it before. The white-knuckle ride of the previous weeks had allowed little room for introspection.

'She's very special, very strong, focused, but gentle too. I think . . . I think we've given each other courage.'

Helena noted something on a small pad. Jack attempted to crane his neck to read it.

'No peeking,' she warned.

'Helena, before we begin . . .'

'But we have begun. I want you to think warm thoughts. Warm, warm thoughts of those closest and dearest to you. Smell

295

them, touch them, bathe in them. Trust me, Jack. Do you trust me, Jack?'

'I do.' He could hear the thickening in his own voice. It sounded distant and strange.

'It is time to go back, to the time you have been hiding from all your life. The thing that most terrifies you, the event you fear ever remembering again. Do you know this place?' Helena Dwyer listened for his response. While his eyes remained open they focused on a personal horizon.

'I know it.' His voice was slightly higher, like a young boy's.

'Calm, nothing can hurt you. Where is this place?'

There was a small sob in his throat as he answered, 'Cyprus.'

'How old are you?'

'Ten, miss.'

'Tell me what you can see . . .'

CHAPTER FORTY-TWO

is head was throbbing with clarity. The memories were horrific but he felt whole again. It was like carrying a secret useless limb that had suddenly sprung into life. His mind felt rusty, unused, but the colour had returned. Now he knew what he had been hiding in the blackness of his memory for all those years. Jack blinked his eyes open. Helena Dwyer's face, unprofessional for once, was marked with the awfulness of his disclosure.

'We need to talk this through, Jack.'

'Another time.'

But she was firm. 'No, now. I had no idea what I was setting free. We need to assess any damage.'

'The damage was done years ago. It can't hurt me any more.'

Helena leaned forward, her eyes earnestly narrowed. 'Regressive hypnotherapy is relatively new. What you have just experienced could have very harmful effects. We don't even know that it's the truth.'

Jack uncrossed his legs, then pushed his arms against the rests to climb from the chair. 'It's the truth, don't doubt that for a moment. I haven't told you everything I know; you don't deserve that burden.'

'Neither do you.'

'It's mine. How I came by it doesn't matter – the point is I have to do something about what I know.'

'You believe it – that doesn't mean it happened. It could be symbolic of some other childhood trauma.'

Jack flexed his shoulders into wakefulness. 'I've always known deep down. Ever since the King Arthur killings began I've been uncomfortable.'

'We all have.'

'I mean more than that. I'm an artist, not a novelist, so I can't explain what I mean properly.'

'Try me.'

She relaxed back into her chair. Jack knew he was meant to do the same. Instead he moved towards the door. 'It was as if I always knew something important about it all, like I had a fast track to the answer about the murders, but couldn't find my way into the arena.'

'Arena is an interesting choice of word. Do you see this as a fight between you and him, while the populace watch?'

Jack put his hand on the wooden door knob. 'I'm not concerned about an audience, but it's a battle all right.'

'And you, whose champion are you? Whom do you see yourself fighting for?'

He opened the door and glanced over his shoulder, she looked worried. Jack opened his mouth to speak but could not frame the words to describe how he felt. How could he explain the painful knowledge that if his amnesia hadn't robbed him of the truth those dead girls would still be alive? 'I know, but I'm not strong enough to say. You can work it out, you know me almost better than anyone else. Thanks, Helena, for everything.' He began to walk away.

'Are you coming back?'

If I'm lucky I may have that choice, he thought as he walked past the sour-faced receptionist.

Jack wanted to touch home base. Outside, the world was going about its business, ignorant of the black secret that was secret no longer. He found a silver-coloured phone booth and telephoned his parents' home. He wanted to talk to them all. He wanted to tell them that he was fine, really fine, at last. His mother answered.

'It's Jack.'

'Anything wrong, dear?'

'No, nothing's wrong. I just wanted to tell you that I'm OK.'

She paused for a moment, he could almost see her smiling. 'You always were.'

He felt a lump form in his throat, then swallowed hard, before he began blubbering like an overemotional schoolboy.

'Is Hollie there?'

'It's Thursday: gymnastics.'

'Just tell her I love her.'

'She knows that, silly. There was a message for you earlier. It sounded important, a man called Jacobson?'

'Go on.'

'He said he'd got the deposition, sounded a little bit drunk, actually.'

'I know him.'

'He gave me an address where you could reach him.'

Jack scribbled it down with a piece of sketching charcoal from his jacket pocket onto an Access slip from a meal with Leone.

'No phone number?'

'I asked, but he said not. He said he's left a message for Leone at home, too.'

Jack felt his heart begin to hammer like a bass guitar. He hadn't warned Jacobson about the surveillance in the flat. Jack tried to keep his voice calm and even – there was no point alerting his keen-eared mother to his alarm.

'How long ago was this?'

'About three hours ago.'

Jack ran back to the Volvo. A parking ticket was glued to the windscreen but at least the wheel hadn't been clamped. A dark painting was growing in his mind and his breath was coming in ragged bursts as he gunned the engine into action. Jack steered the ungainly vehicle into the traffic. Night was plummeting onto London. Should he telephone the police? If so, with what? A couple of ancient stories about a badly scarred man who went on to become not only a successful solicitor, but also a serial killer? Get a grip, Jack, he told himself. The pain in his head suddenly notched up a degree and Jack's hands clenched the steering wheel until his knuckles whitened. The traffic appeared to be driving at state funeral pace. Anxiety inexplicably began to overwhelm him. He sounded the horn repeatedly. On the Old Kent Road, an ambulance and a light-flashing police car forced all traffic to a standstill. He didn't know this dilapidated part of London well enough to attempt a shortcut, but it gave him time to plan a route to New Cross and the tower block where Jacobson would be. Jack hoped that the inebriated PI would play true to form and stay in the pub rather than weave his way home. 'Have another drink, Jake,' he muttered as the traffic began to move again. 'Have a gallon, just don't go home.'

Jack saw the sign to New Cross. It had taken him only one glance at the map to memorise it to perfection; it was all coming back to him. The colours of the spilled light on the glistening roads seemed almost unbearably bright. He squinted to lessen the vividness of the spectrum. Jack followed his route, two lefts, a right, straight on at the roundabout, then the third of three high-rises, Hope House.

That was a laugh. Did the architects really believe that these battery farms for human beings left any room for dignity, let alone hope? Jack saw the entrance to an unwelcoming underground car park. It was too forbidding to risk leaving the car there. Instead, he reversed until the rear of the vehicle was just inside. If he had to escape quickly then this would help. He left the doors unlocked for the same reason. He was calm though his heart thundered. A group of teenage skinheads watched him suspiciously, sipping Carlsberg Special Brew from matt black cans. They looked menacing and ugly. But Jack was in a hurry.

Inside the grim fortress the light was hobbled by darkness. The lifts would be slow or out of operation; he decided to take the stairs. The number his mother had given him was 22; that would mean the second floor. Jack reduced his run to a silent walk as he approached the flat. He spread himself against the wall to the right of the paint-blistered door with the words 'Millwall FC' sprayed diagonally across it, then knocked. He half expected the door to swing open with the gentle force, like a scene from a badly made horror flick, but there was no such cliché. Jack knocked again, this time a little harder: there was still no response. He moved to the front of the door, all the while listening for the telltale clatter of fourteen-hole Doc Martens boots up the stairwell, and bent to the rusted letterbox. It squeaked as he forced it open; they didn't get much mail in these parts. Jack looked through. Inside was variegated darkness.

As his eyes adjusted to the gloom he could just discern a filthy sofa and a thin chair. There was no movement inside the flat. He whispered, then shouted, 'Jake, get up, it's me, Jack Forth.'

The interior answered with silence. He decided to break the door down. It was a drastic measure: Jake could still be in a pub somewhere. He'd just have to forgive him for breaking the place up but something felt wrong. He stood back to make the assault and braced his shoulder for the impact: that was when he heard the thunder of boots on concrete. The sound was coming up the stairs. Flattening himself against the wall, he would have the advantage of seeing whoever it was against the little light available. A shaven head peered around the corner of the stairwell.

'Oi, mister.' The voice was unmistakably a South London whine.

'Some bloke's fucking around with your car; you left the keys in the ignition.'

Jack patted his pockets. Shit, the kid was right, but it could be a trap. 'Back down the stairs facing me all the way or I'll break your fucking legs.'

'Where the fuck are you? I can't see you.'

'Just do it,' Jack screamed, then ran towards the youth. As he had anticipated, the youth turned on his heel and galloped down the stairs. If there were others waiting, he would either stumble into them or flush the little bastards out. Jack walked carefully down the two flights. He could hear the fleeing boy shouting, 'Run for it, he's fucking raving.'

Jack heard the satisfying rumbling splash of feet on wet pavements. The sound was moving away. The Volvo was still there, the front just peeking its blunt end out, but the street was empty. Jack dashed back and checked. The keys swayed slightly, as if they had been recently touched. He glanced into the rear seats but the dull grey velour held no surprises. He crouched down to look underneath the car's stomach. All was in order. A sound split the air. It came from the boot. Cautiously he stood to one side. It came again, a low pitiful moan. He flicked the catch. Slowly it opened. There was a shape. It was a body. It looked like Jacobson, but the face was too damaged to be sure. Both ears were missing. His nose had been split down the centre. 'Jesus, Jake.'

He moaned again. His eyes flickered slightly. There was something in his mouth – Jacobson was chewing on it. It dropped to the side and fell out. It was only then that Jack realised it was his tongue. He felt the bile rising. 'You poor bastard,' he whispered. His peripheral hearing warned him of an approach. Jack spun around. The group of youths had grown. There were older, braver, more dangerous members now; some had bottles. He didn't have much time.

He reached in and pulled the dead weight into his arms, wrenched the rear door open and threw Jacobson into the back. Jack slammed the door shut, then leapt into the front seat. He noticed he was swathed in his friend's blood. The key was there. The engine stalled first time. In the rear-view mirror he watched the group approach with animal stealth.

'Come on, you Swedish piece of shit,' he shouted, 'start.' He turned the key again. The group were alongside him now. Some hands began to scramble for the door handles and the dull thud of

301

boots echoed inside the cab. The engine caught as the passenger door was pulled open. He released the clutch and floored the accelerator. The grinning youth's expression turned to puzzlement as his arm stretched with the vehicle's acceleration, then, with a snap, he disappeared. Jack could see him cartwheeling along the road. He reached out for the door, took the inside handle and slammed it shut. He had to get Jacobson to a hospital, if his rough handling hadn't made it too late anyway. Once away from the scene, Jack pulled over to survey the damage. He wanted to be sure that Jacobson was still breathing. Too many men had died for lack of immediate attention. He might be able to staunch the heavy flow of blood. That at least would give him a chance. The man could be in shock already and well on his way to death. Jack pulled off the main street and up a quiet back lane.

Jacobson was breathing very lightly, his pulse barely discernible. There were terrible wounds over his entire body – at least that was what the pockets of blood suggested. As he leaned forward, Jacobson's eyes opened wide, then half focused. He tried to speak, but the absence of a tongue defeated him. He kept trying.

Jack listened.

'Ack, ack.' Jacobson was trying to say his name. 'Or Famiee Famiee.' Jacobson's eyes were desperate – his hand gripped Jack's arm.

Jack rested his own tongue dead on his palate, in an approximation of speaking without one. He tried out the half words. The F and K consonants would be deadened by the sound. His stomach churning, he repeated the message he thought Jacobson was attempting to communicate.

'Family!' Jake nodded, his gaze beginning to glaze over. He found some more strength and nodded again. 'My family?' Jack didn't want confirmation that he was right, but the man's furiously shaking head gave it anyway.

'Now?' His head began to twist at the neck. 'Is it now? Tell me, is it now?'

With his last vestige of life, Jacobson nodded.

Jack saw the thick black blood spew from his friend's mouth and knew that he was dead. He gently placed a coat over Tony Jacobson. Returning to his seat, Jack fired the engine up and drove away at speed. At the first call box, he drew to a screeching halt, threw a kissing couple out and telephoned home. A single steady tone told him the line was out, probably cut. That must have happened in the last hour or so since he had telephoned his mother. 'What are you, some kind of phantom? In two places at one time?' But Jack had seen Crichton's handiwork at Leone's flat; he knew electrics. A time-delay on an outside fuse box would have the same effect. That would mean that Crichton had been near his parents' home. Jack quickly dialled 999 and left some details of his parents' home address. A disembodied voice asked him for his own details. He didn't have time for this. Jack jumped back into the car. He just prayed he would be in time.

CHAPTER FORTY-THREE

The pages of Leone's notes covered all the available desk space in Jack's old room and spilled down to the wooden floor by her feet. It always helped to get her thoughts down on paper; the mind was an unreliable storage facility for this much information. His mother brought her a mozzarella baguette whilst she worked through the maze of data. She had decided to record everything that she had done and learned in the past few weeks. It was dangerous to chronicle some of the events, but worth the risk should anything happen to her. It was the first time she had acknowledged the possibility of violent death. Crichton had killed on numerous occasions and had shown by his murder of Pat Barraclough that the target group stretched to anyone who stood in his way; that now included her. She had rung work and the receptionist had passed on the gossip that Crichton was in the process of being bought out by the other partners and that something 'big' was on the horizon for him. If Leone had her way that would involve life imprisonment.

Leone's neck still ached from the night spent on the sofa with Jack. She sat back for a moment and remembered his deep breathing, his long lashes fluttering in dream rhythm. Sleep softened the sun-etched wrinkles on his face so he looked younger, innocent. She knew he had seen too much to ever be innocent again. At one stage he had begun to moan miserably: she had stroked his dark curls until a light smile had edged his lips and he had sunk once more into sleep. This sloppy stuff had never been her way, until now. All her past relationships had been shallow by comparison, yet nothing had been said, no promises made to be broken. Perhaps this was how adults behaved. Leone shook her head – there just wasn't time for this stuff now.

Returning her attention to the Speakman case she focused her keen brain on what the defence could prove with the evidence now available. Nobody wanted a guilty man to go free. By the same token, she didn't wish to see an innocent man convicted. There had to be a way around the problem. All the statements from Coombs, Trondl and Barraclough were in the 'Unused material' bundle, and therefore available to the defence. The prosecution had buried it rather than destroyed it; that made a difference. Toby would have to show Sedgewick the statements but not disclose how he had come by them. They were in too deep to worry about a little charade. In any event, the fuddled QC would be unlikely to ask where the information had come from. He would be too concerned about having to do some work.

Leone isolated each statement in her flowchart into how she believed it could help them.

Pat Barraclough's testimony showed that on the night of the first girl's disappearance Colleen had climbed into a car owned by Sir Colin Bigg. It was the last time she was seen alive. Her body was found later in Dosmary Pool.

Speakman's work record for that date showed him to be on a day's sick leave. His home was hundreds of miles from the scene. The prosecution were to claim that he used this time to travel to London and abduct Colleen, keep her alive for twenty-four hours, then blind and drown her at Dosmary. It didn't make sense. All the other abductions took place on his work routes. It meant to Leone that the first killing was an unplanned aberration while the remainder were meticulously planned. It also meant that Crichton would have had access to Speakman's whereabouts. Pat Barraclough was now dead but that did not mean that her evidence was inadmissible. Leone knew of a provision whereby a deceased's evidence could be read to the court: that was the way forward.

That led her to the statement of Dr Ian Coombs. He had examined the original reports and confirmed that the police found the hair clutched in the victim's fist and the four semen samples. This was unlike the later killings, when no samples were found, though all the victims had been sexually assaulted. Coombs attempted a match against Speakman but was unable to find one. The test was by way of a hair sample from the defendant against the strands of hair found on the body. There was in law no property in a witness, so they were entitled to approach the scientist for his views. The one thing they required was a sample from Crichton of some description: how they obtained that was a wholly different matter, but they had to be in a position to show the jury that there was another potential defendant. 'No,' she said to herself, 'we have to do more than that: we have to prove someone else committed the murders.' Things had gone too far for the public, police and, particularly, the jury to accept anything else. There was no smoke without fire. It was almost always the jury's starting point in a criminal trial.

Leone turned to the statement from Brian Stafford, the chauffeur. Although he couldn't identify anyone apart from Sir Colin he was firm about the date and the place. They now had proper continuity from Barraclough to Stafford but no idea what happened to Colleen Bridges at the Knightsbridge address or indeed at any time before her body was discovered. Leone was sure Crichton was the killer; it was now really a question of proving it. Would the Crown call Sir Colin at the trial? Would he agree to give evidence under threat of self-incrimination? Surely they had enough in Stafford's statement to force Sir Colin's hand. He couldn't allow himself to be called a liar in court without attempting to put the record straight. After all, they were virtually acusing him of being a party to the murder. It all seemed so close.

But these were all just threads. It was all so frustrating, but then again criminal defence work was always so. The pack was stacked against a defendant. By the time they stood in front of a jury, they had been arrested and charged. The case had been reviewed by the Crown Prosecution Service with an eye to the evidence and the prospects of conviction. At least that was the idea. Having jumped that hurdle, a defendant was brought before a magistrates' court, and, if the charge was sufficiently serious, sent to the Crown Court for trial. Barristers were then briefed on both sides, conferences held and a trial date set. Then a panel of jurors sat nervously in the back of the court while serious-looking men and women in black robes and white wigs listened to the red- or purple-robed judge's words. Then, after all that, they were sworn in and the charges were put to the defendant.

'For God's sake he must be guilty. You only have to look at him to see.' It was too easy a mistake to make. The fact that he had gone through the entire, imperfect filtering process didn't make him guilty – that was up to the prosecution to prove. But there was a saying in the criminal courts: 'The more serious the offence, the less they listen to defence.'

In Speakman's trial, the crimes were so hideous that she would be surprised if they even bothered to listen at all. That was why they had to make the jury sit up and take notice.

She rang Toby Sloane.

'Leone, how are you getting on?'

She told him of her ideas relating to the witnesses.

'Great work, keep thinking. I've been doing some thinking myself. Crichton has two cars registered in his name. One's a Roller, the other's a Range Rover. The Range Rover's been sighted twice.'

'That's terrific.'

'Afraid not. He has a place on Dartmoor; had every reason to use it at the time and the place. The DVLA records confirm the address. He was spoken to once about it by very deferential CID officers as part of the Trace-Interview-Exclude policy. Not surprisingly, no further action taken.'

'He's too sharp to use his own car.'

'That's what I thought, so that's why I've been out of circulation for a few days. I ran a check through HOLMES on all the hire cars traced in the inquiry; there are thousands. I had to put myself in his place. He wouldn't use his own name, but he likes to be clever and take the piss.'

'What did you come up with?'

'How do you know I have?'

'Because I know barristers: they only ever tell solicitors about their brilliance, never their incompetence.'

Toby laughed. 'Well put. Anyway' – his voice was effervescent with excitement – 'there were three sightings of hire cars from Hertz in Exeter.'

'Not surprising, it's a popular place: the Moors are pretty inaccessible.'

'True, but what are the chances of three people, all men, hiring Ford vans over a three-year period?'

'Not great, who knows?'

'What if the same name turns up on each occasion?'

'Get to the point.' Advocates were all the same: they would try to build the reading of a shopping list up to a shattering climax.

'And what if that name meant something, or would if the reader knew his English history?'

'Continue, Professor.'

Toby paused theatrically, then spoke. 'He used the name Pendragon.' He said it with a satisfied meaningful slowness.

Leone was silent for a moment. 'So?'

'So, Pendragon was the family name of King Arthur. He was leaving a calling card.'

'How does that help us prove it was Crichton who hired them?'

Toby hesitated. In his excitement at the discovery he had not looked at its implications. 'It could if we interview the employees; show them some pictures of Crichton and Speakman.'

'Too dangerous. They'll pick out Speakman every time. His pictures have been over the newspapers for months. They'll convince themselves it was him. Everybody likes to help convict a murderer.'

'I hadn't thought it through. Sorry, Leone.'

'Don't be: it's terrific work, it could be important later. Just keep digging. Everyone makes errors. Crichton is no exception.' Leone picked up her Mont Blanc fountain pen. 'What did you say the address of his cottage was?'

'I didn't. Why do you want it?'

'Just for completeness, in case I discover a tie-in to it from some other source.' She tried to make herself sound convincing.

'Are you sure that's all?'

'Come on, Toby, produce.' She scribbled down the address on her notepad.

'I hope to tomorrow: I'm going to the Explorer's Club. Any news from Jack?'

'Not yet.'

'OK, stay in touch. I think we're getting close to him now.'

So do I, she thought, replacing the receiver.

But as darkness fell on the suburban street Leone didn't realise just how close they were.

CHAPTER FORTY-FOUR

As the police car pulled up at the hospital the sergeant was going through the report. He told the driver to park and wait.

HERTFORDSHIRE FIRE BRIGADE INCIDENT REPORT

CHIEF FIRE OFFICER HAMLIN.

ALERT RECEIVED: 9.26 p.m.

RESPONSE TIME: 20 MINUTES.

REASON FOR DELAY (IF ANY):

1. Blue watch despatched two teams. A team were involved in a road traffic incident (see later report 961 b) with casualties. B team were delayed by the traffic jam caused by the incident. All due diligence was used to attend the reported fire.

ADDRESS OF FIRE INCIDENT: 12 THE GROVE, ST ALBANS.

OCCUPANTS: GRAHAM FORTH 68 (HOUSEHOLDER)
JEAN FORTH 61 (HOUSEHOLDER)
HOLLIE FORTH 8 (GRANDDAUGHTER OF ABOVE)
LEONE STERN 31 (FAMILY FRIEND)

ON ARRIVAL:

Smoke and flames were clearly visible on approach. The road is a narrow crescent with parked cars on either side. Manoeuvrability was difficult, causing delay. A team split into sections. The first organised the removal of vehicles which were blocking the tender's path, the second dragged cannon hoses to begin to dowse the flames. I made enquiries as to the occupants of the house. Mr and Mrs Forth were safe but suffering from smoke inhalation;

Miss Stern too, to a lesser degree. Their granddaughter was still inside the premises. Water power was low thus inhibiting the effectiveness of the hoses. The fire had taken hold. The downstairs was ablaze. Leading Officers Armstrong and Hill made several attempts to enter the building through the front door and front room window. The girl was clearly visible in the front upstairs bedroom. She could be seen attempting to open the sash window without success.

A blue Volvo car appeared on the scene and the driver shunted some of the parked vehicles out of the way with the front end of his own. Several attempts were made to stop the car's progress from interfering with A team's fire-fighting efforts.

The vehicle battered its way through, then drove through the wooden double gates to the premises. It continued on through the flames and burst the door of the garage, adjoining the house. I later saw that there was access to the house from inside the garage. A man emerged from the car: identified by Miss Stern as Jack Forth, son of householder. The downstairs windows exploded out, showering glass on A team (List of Injuries, here annexed to).

Mr Forth was next seen through the smoke at the upstairs front window with his daughter. I could see the paint on the outside frame was badly blistered. He struggled with the sash window (which would have expanded with the intense heat), eventually forcing it open. He had the sense to push his daughter to one side as the surge of cold air from outside was sucked in by the oxygen-starved fire. After the blow-back, Mr Forth dropped his daughter onto a fire-resistant air bag, positioned beneath the window. She was suffering from smoke inhalation. Her clothes were cloaked in protective foam. Later medical examination confirmed there was no permanent injury. Mr Forth attempted to make the jump himself, but the window jamb collapsed. He disappeared from view. Leading Fireman O'Sullivan believed he saw him rise again, though this was unconfirmed by any other source. He must have been correct. It took a further hour to defeat the fire. A body, thought to be male, was recovered from the back of the garage area. Clearly, the deceased attempted to get out the way he had got in.

Whilst Mr Forth's arrival and subsequent driving jeopardised the fire-fighting team, his action in saving his daughter was heroic in the extreme. I commend his bravery to the relevant authorities.

312

THE FIRE

After the blaze I made a detailed search of the area for evidence of the cause of the fire. On examination I discovered two, separate, seats of ignition. Both bear the hallmarks of incendiary devices. This is because they both bore damage consistent with extreme temperature rather than that generated by a normal domestic incident. Some small metal components were discovered that confirmed my opinion. These had been placed:

1. By the front door, possibly inside the middle section of the letter-box mouth.
2. At the rear door, on, or near to, a rabbit hutch.

CONCLUSION

1. This fire was solely caused by an act of deliberate arson.
2. The method of ignition was sophisticated and in all likelihood involved the use of time-delay equipment.
3. By the positioning of the devices, it can safely be said that all the occupants of the house were meant to die in the flames.

RECOMMENDATIONS

1. All members of the watch be commended for their bravery in fighting the fire and ensuring that it did not spread to other properties in the area.
2. The CID be contacted immediately with my findings.
3. I repeat the comment made earlier. Mr Jack Forth gave his life to save his daughter: that bravery must be acknowledged.

A full report will be prepared and forwarded to all relevant authorities in due course.

The sergeant closed the file and began to make his way into the hospital with the unhappy burden of duty plastered all over his face.

Leone knelt down beside Hollie, who lay on the right side of the hospital room. The child's eyes opened with fluttering irregularity. A white-starched cloth cradled a shiny steel kidney dish which Leone held close to Hollie's mouth. She coughed hard once more, bringing up the inky black contents of her smoke-filled lungs. 'Where the hell are you, Jack?' she whispered.

Once the services had arrived everything had happened so swiftly.

She hadn't seen Jack emerge from the flaming house. His parents went away in the first ambulance, their blackened faces peering out of the blankets wound around them like tight woollen cocoons. At least they were alive, but they were clearly in deep shock. Leone had slept in a small room at the front of the house away from the seat of the fire and had escaped severe smoke inhalation because she always slept with the window slightly open.

She looked at Hollie and couldn't fight against the tears straining in her eyes. 'Where are you, Jack?' she asked for the second time.

They had raced along the corridors to the same sort of brightly painted and collage-clad children's ward where, weeks before, she had first seen Hollie performing her puppet show. A doctor had busily examined the child while two nurses fixed the breathing apparatus.

The shock had exhausted Leone and she had flopped heavily into the chair at the child's bedside. She slowly rotated her head from side to side, easing the muscles in her neck. As she relaxed, the fear began to slowly climb her throat carrying its familiar hot flavour. Then suddenly with a jolt it occurred to her that someone must have tried to kill her. Not just her but an eight-year-old girl and Jack's parents. She had never encountered this before – second-hand, yes, through reading papers and defending clients accused of murder; but she'd never been right in there. For an instant her eyes blazed with a rush of self-protective adrenalin. They had to survive, whatever it took, whatever the cost . . .

'Miss Stern?' Leone's eyes opened at the sound of the nurse's voice. She checked Hollie's sleeping form. It was three in the afternoon. It all came flooding back to her. She jolted forward, ignoring the nurse's protestations, then wished she hadn't as a violent splutter erupted deep in her lungs. The nurse rushed to her aid. She eventually calmed down enough for the nurse to speak.

'There's a telephone call for you at the ward desk – a gentleman enquiring about Hollie. He's asked if he could speak with you: do you feel up to it?'

'Did he say who he was?'

'Mr Leath, Hollie's uncle, I believe.'

Leone hadn't heard Jack mention any relatives before; how would they know about the fire so quickly? She picked up the receiver hesitantly.

'Leone Stern speaking.'

'Miss Stern, my name's Tom Leath. I'm a friend of Jack's. I believe you're with Hollie; how is she?'

'She's fine, Mr Leath. Did I hear that you are Hollie's uncle?'

'Not exactly, it's just what he told me to say.'

'Who's he?' asked Leone.

'Jack.'

'Jack!' she exclaimed loudly. 'Thank Christ. Where is he? Is he hurt?'

'I don't really know the answer to either of those questions, Miss Stern. I'm only the messenger boy. He said he'd ring me back in ten minutes to see if Hollie's OK but he wouldn't say where he was. I'm sorry.'

'Who are you?'

'Just a friend; I work at the same agency.'

'Why can't he come to the hospital?'

'I don't know. All he said was to tell you that he's all right. What the hell's going on?'

'Did he say anything else?' Leone carried on, ignoring the question.

'Just that you have to meet him in the morning at eleven o'clock outside the Tate Gallery and not to let the police know that he's alive, if that makes any sense. Look, if he's in some kind of trouble then I can help.'

'It doesn't make sense. Why hasn't he gone to hospital?'

'He sounded strained. I haven't heard him like that before. But I couldn't get anything else out of him.'

Leone could see the door to the ward being opened and two uniformed police officers chatting to the duty sister. 'Look, I have to go. Tell him Hollie swallowed a wedge of smoke but there isn't any serious damage. I'll be there tomorrow. I only hope he knows what he's doing.'

She had just replaced the receiver when one of the officers, a sergeant, stepped forward into her path.

'Miss Stern, I have some news. I'm afraid we have recovered a body from the fire.'

'Oh, God,' Leone exclaimed.

'I'm sorry. All the indications are that it was Mr Forth. Formal identification will have to come from dental records. I'm really very sorry. He was a brave man: he saved lives and sacrificed his own.'

315

Leone sank into the chair and buried her face in her hands: at least it masked her confusion and doubled as the reaction of bereaved girlfriend. If Jack was alive, the obvious question was, whose body had they found in the house?

'I wouldn't say too much to the little girl just yet, Miss Stern, until we've had confirmation from the pathology lab. You may as well prepare her. We'll leave you to get some rest now, but there's bound to be another visit once the full report is to hand,' the policeman said, beginning to adjust the peak of his cap.

'Yes, thank you, Sergeant.'

'Our condolences to you and Mr Forth's family.'

Leone watched him march down the ward and disappear from view before reclining back into the chair at Hollie's bedside. Hollie's little arm had fallen over the edge of the bed. Leone slipped her own hand into the hollow and gently squeezed. For her sake, Jack, you'd better get it right.

CHAPTER FORTY-FIVE

At three minutes past eleven Jack arrived and immediately took her hand into his gauze-covered ones without saying a word. Leone looked at them, horrified, and then into his eyes, which had a familiar distant expression. She surrendered to his lead.

'Jack, your hands—'

'Let's walk.'

'What's going on, Jack?'

'We're in deep.'

'Those understatements!' Leone retorted.

'Sorry. Tell me about Hollie.'

'Fine. They're keeping her in for a couple of days' observation but she's comfortable. Your parents got it worse. I went down to see them this morning. Your mother's cracked a couple of ribs, which isn't helping her breathing, but she copes. But your hands—'

'They'll be OK. What about Dad?'

'He's a strong man, he'll get through.'

They reached San Lorenzo's street café and Jack ushered her inside, indicating the booth furthest away from the door. Jack ordered two large espressos, having to shout over the din of the industrial-sized cappuccino machine. He sat opposite her with his back to the door.

'That bastard tried to kill us, Leone.'

'How do you know?'

'Jacobson told me.'

'Jack, they found a body.'

'Jacobson's,' he said simply.

'What?'

'He was dead already. That's why I went back into the house. He was in the boot of the car.'

317

'Christ, Jack, how? When?' Leone's questions ran one into the other.

'I don't know. How did Crichton abduct and kill seven girls? Leone, this man is a murder machine – pure evil.'

'What about the witness in Oxford?'

'Underground: no chance of finding her again. Jacobson found her but got more than he bargained for.'

'It won't take long before the police discover it's not your body. The autopsy should only take a couple of days; dental records will confirm that it's not you. What are we going to do?'

'I'm sorry, Leone.'

'Forget the apologies. You're going to be in the frame as number-one suspect in a murder enquiry. We have to go to the police with what we've got.'

'In case you've forgotten, we don't have any evidence to prove what we know. You said it to me once before: the Crown believe they have the right man in the dock. There's nothing we can show them that would alter that opinion.'

Leone realised that he was right. Despite all the suspicions they had, they were no more than that: just suspicions. Jack told her about his visit to Exeter, but again it was only another indicator, not real evidence.

'Jack, when the police find out about Jacobson's body there'll be a warrant for your arrest. They're bound to come to me. You're asking me to lie. I've lied to them already; that makes me an accessory.'

'I didn't kill Jacobson, you know that, but if I tell them what I think then they'll probably lock me away in a psycho ward. You have to stay with me on this, Leone.'

'What about Hollie? What shall I say to her, Jack? Have you thought about that? When she wakes up, should I tell her that her Daddy's dead, or shall I just say you're on the run from the police because they think you've killed someone? Do you want to run through that scene for me so I can get it straight in my mind?' Leone asked bitterly.

'I didn't plan any of this. I'm just reacting on the move. I tried to get Jacobson's body out of the house but the door to the kitchen caved in on me as I was dragging him. It just hit me that I wouldn't stand a chance trying to explain any of this rationally, so I took the risk and escaped out the back.'

'Better than trying to explain it after you've been on some kind of fugitive jaunt. Jack, it has to end here.'

'No, it doesn't,' he said quietly.

'What do you mean?'

'I saw Helena Dwyer yesterday.'

'That's great. I'm looking after your family while you're relaxing on your shrink's couch. Get real. Speakman's trial starts on Monday; that's only four days away. We don't have anything concrete against Crichton. There's only one way forward: give yourself up to the police. Just tell them everything you know. Even if it does mean that they'll be sceptical about it, they can't prove anything against you. Tell them you fled in panic after the fire, lost your memory – that's not going to be too difficult to establish – anything, but get it sorted out. We'll figure it, together. Please, Jack.'

He could see that she was genuinely pleading with him, born out of a deep concern that he hadn't experienced since Fiona was alive.

'If I hadn't seen the truth, Leone, I would agree; but I have.'

'We know what the truth is: that Speakman is innocent. We have to have evidence. As much as I want to believe in you, there's no avoiding the fact. We can't call you to testify about your dreams, can we?'

'I'm not suggesting that.'

'What are you suggesting?'

'I'm suggesting that you and I take a holiday.'

'Have you gone out of your mind?'

'No, in fact I've just found it. Look, call Toby and tell him to kick up a big stink at TWC. Speak to Crichton direct and inform him the Speakman case is a shambles and that afterwards you're going away on holiday with your boyfriend.'

'This is crazy, Jack.'

'It's the only way we have to get Crichton out of the country. He has to know I've gone: if he believes he can take me out abroad he's bound to go for it. I'll be the bait; you can hole up in Exeter ready for the trial.'

'He won't go for it, Jack.'

'He will, Leone: I've seen the first murder.'

'What?'

'I was the only witness and he'll know it when Toby tells him where we've gone.'

'I don't understand. Where?' she exclaimed, utterly bemused.

'Cyprus, Leone: it's a long shot but it's the only way.'

CHAPTER FORTY-SIX

Friday morning at seven o'clock, Leone slipped out of bed. Her stomach threw cartwheels and her mouth was firestick dry. Jack's words hadn't stopped racing through her head since she had left him yesterday. She found a hotel in the Aussie district of Earl's Court because she couldn't return to her flat. Crichton had tried to kill them; there was no way she was going to invite another attempt. She bought what she needed en route and hadn't ventured across the threshold of the barren little traveller's room since late yesterday. With only a mini bar for company it had been a rough night. The game plan had seemed so possible yesterday; today it seemed futile.

She made a shaky run to the bathroom and pressed a warm flannel against her face. Tensing the muscles in her legs, she tried to stop the weakness brought on by fear. Suddenly, the saliva prepared her throat; she retched green bile.

The beast hadn't seemed so real last night. Then, as the dark set in and the doubles of Londonderry gin clinched her in their dishonest wet arms, facing him out didn't present a problem. Now, as she stared into her own eyes, penetrating deep beyond the mirror's silvery plane, Leone Stern was petrified.

She showered slowly, awaiting the charade ahead, then she washed her hair, trying to massage the reality into her numb skull. 'It's not someone else's life,' she kept on repeating, 'it's mine.' Gradually, the wheels slowed down. Her focus began forging its uncertain way back from the edge of submission. She had to be ready. It wasn't something negotiable. Jack had told her to 'control' and 'manipulate', so instead of worrying she spent fifteen minutes delicately and perfectly painting her nails. Plan your work and work your plan, Leone.

Leone dried her hair, then extracted the new charcoal-grey suit she had bought from the wardrobe. She made two calls: one that Jack had asked her to make to Moira and Andy, Hollie's grandparents, in Loch Awe, and the other to Dr Ian Coombs, the DNA expert.

A taxi dropped her outside the office at 9.30 a.m. She cruised confidently across the foyer; her knees weakened slightly but she managed to make it to the lift. One movement at a time, she told herself. Everything seemed so unreal. Around her the faces of familiar people were suddenly two-dimensional. They walked around her like flat cardboard pastiches, opening their mouths but saying nothing; talking but not letting you know their secrets. How well do we know anything? she thought. All these people, conned and controlled by a murdering bastard. The fuel in her tank was beginning to benefit from the high-octane rush of adrenalin. She was scared, but she was ready.

Leone spoke to all the five secretaries simultaneously; she didn't wait for a refusal. There wouldn't be one. She knew it because it had to work this way. She would be in the partners' boardroom at ten o'clock. There was only one visit yet to make: the personnel department of TWC. That done, she would soon be sitting opposite the beast.

At two minutes to ten, Simon Windle was talking animatedly to Stephen Teal. They sat at the head of the conference table, where they always sat for partners' meetings. But this was an Extraordinary General Meeting called by an employee. Neither of them could remember an occasion such as this. What on earth was the firm coming to when meetings were scheduled at the drop of a hat by a junior salaried solicitor? They weren't pleased. The firm was run by rules and order; that was the way it had always been. Whatever she had to say, surely it couldn't be so important as to interfere with lunch. Today, like every day, it should start at 10.45 with sherry in the boardroom while they waited for the car to take them to the club by noon.

Freddy Foster and Dan Morgan were both on telephones at opposite sides of the room, looking equally harassed at the change in schedule. The fact that their secretaries' presence was also requested at this meeting was another unprecedented outrage. Mr Windle reminded Mr Teal that this was the self-same girl who had created so many problems over that enquiry business last year. Couldn't he recall, when that young thug topped himself?

A dreadful troublemaker. That was the biography that preceded Leone as she walked through the door at one minute to ten.

The two senior partners rose from their seats, through breeding rather than choice. Leone checked the clock. She knew that the door behind her would open in thirty seconds; she wasn't disappointed. As the hour struck, the gleaming brass handle opened smoothly, quietly.

It had been a long time since Leone had studied Rex Crichton's face. He glided the length of the room without looking at her; controlled strides of perfectly regulated motion. The room was hushed as he took his place between the older, but in reality junior, partners.

Now was the time. She could hear Jack's voice echoing, 'Look at him, Leone, look right into him and see behind the mask. Don't be afraid.' She waited for Crichton's secretary to position herself at his left shoulder, then deliberately and slowly raised her eyes to meet his. With the flashing speed of a liar's glance he left her gazing into space; he had seen all he wanted to see. It was a strange lacuna – it confirmed everything she believed. The charade began.

She recovered with the scent of a wispy new confidence in the embarrassed silence that ensued. Morgan finished correcting a writ on the telephone. Crichton realigned an already perfect ink blotter. Leone watched the precision with which he adjusted the water tumbler at his side and peered at his manicured nails on muscular hands. Those hands had killed! Seven years earlier she had sat before him in this same room. His eyes had seemed full of promise then. He'd been a defender of the meritocracy, a man who was willing to give her the chance that no one else would. But what was he in reality? A merciless, murdering sociopath – 'with an overwhelming power drive': the words of the FBI profiling report. An extreme schizoid, who couldn't be controlled by anyone, such was the strength of his desire.

She swallowed hard as all five men signalled their readiness with a collective scowl.

'We're waiting, Miss Stern,' Crichton opened. 'In case it had escaped your attention, the meeting you requested is now assembled, at great personal inconvenience, I might add, to all of us. However, in deference to the degree of urgency which you communicated, we are here. Let us hope it warrants the priority you

323

feel it deserves.' Crichton's voice stank of lawyer's pragmatism overlaid with a frosty hue.

'I called this meeting in the hope that we all arrive at the same conclusion, sir,' Leone retorted, but avoided Crichton's studious eyes.

'Get on with it,' Stephen Teal implored.

'The situation is this. As I'm sure you're aware, I am representing Trevor Speakman on behalf of this firm and I believe that there is a risk of a serious miscarriage of justice occurring when this man begins his trial next week. I have asked to see you because I have been placed in a position of difficulty and I need some guidance.' Leone's voice quivered with a hint of unfamiliar vulnerability.

'What kind of difficulty, Miss Stern?' Crichton asked, direct and sharp, seeking the issue immediately. She sensed how hungry he was for knowledge of how much she had learned. She appealed instead to his partner, Simon Windle – don't allow Crichton any space, she counselled herself.

'A short time ago I discovered a discrepancy in the funding of Speakman's defence. I believed he had the benefit of legal aid to cover the costs; it turns out that he does not. There is no prospect of a retrospective application, and the firm is now at risk as to those costs.'

'Cancel lunch, Miss Wilson,' Teal shouted over his shoulder to his secretary. 'This is serious, Miss Stern; who's responsible for the oversight?'

'I don't know exactly, but it's just one more on a list of irregularities in the case. It leads me to believe that the firm will be compromised as a result of deliberate sabotage by one of the partners.' She couldn't have dropped a more potent bombshell; the room went silent. She couldn't bear to look at Crichton. 'My own position is clear. I intend to offer my resignation effective from the end of Speakman's trial. I shall be leaving the office today to travel to Exeter for that.'

'How did you come across this?' Windle asked suspiciously.

'Inadvertently, investigating the correspondence file. The first person to see Speakman, according to my information, was a man by the name of David Taylor, who was an articled clerk here some time ago. He made a note on the file that Speakman's insurance policy would cover any costs arising from a prosecution. That note was forged. Furthermore, it implicates me in the process.'

'What nonsense,' Teal added impatiently.

'I was led to believe, by the management committee, that the Speakman case was an oversight, yet someone, purporting to be David Taylor, had made visits to the defendant and deliberately stalled the prosecution.'

'So you say, Miss Stern,' Crichton hissed. 'Whatever the position is, it is abundantly obvious that this firm is now funding the entire case out of its *own* pocket.'

'I was only brought on very late in the day,' she replied, icily facing him out.

'What about Taylor?' Teal asked.

'I was hoping you could tell me that, sir.'

'Explain, Miss Stern.'

'I have every reason to believe that David Taylor stumbled across a substantial fraud being perpetrated from these offices. I have looked for his personnel files; they don't exist. It appears he left these offices with an unblemished character; apparently enough to get him a smart position in the City and some "shut-up" money.'

'Serious allegations.'

'I'm fully aware of that, sir.'

'What sort of fraud are we talking about?' Windle demanded.

'I believe that Taylor discovered that a partner in this firm and someone by the name of Jonathan Berkeley were insider dealing,' she said.

'Is there a loss to the client account?' Danny Morgan chipped in.

'No, Mr Morgan.'

'That's something. This matter must be investigated further.'

'If there is no loss to the firm then that's the matter closed and this is a waste of time, Miss Stern,' Crichton said, shifting his position in the chair and leaning back. But his partners shuffled forward, eager for more information.

'Rex, with the greatest of respect, and given your imminent departure, shouldn't you better stay out of any decision?' Windle said politely but firmly. Leone looked puzzled.

'You may as well know, Miss Stern, that Mr Crichton will become Mr Justice Crichton as of two weeks from today. He leaves the firm officially next week,' Foster explained. He looked frazzled to the core.

'Congratulations, sir,' she muttered, her voice cracking. They were making him a judge?

'You cannot leave the firm until this matter is resolved, Miss Stern. After all, you may be vindicated,' Morgan said with uncharacteristic fairness.

'Thanks for the vote, sir, but it's not the only reason I have tendered my resignation.'

'Go on.'

'Regrettably, sir, I have become involved with a potential witness.'

'Good God,' Teal exploded. 'What sort of solicitor are you?'

'Before you go any further, sir, please allow me to explain the circumstances.'

CHAPTER FORTY-SEVEN

J ack flew via Cyprus Airways into Larnaca. It was time to go back and face the thing he had spent the majority of his life sprinting away from. In the three hours of the flight his barbecued hands had throbbed and wept beneath their covering gauze. He'd gratefully drunk a complimentary double Scotch in double-quick time using the fiery liquid to wash down a triple dose of painkillers. It hurt like hell.

At least he was alive. Not like Jacobson. It was awful; the snarling fire had stopped him from rescuing Jacobson's corpse from the flames. Leone had assured him that a routine dental comparison would take about a week. The time to act was now. It wasn't exactly how he'd seen his life progressing, but it had given him time to get out of the country and into Cyprus.

He'd liked Jake. Jake just wasn't good enough; he himself had to be. The answer was here if it was anywhere. But it wasn't an answer he was seeking: it was proof. The proof of the killing he had witnessed but had secreted in the back of his head for twenty-two years. Crichton hadn't only taken the girl's life, he'd also murdered Jack's future.

It was midnight in Larnaca. His progress through Immigration was swift, his only excess baggage the knowledge of the truth. He now knew this place; remembered its citrus tang and balmy air, still warm in the darkness. Sleepy, dark-skinned taxi drivers listened to blaring rock music, waiting for a late-night fare. Arguing families in matching shell-suits pushed trolleys of belongings along the smooth pavement. A grinning, gold-toothed Cesar Romero lookalike swung Jack's holdall into the car's boot.

'First time you visit?' he asked lazily, driving the battered Renault with one hand on the wheel.

'I used to live here.'

'You back to stay?'

'No, I'm here to work.'

'Cyprus, a nice place for holiday, not so good for work. You have hotel? I know good one, my cousin, best English breakfast on island, frie bread, the lot.'

The driver's easy way was another reminder of Jack's newfound memory of the place.

'Take me there, I'm sure it's fine.'

'Not so clean though. My other cousin has clean place. You rich?'

The car negotiated a sharp left-hand bend at speed. Jack swayed with the movement.

'Not rich.'

'Everything relative,' the driver replied nonchalantly.

He was right. Jack's life had been a carefree one until he had become a reluctant witness to Crichton's crime. His reluctance to remember the truth was a cop-out from his human duty to see right done.

'Here you are,' the driver announced, grinning, 'Hotel Emerald. You can even see the planes land from your balcony.'

Jack could have walked the distance, but the driver's cheek had lifted some of the gloom from his shoulders and he happily paid the exorbitant fare. What he had said to the taxi driver was correct: he was here to work. He was here to find the evidence that would clear Speakman of the murders. Leone had been unimpressed by his idea at first, but was eventually persuaded that, whilst it was a very long shot, it was the only real shot they had.

The chipped marble flooring of the hotel's interior told its story. His room provided conclusive evidence of its faded glory and uncertain future. They would be looking for him soon, but it wasn't the authorities he was concerned with: it was Crichton. He wanted Crichton here, looking for him, whilst he garnered the evidence that would lock the sick bastard up for good. It was really personal now. Crichton had messed with his head, but now he was messing with his family.

He unwound the bandages from his painful hands. Blisters bulged from his tortured skin, white balloons of serous fluid squishing as the cold water allowed him momentary relief from their painful pulse. Jack pulled fresh bandages from his scant luggage, then rebound his hands. He spread a map of the island on the cream candlewick bedspread.

Cyprus was split unevenly into two segments: the north, which was Turkish-held, and the south, which the more easygoing Greeks protected so volubly. The 'Green Line' ran between the divided nations, each nationality with its own stand-off border posts and hostile guards.

He outlined the lake in red marker pen. Before he began his grisly search he needed confirmation that the girl's body was still there. There was only one man who would possess that important knowledge: her father.

He could be dead by now, or moved on. The taverna was on the periphery of the Green Line. Jack could now recall the grim mood, the tattered tablecloths and the florid face of the soon-to-be-grieving figure. He had called Crichton a freak and leper, a monster and a pig. The quivering girl's large eyes and distended stomach formed the core of the man's fury. It was twenty years on, but if the man was still alive he would know if her body had ever been recovered. The child must have been Crichton's. Its remains would share its father's DNA. Coombs's report was the key to all this: the hairs found clutched in Colleen's dead hands must have come from Crichton; the report proved that they didn't emanate from Speakman. If Jack could secure a sample that matched the strands it would prove conclusively that Speakman was innocent of the crime. Then, using the prosecution's own argument against itself, if the same man killed them all, and Speakman was provably innocent, he was not King Arthur; that was simply how Crichton had intended it to look.

Outside, the aeroplanes' thunderous departures and arrivals scarred the air every twenty minutes, forcing him to remain awake. Painfully, Jack jotted his thoughts on a piece of notebook paper. He had to be seen, to be traceable. If Leone's part of the game plan worked then Crichton would soon be searching for him. Jack didn't want Rex to be disappointed. The point of her ploy was to flush the solicitor out into the open. While that placed Jack in danger, he was more than willing to run that risk if it kept Leone and his family safe. Leone had argued against it, but was eventually persuaded that it was the only way forward.

He wasn't afraid now. The final session with Helena Dwyer had lanced the boil of his terror and swabbed the pus of his dark secret. It had blighted his life. Witnessing real horror was a system overload of the mind. While sketching killers or serial rapists, he had been annoyed at the witnesses' inability to get their stories straight. Now he understood that the brain attempted to protect its host by the healing process of forgetfulness. Some events were just too real, too awful to recollect accurately. But he knew the truth of what he had witnessed as a boy. The killing, the first slaying by King Arthur – the dead Cypriot girl, the long-dead mother of the murderer's child. He thought of its tiny bones, curled in an unending sleep in the cavity of her womb, robbed of life without ever taking a breath of the future. He wanted to do this, to get this bit right. His amnesia had stayed justice for over two decades. Now that he could remember, he had a duty to see it through and allow them to be avenged – all of them, all the girls, King Arthur's watery Ladies of the Lake. The truth had to be screamed at the world: *He* did this, yes him. I know. He'll never tell you, but we will; we can prove it.

His head was throbbing madly. His notes reflected the desperation of his position. He was tired – dog, cat and artist tired – but now wasn't the time to sleep. Dawn began to seep through the rice-paper-thin curtains; another 747 grumbled its departure from the tarmac as Jack pulled the white cord to crank the wheezing shower into action.

As he scrubbed his aching, blistered body, as the stinging water pummelled his shoulders into semi-relaxation, Jack accepted that it would soon be time to return to the water. It had scarred Crichton's soul, and, after Fiona's death, it had almost broken his own, but he would have to go back in. At Hollie's swimming accident he had been nailed impotently to the spot, frozen by terror and a half memory. Crichton owed him; he owed him half a lifetime. The water. It had begun there, it would end there too.

The shower lost its battle with the production of heat. Freezing water hammered his grateful body. The army had taught him that discomfort was good for the soldier: it kept him awake and alert, ready to perform his duty. Jack had thought the idea risible at the time, just another jingoistic anachronism. Now he saw the truth in the proposition. The chill water hammered a tattoo of wakefulness that he hadn't experienced since the Gulf War. In a very few hours he would seek out the owner of the taverna, or trace his whereabouts. He felt an unspoken debt to the man that could only be resolved by the truth of what he had seen. How the disclosure would be received was another matter. If Hollie had vanished without explanation, and twenty years later a stranger appeared with a sick story of her disappearance, the storyteller would be given short shrift and a couple of black eyes for his tale. Why should the Cypriot father react differently?

Jack towelled himself dry, careful not to anger his burns. They would scar, but didn't everything? He dressed in some faded Levi's and a white long-sleeved shirt. He opened the sliding door to the balcony and rested his stubbled chin on its aluminium top. Larnaca was waking up. Outside, noisy pigeons goosestepped to gather the falling debris from a refuse truck. A rosy winter sun backlit the pastiche scene, spreading dull warmth to the early risers. The light was beautifully unreal. He had misplaced his artist's awe of Mediterranean dawn – it was yet another example of that which Rex had stolen from him – but it had now re-emerged with a purposeful vengeance.

A young girl wandered along the tarmacked street, gazing longingly into shop windows. She was around the same age as Hollie – slightly taller, but her hair spilled out in the same way.

She was really what this whole thing was about, his Hollie. She represented all the little girls who needed protection from the likes of Crichton. There were too many of them. Sick, sick bastards in a sick, sick world. Paedophilia and murder weren't new, they just got more column space. He had watched her grow, become more like her mother in thought and deed, as the years glided past. Sometimes it was too painful to witness their alikeness. A glance, a smirk of amusement, or the way her gentle eyes rested on a sad scene propelled him back to his Fiona.

'You're smiling, Jack, is something wrong?' she'd said.

It was an hour after their wedding. Fiona sat astride him in the hotel room. They were supposed to be changing for the bride's and groom's grand departure. Instead, she French kissed him into helplessness.

'I'm happy,' he replied truthfully.

'You should be, I'm a great lay.'

'So I heard.'

'Pig.' She moved her hips in a tight circle. 'It's legal now, enjoy.'

'It's the illegal bits that I'm more interested in.'

She bent down and kissed him wetly on his mouth. 'Give me a baby, Jack, I want that: I want to see our baby grow up like you.'

He groaned.

'Don't be like that,' she warned.

'If we have a baby, I want her to be like you: undamaged, real.'

She had stopped moving and gazed sadly into his eyes. 'You're real, Jack, very real.'

She reached a hand to where his body joined hers, and gently squeezed. 'Feel that? Real.' She took his hands and placed them on her sex-swollen breasts. 'Me too; one life, one chance.'

'I know,' he accepted.

It had been long years since he had been able to remember without torment. Now he could feel the loss, but realise that what they'd had was very special, undamaged, real. On the balcony he cried tears – tears of gratitude, not pain. He had loved and she had died. In her passing she gave him Hollie, in her last breath and in her memory; she was a worthy memorial. The Cypriot girl had disappeared without trace.

Larnaca had woken and was now rising to meet the day ahead. Jack gathered his belongings, then walked out of the hotel into the future.

CHAPTER FORTY-EIGHT

The first day of the trial of R versus Speakman was worse than Toby Sloane had expected. Roger Fry's opening address to the jury carried the sombre authority of his experience and the full horror of the crimes. When a woman juror began to weep as he outlined the young lives snuffed out by King Arthur the temperature in the packed courtroom dropped from freezing to Antarctic.

Toby had known many murder cases in his career, but none that reeked of such understandable hostility towards the accused. The problem was that Toby knew that Speakman was innocent. He was alone in that view, at least for the present.

The outline of the prosecution case ground on for a grim two hours. Fry wasn't talking for the sake of it: there was just a vast amount of detail involved, all of it pointing directly at Speakman. Mr Justice Singleton had adjourned after the emotionally charged address had ended, pausing only to glare at the defendant before rising imperiously for his chambers. The jury could not help but see the judge's attitude, for that was what he intended. Singleton would not be granting the defence any favours.

During the course of the afternoon, Fry had called the arresting police officers to outline how they had discovered the drugged form of the girl in the back of Speakman's trailer. It was then that Sedgewick began to feel ill. His normal funeral-parlour pallor had deepened to a corpse-like grey.

Sitting behind his leading counsel's benches, Toby saw Sedgewick mopping his brow with a ragged silk handkerchief. As the moment arrived for his cross-examination, the QC had climbed unsteadily to his feet and in a wavering voice asked that he be allowed to conduct that task the next day. It was obvious that the man was ill, though Justice Singleton ignored that fact for some minutes before granting the adjournment. Sedgewick's sigh of relief could have been heard on the Strand. A few brief minutes later he fainted in the robing room. An ambulance whisked the frail man away to hospital. Roger Fry, his face troubled by how this would affect the progress of the case, had approached Toby.

'The old boy's been overdoing it.'

'It appears so,' he replied, unwilling to enter a debate with the silk.

'Quite a strain, a case of this magnitude.'

'On all of us,' Toby answered truthfully, untying the bands from around his starched wing collar.

'How are you bearing up?' Fry asked, when what he meant was, 'What are you going to do?'

'Considering the options.' Toby's brusque, incisive answer caused the QC to pucker his lips and remove his black, silk gown.

'We must speak to the judge,' Fry commanded.

'I've sent an usher with the information. He'll speak to the judge's clerk. No doubt Singleton will wish to speak to us.'

Fry scratched his chin thoughtfully. 'An adjournment at this stage would be very tiresome.'

'It may be very necessary.'

'Of course. A man is entitled to be properly represented. I hear you're very able.'

Toby smiled grimly. He had been waiting for this gambit. The trial had taken months of careful planning to arrive at this stage – he wouldn't see it aborted easily. The buttering process had begun. 'I try to do my job.'

'And very well too, or so I'm told.'

Toby doubted this proposition. 'We need to know what the doctors say, Fry.'

'Of course. We all pray for the best. It would be most unfortunate if Sedgewick weren't able to continue, but perhaps a little dangerous if he did.'

Toby knew that Fry was referring to the launch of an appeal if Speakman was convicted on the grounds that Sedgewick was in no fit state to conduct the case.

'I prefer not to bury people before they are dead.'

Toby had spoken his thoughts. Fry glared in return.

'You're being unreasonable, Sloane.'

The statement carried throughout the room; the other occupants froze in anticipation. Toby felt the blood rushing to his cheeks.

'I'm being realistic.' His voice caught a little in his throat. Junior barristers avoided a confrontation with QCs like the Black Death – they all tended to result in the same end.

'You need to grow a longer beard to be so arrogantly realistic.'

The men stood face to face, eyes locked in mutual antagonism. Toby knew he could not afford to push this any further, at least for the moment.

'Roger, you're right. I'm just a little upset about Sedgewick.' His public climb-down produced a caring smile from his opposition.

'Dear boy, we all are. It's clear to me that you know what you're doing, but it might be an idea to trot down to the cells and tell Speakman all that has occurred. I'll send a note through to Singleton about the position.'

Toby had entered the grim holding cells in the belly of the court and been shown to an interview room. Speakman was presented minutes later.

'Trevor, I've got some bad news.'

Speakman's doughy face was blank. 'I already heard about Mr Sedgewick.' He stared at the bare wall. 'Just another nail in the coffin, Mr Sloane.'

'You have options.' Speakman's face failed to register any response. 'It's unlikely that Mr Sedgewick will be able to continue, at least for the present. I will apply for an adjournment.'

'You said options. What are the others?'

'There's only one other.'

'Which is?'

Toby took a deep breath. 'That I represent you on my own.'

'OK.' Speakman's voice was flat as stagnant water.

'What do you mean, "OK"?' Toby's voice was angry. Speakman flushed.

'I mean, yes, that's what I want. It's not going to make one difference to the outcome, so I might as well have that.'

'It isn't that simple.'

'I just want it over and done with. I know you'll do your best. You've always been all right with me, never tried to get me to plead guilty or nothing. That's what I want. I'll tell the judge that too.'

'Trevor, listen to me. This could be the most important decision you make in your entire life. Take some time to think about it.'

'Don't need to, Mr Sloane. You'll do for me and I won't blame you when they find me guilty.'

'Think about it overnight.'

Speakman rose from his chair, his face slack with resignation. 'Try and get some sleep, Mr Sloane, and try not to worry too much.'

'How can you be so calm about this?' Toby was genuinely perplexed. He was the professional – he was supposed to be the calm one.

'When I heard that prosecutor make his speech about those poor little girls I would have convicted myself. I don't have a prayer, but you'll do your best and that's good enough for me.'

Speakman rapped on the window. A prison officer meandered over and unlocked the door.

'In a way, I'm glad it's you, Mr Sloane.'

Toby made his way back to the robing room. Fry and his junior were in conversation with the judge's clerk.

'Toby,' Fry began, 'the hospital called and the news is not good.'

'How is he?'

'Mild stroke, I'm afraid: could be months.'

The clerk, a tall, bearded former chief petty officer in a Royal Navy tie, spoke. 'His Lordship would like to see you all in his chambers. Tread carefully; calm head, Mr Sloane. He doesn't like it when things don't run smoothly.'

Toby flashed a glance at Fry, who at least had the decency to look away. He had obviously informed the clerk about their earlier argument.

'I'm ready to see him.'

'No,' said the clerk, 'he's ready to see you, sir.'

Minutes later they were led into the plush interior of Singleton's chambers. The judge sat at an antique oak desk reading a leatherbound law report. He didn't glance up when they were shown in. He flicked a page over, before waving his hand to indicate that they might sit. Toby was uncomfortable in the silence. Fry and his junior waited patiently for the judge to make the pace.

'Pity about Sedgewick,' he muttered, idly scratching the red sideboards on his right cheek. 'Still, better to go in harness than bored in a field.' He glanced up at them, raising his bushy eyebrows.

'It does present us with a problem. Has the defendant been informed about the occurrence?'

'He has, my Lord, I've seen him in conference,' Toby replied.

'And the options have been fully explained to him?'

'They have.'

Singleton watched Toby's face carefully and willed him to continue. Toby waited for another question: he didn't have to make it too easy.

'Well?'

'I have asked him to reserve his final decision until the morning.'

Singleton sucked in his cheeks in irritation. 'What is his preliminary view?'

Toby looked at Fry and his junior, who were watching him keenly. 'That the case should proceed and that I should take over full conduct of it.'

Out of the corner of his eye, Toby could see the smirk on Fry's face. Singleton's was grave, watchful.

'Will he sign a declaration to that effect?' the judge asked.

'If he doesn't change his mind overnight, and I am still unable to persuade him that it would be unwise.'

Singleton stared at Toby, calculating how to play the difficult young man. 'Do you feel yourself incompetent to take the case?'

Toby gritted his teeth at the unfairness of the loaded question. It was like asking a defendant when had he stopped beating his wife. 'The case is a complex one.'

'I'm aware of that, but it doesn't answer my question.' Singleton drummed his fingers on the desk top awaiting an answer.

'Inexperienced, yes, incompetent, no.'

'Practice makes perfect, Mr Sloane. When I was at the bar one either learned to swim or one drowned. Murders generally are straightforward: at least there are no victims to cross-examine.'

Fry tittered sycophantically; his junior, always a quick learner, followed suit. Toby locked eyes with Singleton, fully aware that he was being backed into a corner.

'So, Mr Sloane, it is your position that you hold yourself out as competent to take conduct of the case.' Toby didn't respond; besides it wasn't a question. 'And you have the defendant's confidence. I would be very disappointed if anything should happen before the court sits that might lose that confidence. Do we understand each other, Mr Sloane?'

'Perfectly, Judge, but I cannot guarantee that he won't change his mind for other reasons.'

Singleton smiled thinly; he was enjoying himself. 'But none that revolves around your competence.'

'I shall speak to him in the morning and fulfil my professional duty.'

'Your first duty should be to the court.'

Toby knew he was being bullied; it was something he had hated at school and that feeling had not diminished with the passage of time.

'With all due respect, that is *your* first duty: mine is to Speakman.'

Singleton's ruddy cheeks reddened: it was a well-known fact within the law that anything prefaced 'with all due respect' meant exactly the opposite.

'You go too far, Sloane.'

Toby dropped his eyes. The day's events had not improved his future. 'I meant no offence, my Lord: if I have caused any then I apologise.'

Singleton nodded slowly, Fry coughed, his junior studied his Oxford shoes. Toby raised his eyes again. He felt he was being measured by the hangman for the drop.

'Then we shall continue the trial in the morning. I shall look forward to your cross-examinations, Mr Sloane, if this performance is anything to judge by.'

'That is, if the defendant doesn't change his mind.'

'He knows himself to be in good hands,' Singleton said slowly. 'I have a feeling that he will be of the same opinion come the morning. Till then,' the judge said, smiling warmly at Fry, 'Roger.' He flipped his face to Toby, banished the smile and said coldly, 'Sloane.'

No, all in all the first day of the trial of R versus Speakman had been worse than he had imagined; the worst day of his life in fact, but that might change by the morning.

CHAPTER FORTY-NINE

J ack retraced his childhood steps, but Cyprus had changed – like most things, for the worse. It retained its Englishness – red postboxes, traffic driving on the left, even the currency was the pound – but it had been divided by hostility and scarred by that separation.

It was a simple matter to arrange the hire of a Fiat, and drive towards the Akamas Peninsula. One of the conditions of Cypriot independence was the British reservation of retained sites on the island; the peninsula hosted a massive artillery range on its deforested surface. Jack's father had been second in command from 1972 to 1973. The family home, a cramped villa among pine-scented saplings, stood at Loutra Afrodhitis, the baths of Aphrodite, but Jack felt no compulsion to return there. The legend was that the goddess bathed there before and after entertaining her lovers: the disappointing reality was a four-metre grotto, with dripping water, surrounded by ugly flagstones and notices forbidding everything but breathing. Like most things in life, it rarely matched the hype.

He was heading for Latchi, where the taverna had stood twenty-five years before. The roads were quiet. In the summer it would be humming with the noisy throttle of tourist-driven mopeds. Now the twisting, pot-holed route was his alone. If his memory was right, then Latchi would be coming up soon, and in Latchi was Jangos's taverna. Jack's father used to visit the watering hole as the noticeboard there was the only reliable source as to when the artillery range was active. He had trusted Jangos more than his commanding officer. Jack hadn't been allowed to go there, but had still crept away occasionally with his sketchpad in hand. Towards the end, the atmosphere on the island had been hostile, nowhere more so than the popular taverna, where angry moustached men banged glasses violently on the table tops. He could see it clearly in his mind's eye. Helena Dwyer had released the memory from its mental prison: it vied for his attention, demanded that he see.

At thirteen, Jack had been a gangly boy in Bermuda shorts, roaming the island, searching for scenes to draw. He had walked miles that morning: along the Fontana Amorosa, overlooking the crashing waves of Khrysokhou Bay, towards Cape Arnaoutis and the steep cliffs to the Mediterranean sea below. The warm sun made him sweat as he walked through the pines and goat paths towards a lifesaving lemonade at Jangos's. Jack's father had forbidden him to roam far that day: he had seemed worried, at least more worried than usual. Now Jack knew that his father had suspected an invasion was imminent, but to the schoolboy his concern appeared unnecessary. What could go wrong on a day like this in this wonderful place? The answer was everything.

Jack had sat at the only spare table. The mood in the taverna was ugly. Bottles of zivania – the local fire-water, nearly pure grape alcohol – were drunk at speed. Arguments spread from table to table, the volatile Greek Cypriots shouting at each other and the skies in fear and confusion. He was eventually served with his cloudy lemonade by a dark-skinned girl with almond eyes whose rounded belly eloquently told her tale. She couldn't have been more than thirteen or fourteen. There was no band of gold on her finger. In a staunchly Catholic society her disgrace would not be readily overlooked. Jack risked a smile at her – she shook her head.

'This no place for little English boy today.'

'I'm not little,' he replied, hurt by the put-down.

'My people not happy with your people, finish your drink. I not wish you harm, but others have been swilling raki and zivania, makes them crazy.'

'I'm staying.'

Her large eyes rested sadly on the stubborn schoolboy. 'Please: you get hurt.'

Jack remembered thrusting his chin out ridiculously.

'You English all the same: stubborn as donkeys, but not as bright.'

A voice shouted a name from the taverna's interior. 'Kyra.'

The girl swivelled around to face her father as he emerged through the crowded doorway: a huge, stocky man in his late thirties, red-faced with worry and drink. 'Keep away from English, English brought you enough trouble already, bring us all trouble.'

The girl's face crumpled with the public humiliation of the scene. 'He just a boy,' she replied quietly.

'So is other one; he give you man-sized trouble in your belly.'

An English voice cut through their argument. 'Leave her alone, Jangos.' It was the tall, slim figure of Rex Crichton. He wore long white trousers and a long-sleeved shirt, his handsome face unblemished.

Jangos spun around. 'You should have left her alone. You are bastard and you give her a bastard.'

The other drinkers abandoned their own disagreements to concentrate on the encounter.

'Shut up,' Rex ordered. Though Crichton couldn't have been more than seventeen he had a menacing presence, but the burly Cypriot was not going to stand down in front of his friends and customers.

'No, you shut up. You freak, I seen your body, you ugly as leper. Go away, leper, fly home before your body get more hurt.'

Jangos had scored a direct hit. Crichton's eyes blazed with seething fury. The Cypriot knew Rex's weak point, the soft underbelly of his secret. Crichton glared at the hard, unwavering faces of the other Cypriots. Jack could see tears of outrage and frustration in his eyes. He turned to Kyra, who dropped her gaze to the ground.

'You too,' he screamed. 'Look at me.' She shook her head violently, but kept her gaze on the dusty ground.

'Kyra does not want to look at ugly freak,' Jangos roared. 'Join circus, people pay to look at such horror.'

Crichton turned away then; his walk became a run, then a sprint.

'That right, run, run away, like all English,' Jangos screamed at the disappearing figure. 'Keep running, Jangos will be behind you all your life.'

It was after Rex disappeared from sight, and after Jangos re-entered the taverna, that Jack watched Kyra slip out of the back, around the cars, to the track where her lover had gone. He hadn't meant to follow her, it just sort of happened.

It was the worst decision he had ever made.

Jack steered the Fiat around a steep curve in the mountain path. As the vehicle's nose negotiated the turn he saw the taverna, and it still bore the same sign, 'Jangos'. Even after more than twenty years the place appeared exactly the same. Though the summer tables had been stored away, the awning and decor were as he remembered.

He parked the car and went into the sleepy taverna. The restaurant was deserted. A young boy idly washed glasses; he didn't look up as Jack approached.

'Is Jangos here?'

The boy ignored the question, but a thick voice behind answered, 'Who wants him?'

Jack turned to see how the years had treated the innkeeper. He looked well lined by the years of constant sun, and appeared as strong as he ever was, but his eyes had lost their passion.

Jack held out his hand. He remembered how tactile the Cypriots were, that every meeting was conducted with handshakes or kisses.

Jangos shook firmly. 'What can I do for you?' His voice was mellow with middle age, not the screaming drunk of 1974.

'My name is Jack. I lived here as a boy.'

'Army?'

'That's right; my father had the villa at Aphrodite's Bath.'

Jangos peered at him, attempting to see the boy in the man. 'What your father called?'

'Forth, Colonel Graham Forth.'

Jangos nodded approvingly. 'He good man; still alive?' Jack nodded. 'Quiet man, but honest; I trusted him. When you see him, tell him Jangos is happy he's still alive.' Jangos pulled out a chair and pushed it towards Jack. 'Tell me what Colonel Forth's son wants. You haven't come here to say hello to an old man.'

'No, no, I haven't.'

Where did he start? How could he get the man's help, when all those years ago he had failed to help his daughter?

'All I ask you to do is hear me out. What I have to tell you will be painful: you may be angry with me or with yourself, but I ask you as my father's son to let me finish before you make your mind up.'

The Cypriot stared at Jack before replying. 'I know you now: Little Picasso we called you, always wandering, always drawing, head in the clouds, fingers on pencils. You still drawing?'

Jack nodded. 'Of sorts. Jangos?'

'Yes.'

'It's about Kyra.' His face went slack at the mention of her name. 'I don't want to upset you, but you need to know the truth.'

'Kyra, my little Kyra. I was to blame. She ran from me into the arms of the bastard Turks when they invaded.'

'No, she didn't.'

Jangos looked deeply into Jack's eyes, searching for sincerity. 'What do you know, Little Picasso? Tell this sad old man your secret.'

'I was here that day, the day she went after her lover, the day before the invasion. I saw your argument with him.'

Jangos nodded sadly. 'I drank with worry, an unwise pastime for an innkeeper. There were terrible pressures. I struck out at my little Kyra and lost her and my grandchild that day. I have never taken another drink since. I pray to the gods, any gods, to send her home to me. My weakness for drink pushed her away. I gave it up, but she will never walk through the door again, will she, Jack Forth?'

Jack returned the Cypriot's pleading stare. 'No, Jangos, she won't; there isn't any hope.'

'How can you be so sure? Why rob her father of his hope?'

'I saw her murder.'

'You saw what?'

'He killed her at the lake, Jangos, I saw it, saw him.'

He had thought he had lost her on the mountain path. Kyra walked with a determined stride. She appeared to know where she was going. Jack followed. He knew he shouldn't, but the little boy in him won the brief battle with the decision. The walk was hard going: he didn't want to get too close, or she would see him; any further back and he would lose her. It was never this hard in the films he saw at the cinema.

She turned around a couple of times as she marched along the rough terrain, checking to see whether her father was following. That made Jack copy the action – he didn't want to be caught trailing the pregnant daughter of an irate islander. The path shelved down steeply through the scented lime trees towards the shore of the lake. If he went any further he would certainly be spotted as the trees thinned out to low scrub and dry earth.

The young man, her lover, was standing with his back to her approach. Jack squeezed between two rocks and watched her move towards Rex Crichton. He was roughly 200 yards from them. A heat haze rippled from the lake's still surface, they had the water to themselves. Rex reacted to her presence by spinning towards her and slapping her face. Jack could hear the crack of the blow in the silence of the deserted countryside. She held her face where he had struck.

Rex began to shed his clothing. As his shirt was discarded, Jack could see the livid scars stretch from his chest to his waist. As the trousers and underwear were pulled off, Jack saw the purple scarring continue along his groin and buttocks. Rex held out his arms in cruciform: Kyra stood, frozen by the action. Crichton's face was blank, there was no primal scream or bellowing fury; he appeared to be in some sort of trance. He reached for Kyra, she backed away. He spread his arms wide, as if to cloak her body in his own. Slowly she moved inside his embrace. He laid her gently on the ground, then sat astride her full belly. Jack watched them silently. Crichton pushed her hands beneath his knees. Jack could see he was smiling, the girl mesmerised by his performance. Crichton bent down to the girl's ear and whispered something. She began to struggle, but was helpless in his embrace. He leaned to her ear again; as he did so, the girl snapped her head around and sank her teeth into his face. Crichton shrieked in pain, and struggled to unlock her jaw from his right cheek. Blood flowed, she clung on. Jack felt sick, he wanted to pee, he wanted to run, he wanted to help. He was frightened beyond experience.

Crichton wrestled her from his face. Blood was showering from the wounds her perfect white teeth had inflicted, but Crichton was smiling. He reached up a hand to the sticky wetness, looked at the crimson path across his palm, then smeared some across the girl's forehead in a cross. She had begun to scream. Jack's fear nailed him to the rock; he was afraid to watch and afraid to turn away. Crichton smiled sweetly at Kyra. 'See me now,' he shouted across the water, 'see me as I am, now and for eternity.'

His thumbs plunged into Kyra's eye sockets, expelling her eyeballs onto her face. Jack passed out. When he came to, Crichton was at the water's edge. He had tied and weighted her body with her own clothing and some rocks. Jack saw the bubbles as he launched her body into the depths of the lake. As Crichton stood watch over his achievement, Jack had run, his mind racing, already blanking out what he'd seen. The Turks invaded the next day. The island was a maelstrom of confusion. What was a missing girl among so many fatalities?

That was when his mind had sought to protect itself from the knowledge – when his breakdown shaped his future and denied him the truth.

Jangos's face was awash with tears. He dropped his head into his hands and sobbed. Jack hadn't seen this level of misery since Fiona died. 'I'm sorry, Jangos. I could have helped her.'

The man's huge shoulders shuddered with each racking gulp of grief. He was crying the tears that the absence of the truth had denied him for over twenty years.

'I'm so sorry.'

'Why? You were a boy, not a man. If you had helped you too would sleep in the lake with my Kyra.'

'You mean her body's never been recovered?'

'The lake has not been searched; I shall put that right. You must tell the authorities what you have told me.'

'I can't.'

'You must: you are not Little Picasso any more, you are man with all that brings.'

'Jangos, by now the police in my own country will be looking for me. The man who killed Kyra is still out there, and he's still killing.'

The Cypriot dried his eyes. 'Why do your police seek you? For all I know, you could have killed my Kyra.'

'I'm no murderer, but I should have helped her. I want to make amends. Help me find her, Jangos: we can find her and lay her to a proper rest. She carries within her the evidence that will lock him up forever.'

'You talk of evidence, but you mean my daughter.'

'No, look, this is difficult for me too, but it's your unborn grandchild that carries its father's DNA.'

Jangos's hand shot out and slapped Jack's face. It stung. The clap echoed through the premises. 'Have you no soul? You pretend to care then talk of desecration.'

Jack spoke quietly. 'Don't let your temper deny you your daughter again.'

The words caused more pain than a thousand slaps. Jangos slumped onto his hands.

'We can revenge her death by making him pay for his crimes. There are other dead girls, with fathers who miss them every day. Like you, they are angry; like you, they strike out in frustration; but you can make the difference, they are powerless.'

'If you lie, I will kill you.'

'If I have lied I don't deserve to live.'

'Well spoken, Graham Forth's son. But why should I believe your story?'

'You trusted my father; he is a man of honour. I am his son, he has taught me well. I live by honour, believe me for his sake.'

Jangos smoothed his hair with his fingers. 'You ask a lot.'

'I know. It's more than any father should have to bear.'

'Do you have children?'

'A girl, Hollie.'

'And you love her?'

'Yes.'

'Then swear an oath on her life that what you say is true. The gods will hear you, and will know you through your face. This is solemn in my country. Lie to me and you will damn her.' Jack raised his hand. 'No, place it on your heart: the heart does not lie, only men.'

Jack moved his hand to the left side of his chest. 'All I have told you is true. I swear it on my life and on the life of my only child.'

Jangos nodded slowly. 'You show no fear in your oath. I believe you.'

'Thank you.'

'You must tell me your story, from the beginning. Leave nothing out. I want to know what brings you to my door, Jack Forth.'

Jack took a deep breath. 'I draw killers for the newspapers . . .'

Rex Crichton sipped a glass of Chardonnay as the pilot announced that they would be landing at Larnaca in the next fifteen minutes. The executive-class seat was comfortable. He had purchased two side by side – he didn't require company. Cream chino trousers and a Ralph Lauren polo shirt would match the expected weather. She had forced him to this action: Leone Stern had proved more troublesome than he had ever imagined. But the girl had bigger balls than a gladiator. He would never let it be said that talent should not be recognised; he acknowledged hers. One day he might well have the opportunity to show her his own talent. Before that he needed to settle with Forth.

Things were too close now, too near his grasp to allow Leone and Forth to interfere. He had never wished to return to this place, where he had taken the first one to his bosom. He had shown her his magnificence and she had trembled in awe. Her eyes had focused on the truth before they had been plucked, his image graven on their retinas: a testament to his fearsome beauty. But to return was dangerous. He had always chosen different venues for disclosures. The girls had touched his soul, and he had saved them from corruption. Life would have just given them varicose veins, pot bellies and shifty husbands. He had saved them from mediocrity. They were pure now, cloaked in his revelation, warm forever.

He fastened his seatbelt at the pilot's request. He expected the country to be different. The changes brought by the 1974 troubles would ensure that. The invasion had been an intercession by the dark gods on his behalf, he was sure of it. They looked after their own. He would join them one day, when he was ready, but the earth had to be cleansed first.

Young females had the potential to be dirty, dirty girls who would snigger behind their painted hands while dreaming of fucking their fathers and brothers. He knew all their dirty secrets and some they didn't know themselves. It was only by expanding their minds that their future moral cancer could be eliminated before it laid waste their potential. His mother had suffered: oh, how that wonderful woman had been tormented by the sickness of desire. He would have released her from the bondage of her sex, if she hadn't done so herself. She was a clean woman, soiled by her husband and his demands on her libido. When she went into the water, she had known instinctively that it would wash away the grime, and she would be renewed, reborn, fresh and virginal, hymen intact forever.

It had taken the episode in Cyprus to allow him this clarity of viewpoint. They had forced his hand. The girl had volunteered: she had followed him to the lake, and the figure he had seen fleeing the mountain must have been Forth as a boy. The dark ones were testing him, stretching his resourcefulness to its limit; he would not fail them. If he was right then locating Forth would be a simple matter. The only reason he would travel to Cyprus was for evidence, and that evidence could only be little Kyra's body. The lake would still be there. He would watch until the moment was right. What Forth knew, others might too. He would wait until Forth's search was over. It would be nice to see Kyra again.

CHAPTER FIFTY

T he lake was still. Early morning light threw long shadows from eucalyptus and citrus trees across the flat water, like fat black fingers reaching into the lake's heart. Jack was cold. It wasn't the temperature, it was the fear: it was nearly time to go back into the water. Jangos had insisted that he lodge at the taverna. A neat, whitewashed room with sparkling linen provided a few hours' sleep.

They had talked deep into the night; there were few customers. Jangos insisted on cooking him something special, claiming that he needed all his strength for the dive. Jack didn't have the heart to tell his Cypriot friend that he was terrified of the water. A huge *rifi*, a whole lamb on a spit, was produced with great ceremony and obvious pride. Jack did his best to do it justice. Jangos offered him wine. Jack had two glasses. Jangos sniffed the rough bouquet approvingly and explained that he was 'just saying hello to an old friend'. He drank thick black coffee as the *rifi* was reduced to a carcass. Jack told him everything; he had a right to know.

Jangos in return described his long search for Kyra. After the partition, Cyprus had remained in a state of utter confusion. There was no chance of help from the Turkish militia. Hundreds had disappeared as each side, Greek and Turk, rushed inside their own demarcation lines. An ancient dispute had catapulted the island into national schizophrenia. Jangos had looked without success for the boy who had impregnated his daughter. In the panic of partition many records were lost or intentionally destroyed. Bureaucracy ruled supreme. He searched for years, even risking several illegal border crossings in order to continue his quest. All the time she had been resting in the lake, no more than two kilometres away.

That water now stretched before him. Jangos had provided diving suits and oxygen tanks. Jack pulled on the black wetsuit, feeling its rubbery snap as he stretched the casing over his chest. A small semi-rigid inflatable lay on the water's surface; its outboard motor was ready for action.

'We need to divide the lake into sections, Jangos.'

The Cypriot was squeezing his stomach into his own suit. 'OK, Jack Forth. We start where you saw him push Kyra into the water. There are currents in this water, though. The surface not the truth. Like Greek: calm on top, passionate underneath.' He flashed a thin smile.

'You don't have to do this, Jangos.'

'You wrong. My duty to Kyra takes me into the water. What makes you swim?'

Jack shrugged. 'The same.'

Jangos studied Jack's face. 'I think so, but there's more. You want to save all the little girls from the water.'

Jack knew he was right. 'Someone has to.'

Jangos walked towards him, then placed his huge hands on Jack's shoulders. 'Listen to me. You cannot carry all the world's problems. It's not your fault, Jack. This man is evil, you are a good man. You will stop him: it is meant to be, just not so easy.'

Jack appreciated the man's understanding way. He needed to be honest with him, otherwise it could jeopardise their safety. 'I'm frightened of the water.'

Jangos punched him playfully on the shoulder. 'I know, I see the fear in your eyes; but not in your heart, eh? Wise man is always afraid, the world is a dangerous place. Wise man know this and take more care; live to be old wise man. You will swim because is right thing to do, only thing to do.'

They loaded the equipment onto the inflatable. Jangos had returned from Larnaca Bay armed to the teeth with it just as Jack had risen from a brief sleep. Other than the wetsuits and oxygen cylinders, he had scrounged the use of an elderly air generator.

'For when we start gasping. It refills the tank,' he had explained as the wheezing contraption coughed into life. 'These tanks give thirty minutes' air. Here is watch, pressurised. Set alarm at twenty-five. Not like bed: when it goes off, you come up. No lie-in on the sea bed, or lasts for good.'

Jack was curious when Jangos removed a long, ribbed trunk which he connected to the generator.

'Sand-blaster,' he explained. 'Kyra down there a long time,

too long,' he added sadly. 'My friend Peter in Larnaca tell me about slit.'

'You mean silt.'

'Crap, garbage, whatever the name. This blasts it off, let us see. Peter said we must be calm, wait until silt calm too. Then we see proper.'

Jangos walked to his Ford truck and withdrew two long, slim objects. They were spear guns; he had half a dozen barbed shafts.

'For the fish?'

Jangos smiled, but his eyes were obsidian. 'For the shark. If he comes, Jangos will be ready to spear him.'

There was nothing more to say. Jack walked into the water, and felt its cold fingers grip his legs, then his groin – though his testes were already shrivelling in anticipation of the experience ahead. He hauled himself into the boat and sat on the slatted pine seat. Jangos followed, carrying the remaining equipment chest high. Jack took it from him and laid the spear guns down carefully. He heard the rush of water as the Cypriot threw his bulk into the boat, which rocked from side to side. Jack clutched both hands to the rubber sides until the swell subsided.

Jangos sat at the stern, then whipped back the starter cord on the motor; it growled into life. He plunged the whirling blades into the black water and the vessel began to move.

'First we have pleasure cruise of lake; get you in the mood to swim.'

'I'm ready now,' Jack replied half-heartedly.

'No, you're not, but you will be.'

He increased the throttle speed to maximum; the prow rose alarmingly as they sped away. Jack gripped on.

'You be glad to get in the water by the end of pleasure cruise.' Jangos laughed loud and strong, exposing white teeth interleaved with gold.

Jack was tense. Then, as the wind threw his hair around his head, he began to laugh himself. What the hell was he doing in Cyprus on a lake with an insane innkeeper looking for his long-dead daughter? The absurdity of it all struck him forcefully. He realised it was the first real belly laugh he had experienced in his adult life. There had been smiles, giggles and wry grins, but not the stomach-deep, helpless braying at the ludicrous life

351

they all lived. Jangos nodded his approval, through his tears of mirth. As one of them calmed down, the other then spluttered into laughter and the first followed suit. By the time they had sped around the lake, Jack's stomach was painful. Jangos glided the boat to a stop at their point of departure and, dropping a small anchor, he killed the engine. Silence descended on the deserted lake and its domain. Jangos glanced at him and raised one cocked finger, which he pointed at the water.

'Now. Now you are ready, Jack Forth.'

He was as ready as he ever would be.

'I go in first,' Jangos muttered as he grabbed an oxygen tank and face mask.

'No, Jangos, it's time.'

The Cypriot's eyes were hooded as he considered Jack's words. Without replying he handed the equipment over. Jack struggled into the tank harness. He had learned how to dive on a trip to Barbados with Fiona. Then it had been two days in a hotel swimming pool, in shallow water, to gain his PADI certificate, before a single dive on a safe coral reef under supervision. This couldn't be that different – could it?

He couldn't produce any spit to coat the inside of his face mask to prevent it from steaming over. Twice he attempted the exercise without success. Jangos reached for it, gobbed heartily into its interior then ran his fingers to spread the moisture evenly.

'Greek Cypriot spit; best in world.'

Jack smiled: though his friend's English was faltering, his heart was not.

He fastened a thin rope around Jack's ankle. 'You get in trouble, tug this three times. Now swim, little fish, bring my Kyra home.'

Jack decided against a flashy entrance to the water's mouth: a backward somersault might look flashy in a swimming pool but could lead to an early disaster in the lake. He turned and lowered himself into the chill. Jack could feel his heart hammering through his skin and onto the rubber of the suit. Jangos gave him a meaty thumbs-up, which he then rotated through 180 degrees. Jack followed his command and submerged.

He lay three feet below the surface to orientate himself with the water. It pushed at him, even at this depth. He felt its weight, the pressure of the lake's contents driving against his tense body.

He began to feel the insistent tug of panic begin in his stomach and lungs. He was supposed to breathe slow and deep, but felt his breathing rate soar.

Then he saw the colours. The gradated light split into fantastic prisms where it refracted in the water's touch. All the colours of the spectrum showed themselves singularly to him. It was truly wondrous. He glanced down to follow the refracted beams until they disappeared into the depths. There would be colour there too – you just needed the right vision to see it. Jack noticed his breathing rate had slowed to a steady pulse. He could hear the exaggerated sound of his own life.

Jack took one deep lungful and kicked down to the lake's waiting bed.

CHAPTER FIFTY-ONE

'Yes, Mr Sloane,' Justice Singleton said brightly with a sympathetic smile in his direction which, Toby was aware, was purely for the benefit of the jury. Singleton wasn't going to alienate them by appearing unfair to a young advocate thrust into the maelstrom of legal battle. Earlier on, Singleton had explained the position to them. Some had smiled sympathetically in his direction; others were too far down the road to conviction to care.

He had suffered a sleepless night preparing his cross-examination for the day's witnesses, but there was such a thing as over-preparation. It made the questions stale, the answers mechanical. He had to be at his very best, his sharpest. Evidence as read on paper could change dramatically during its presentation before the jury. It could be the emphasis on a word or phrase that altered its meaning. In itself it might appear of minor consequence, but could, when viewed against the larger canvas, be of crucial significance to the case as a whole.

Toby breathed out slowly, then climbed steadily to his feet. In the witness box Sergeant Hall stood upright, buttons gleaming on his freshly pressed uniform. He was young to wear the three stripes. Toby turned to him, ready to cross-examine.

'Now, to recap, you were one of the officers who discovered Joanna Cheem in the back of the defendant's lorry trailer?'

'I was, sir.'

'You told us you were on mobile patrol in the area and you were told, as the nearest unit, to proceed to the lorry with all haste.'

'Yes, sir.'

'That involved the use of a siren and flashing lights?'

'It did.'

'Those sirens are meant to attract attention, are they not?'

'They are.'

355

'Yet when you forced open the doors to the trailer, Mr Speakman approached you and asked what was going on.'

The sergeant appeared puzzled. 'He did, sir.'

'Did he at any time attempt to stop you forcing the door?'

'Not as such, but he wasn't very happy.'

'He offered you the keys, didn't he?'

'He did, but we had strict instructions to act as quickly as possible.'

'Did he ever attempt to run away?'

'No, sir, but there were two of us.'

'Yes,' Toby continued, 'and you were both involved in jemmying open the doors. He could have run at any moment. Indeed, he could have disappeared when he heard your siren. At the crucial time he could have escaped.'

The sergeant turned his eyes towards the jury. 'We would have known who we were looking for, sir: it was his lorry.'

'By which time he could have killed again.'

'Mr Sloane?'

It was the judge, still wearing a frown of insincerity. 'Please correct me if I misunderstand, but are you accepting on your client's behalf that he had killed in the past? If that is so, why are we having this trial?'

Toby breathed out slowly, almost a sigh. To the uninitiated, it appeared that Singleton had asked a reasonable question; to the knowledgeable he was sealing his thumbprint on the case.

'No, my Lord, I am suggesting that if the defendant had anything to escape from he had ample opportunity to do so.'

Singleton sniffed, then raised one eyebrow in the jury's direction.

'I see, continue.'

'The girl was positioned near the door?'

'Yes, sir.'

'So that she was immediately in view?'

'Correct.' The sergeant was enjoying himself. Toby pressed on.

'This trailer is some forty feet long, yet she was positioned at the front?'

'Correct again. I've said all this.'

'Just trying to get the full picture, Sergeant. You later made a full search of the lorry and found tarpaulin sheets.'

'That's correct, at the very rear of the trailer.'

'She wasn't covered by a sheet, was she? Just there in plain sight?'

'Lucky for her, sir.'

'As if she was meant to be found.'

Fry QC sprang to his feet. 'My Lord, really, I sympathise with my learned friend's lack of experience, but that was a comment best directed to the jury at the close of the case in his closing speech.'

Fry's face appeared saddened that he had to do his duty; Singleton clucked.

'Disregard what Mr Sloane has just said, members of the jury. Mr Sloane, please restrict yourself to asking questions: fanciful scenarios can be saved for your final speech.'

Toby had anticipated the judicial reprimand, but his intention was to plant the seeds of a set-up in the jury's mind as soon as possible.

'Sergeant,' he continued, 'the door opened easily, didn't it? As if it wasn't locked at all?'

'How did you . . . ?' the witness began, then tailed off. Toby had been right. Crichton would have had to force the door himself earlier in order to deposit the girl in the trailer, then make it appear locked.

'It virtually sprang open, didn't it?'

Sergeant Hall was beginning to look uncomfortable. 'It was easier than I had imagined; perhaps I don't know my own strength.'

'Perhaps it had already been broken into earlier.'

'Mr Sloane,' Singleton hissed.

'I withdraw that question, my Lord.'

'That comment,' Fry whispered loudly and towards the jury. Toby kept his eyes from the judge's but could feel their heat on him.

'Was the lock ever examined for other damage?'

'Not that I am aware of, sir.'

'Pity,' he muttered, loud enough for the jury to hear, but also with sufficient volume for another courtroom bollocking. He noticed one member of the jury, a sharp-faced woman in a smart suit, begin to write notes of his cross-examination.

'Mr Speakman appeared surprised at what you found: indeed,

he said, and I quote from your evidence yesterday, "What the hell is she doing there?"'

Hall stuck his chin out firmly before replying. 'Wouldn't be the first murderer caught bang to rights to deny what he'd done, sir.'

Toby turned his attention to Singleton. 'My Lord, really.'

'You asked the question, Mr Sloane.'

'With respect, my Lord, I asked a question and the witness chose to ignore it. I asked whether he had said it, not what it meant; there is a difference.'

The jury's faces were gripped by the encounter; now this was what they wanted in a trial. Singleton glanced to the policeman.

'Did he say that, officer?' The judge's voice carried the tireless patience of a long-suffering father with an errant child.

'He did, my Lord.'

The judge smiled indulgently at the jury as if to say, 'So what? He would, wouldn't he?'

'So, Sergeant Hall,' Toby continued, 'from the earliest opportunity the defendant denied any involvement with the drugged girl?'

'It seems so.'

'The interior of the trailer was extremely dusty, wasn't it, Sergeant?'

'It was. I had quite a lot of it on my uniform; had to have it dry-cleaned.'

'Yet not one fingerprint belonging to the defendant was found on the masking tape around the girl's eyes, mouth, arms or legs. Indeed, there was no forensic evidence to link him with the girl's abduction, was there?'

'Must have worn gloves,' the sergeant replied with vicious glee.

'Answer the question, Sergeant Hall.' Toby shouted across the courtroom: he locked eyes with the policeman, who stared back until he dropped his gaze from Toby's furious face.

'No, sir,' he answered quietly.

'Yet Mr Speakman's fingerprints were found all over the rest of the lorry and trailer?'

'So I believe.'

Toby turned to Singleton.

'My Lord, it is agreed evidence between the prosecution and

the defence.' The judge scowled for him to continue. 'One more thing before I conclude, Sergeant Hall.'

The officer had lost his cockiness and appeared grateful that the end was in sight. 'Sir?'

'There was a fifty-thousand-pound reward for the arrest and conviction of King Arthur. Were you aware of that?'

'The whole country was aware of that.'

'Yet the tip-off the police switchboard received about the girl's whereabouts was anonymous?'

'So I believe.'

Fry rose to his feet, his voice not so forgiving.

'That is hearsay, and my learned friend knows it.'

'I can prove it by other means: your Lordship will find this evidence at page four hundred and thirty-one of the bundle of agreed evidence.'

Toby watched with no small satisfaction as the prosecuting QC spun around to his junior, whose fingers quickly found the page in question and showed its contents to the red-faced Fry. Singleton didn't need to look: he was aware of everything in the case. Fry took his seat once more without further comment. Toby risked a glance at the jury. The woman taking notes had been joined in a similar task by a middle-aged man in a Barbour jacket.

'Sergeant Hall, you know that to be true, do you not?'

'I do, sir.'

'And as yet no one has come forward to claim the reward?'

'Not that I am aware of.'

'You as a serving police officer cannot claim the money, can you, Sergeant?'

'No, sir, just doing my job.'

'You know it was a man that phoned in?' Toby turned to Fry and whispered loudly, 'Page two six two: it's all in there, and on tape.'

Fry looked away, attempting to appear bored by the proceedings.

'I heard that.' Sergeant Hall was sweating profusely. He reached into his pocket and produced a white handkerchief to mop it away.

'If you could claim the reward, would you?'

'That's an improper question, Mr Sloane, and hypothetical to boot,' Singleton warned. Toby ignored him: there was no going back now.

'But, then again, you have nothing to hide, do you?'

Toby sat down immediately. It wasn't a question that required an answer. Justice Singleton coldly asked the jury to retire and Toby Sloane awaited his punishment. As the jury were leaving he caught the eye of his first convert; she nodded before leaving for the jury room. Round one was over.

The day dawned bright through Crichton's hotel window. He had slept well; but when he'd dreamed, he'd dreamed of her. Her features had blurred with time but he could feel her spirit, strong and unafraid. It ran through his blood; he could feel the crackling of its ferocity.

He showered, turning the dial to its coldest point and luxuriating in its needlepoint sharpness. There was no rush, he did not have to make haste. The man Forth would be there for some time, diving for bones: Kyra's and his child's.

It was a curious experience returning to this stifling place after so long. Over twenty years: twenty good years and the island still carried its head underneath its arm, wailing about *enosis* – unity, the reality that could not exist. In that dry summer, his guardian had brought him here for a lengthy stay. He had owned a villa near the lake at Ayia Ekaterina for many years. The invasion had seen it burned to ash. There had never been a reason to return, until now.

He had met the girl out swimming one day. They had swum together: she because she was attracted to him, he because he wanted to experiment with sex. His public school saw little heterosexual activity. His guardian had warned him against the locals but that only served to add relish to what proved to be a dull dish. She had been a virgin. It took him several weeks, and many turgid poems painstakingly translated into Greek, to allow him into the secret nest of her body. He had thought then, and retained the belief, that if that was what normality had to offer he was delighted to be different; but oh, so different.

Little Kyra had become pregnant. His guardian bought her father's anger off with many Cypriot pounds.

'Every man, particularly a proud man, has his price. Show me a man with no pride then I will tremble, for he is dangerous, Rex.'

His guardian was proud of these esoteric utterances, showing a particular fascination for the Chinese philosopher and warlord Lao Tzu, quoting him regularly, both in and out of context. Rex patronised him by quoting the teachings back, always in context.

He had been deeply moved by Kyra's final voyage. It burned his mind with his true destiny. She was his first in every way. Rex smiled at the memory of her touch on his skin, her oval face set in sympathy as she traced his mother's bequest with her tiny soft hands. There were no questions. Never once did she ask how he had become like that. Kyra was too beautiful to be spoiled by this world. He had no choice but to send her on.

Rex left the shower cubicle, towelling himself dry with wistful rubs. All the mirrors in his room were turned towards the wall. He would be seen only when he chose to be seen.

Breakfast was a simple matter: Normandy croissants and viscous Java, consumed in the pleasant surroundings of a sheltered tree-lined café. The four-wheeled jeep he had hired at the airport was parked nearby. For all intents and purposes he was David Taylor, an ex-employee of Teal, Windle and Crichton. Taylor had proved himself useful during the Bigg Truck Haulage flotation, but had become more effective since his timely disappearance. It had been a simple matter to invent the bogus job in the USA for the ambitious young lawyer. He had believed in himself so completely that suspicion that one so young should be offered so much for so little never once tripped across his greedy mind. Rex had made it clean and quick for the young man. He believed in honouring debts and the lethal injection was a reasonable pay-out to the youngster. The world was such a large place. People disappeared so easily. Once he had Taylor's passport and birth certificate, his new identity became readily available.

A pretty young waitress cleared his table. She had the look. Her eager face told of her needs: like so many, she wished to know. Perhaps, before he left the island, he would show her, but there was business to attend to first.

He spent the morning in Limassol gathering various items which would furnish him with all he needed for the campaign. He would camp in the woods near the lake and watch Forth. Then it would be time to meet Leone's lover. He too needed to see the way of things.

CHAPTER FIFTY-TWO

Roger Fry QC cleaned his half-rim spectacles with the Liberty handkerchief from his top pocket for the twentieth time during that long, dull day. This was the guts of the prosecution case.

After Speakman's arrest the search into his movements over the previous five years had been thoroughly investigated. The evidence that the jury had been hearing detailed his work records and deliveries during that lengthy period. Fry's junior was taking the witnesses through their records in meticulous detail; it had to be so. If there were any gaps in his provable whereabouts then the jury might be uncertain that the same man had committed all the offences. Various employees from the Bigg Truck Company passed through the courtroom with little or no cross-examination from Sloane.

The young barrister had been surprising the previous day. His questions had been brief and to the point and raised doubt in the expressions of some of the jury. Sloane had to be watched. He would go far, but not in this trial. By his attitude to the witnesses it was clear that Sloane was accepting that his client was in the right place at the right time. No alibi notice, detailing a contrary view, had been served by the defence on the prosecution. It seemed cut and dried, but in Fry's lengthy experience many foregone conclusions had been turned on their heads by intelligent defence battle plans.

Mr Justice Singleton watched the proceedings with ill-disguised boredom. On several occasions he had quizzed the young advocate as to why this or that witness had been compelled to attend. Sloane thought well on his feet and had till now provided reasonable explanations for all that took place. The hidden reasoning was Sedgewick's previous handling of the case, and Singleton fought against the prospect of appearing unfair to Speakman.

The defendant hadn't moved throughout the hearing. His pudgy face stared continually at the floor inside the dock. At each adjournment he had trudged away, still handcuffed to the burly prison officers, without a glance at the public gallery. He refused to appear surly or defiant, as if accepting the inevitability of the case's outcome. Fry hoped so.

Returning his glasses to the bridge of his nose he listened as the police officer in charge of the collation of all Speakman's work records concluded his evidence. Fry watched Sloane, to his left, shuffle through a sheaf of notes, before pulling his black gown around his shoulders to begin his questioning.

'Chief Inspector Oates.' The senior policeman straightened his back and turned his attention to Sloane. 'You are to be congratulated on your work. It must have taken some months to compile all this information.'

'There was a lot to collate, sir.'

'But it was readily available?'

'That's right, sir. The company was more than helpful in providing it.'

'And that company has all its records on computer?'

'Correct. The earlier information had been changed from card file to disk: it was all there, but it just took a long time to put it together.'

'As the jury have heard, credit card vouchers for diesel formed a large part of your database?'

'Correct again: their advantage is that they were dated and timed.'

Toby turned slightly towards the jury.

'Let's not beat about the bush: they clearly show Mr Speakman in the right place at the right time for the abductions?'

'That is the prosecution case, sir.'

'Exactly, and the defendant's signature appeared on each and every one, and he has accepted that signature as his?'

'He was interviewed about the matter and agreed that it was his writing.'

'Indeed, a handwriting expert confirmed that admission.'

'So I believe.'

'Therefore, he made no effort to disguise his signature when these stops were within a brief period of the abduction of another girl?'

The chief inspector paused, attempting to gauge where Sloane was heading with his questions.

'Not according to the expert.'

'From your investigations, it would appear that Speakman made no efforts to hide his tracks at all?'

'I wouldn't like to comment on that.'

Singleton had awoken from his stupor and watched the scene carefully.

'Come on, Chief Inspector, you must have been involved in many murder enquiries.'

'Too many, sir.' The policeman meant what he had said.

'And among those have there been any so-called serial killings?'

'A few.'

Toby was beginning to approach dangerous territory. It would be counterproductive to have the jury know how many repeat murderers walked the safe streets of Britain.

'They all attempted to cover their tracks, didn't they?'

'I suppose they did, in their own particular fashion.'

'But at least they made some effort.' The officer nodded curtly. 'Yet here we have Trevor Speakman, almost advertising the fact that he was there, in a forty-foot lorry with the words "Bigg Truck Haulage" in six-foot letters on its side.'

Singleton had heard enough for the moment. 'Mr Sloane, I warned you yesterday about making speeches to the jury during your cross-examination.'

Toby heard Fry mutter, 'Quite right.'

Singleton continued, his cheeks almost matching the colour of his Edwardian sideboards. 'And this court will not tolerate that behaviour any further.'

Toby felt his own face begin to redden. Chief Inspector Oates spoke. 'I'd like to answer that question, if I may.'

'It wasn't a question,' Singleton snapped, then realised he was beginning to trample on too many toes in the same foot-stamping exercise. 'Oh, very well, officer, but be brief.'

Oates stared directly at the jury before replying. 'Perhaps he wanted to be caught.'

The public gallery began to murmur their approval. Toby waited for the glare from the judge to silence them. He nodded his head.

'Perhaps, Chief Inspector, perhaps, but there is another possibility.'

'Sir?'

'That he had nothing to hide in the first place.'

Toby sat down quickly before Singleton had another opportunity to reprimand him in public. Instead, the judge tapped his fingers slowly on the polished oak surface of his bench. He was fighting to keep control of his temper and he succeeded, but only just. Instead, he spun his chair to face the jury and beamed a smile that should have had them edging towards the exit.

'Jury members, it has been a very trying day for all of us. I am going to adjourn the proceedings a little earlier than anticipated. I remind you of the warning I gave before this trial commenced. Do not speak to any person about what takes place in this court. That includes the members of your own family. They may have a point of view, but they are not on this jury. They have not heard what you have heard and, like others in this court' – his eyes flicked momentarily towards Toby – 'may be woefully misguided. Until tomorrow.'

Mr Justice Singleton leaned towards his clerk and spoke behind his hand, before departing for his chambers. Toby rose with the rest of the court and turned towards the dock as Speakman was being led away. He had a fair idea what the conversation between the judge and his clerk involved and wanted to make a quick exit.

In the walnut-walled robing room he quickly slipped out of his wig, gown, white bands and wing collar. Fry sauntered up to him, battered wig in hand.

'You appear to have upset the old boy.'

Toby loathed this affected reference to any judge, as if he were a lovable, crotchety uncle.

'Seems so,' he replied, placing his collar in its box and horsehair wig in its tin with his initials on the top.

'Powerful man; bad enemy,' Fry continued nonchalantly.

'So I've heard.'

'Yes.' Fry removed some imaginary lint from his dark, silk waistcoat. 'Can make them or break them, but a good man to have in your corner.'

Toby wrapped his robes into his blue advocate's bag, then turned to appraise the QC.

'I'm a barrister, not a boxer.'

Fry smiled thinly. 'It's his "ring". This is a prize fight.'

Toby walked to the coat rack and removed his black crombie. 'And which round would you like me to take a dive in?'

Fry didn't have a chance to answer. The tall figure of Singleton's clerk approached him from the door.

'Mr Fry, sir, the judge is delighted to accept your invitation for dinner tonight at the club. Seven-thirty for eight.'

The QC nodded. 'Splendid.'

Toby began to walk towards the door.

'Mr Sloane, sir?' His voice had lost the obsequious chumminess of the preceeding moment. 'The judge will see you in his chambers now.'

'About what?' Toby replied, seeing his fast exit ruined by dallying with Fry.

'A personal matter, sir.'

Toby tried to think quickly. Whatever Singleton had to say had to involve the trial.

'I'd like the shorthand writer to attend.'

'She's gone home, sir.'

'Then she must have been quicker than me.'

The judge's clerk smiled in grim appreciation. They both knew that he had no choice in the matter. To delay the meeting would only serve to exacerbate the position. He removed his coat, and placed it over his arm.

'Very well.'

'Follow me, sir.'

As Toby did as he was told and passed through the doorway, he heard Fry shout, 'Keep your guard up.'

He was shown into Singleton's chambers. To his surprise the judge was down to shirt-sleeves, a decanter of pale sherry and two crystal tulip glasses in front of him. His clerk didn't ask: he merely poured two full glasses and handed one to Toby, as the judge indicated he should sit. The clerk left the room; they were alone.

Singleton looked at him for some time, thoughtfully sipping from his glass.

'I have it imported from Cyprus, a place not noted for its fortified wines, but I acquired a taste for it some years ago and never lost it.'

Toby took a small mouthful. It tasted oily, bitter. He tried not to grimace.

'As I said, an acquired taste.'

'You wanted to speak to me: something personal, I believe.'

'But isn't everything in one way or another?'

Toby waited for Singleton to continue. His master in the law had taught him a very valuable lesson: 'If you want to learn something, then learn how to be a good listener. Any fool can shoot off at the mouth, but the man who listens learns.'

'It is personal, because it relates to how you are pursuing your profession.' The judge looked earnest. 'There is nothing more personal than that.'

Toby remained silent.

'We in the law have heavy burdens placed upon us on a daily basis. Have we given the right advice to a client? Was the cross-examination up to scratch? Was my closing speech sufficiently well prepared and delivered?'

'I'm not complaining, Judge.'

'Nor should you, Sloane. Many aspire but few are chosen: even those that are can still fail to achieve their full potential. A young man can have all the hallmarks of future success, yet the wrong marriage, financial mismanagement or a weakness for the fruit of the grape can cause him to fail. We have all seen it happen.'

'I trust that I don't fit into any of those categories,' Toby answered quietly. He could now see the destination of this 'chat'.

'They were not categories, they were examples. There are as many ways to fail as there are days of the year.'

It was on the third day of diving that Jack found the locket. They had divided the lake into sections, following the currents north-east from the point at which Crichton had pushed her body into the water. Neither of them was an expert, so guesswork played a large role in their work plan. They each dived an hour at a time, coming up to the surface for newly filled water tanks in between. It was heartaching, backbreaking work, but Jangos was a rock. He would not tire of the task until he had found her.

'I drink the lake dry, if need be,' he had announced over stuffed vine leaves the night before. His cousin, Dimitri, had taken over the running of the taverna and the food wasn't up to Jangos's standard. 'It is meant that we find her, Jack.'

They had become firm friends rather then necessary allies over the past few days. When one was exhausted and talked of ending the day's dives, the other would bully or cajole another round of submersions. It was always dusk when they retired for much-needed rest. Jack had never felt so weary or slept so well. He scanned the hills for Rex. But that wasn't his way, to be seen. You always saw him too late.

The light had been fading fast as Jack had plunged down to the lake bed. It was agreed that this was the end of the day's labours. He had dragged the truncated sand-blaster with him and began to shift the silt and pebbles aside. A compass kept him on a true path, just over four feet wide. If he deviated from that course, Jack would feel a sharp tug on the rope around his ankle. So far there had been no reason for either of the submerged men to pull the tether for help.

It was slow work. A blast from the compressed air would activate a maelstrom of debris to momentarily blind him. The first time, Jack had been terrified, but forced himself to remain calm at all costs. It took between ten and fifteen seconds for the disturbed debris to settle, then the process began again. Though the eyes searched and the hands dug and fiddled, the mind was free to roam, the peace unbelievable. During his spells up top, while Jangos searched, Jack daydreamed the hours away, using his newly recovered vision to capture the scenery. One day he would draw all this and impart to the picture how it felt to be in this place, at this time.

They would all be thinking him dead or, if not dead, a man with an explanation for Jacobson's body. Jack had been lucky to escape. When the window frame had crashed in, he'd thought it was all over. The heat was ferocious. When he had come to his senses and vaulted across the fireball of Hollie's bed the soles of his shoes had begun to melt. The staircarpet was fire-resistant and he had been able to dash down the stairs towards the garage, which by then was an inferno.

It was only when he had kicked the back wall of the slate garage open that he remembered Jacobson's body. His first instinct was to leave him; he was dead anyway. Then he tried to drag him out. He had known every moment was vital but it seemed wrong to leave him to turn to a crisp in the flames. He had failed. A beam from the roof caved in on Jacobson's body and he was ablaze in seconds. It was horrible.

It was only when he breathed in the clean, cold air from the back garden that his mind clicked into gear. While he was alive, his family would be in danger. Crichton must have discovered his parents' address and tried to take him out of the action by murdering his family. He kept running: the woods to the rear of the house had provided sufficient cover for his painful escape.

The salt had helped to heal his wounds but, like Crichton, he would be scarred for life. His hands still stung and throbbed, but there was much to take his mind off the pain. His family would be grieving over his death. Jack felt terrible. How would Hollie take this? It would all come good some day, but that was small recompense to a little girl who believed herself an orphan. It was too dangerous to let them know he was OK. Not until he knew for certain that Crichton was in Cyprus could he spare them the torment of his death: there was no other option.

Jack had waited until the sand and silt resettled on the lake bed; that was when he had noticed a stringlike shape. He had moved closer and dug around it, eventually finding that it was a small chain, with something attached to it. It was heavily encrusted with mud – there was no shine – but when he was sure that it was a complete object, he became excited. There were still ten minutes of oxygen left, but he had decided to swim up to the surface with his discovery.

Jangos was surprised to see him until Jack thrust the chain into his hand. The Cypriot nodded, then got to work with some white spirit to clean away the debris of the years. It took some time. For a big man, Jangos worked with great delicacy. He took out a small brush to flick away the last of the small flakes that remained. Though it was heavily tarnished by the corrosive water it could be identified as a circular locket. Jangos nodded at his handiwork, but appeared hesitant about what to do next. Jack didn't want to force the Cypriot into action: if he hesitated, then there was a reason for that hesitation.

Jangos fingered the locket like a rosary, moving it back and forth, while all the time gazing over the lake's still surface. They were silent. Jack watched his friend's face with concern. He was obviously fighting some internal battle. Finally, Jangos gently pushed his thumbnail into the locket's joint, his face a mask of concentrated strength. The years had made it stiff. He grunted, applying pressure in a steady push. It flipped open. Jangos's eyes stared ahead; he was afraid to look inside. He took a deep breath, then dropped his eyes to the object. He nodded twice then, squeezing his eyes closed, Jangos began to rock back and forth. He brought the locket up to his lips and kissed it, whispering one word: 'Kyra.'

Jack watched the pain bite into his face, saw the tears begin to trickle down his cheeks. He silently slipped into the water. Jangos needed to find his peace. Jack began to swim for the shore, scanning the horizon, hoping and not really hoping that Rex was watching.

Hawk moths fluttered around Crichton's campfire on the hillside, almost distracting him from his real purpose. Their love of flames reflected his affair with the water. He had pitched his tent some distance from the lake two days before. The days had been spent in an easily constructed hide within binocular range, watching Forth and the Cypriot dive.

He recognised Kyra's father immediately. Forth had been ingenious. In engaging the assistance of Jangos he had increased the prospects of success. The taverna-keeper must have been told the truth about his daughter's death: it would make for an interesting reunion. In the meantime things had to be monitored.

In all his years as a solicitor – in delicate negotiations, over labyrinthine contracts – he had always waited for the first sign of weakness before severing the head from the negotiative neck. To show oneself was to include the idea of weakness: that would never do; not then, not now. No, rather assess the relative strengths of the opposition and use it against them. Allow them to forge the hammer, then crash it down on the maker with outrage. But then, as now, it was merely a job: something to do, brush the hands after, and say, 'Not bad, not bad at all.'

It should never have come this far, but Rex was pleasantly surprised at Forth's resilience. It had all become a little too pat recently. Too easy. Like the girls. No one was ever there for them. Didn't their parents realise that there were dangerous people about? Too sad; too, too sad.

This was more like it. Rex remembered the great days of ripping the deals from foolish, hungry boys' mouths, still snapping as he slapped them down with the knowledge that they had lost the great race. Forth would lose, Jangos would lose, in time: all in time. Are you watching for me, Jack?

CHAPTER FIFTY-THREE

The case for the defence was about to be put. Toby stood up slowly and deliberately. He adjusted his robe where it had fallen off his shoulders and took a deep breath. He knew it would be a moment that would never leave his memory as long as he lived. If Leone was nervous she didn't show it as he gave her one last look.

'Ladies and gentlemen of the jury,' he began. 'The prosecution, as you are now aware—' The quiet that had descended on the court-room was suddenly shattered as Roger Fry jumped to his feet.

'My Lord, this is highly irregular,' Fry started. Toby sat down in deference to him, although he had already anticipated the objection.

'Yes, Mr Fry, I quite agree. What is the meaning of this, Mr Sloane? Are we to understand from your comments that you intend to make an opening speech to the jury?'

'I should have thought that obvious, my Lord,' said Toby angrily, clambering to his feet again.

'You do appreciate that such a right only exists where you intend to call evidence as to the facts of the case,' Singleton said sharply. 'Perhaps I should ask the jury to retire for one or two moments.'

'There is no need, my Lord, unless of course your Lordship wishes them to be denied the opportunity of hearing the reasoning behind this interruption.' Toby scored a rare point at Singleton's expense.

'Have it your own way, Mr Sloane, but I must warn you again—'

'I hesitate to interrupt your Lordship but I am fully aware that the defence right to make on opening speech is restricted: I do indeed propose to call evidence as to the facts in addition to character evidence on Mr Speakman's behalf.' He'd practised the line a hundred times and he swivelled to watch the reaction from Fry.

'My Lord, the Crown have received no prior notification of any defence alibi witnesses. Furthermore, I am sure I do not need to remind your Lordship that my learned friend has accepted virtually all of the Crown's evidence as to the facts,' Fry stated.

'Well, Mr Sloane?' Singleton nodded for Fry to resume his seat. 'Mr Fry is correct, is he not? I do not have a notice of alibi in my bundle. Perhaps you can enlighten us.' The repeated insinuation of agreement between the judge and the Crown was beginning to grate on Toby: he could only hope that it permeated through to the jury in the same way.

'My Lord, I trust that I have not misled the court in any way, but for the sake of clarity I confirm that I do not intend to call alibi evidence,' Toby said accurately, before sitting down with an exasperated expression.

'I see. Mr Fry, do you have anything further to add?'

In his mind, Toby counted the seconds of silence. What would Fry's reaction be to this cryptic situation? The Crown would now be completely in the dark. They would have no idea what evidence Toby intended to call, nor were they entitled to know. One, two, three, four – he heard frantic shuffling of papers from the juniors behind Fry – five, six, seven . . . too long.

Toby jumped back up and looked in an exaggerated fashion between Singleton and Fry. 'If I might be allowed to continue with my address to the jury, my Lord . . .' He trailed off as Fry waved a dismissive hand in his direction.

'I am most obliged,' Toby said graciously, before continuing. 'Ladies and gentlemen, you have been treated to an overwhelming mountain of evidence, all pointing to the fact that one person alone is responsible for these hideous crimes. The Crown have told you this in their lengthy opening to you and they have repeated it by implication during the course of their highly circumstantial case. Let me say at the outset that I do not seek to persuade you any differently.' He paused and looked each juror in the eye.

'What I do seek to persuade you to conclude is that this man' – he turned and pointed at Speakman's pathetic form in the dock – 'this shell of a creature is not the person this country should be striving to convict. You have heard already his account in the interviews he gave to the police when first arrested. He can't tell you any more and I shall not be calling on him to tell you once more about his poor memory. I will not be inviting you to look at the

374

columns of figures, petrol receipts and hoards of tachograph charts. I will not try to prove that Trevor Speakman wasn't in or around the abduction sites at the relevant times. I will not, furthermore, invite you to search for ways of discrediting the many witnesses we have heard from who may have seen Mr Speakman's lorry at the relevant times.

'No, ladies and gentlemen, I simply ask you to consider, when you have heard the defence evidence, whether you think the prosecution cloak could fit someone else as well as Trevor Speakman, or perhaps even better. The Crown have said, have they not, that if you are sure Speakman committed one murder you can be sure he committed them all? Ladies and gentlemen, using that very same criterion it must then follow that, if it can be proved he didn't commit one of the murders, then he cannot be convicted of any.'

Toby paused again, this time reaching down for the water carafe to his left. If they were to get anywhere it was essential the jury understood. Pouring the water slowly into a glass, he continued. 'The prosecution may put it this way' – then he took a sip and replaced the glass, saying quietly and sincerely – 'it is one for all and all for one . . .'

Singleton threw down his fountain pen in disgust, but the jury had taken it on board.

Later that same day Sloane paused again.

'My Lord, with your leave I call Mr Malcolm Hurst.' Toby waited for the objection. He wasn't disappointed as Fry pushed himself up from the bench and demanded that the jury be sent to their room. When they had trundled out of the box with the jury bailiff, Fry spoke again.

'My Lord, I am familiar with Mr Hurst: he is, I believe, an expert witness in forensic psychiatry. As my learned friend ought to be aware, under the provisions of the Crown Court Rules, Advance Notice of Expert Evidence, a statutory instrument which I think has been in force since 1987, the defence cannot call this witness without leave of the court.'

'But, my Lord, leave is only required if service of the witness statement has not been effected. If your Lordship will allow me just one moment, I'm sure my instructing solicitor will have a record of the date of service,' Toby lied, whilst turning round to Leone. She pulled out the forged recorded delivery slip with a poker face and handed it to Toby. 'Yes, my Lord, here it is dated the fifteenth of October, addressed to Mr Dexter of the Crown Prosecution Service. The post office have not returned it, therefore service is good. The defence cannot be impeded merely because documents have not been passed on from solicitor to counsel.'

Toby handed the slip to the court usher, who proceeded quickly to the judge. Dexter glared over at them, then tugged on Fry's gown hastily to absolve himself from responsibility.

'Well, Mr Fry,' said Singleton reluctantly, 'it does seem proper service has been made.'

'But, my Lord, Mr Dexter has no knowledge of this statement.'

'That may be so, but I am bound by this.' He waved the slip. 'Carry on, Mr Sloane.'

The jury were brought back and Malcolm Hurst was sworn in. He was led by Toby through his evidence regarding his examination of Speakman and concluded forcefully that in his opinion Speakman did not have the fundamental propensity to commit these crimes. One or two members of the jury switched off completely until Fry stood to cross-examine. Toby noticed that Fry had sent out his junior, no doubt to dig some discrediting material to throw at Hurst.

'Mr Hurst, or should I say Dr Hurst, basically your interest is in the study of the human mind, is that correct?'

'Yes, basically.'

'Thank you,' said Fry, snidely, 'and would it be further correct to say that, unlike mathematics or physiology, it is not an exact science?'

'I would agree with the statement,' the witness replied, a little uneasily.

'For instance, unlike other more precise sciences, you could look at a given subject and come to a completely different conclusion or diagnosis from that of one of your fellow psychiatrists.'

'It has been known for people to disagree occasionally, Mr Fry, yes.'

'I see. Would you say, therefore, that it would be possible for the Crown to instruct their own expert, or perhaps two experts, or five even, and for each of them to come to a different conclusion about a person's motivations and propensities, as you put it earlier.'

'It's possible, but I would say unlikely.'

'Unlikely, you say, but certainly possible.' The twists on his words echoed ominously round the room.

'Yes.'

'Not dissimilar from lawyers, in a sense, would you say?'

'I'd go further than that and say we disagree substantially less than members of your own profession, Mr Fry.'

'Yes, that may be so, Dr Hurst: we seem to be witnessing that very phenomenon in this courtroom.' Fry smiled sneeringly as his junior returned and handed him a document. Fry looked at it for a while, aware that everyone was looking at him. He placed it on the bench in front and continued calmly. 'Now, your opinion, it seems, is that Trevor Speakman could not have killed anyone. Is that right?'

'Not strictly true, Mr Fry. I said, in my opinion he does not present himself as a man who exhibits any of the traits normally associated with killers of this nature.'

'So you're saying it's possible he could have killed someone?'

'It's a rare individual who could not, in certain circumstances of self-preservation or defence of loved ones, say. But I reiterate—'

'There's no need, Doctor, I quite understand. Let me ask you, by the way, if you were made aware that Speakman suffers from seizures which lead to blackouts.'

'I had access to his medical records, yes.'

'And it doesn't alter your opinion that there are areas of his brain which must remain forever a mystery to us all, including learned medical men like your good self?'

'I conducted several specialised tests from verbal reasoning skills to personality analysis evaluations—'

'Ah, tests, Doctor, they can produce odd results, especially if the subject is determined to mislead the examiner, can they not?'

'What do you mean?'

'Did it never occur to you that the defendant has been misleading his employers and the vehicle licensing authorities for years? Surely, Doctor, those people are in no different a position to yourself. They too didn't think there was anything wrong with Trevor Speakman because he chose not to tell them about his blackouts in the knowledge that he would certainly lose his licence and his job.'

'It's hardly the same, Mr Fry.'

'Really, Doctor, I'm not sure I would agree with you, but then again, I don't have to decide this case. The jury do, however . . .'

He looked over to them, forcing his eyebrows together in a frown.

Toby didn't even bother to object to the comment. All eyes were on Fry as he sat down with a heavy sigh.

After the short adjournment for lunch, Toby breezed into the empty courtroom and strode straight up to Fry, who was busy reading through Archbold, the criminal practitioner's bible.

'You'd better keep that out, Fry,' said Toby, gesturing to the hefty volume.

'Why's that then, Sloane? It doesn't have much in it about pulling fast strokes, young man,' Fry replied without looking up.

'Not that you'd need any tuition in that direction,' Toby replied flatly.

'I don't know what it is that you're implying, Sloane, but I certainly don't like the tone of it.'

'OK, where should I start? Sven Trondl, I think.'

'What?'

'You heard, Fry. The question is, are you going to object when I apply to have his statement read aloud: section nine?' He couldn't have dropped a bigger bombshell on the silk.

'Never heard of him. Is he one of your surprise witnesses?' He was lying and Toby knew it. Toby pushed home the advantage.

'Not mine, Fry, old boy, yours. I think you'll find it at page one eighty-nine of the thirteenth volume of unused evidence hidden among TIE statements. So, on the contrary, I'm surprised you haven't heard of him.'

'All right, where did you get hold of that statement?'

'You should know: you're probably the one who gave the order for it to be hidden in the first place.'

'I resent that remark, Sloane.'

'I don't care, Fry. The question is, what are you going to do about it?' Toby glared at the silk, daring him to go further. Fry could object and demand that Trondl be called to give live evidence but the beauty of the situation was that he couldn't cross-examine his own witness. He had to concede, but he wasn't happy.

'"The prosecution enjoy no victories"—'

'"And suffer no defeats."' Toby finished the last line for him. 'Save it for the press, Fry, because I'm going to make sure they know all about this when the case is over.'

'Read the damn statement, then,' the silk said angrily before storming out: Toby sat back with a smile. It was the first time he had ever seen Fry rattled. What was more, he was beginning to enjoy himself.

When the court reassembled, Toby read the statement of Sven Trondl, the FBI profiler, to the jury. He read it slowly and carefully, emphasising each segment that confirmed Hurst's evidence. When he'd finished he noticed that a couple of jurors were beginning to sneak glances towards Speakman in the dock: something that hadn't happened before. It meant they were lowering their resistance to him. At the very least, they were starting to think about things properly instead of simply accepting everything they had been told during the prosecution case.

'May it please you, my Lord, I apply to read the statement of Patricia Barraclough,' Toby announced. There was a scuffle to his left as the Crown team frantically searched through the files.

'We object, my Lord,' said Fry, rather weakly.

'My Lord, this witness appears at page four eight seven seven in the seventeenth volume of unused material served by the Crown on the defence; they can hardly object. Further, my Lord, the witness is now regrettably deceased and I respectfully apply to invoke the provisions of Section 23 of the Criminal Justice Act, 1988.'

'I am fully acquainted with the statute, Mr Sloane,' Singleton shouted, causing even Toby to jump. Why had he become so irate?

'I apologise if I have offended the court, my Lord, but this statement is essential to the proper conduct of the defence case. I am not obliged to give the Crown notice of intention and, as I understand the situation, it falls to your Lordship's discretion to admit the statement in evidence.'

'Precisely, Mr Sloane,' Singleton said. 'Is there a death certificate you can produce to confirm what you say?'

'No, my Lord, I rely on common knowledge. The murder of this individual is well documented elsewhere, but, if your Lordship would allow me a short time, I'm sure we can call the pathologist.' Toby gambled that the judge wouldn't waste time simply to wait for the inevitable. He was right, but there was something else that worried him about Singleton's demeanour. The courtroom went deathly silent for what seemed like an hour, but was no more than seconds, as Singleton stared at Sloane with glazed eyes.

'Is your Lordship feeling unwell?' Toby enquired to break the moment.

'Yes, quite all right, Mr Sloane,' Singleton replied, a little too distantly. If the judge didn't allow the statement of Pat Barraclough to be read to the jury, Toby was sure that would be at least one point to take to the Court of Appeal. 'You have my permission, Mr Sloane.'

'Thank you, my Lord. Ladies and gentlemen of the jury . . .' Toby began to recount Barraclough's original statement identifying for the first time the possibility that someone had definitely seen Colleen Bridges alive three days before her body was found in the culvert at Dosmary Pool. There was a collective gasp from the court when he revealed that she had given the police a full vehicle registration mark.

'As my next witness I call Dr Ian Coombs.' As he said it he could hear the eruption to his left. Roger Fry had never moved so quickly to his feet.

'My Lord, this witness is, as your Lordship is well aware, the Home Office forensic scientist. He was asked by the Crown to provide a report collating information garnered from the original autopsies. His report has not been relied upon by the Crown but he is essentially a prosecution witness; the defence were served with that report as unused material. If my learned friend had any questions for the witness he ought to have requested his presence during the prosecution case to give oral testimony. This is merely a time-wasting exercise by my learned friend.'

'I understand, and indeed share, your frustration, Mr Fry, but regrettably my hands are tied. There is no property in a witness and if Mr Sloane wishes to call him I cannot prevent him, although I would like to see a copy of his report before continuing.' Singleton glared at Toby who calmly remained sitting as the papers were handed up to the judge. He looked at the report for no more than a couple of minutes before throwing it down beside his red notebook.

'Mr Sloane, I cannot see that there is anything remotely controversial in the professor's statement, which is probably why the Crown have served it quite properly upon you as unused material. Why do you wish to call him?'

'Because, my Lord, I believe the report before you is incomplete.'

'What nonsense,' Singleton snorted. 'This man is an eminent scientist and his credentials are of the highest calibre. You do not, surely, suggest otherwise?'

'My Lord, I am grateful that you acknowledge the learned doctor's skill and I can assure the court that I do not seek to discredit him in any manner. On the contrary, I simply wish to give him the opportunity of delivering his full findings.' He waited for the words to sink in.

'What do you mean, his full findings?' Singleton was becoming agitated, while Fry was puce with anger.

'I hesitate to guess at the reason why, but it appears that – by some administrative oversight, if I can put it that way – the document before you represents only half of the report commissioned by the Crown.' Toby was treading very carefully. Fry and Dexter were well aware of what he was referring to but could hardly object any more for fear of exposure. Toby wished secretly that he could have told the judge the real reason why only half of Coombs's report had found its way into the trial bundle, but that would involve an investigation into how he had come across the missing half.

Singleton seemed extremely shaky; perhaps he wasn't used to being forced into a corner. But Toby's instinct kept forcing him in another direction. What was it that he saw in those eyes? For a moment, he was lost in thought and the only thing that flashed across his brain was the smell of fear. But why should Singleton be so afraid? Seconds later the judge had regained his normal composure and reluctantly gave his blessing for Coombs to be sworn.

The big man recited the oath and, without prompting, listed his professional address and qualifications, as is customary among experts. Toby asked him to produce his full report and watched for the jury's reaction as he told them about the hair sample.

Now we're getting somewhere, he thought as one or two began to look at each other with raised eyebrows, and at Speakman in a different light. It was beginning to work. The delicate web that Toby was trying to weave for them was actually starting to hang together. Pat Barraclough's eyewitness account of the disappearance of Colleen Bridges; the fact that she had seen four people in the car that night; the fact that four semen samples were discovered; the strands of hair and the fact that Speakman matched none of them.

Fry didn't cross-examine for long. He didn't have any material to refute Coombs's findings and the best he could come up with to shore up the Crown's case was a suggestion that the hair sample was of no relevance given that it could have floated down the culvert from the reservoir of Dosmary Pool.

'So it could have come from anyone, Doctor – wouldn't that be a fair assessment?' Fry concluded his questioning.

Coombs, however, had a response which, even in his wildest moments, Toby could never have hoped for.

'I anticipated that question, Mr Fry, because Mr Dexter held exactly the same view when he visited my laboratory. Out of curiosity I cross-matched the hair sample with all the semen samples recovered from the body and the results show a match with sample number three. I conclude, therefore, that the hair was grasped from the head of the assailant and locked in the hand by way of cardiovascular spasm. There can be no other reasonable explanation.'

All for one and one for all, Toby willed into the jury's minds.

CHAPTER FIFTY-FOUR

Daybreak over the lake arrived with the departure of the screeching bats, flapping home to a guano-strewn cave in the nearby hills. Jangos was grimly quiet as they loaded the gear onto the boat. Each of them knew without words how close they might be. Jack prayed he would be the one to find Kyra, however awful that discovery would be. The buoy Jangos had anchored to the lake bed swayed slightly in the breeze, casting small ripples on the lake's still surface.

Jack felt certain that they would find her today, but that was only the start of the next headache. He could not afford to have the Cypriot authorities involved. Give or take a little graft, bureaucracies were the same the world over, with enough red tape between them to stretch around the earth's circumference.

Jangos gunned the boat's engine into life. Its prow rose slightly as he dipped the whirling blades into the accepting water. Overhead, dark clouds pushed their snouts over looming hills and began to shut out the new day's light. Jack shuddered and glanced back at his friend. The Cypriot was in a deep, dark place of his own, lost in the thought of how different it could have been, should have been. Jack noticed that a spear gun was loaded and nestled next to the silent Cypriot inside the boat.

Three hours later it was Jack's turn to dive; there had been minimal conversation. The lack of available sunlight had been reduced further by the storm-threatening clouds that now covered the sky above. Jack shivered. His wetsuit should have kept his body temperature constant, but he felt cold nonetheless.

'No light down there today, Jack, getting worse,' Jangos muttered, as he ripped off his face mask and threw it into the bottom of the boat.

'I'll take my turn, Jangos, it's only fair.'

Jangos flashed a quick glance towards him. 'You English. Always fairness, never what is right.'

Jack didn't want to argue with his friend about national characteristics, as that wasn't what his words were about. How would he feel sitting here day after day searching for Hollie's body? He didn't know, couldn't know, didn't want to know. 'If it gets any worse, we'll call it a day.'

Jangos nodded curtly. Jack spat into his face mask, whisked his legs over the side and ducked into the lake's embrace. Jangos was right: it was pitch-black down there He felt his way down to the blaster by the compression cable attached to its trigger. It felt colder than he had ever known. If his teeth had not been clamped on the rubber mouthpiece of his aqualung they would have chattered together like icy castanets.

Jack began to blast the lake bed with the compressed air. He worked patiently, waiting for each dark cloud of swirling debris to settle before probing with his fingers into the disturbed area. He was twenty minutes into his first tankful of oxygen when a flash of white caught his eye. It stood out against the darkness and, though it was a tiny glimpse, it demanded his attention. Jack laid the blaster on the lake bed. It was heavier than water and nestled gently on the bottom. He moved closer to the area of inspection, until he was inches away. He removed a jagged diver's knife from its leg sheath and began to scrape away the surface area. It was slow work. With each fresh rendering a small but still blinding whirlwind obstructed his vision. He realised he was breathing hard and forced himself back into the slow deliberate rhythm that this task demanded.

There was white, at least a circumference of white surrounding a dark circle about an inch and a half in diameter. He placed his finger in the hole to test its depth, but his finger wasn't long enough to reach the back of whatever it was; that was if it had a back. Instead, he waggled his finger to the right and could feel a bridge of some sort, then felt another hole. Jack watched in fascination as his questing digit appeared through the sand about an inch to the right of the first hole. With his free hand he scraped away the sand of the space between. With each scrape he was a little closer to his goal. Time was beginning to work against him.

Checking his watch, he saw that he had stayed down beyond

the agreed span and in confirmation felt a sharp tug on the rope secured to his ankle. Jack ignored it: he was nearly there. Whatever lay between his fingers would present itself soon. Motes and dust shimmied in his face before its weight compelled it to return to its bed. As it did he saw that he had his finger through the eye sockets of a bone-white skull. Jack vomited into his mouthpiece, which sprang out and expelled a blast of bubbles and stale breakfast coffee into the water.

He felt the surge of horrified panic. His natural instinct was to break for the surface. He fought his fear and, though all life-giving oxygen had exited his starved lungs, plunged his knife deep into the bed next to the skull. They had found her, he thought, as his pressed lungs craved fresh air.

He kicked as slowly as he could and finally felt the rope pulling him up to the boat. He surfaced with a wallowing thrash and grasped for the side of the boat, gasping for air.

Crichton watched the scene through the mounting gloom; it had begun to rain heavily. They had found something, that was clear. The old Cypriot was still strong. Rex watched in admiration as Forth was plucked from the water and placed carefully into the belly of the boat. He trained the binoculars onto Jangos's face, which was knotted with concern at Forth's distress. He increased the focus to its maximum. How Jangos reacted would tell him all. His expression changed from concern to slack concentration, then to bewilderment, then Rex saw the tears course down the Cypriot's face. Jangos threw back his head and bellowed one word into the driving rain. Crichton heard it carry in the natural amphitheatre of the hills: 'Kyra.'

Jangos stood, arms outstretched to the heavens, his tears mingling with the clean, hard rain. Crichton had seen enough. He picked up his bag and began to skirt the lake's edge, hidden from view by the citrus trees bending under the weight of the deluge and the wind that had sprung up and swept down the contours of the hills into the heart of the lake.

Leone was nervous. Her hands felt damp against the leather steering wheel as she manoeuvred her car around the tight corners that hugged the vast gloomy expanse of Exmoor. The slight available light from a milky afternoon sun seeped away as the day began to close in on her journey.

She was already regretting her decision to visit Crichton's cottage. There was no guarantee that he would not be there, but his absence from the firm suggested that he might well have swallowed the bait. Leone swallowed hard herself when she remembered that the 'bait' was Jack.

They had discovered the cottage's address through Toby's trawl of the HOLMES system some days before, but it was only when Trondl had focused once more on the killer's 'trophies' or souvenirs that she had made her final decision to visit this bleak place. Leone wasn't sure what it was she was looking for but suspected that it – if it existed – would be obvious once discovered.

The road swept away from a dark tract of boggy land, down into a dip, then upward towards one of the few hills this part of the moor possessed. Leone switched her headlights to full beam, though this did little to cut through the banks of drifting fog that were the area's signature. It couldn't be far now. The detailed Ordnance Survey map of the area that lay on the passenger seat had a small red circle around a building: Crichton's cottage. As she drove, slowly now, in second gear, car engine at a low hum, Leone glanced to her left and, though visibility was decreasing with each passing second, could just discern a dark shadow, more solid than the mist. Leone parked the car around the next slight bend in the rough road, just out of sight of the dwelling. She decided not to leave the keys in the vehicle, even though the moor was so remote, but left the car unlocked in case she needed to make a hasty exit.

The evening air was cold against her exposed throat, but she felt colder than the temperature demanded. The hefty rubber flashlight felt comfortable in her hand as she began to walk through the ever-mounting gloom to King Arthur's lair. Jesus, she thought, it's like *The Hound of the Baskervilles*. The gravel crackled under her feet; the cottage was no more than sixty feet away.

Toby knew Brian Stafford was waiting nervously outside.

'Mr Sloane, are we to wait all afternoon for your next evidence?' the judge boomed.

Toby turned quickly, took a deep breath and said, 'No, my Lord, the defence call Brian Stafford.' He looked around at Fry, who was peering over his half-rims, eyebrows clenched in confusion. The call went down the corridor outside the court and shortly afterwards a tall, thin man in a grey suit with even greyer skin walked confidently to the witness box to be sworn in. Despite his pallor he had a remarkably cheerful face with bright, blue eyes.

'Repeat the words from the card and take the Bible in your right hand,' the usher said to him.

'I swear by almighty God to tell the truth, the whole truth and nothing but the truth.'

Leone progressed with painful caution. She had decided against the use of the torch unless it was absolutely necessary, as it not only illuminated the way but also drew attention to its user. Her eyes had become accustomed to the encroaching darkness.

Is this where you brought them, Rex? Is this where you played with them before the end? The last home they would ever know before the water? The thought made her angry but more watchful, aware of the unthinkable danger she might face.

Leone hid herself in a gnarled copse of twisted trees forty feet to the left of the building, from where she had an unobstructed view. It was single storey, oblong in shape, low but long and dark grey in colour, almost camouflaged amongst the hues of the moor. There were few windows along its exterior and those that existed were not designed to promote a feeling of light and space. She was relieved that none of them was lit.

Keeping low, Leone scouted around to the rear of the cottage where the track from the road ended at a hard-stand yard; there was no car or garage to park one in.

'So far, so gut-wrenching,' she whispered to the increasingly cold air as she crept towards the rear door. This was not a picture-box cottage. Rotten wooden window boxes showed no sign of care, the soil unturned and crusty as she touched its surface. Rusted farming tools lay around the sides of the house, age-spotted brown by abandonment.

Not really a man of the soil, are you, Rex? she thought as she turned the tarnished metal door handle. It wouldn't open. She wasn't surprised. A man as careful as Crichton was hardly likely to forget to cancel the milk or leave a window open for fresh air. Leone stooped down and retrieved one of the discarded farm tools.

387

The warped oak door bent away from the true of the frame in an area just above the locking mechanism. She forced the item's spike into the gap and began to apply increasing pressure on the lever, then a sharp crack of splintered wood sliced through the brooding silence. She stopped immediately, dropped down below the poky window's level and held her breath. Leone felt a pulse in her right temple pounding. Her vision, sharpened by surging adrenalin, was now almost nocturnal. There was no movement. No response. No one home.

She allowed a now stale pocket of air to escape from between her lips, then realised how fiercely her breaking-and-entering tool was held in her hand, like a club, which Leone knew she would use, if it came to that.

She replaced it where the fractured wood, lighter in colour, splayed out. Burglary, she thought: the old man would have been proud.

Leone pushed harder, widening the crack with a rocking motion until, with what sounded like an explosion in the still air, it yawned open.

Jack's head was buzzing. He was exhausted. The wind began to rock the inflatable from side to side as he lay slumped, still gasping for air. He looked up to where Jangos, his friend the Cypriot, still stood, eyes turned up to the old gods.

'Jangos,' Jack shouted over the wind's whip and crack, 'Jangos, sit down, please, sit down or we'll go over.'

He moved his body into the craft's centre of balance striving for some stability. Jangos's great face stared down at him, eyes hard as obsidian, his teeth exposed in a snarl. He was breathing quickly.

'Jangos, for God's sake, sit down.'

The Cypriot's eyes flicked back to the huge black clouds. 'There is no God,' he screamed over the tumult's shriek. Jack stretched across for the loaded spear gun. He grasped it and felt for the trigger, then swung it around to point at his friend's chest.

'Jangos,' he shouted, and was rewarded with an appraising sneer. 'Sit the fuck down, for both our sakes.'

Jangos ignored him as he reached for an oxygen tank and threw it around his burly shoulders.

'You can't go down, not in this, it's too dangerous.'

Jangos grabbed a face mask and fixed it on his forehead. He

turned to Jack. 'No, pointing that at me is dangerous for you. Never threaten a Cypriot unless you willing to carry it out.'

Jack laid the weapon down but still within reach should it become necessary. 'I'm sorry, Jangos.' He held his palms out in supplication. The big man nodded once. 'We can come back tomorrow.'

'No,' he said as he moved to the boat's side. 'She down there too long already.'

'Then another day won't make a difference.'

Jangos pointed a large finger into his face. 'It make a difference to me. You take boat back, or swim, whatever you want, I go for my Kyra. I have never seen a storm like this. It could move her, now you disturb bed of lake. And my Kyra.'

As the great man's bulk shifted, Jack threw himself to the other side to counterbalance the change in weight.

'I'll be here, Jangos,' he shouted as his grieving comrade grasped a plastic bag to collect his long-dead daughter's remains. He slipped beneath the swell of the surface.

It took half an hour: thirty minutes of lurching movement, the inflatable threatening to pitch at any moment. As it began to tip, Jack threw himself from side to side to keep himself afloat. Lashing rain hammered horizontally into his face, causing him to don a face mask to avoid its searing bite. With a rush of water, Jangos appeared and carefully placed the black bag inside the boat. Jack didn't dare to help Jangos in, as with the yaw and pitch of their movement any loss of balance would be disastrous. Jangos plumped down at the stern. The engine responded only after several pulls on the motor cord.

'Now we go back, Jack Forth, and decide what we do with my Kyra.'

He angled the motor's blades to take them back to the safety of the land.

Jangos took the boat right up to the lake's edge, close to where his truck was parked. Jack was torn between relief and exhaustion as he scampered onto the certain surface of dry land. Around them the leaves were in rushing turmoil, the storm was increasing in ferocity. It took them a couple of minutes to drag the boat out. At least this part was over.

Leone surveyed the dank interior of the cottage. In her left hand the torch's beam cut through the darkness, illuminating crammed bookshelves and an overstuffed armchair. In her dominant hand, her jemmy was hefted as a weapon.

She shuffled forward, feeling her way with her feet and using the beam to search for a light switch. After some seconds Leone knew that this place was without electricity and that her torch was her only aid. Her heart was racing even though she knew the cottage was deserted. It felt as though she were acting in a bad schlock horror film, where the baseball-jacketed high-school kids were warned, 'Under no, and I mean *no*, circumstances go into the attic.' But that was just what Leone had, in a sense, done.

She sniffed the air: it smelled bad, like a kipper on a car radiator but worse. The room was low, as she had expected from the exterior view. The light picked out thick black beams of wood embedded in the coarse ceiling, that ran to similar beams reaching vertically from the floor. This was obviously the living room, if anything in the morbid place could be described as living.

To the right another door stood half open, inviting her to push through and enter the next room into the kitchen. The range was filthy with grime, caked black in its decrepitude. A dwarf Welsh dresser skulked in one corner behind a rough-hewn table and one tired stool.

'Not one for dinner parties either, I see,' she whispered to keep herself company and the fear at bay. The porcelain sink, once white, now Windsor-soup brown, gave her little assistance in her search for evidence or clues. As she swept the beam away her eyes alighted on a flash of bright white that stood starkly against the room's other objects. Leone walked towards it, bent and scooped up what turned out to be a paper bag. She trained the light upon it and could see that it was from a medical supplies company and had once contained a colostomy bag. She could not discern what possible use the bag could have had, but realised that Crichton had long passed his 'psycho proficiency' test. Pleased with her grim joke Leone tucked the bag into her back pocket, scanned the rest of the room without success, then left by another adjoining door. She checked her watch: 4 p.m., yet it felt like midnight. She wanted to be back in the light away from all this; with Jack or with Toby in the courtroom. She wondered how they were feeling now.

'Mr Stafford, you were in the employ of Sir Colin Bigg, were you not, in the capacity of driver?'

'Chauffeur, sir.'

'I do apologise; chauffeur,' Toby repeated in deference. 'And would I be right in saying that you were so employed during the years 1987 to 1990?'

'That's right, sir.'

'Specifically, Mr Stafford, can you confirm for us that during 1990 you drove Sir Colin's green Bentley?'

'Bentley turbo, yes, sir.'

'Registration number G65 CTB?' The mention of the same number as appeared in Barraclough's statement, and of Sir Colin Bigg, caused a ripple of anticipation around the court.

'That's correct, sir.'

'And can you further confirm that on the night of the fourteenth of September 1990 you were on duty, driving Sir Colin, among other places, to central London?'

'Yes, sir, I can.' The man smiled to the jury.

'On that night, did Sir Colin have company?'

'He did, sir.'

'Do you know who travelled with him?'

'No, sir.'

'Do you know how many people were in the car that night at around eleven forty-five p.m.?'

'Sir Colin and three guests, sir.'

'And did you stop the vehicle to pick up anyone else?'

'We did, sir.'

'And who was that?'

'The young girl I've seen the picture of.'

'Take a look at this, if you would.' Toby handed up a photograph of Colleen Bridges. 'Is this the girl?'

'That's her, sir, only she wasn't dressed quite like that,' he said, examining the photograph of Colleen dressed in school uniform: the last taken before she had run away from Ireland.

'And where did you take her that night?'

'I dropped them all at an address in Knightsbridge and waited for about two hours before Sir Colin returned and directed me to take him home.'

'And are you sure about the date?'

'I've checked it in my diary, sir.'

'Mr Stafford, did you ever see the girl again?'

'No, sir.'

'And were you ever approached by the police for this information at any time during the last five years?'

'No, sir, I was not.'

The effect was stunning. Singleton was glaring at Fry, who was in animated discussion with his juniors. The evidence couldn't have come out better. Toby had managed to shift the goalposts. There was now a definitive link between Pat Barraclough's sighting of the car and the actual driver who had just testified that Sir Colin Bigg, one of Britain's most renowned industrialists, had seen Colleen Bridges alive only twenty-four hours before her body had been discovered.

Toby had cast the line he hoped would be taken by the Crown: they had to call Sir Colin to give evidence in rebuttal to discredit Stafford.

Leone, though still cold, was damp with dread. The odour she had detected on her entrance to the cottage remained but had become more rank, more intimidating. The other rooms she searched offered up few secrets other than a love of taxidermy. There was a regiment of stuffed animals lining the walls. Leone had seen many such exhibits before, but they had been fixed in snarling contempt of their killers: Crichton's merely registered expressions of pain and bewilderment at their predicament.

'Was it like this with the girls, Rex? Is that what you wanted to see?' she asked the moth-ravaged figure of a cowering fox. Curiously she felt close to some truth, some revelation, herself.

Leone had been travelling in an anticlockwise circle. The cottage was two rooms deep; that meant that she would soon return to her point of entry. Another closed door faced her. Leone clicked the top latch and pushed it open. She trained the beam of light about the place, but it was here that the smell was strongest, as if the other rooms were a mere taster of the real thing. She tried to breathe through her mouth to cancel out the vile odour, but it still seeped through to her olfactory nerves. It was the smell of piss, excreta and fear.

Leone knew it, as she had known nothing more certainly in her life: human beings had died here in hopelessness and misery. Some said that the concentration camps of Nazi Germany had the echoes of misery ringing through their quiet abandoned huts, that the earth outside was rotten with corruption, cool and creeping to the touch; now she believed that. This place was a killing and torture ground. Waves of shivers ran through her body, the torch shaking in her hand.

As the tremors passed she picked out a large chair with bindings attached that faced a blank wall, with nothing to distract a victim's attention away from the inevitablity of their fate. She fought her fear. There might well be ghosts in this place, but they would mean her no harm. At the foot of the grim chair, she found a hypodermic needle from a syringe and carefully placed it inside the medical supply bag in the back pocket of her trousers. She didn't want to stay in this room any longer, but forced herself painstakingly to scour its interior for evidence. There was nothing more to find. Trondl had been wrong, there were no 'souvenirs'. But the 'Mind-Hunter' had seemed so certain of his conclusion.

'He will have kept something from all of them, he has to: it's his way of reliving the moment. Maybe a video, or photograph, who knows, but something.' She could remember his words, almost see them as solid entities in the air. She had to keep looking. Leone mentally retraced her steps and counted off the rooms she had searched. All that was missing was a bedroom, somewhere for the sick bastard to rest his head when the 'work' was done. In front of her a steel padlock glinted dully in the torch light barring her entrance to another room.

Jack didn't want to look into the bag. He knew that if he were to succeed he must, but now wasn't the right time. Jangos ducked around the back of the truck out of his vision just before Jack heard a muffled thud as Jangos dropped backwards and down to the ground with a crash. Jack could see that he was bleeding heavily from a head wound. He began to rush towards the unconscious figure when another appeared, holding a spear gun: Crichton. He nodded to Jack before kicking Jangos savagely on the head with the deadly barb still trained on his chest.

'Down on your knees, Mr Forth,' he shouted. 'I don't ask twice.'

Dropping down, Jack scanned the area for a weapon, something to give him an edge.

'Hands behind your back.' Jack complied. Crichton moved behind him. Jack felt a nerve-jangling blow to the base of his neck. He pitched forward to the mud of the sodden ground and tasted its bitterness. A blinding light pierced his vision in response to the assault. His ears rang with pain. He could feel the sharpness of the spear gun's tip on the back of his skull.

'This should come straight out of your left eye, Mr Forth: most satisfactory. When you are no longer with us I'll take the other out too.' Crichton's voice carried with the wind.

'A calling card?' Jack shouted.

'An amusement,' Crichton replied. 'I'd say it's been fun, but that would be disingenuous. Anyway, goodbye.'

Jack felt the pressure of Crichton's foot begin to tense for the *coup de grâce*.

'I know all about you, you motherfucker,' Jack bellowed. Crichton hesitated, for a second, then Jack felt a vicious blow to the back of his head. He shook it to see off the pain.

'Perhaps I'll take a little longer with you than I had intended,' Crichton hissed in his ear. 'What about a firebrand blinding? It won't kill you, at least not immediately, but the pain will keep you warm.'

Jack ignored him. 'You wanted her, didn't you, the drunken bitch? But she didn't want you once she scalded you into ugliness.'

He felt another blow to his head, this time his ear took the brunt.

'I will make you my finest piece of work, Forth. A gutting knife should be fine: I'll save your genitals until last.'

When Toby walked into the robing room the next morning he knew that it had worked. It felt like the most important day of his life. Fry avoided him and was huddled with his juniors, who were forming a barrier around him in the corner. They were whispering but he could guess the gist of the conversation as he robed up.

The fact that he had now closed his case with the damning evidence of Stafford meant only one thing: the Crown would have to call Sir Colin Bigg. Fry's cross-examination of Stafford had been ineffectual: the man hadn't so much as a parking ticket and no axe to grind. He was certain that he never made mistakes in his diary and no matter which way the questions were put he wouldn't be moved. One of the country's most eminent industrialists had therefore been implicated in association with a teenage prostitute who had been found dead only hours later. The Crown couldn't allow Stafford's evidence to remain unchallenged. Fry didn't know that Toby had already seen the TIE statement wherein Sir Colin had told the police the car was safely in the garage at his home at the relevant time. Whichever way he looked at it, Toby couldn't see a way out: they had to call him. And Toby was ready.

Singleton lumbered onto the bench at exactly 10.30. His eyes looked heavy and strangely distant. Toby hoped he wasn't about to collapse on them: that would inevitably mean a discharged jury and he was beginning to like the one they had. Everyone rose and waited a few moments for Singleton to settle himself. The court clerk bellowed out the usual opening: 'All persons having business before Her Majesty's justices draw near and give their attendance.' Toby felt a rush of adrenalin and a tingle at the base of his neck. Roger Fry stood.

'My Lord, with your leave, the Crown seeks to call evidence in rebuttal.'

'I thought you might have that application, Mr Fry, and I have addressed my mind to it overnight. That is why I have asked the jury to remain in their room for a while until we have taken stock. It appears to me that you are now in some difficulty, are you not, in particular with regard to count one?'

'My Lord . . .' Fry looked startled and Toby's instincts forced him bolt upright. What was the judge saying? That the Crown's case had collapsed on count one? If so, then surely it would mean— His thoughts were interrupted.

'The evidence of Mr Stafford demonstrates a lacuna in the Crown's case: there is no direct evidence that Speakman had contact with Colleen Bridges between the time of her disappearance and her death, yet there is clear evidence that someone else did.'

'My Lord, the Crown does not accept Stafford's account and I have evidence in rebuttal which, in my respectful submission, the jury must have the opportunity of weighing for themselves.'

'Your evidence being Sir Colin Bigg, I anticipate.'

'Exactly, my Lord.'

Toby's brain was racing. What was the judge doing? He had been playing tag with the Crown since the case began. What had changed his mind? While Toby knew Stafford's evidence was damning there was still room for the jury to conclude that Speakman had picked the girl up after she left the Knightsbridge area. Something wasn't right. Fry was demanding the right to call the evidence because he knew that if he didn't the jury would be forced to accept Stafford's account. If they then concluded Speakman was not guilty on the Colleen Bridges murder, surely he was not guilty on them all because that was the way the case had been put throughout.

Toby looked up to the judge. He was cupping his face in his hands and an almost vacant expression dwelled on his broad features. The room was so quiet that the only sound to be heard was the soft buzzing of electricity from the fluorescent tubes overhead.

'I want you to reconsider your position, Mr Fry. Take instructions from the Attorney General and the Director of Public Prosecutions. I believe your case to be fundamentally flawed,' Singleton said slowly.

'I do not need to take instructions,' Fry erupted. 'The Crown's case is sound and I repeat my demand for the right to call Sir Colin Bigg. You have no discretion in these circumstances.' He was furious.

Toby could hardly believe what was taking place as Singleton replied sadly, 'So be it, Mr Fry. So be it.'

'Warmer, warmer, hot,' she chanted, reliving the childhood game as once again her newfound skills as a burglar were put to the test. But this was no crumbling wooden door, weakened by the elements. The hasps were firmly screwed into the frame and, despite pitting her full strength with it, she could not shift it a millimetre. Whatever was in there had to be worth seeing, and she had to get in. Leone attempted to unscrew the steel heads of the hasps, but they were firmly entrenched.

'What would a decent cat burglar do? Come on, Leone girl, think!'

She walked back through the cottage until she was back outside, at her point of entry. By her reckoning the next window to the left of the door had to be the window to the sealed room. It was shuttered – the only one that was. That told her she was right. Leone began to force the shutters away from the crumbling plasterwork, which cascaded onto her feet. One part of her didn't want to gain entry, the other knew that she must. Eventually one of them gave way. She used the leverage gained to force the other open. The glass of the window was filthy with neglect. It must have been years since the sun had illuminated the room's interior.

'But that's the way you like it, isn't it, Rex?' she said as she smashed the window with her makeshift jemmy. Fetid air seemed to hiss from inside. Reaching down, Leone released the catch on the window, then heaved it open, and, knocking loose shards of glass away, climbed gingerly inside.

To her left Leone could make out a single bed with a dishevelled duvet hanging down to the rough flagstone floor beneath. The room had a small table and chair set to the back wall, to the left of the door that had denied her access to his sleeping quarters. A small bookcase stood next to the other side of the door. It had few books on it. Leone approached, shining the flashlight before her, and stooped to view the printed works.

First to demand her attention was a small battered tome entitled *The Thoughts of Lao Tzu*, next to that the works of the American poet T. S. Eliot: that too was well thumbed, particularly at *The Waste Land* and *Four Quartets*.

Jack's breathing was ragged now. He had to focus. 'How are your own balls, Crichton? You fucking deformed freak: must be smooth as lava down there.'

Jack felt himself being rolled over and kicked until he was at the side of the truck. Shielding his head from the blows, he continued to shout, 'Your own baby, your own blood, you!'

The attack ceased. Jack looked up through the blinding rain and rubbed some of the blood from his eyes. Crichton was towering over him, his face consumed with fury, but then he stopped and flashed a smile. He placed the barb against Jack's eye. 'You die, that is all. No apology, no explanation.'

Jack could tell by the cold grin that it was over. He clenched his eyes shut waiting for the spear to pierce his brain. His last thoughts were of Hollie, Fiona and Leone and he felt almost peaceful as he waited for his life candle to be snuffed.

From above he heard a thump, then a scream: it was Crichton's voice. Looking up, he saw that Crichton's hand had been pinned to the thin metal of the truck door by another spear. Jack spun round to see the bleeding shape of Jangos discard the empty spear gun and move towards Crichton, his hands outstretched. Crichton pointed his own weapon at the approaching figure as he struggled to pull his pinned and bleeding hand from the truck.

'Get back, old man.'

*   *   *

Toby took a full note of every lying word that fell from Sir Colin's fleshy lips during the examination in chief. He looked uncomfortable and sharkish dressed in a blue Bengal-striped shirt and yellow tie underneath an expensive, grey chalkstripe suit. At times he had attempted indignation but Toby knew he was faking. All he had to do now was to prove it.

'Your witness,' Fry said to Toby when he had finished extracting the last lie. Toby made one final check in the briefcase at his feet for the book. It was still there. Rising to his feet, he and Sir Colin locked eyes.

'Sir Colin,' he began, 'I have never been one for unnecessary cruelty, nor do I enjoy watching others suffer, so I will ask you right at the outset to retract everything that you have said in answer to my learned friend's questions and give this court the truth. Will you do that, sir?'

'I have told the truth already.'

'Are you sure, Sir Colin?'

'Of course I'm sure: what is this?'

'You are here to answer questions, not ask them, Sir Colin. Now, are you quite clear that on the night in question you were at home and that your car was also garaged.'

'Quite sure: I've said so already.'

'So Mr Stafford, your ex-chauffeur, has invented this entire fantasy?'

'Yes.'

'What, all of this detail he has given to the court: the guests in your car, the visit to the Explorer's Club, the prostitute, the Knightsbridge apartment, everything?'

'Yes.'

'Why?'

'I have no idea. I'm a very rich man; a lot of people bear grudges.'

'But not Mr Stafford: he told us he only wanted to tell the truth.'

'Everyone has an agenda but sometimes it's hidden so deep you can't dig it out.'

'Is that right?'

'I believe so. At least my experience in the business world makes me believe so.'

'Seeing as you've brought up your business experience I may as well ask you, have you ever had any dealings with a man called Jonathan Berkeley?' Toby delivered the line in an almost casual tone and he could detect the faintest twitch of Sir Colin's mouth. Fry jumped up before he could answer.

'My Lord, I fail to see what relevance this has to the issues.'

Before the judge could rule, Sir Colin answered, 'No, I don't believe we ever met.'

'I see,' said Toby, 'but you are aware that he is now dead so it would be difficult for me to prove you wrong about that, wouldn't it, Sir Colin?'

'I suppose so.' He was beginning to look very uncomfortable. Now was the time. Toby reached down into his briefcase and pulled out the black leather volume.

'I wonder whether you could look at this for me, Sir Colin. Just read the flagged page to yourself for a moment, please.' The usher took the book from Toby and walked slowly around to the witness box. The press were scribbling ferociously into their jotters while Fry looked on bemused. The colour visibly drained away from Sir Colin's face. He snorted as he snapped the book shut.

'Now that you've had the opportunity I wonder whether you would be so good as to enlighten the court as to what it actually is.'

'You know damn well what it is!' he exploded.

'Very well. For the sake of the record, the witness has just been given defence exhibit number one, the visitor's book from the Explorer's Club flagged at the fourteenth of September 1990, the night of Colleen Bridges' disappearance.' Toby turned back to Sir Colin. 'It shows, does it not, that you were present in the club that evening with two other guests?'

'You know it does.' The courtroom exploded in a collective gasp.

'You accept, therefore, that you have lied on oath earlier today, Sir Colin.'

Silence.

'You must further accept, Sir Colin, that when you were interviewed by the police investigating the murder of Colleen Bridges you also lied.'

More deathly silence. The man stood shakily in the box staring at Toby, his eyes transfixed.

'You have pilloried the good character of Mr Stafford in an

attempt to conceal the truth, Sir Colin, and I implore you once more, in the name of justice: give this court the truth.'

Bigg collapsed with a heavy thud against the brass rail as Singleton gave him a warning about self-incrimination. Journalists ran out of the courtroom to the telephones: the City would know by now what was going on. Slowly, Bigg lifted his head. Toby could see the veins in his neck pumping the blood to his brain.

'Sir Colin, did you pick up Colleen Bridges that night?'

'Yes.'

'Did you have sex with her?'

'Yes, we all did.'

'Tell the court who you were with that night.'

'Jonathan Berkeley and Rex Crichton.' At the mention of these names the public gallery lost control: shouts of 'scum', 'bastards' and tears of grief from distraught parents all melted into the chaos.

'Did you murder Colleen Bridges?' Toby shouted through the mêlée.

'No, no, no, for Christ's sake, no. She blacked out on us. Crichton had given her a loaded cocktail but she was still alive when I left. Crichton said he would drop her near King's Cross. Oh, Christ, forgive me. I wish it had never happened.' He broke down, sobbing uncontrollably.

'Do you have any knowledge about the other girls in this case?' Toby said with a steel edge to his voice.

'As God is my witness, Speakman,' Sir Colin shouted to the bewildered accused, 'it was out of my control.'

'Sir Colin, I repeat, do you have any knowledge of the other victims in this case?'

Toby watched as Sir Colin's watery eyes flickered from him to Singleton. Suddenly he clutched at his chest and in a rasping, throaty drawl he said, 'Rex Crichton is the Devil himself. May God forgive us all.' Then the industrialist crashed to the floor, spilling out of the box, his face the colour of a winter's sky.

Singleton threw his pen down and stormed off the bench without waiting to witness any more. Fry buried his face in his hands and Toby stood there mesmerised with one question hanging off his tongue.

'Who was the fourth man, Sir Colin? Who was the fourth man?'

Sir Colin raised a finger and pointed at the back of the disappearing judge.

'Bedtime reading, Rex?' Leone muttered, replacing the aged book to its original place. There had to be something more than this. It still wasn't proof. She searched the rest of the room in vain. There had to be more. Crichton would not have gone to the trouble of protecting its interior unless there was something valuable to protect. Try as she might Leone could not discover what that was. She had felt so certain, but now that certainty had vanished with the last paltry rays of the sun.

Leone slumped down on the hard bed and dropped her tired head into her damp hands. She massaged the veins in her forehead and dropped her eyes down to the floor. That was when she noticed the uneven flagstone. It stood prouder than the rest by a centimetre or so. The area around it was correspondingly lower. Leone dropped down to her hands and knees to examine it more closely. She pushed against its right-hand side and could feel a slight rocking motion, suggesting that it was not properly bedded in with the others. Leone forced the jemmy, now a familiar friend, into the slight crack that appeared with the motion and began to force the flag away. It was easier than she had expected, as if it were well used to this movement. With a grating moan it was pushed to one side. She trained the torch beam inside the hole beneath.

There was a large box in the excavated area. She reached in and with some effort pulled the casket from its hiding place. Two feet by three, it was simple woodwork, as if a statement against elaboration. There was no padlock upon its exterior or lock or bar to its entrance. Leone grasped both sides and pulled open the lid.

'Look for trophies.'

Jangos continued walking slowly towards him. Crichton took careful aim and pulled the trigger. The deadly barb took Jangos through the throat. He swayed slightly. Most men would have been propelled onto their backs, but Jangos felt for the arrow and pulled it from his neck. Blood fountained from it. He began to walk again. Crichton screamed as he pulled his hand away from the door: the spear was still embedded in it: he had pushed his hand right down its shaft.

Jack's strength was beginning to return with the change in events. He threw himself at Crichton's legs. But Crichton dodged him easily and delivered a stinging kick to his temple. Jack slumped back down to the ground. Then Jangos was upon the solicitor, who hit him repeatedly in the face with the butt of the spear gun, but it made no difference. Jangos picked Crichton up and began to walk towards the water. Jack's vision was blurred but he could hear the Cypriot's guttural words. 'To the water,' he said through thick blood.

Jack attempted to climb to his feet, but his knees buckled under him. Instead, he began to crawl behind Jangos's inexorable progress towards the lake. Even when Crichton bit off one of his ears and spat it to the ground, the Cypriot continued his slow progress to the storm-whipped water.

'Not the water,' Crichton screamed, 'please, not the water.'

Jangos's remaining ear was deaf to his plea. Jack pulled himself forward inch by inch. The last thing he saw before he passed out was the two figures disappear into the water and from his view. Jangos's huge head turned to look at him briefly then returned to his task. They were gone.

Trondl's words punched through her mind: was this what she was looking for? A red velvet cover masked what was beneath. Taking a deep breath Leone tore the sheet away with a flourish. Inside were what looked like seven white grapefruits. It was only by peering closer that Leone could see they were the heads of seven bald, children's dolls.

'Very weird, Rex,' she muttered, feeling disquieted by the discovery, but still unsure what it was she had discovered. Reaching in, Leone felt the plumpness of one of the dolls' heads in her hand like a fat, cold cricket ball. She manoeuvred the object in her hand until she could see its face. The features were finely drawn. A rosebud mouth, lightly arched eyebrows and snub nose. But the eyes were very realistic. She looked closer and noticed a thin film over the orbs and could smell formaldehyde. It was then and only then, her heart fluttering like a trapped bird, that she realised, knew that she had found what she was looking for.

'Look for a trophy, a souvenir.' What is it that he wants from them? What does he take? And here before her was the answer. He'd taken them all, forced them with his thumbs from their sockets and mounted them inside these broken, innocent childhood effigies.

Leone's head began to carousel. She had found the proof, the undeniable evidence of Speakman's innocence and Crichton's guilt.

Leone swallowed the rising bile in her mouth. She wept for the little ones that Crichton had taken and reduced to this end. There was no joy in this victory, only relief in the certainty that it was over.

When he woke, the storm had passed. The lake was deserted. He climbed painfully to his feet, legs still weak. He scanned the lake's surface but could see nothing. He knew his friend and Crichton were dead. There was an overhanging ledge a few metres out. Jack suspected that Jangos had wedged the two of them there and waited for the end.

He turned to the truck with the spear still protruding from it. Looking closer, he now understood why Crichton had not been able to pull his hand free: one of his fingers was still nailed to the door. Jack didn't have time to mourn his friend, not yet. Instead, he wrenched the shaft out, recovered the finger and placed it inside a plastic bag. From it they would be able to cross-match the other samples from the first dead girl's body. But first there was another, more grisly, task to perform.

Jack took a deep breath before opening the bag of Kyra's bones. A tear ran down his face as he peered inside. Her ribcage held something. It carried the small, hardly formed bones of Rex Crichton's child. It carried his genes, his DNA, and the key to Speakman's acquittal. He pulled the baby free and placed it in a separate bag.

Before leaving the lake forever, he dug a shallow grave underneath a eucalyptus tree and buried Kyra there. She had been in the water too long. He had been afraid for too long.

It was time to go home.

EPILOGUE

Leone Forth watched her husband's sleeping form shuffle inside the quilted duvet. Since her partnership with Foster-Morgan associates had been announced, the workload had tripled. Teal and Windle had taken their places on the golf course and the riverbank respectively after the inquest into Rex Crichton's death. Reliving the past had been hard on Jack. He had wept at the memory of the death of his friend Jangos. Their bodies had been recovered by the Cypriot authorities and Crichton's flown home for a desolate funeral that Jack had insisted on attending.

'Just making sure, Leone, that's all.'

The brave Cypriot's funeral had been a vast bittersweet party attended by thousands, including Leone's husband. After Speakman's acquittal the world had continued to turn. Jack was whole again, or as whole as the past would allow him to be. He had encapsulated it so accurately after the file on King Arthur was closed for good:

'It's the fractures in a man's heart that make the present more intelligible.'

The letter from Toby Sloane had arrived that morning. It lay on the pine bedside table. Jack had feigned disinterest, but she had caught him reading it shortly before Hollie went to bed. He didn't comment, just nodded his head once as if satisfied at the news.

Leone reached for it and scanned over the news of yet another hopeless murder trial until she came to its real point.

'La Saux left them all a legacy. He had duplicated the video of the orgy with Colleen Bridges a thousand times. The crate was discovered at customs after the publicity following the trial. Bigg has left the country, apparently to join the Nazis in South America (he should feel at home) and Singleton's retirement may well be interrupted by a heavy knock on the door. All in all, to quote the Winslow Boy, "Right was done".'

Jack murmured in his sleep and Leone hugged her stomach and his child within. He didn't know yet. She was saving the news until his birthday the following morning. Leone reached out and stroked his forehead where the curls were damp. The nightmares had not disappeared completely, but they would in time.

She watched him reach out a hand to where the telephone had once been until she had insisted on its removal, and pick up a phantom receiver.

The telephone's insistent ring cut through Jack Forth's dream. Groaning slightly he plucked the Bakelite mouthpiece from its cradle and listened.

'Jack, it's Rex.'

'No, you're dead.'

'Depends on how you define dead, Jack. Gone but not forgotten, if you like.'

'It doesn't matter, this is a dream.'

'Whatever. Anyway, I thought congratulations were in order.'

'Get on with it, Crichton, then I can get rid of this dream.'

'She's pregnant: a girl, lovely.'

'You sick f—'

'Hollie's a little old for my tastes, but I'll be patient.'

The fury coursed through his body.

'I'll be seeing you, Jack.'

'Jack, wake up, you're dreaming.'

Leone shook him out of the palpitating terror. He flushed open his eyes, then relaxed their startled gaze as he found her. But he couldn't smile. He desperately needed the answer to a question first.

'Leone, are you pregnant?'

Her face was questioning, troubled.

'How do you know, Jack? Jack, tell me how you know.'

As the waters fail from the sea, and the flood decayeth
and drieth up, so man lieth down. He shall not awake.

Job 11:12